Praise for **GRIDLEY** *Girls*

I eagerly await more from the brilliant Ms. First
Amy Gronholz

Cleverly captured the fun and innocence of a spirited girl and her friends growing up in a small town.
Mary Ann Haro

Couldn't put it down!
Jean Baty

I found myself laughing and crying throughout the entire book.
Jackie K.

I thoroughly enjoyed Gridley Girls. The glossary alone will generate some very funny cross generational conversations. I was sorry to get to the end of the book. I hope there will be more Gridley Girl stories and that we will get the chance to follow Meg through the rest of her high school years.
Anne S.

Can't wait for the next book!
Paula Taylor

Loved this story!
Karen Harp

GRIDLEY *Girls*

A True-Life Novel

_____

Meredith First

www.gridleygirls.com

ISBN: 978-0-9887822-8-0

While this story is inspired by actual events, certain characters, characterizations, incidents, locations and dialogue were fictionalized or invented for purposes of dramatization. With respect to such fictionalization or invention, any similarity to the name or to the actual character or history of any person, living or dead, or any product or entity or actual incident is entirely for dramatic purpose and not intended to reflect on any actual character, history, product or entity.

Published by Gridley Girls, LLC
Established 2005

www.GridleyGirls.com
www.MeredithFirst.com

For information about special discounts for bulk purchases or rights inquiries please email Business@GridleyGirls.com.

Printed in Brainerd, Minnesota, USA

Cover design by Stewart Anstead
Book design by Patti Frazee
ebook formatting by Guido Henkel

For Lance
The moment we met, you brought color into my life.

Author's Note to Readers Under 30
Since much of this book takes place in high school in the
seventies, make sure you read the *Gridley Girls' Glossary to
Seventies Pop Culture* in the back of the book. Here I attempt
to define your mother's generation in hopes that we'll
all remember that while things have changed so much,
they've also stayed exactly the same.

Foreword

Jimmer Anderson, RoseMarie Curcuru, Stacie Sormano Walker,
Meredith Carlin First
2012, Lake Tahoe, California

When you meet your friends in kindergarten, nobody tells you what that means. You're five years old, what do you care? You play with the fun girl from the slide, and you share your cookies with the cute boy on the merry-go-round. You don't foresee the fights, heartbreak, betrayal, loss, warmth, love, redemption, and forgiveness.

All you see are the kids you want to play with.

This book is my thank you to those kids I wanted to play with — those friends who have been by my side every step of the way, and those who are here in spirit only. <3

Seeing Jesus and The Virgin Diaries

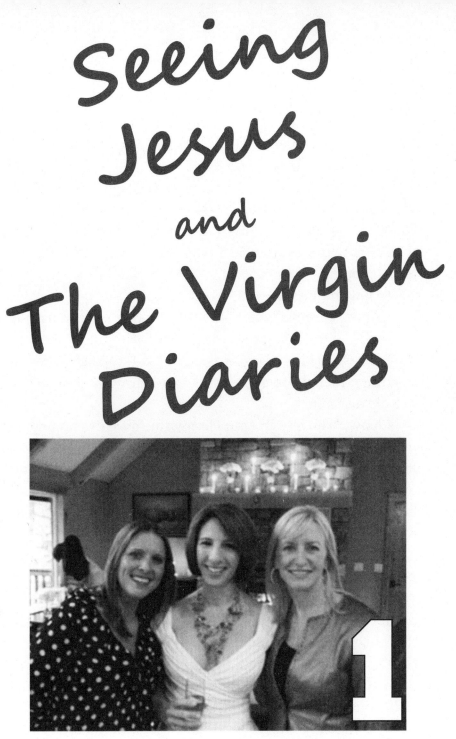

Stacie Sormano and Michael Walker's Wedding
March, 2012, Lake Tahoe, California
RoseMarie Curcuru, Stacie Sormano Walker, Meredith Carlin First

2008

If people saw us now, they'd never believe that as teenagers I once betrayed one of my best friends (there's never just one), AnneMarie Calzaretta, in an unforgiveable way. It wasn't over a boy or a catty teenage girl prank. It was because of God. I broke the solemn trust of a lifelong friend because I was a misguided, religiously confused girl who was told a secret that I was incapable of hearing, let alone keeping.

That and because of God.

Anne forgave me. She understood my religious confusion, but the betrayal was always with me. Not every day, sometimes not every week, but I know when I die the first thing I'll have to atone for is that betrayal and inability to keep a secret.

Now, we were in spin class with my hair clinging to my head and sweat flying off my body in ways I never knew existed. My heart beat faster than the horrible techno music. I looked over at Anne, her sandy blond ponytail blowing from the spin room fans like a music video, and remembered the secret and the betrayal.

I don't believe in sweating. I'm not an athlete or a cardio person. I'm a yoga mom, a Pilates girl, a former swimmer. I am not a spinner. It's the twenty-first century, and we're in our forties, so why were we in a darkened room of a gym, in the 'burbs of Sacramento, riding bikes to nowhere? The last time I saw this many black lights was after we won them in the magazine selling contest in seventh grade. And that was 1976. It made sense. This was an alternate universe.

"Omigod, I think I just saw Jesus. Seriously. There was white light and everything." I almost shouted this in my best whisper-scream to Anne from the helm of my evil exercise bike. I can be a bit dramatic about heart attacks because of my family history of heart disease. You can call it hypochondria. I call it PTSD from a fear of sudden death that I've had ever since my cousin David died when he was twenty-one and I was nine. I didn't figure out the connection until I watched an episode of Oprah on fear. All I really needed to know I learned from watching Oprah.

"White light?" Anne laughed. "You're killing me, Meg. 'Go away from the light. Go away from the light' ". Anne whisper-screamed back to me in her best *Poltergeist* voice.

Until recently, I thought there were a lot of crafty women in the world. So many people had taken up spinning I thought they were weaving on looms or knitting. I swear to everything holy I thought that. Even when I watched *Sex and the City*, I thought Miranda was a crafty, little weaver when she left for spin class. I had no idea intelligent people holed themselves up in stinky rooms and rode stationary bikes to hip-hop music, while a blond pony-tailed drill sergeant disguised as a perky little instructor shouted orders at them.

I was in spin class because Anne was trying to save me from my lack of athleticism. Growing up together, Anne played every sport possible...and was fabulous at everything. We played soccer together in the seventh grade on what I'm pretty sure was the first post Title IX soccer team in Gridley. I was a forward. She was a forward/bodyguard. That's when Anne officially became my bodyguard. I stank at all sports and would sometimes be targeted by bullies on the other team. She would yell at the ref for not calling a foul on another girl when they kicked me. Or she'd just get in the other girl's face and tell her off.

I didn't even get offended when she'd look over at me,

point to my Dorothy Hamill haircut and toothpick legs, and say to our opponent, "Look at her. You're seriously going to attack a seventy-pound weakling like that? When you're... what?" She'd eyeball the girl, up and down, to get her point across. "A hundred and fifty pounds yourself? That's more than double. Pick on somebody your own size." That would start a fight since no one wanted to be called 150 pounds in the seventh grade. Anne would just scurry off the field, never actually participating in the fight but always proud of her math. "Did ya like that? Seventy *is* around half of 150, right?" She'd look me over just like she did the mean girl. "Do you even weigh seventy pounds?" She knew the math but liked to play dumb. It worked for her.

Anne is the kind of physically fit, beautiful woman that most women love to hate. I would join you in your hatred if I didn't love her so much. A classic Italian beauty though like so many of my Italian friends, her hair was dyed blond now that we were in our forties. Having a perfect body and gorgeous eyes doesn't change the fact that, as you age, it's harder to keep the gray hair out without going blond. She even has the Shirley Temple dimples she was born with.

Anne was determined to take me to "the next level" in my fitness regime. I had been in physical therapy for a nasty back injury for the past year and was forced into the athletic world just to fight off the chronic pain. It was working, but I had no idea people who *liked* to exercise existed. Didn't they know that running was invented to keep us from being eaten by larger animals? And now, in civilized society, we only need to run if we're being chased by someone. And we only have to run *fast* if we're being chased by someone with a weapon.

After the white light and Jesus went away the

endorphins kicked in, and I could talk like the instructor told us to. She's the only teacher I've ever had who asked me to talk during class. Usually, they're on *Chatty Cathy* (that would be me) to just shut up, but this one was asking us to talk to each other so we could make sure we were working "in the right zone." Anne was going to get me in cardio-shape if it killed her. I was just hoping it didn't kill me first.

"We're supposed to talk now, so say something," she instructed.

"I just want out of this class without a heart attack. Talking is not a high priority," I said, as I tried to get my blond hair out of my sweaty eyes.

"Okay, I'll talk but you have to answer." I nodded yes. It was my first class. *There should be no talking. There should just be spinning and breathing so one can stay alive on this evil bike.* "I was thinking of *The Virgin Diaries* the other day. Do you still have them?" she asked.

"That's so weird that you asked that." I huffed. She was pushing it. "I was just looking at them the other day. My dad brought me a box of stuff from the garage and they were in it. I meant to call you and got distracted." I was out of breath. But that was the first time I had spoken since we started, and I didn't have a heart attack so that was a good sign.

My heart was beating so hard it felt like it was going to fly right out of my chest. Seriously. When I was in labor with my first baby, I was induced because all my internal organs had shut down. It was good fun. In my case, that meant my labor was sped up into what I affectionately called turbo labor. When my water broke, I looked down at my belly and screamed to my husband, "Did you see that?" I patted all over my belly, convinced a baby hand or foot was sticking out. "Do you see it?" He looked at me puzzled, as I continued to feel my way around my belly. Whether or not that was the painkiller talking or my own craziness since I'd been bedridden for two months prior to the birth, I will never know. All I knew was the force of my water breaking was so powerful that I thought for sure there was an alien-like moment happening to me. It was with that same conviction that I thought my heart might very well be flying out of my chest, right there in that spin class.

"See," said Anne, beaming with pride. "You talked. A lot. I knew you could do it. You're going to be a pro at this after a few more classes." Who knew that my cardio fitness could mean so much to her?

At that point, the instructor/drill sergeant danced over to our bikes, chanting something indecipherable. She threw her arm in the air like a cheerleader and hollered into the sea of bikes as she walked straight to me. With her fist pumping, she howled right in my face. "Ooo-wah. Ooo-wah." To inspire me? To scare me into riding my bike-to-nowhere faster? She was accomplishing both; I was afraid of her and her little cheerleading moves.

Anne slipped off her bike, she laughed so hard. Holding her handlebars tighter, she yelled, "You should see your face. You look horrified. You'll get used to her, Meg. She means well. It's the endorphins. It makes people act like they've been drinking, when usually they haven't. It's fun."

"Fun? Hmm. I don't think I'd go straight to fun, but I could probably use a cocktail right about now." At least Anne laughed at my pain.

The interminable class ended—for me. If you wanted only forty-five minutes of the torture, you could dismount and leave. I had to stay for Anne (she was my ride, which ensured my attendance), so I jumped off my bike and stretched while she spun her fool head off for fifteen more minutes.

We left in a trail of sweat and a waft of onions (I've long thought that body odor smells like the onions on a hamburger). Of course, we thanked the drill sergeant as we left. The world's strongest snip of a girl gave us an enthusiastic farewell. "You did great for the first time. Come back soon." She reassured me with her fabulous smile and adorable blonde ponytail, hoping I'd join her cycling-to-nowhere-gang.

"I will. See you on Friday." *Did I say that? I can't come back for more of this. What was I thinking?* I clearly was not, and now they'd sucked me into their spinning cult. Only one class in and I was one of those crafty little people off to spin class only to return sweaty and without so much as a tiny piece of fabric to show for my efforts. The least they could do was hook up a loom to the bikes so we could be productive. Or maybe some windmills so we could be creating energy out of our sweat. It doesn't make sense to work so hard on those darn bikes and go nowhere and produce nothing. Where was our American ingenuity?

All I knew was that I was going to have to get a blond ponytail. Quick.

"Margaret MacGregor Monahan, I am so proud of you," Anne chirped, almost as perky as the instructor, as we walked out of the gym. "You did it. You finished a whole spin class and you sweated. I witnessed a real, live Monahan girl sweating. I feel so honored to have shared this with you." Anne was dead serious. That was the funny part.

I am the youngest of four girls who, while somewhat fit and very active, do not believe in sweating. Call it the long line of proper English women we come from. Oh, we're American. We just come from a line of straight-off-the-Mayflower-women, so the gene pool didn't get diluted enough. They still use phrases like "jolly well" (not *this* generation, thankfully), have way too much bone china, and have serious stiff upper lips. Call it lazy (i.e. we don't like to have to re-do our hair and makeup). Call it crazy. Call it what you want. We Monahan women do not sweat. That whole "Horses sweat, men perspire, and women simply glow," thing is taken seriously in our family.

"I did. Didn't I? We should call Katie and tell her. This *is* big news." Katie, the second of my three sisters, is five years older and like a second mom to us. With her dark hair and olive skin, she looks as much like Anne as she does me, and has always been the big sister that Anne never had.

"Katie would be very proud of you, Meg. I haven't heard from her yet. Is she coming to the wedding?" The big wedding. Well, it won't be *that* big, but it is exciting. Anne is getting married in my backyard.

"Of course she's coming. She wouldn't miss it. She'll respond, don't worry. Katie is Jayne's daughter. No shortage on manners. Besides, it's still three weeks away. The invitations just went out." Anne gave me an "oh yeah" shrug, and I looked at her carefully since she was acting odd.

Jayne Monahan is my mother, but she's also everyone's mother. Both my parents are middle school teachers. Have been forever. My mother was the eighth grade English teacher in our hometown of Great Gridley, California, just sixty miles north of Sacramento. Population 3,000 back then. In the small farm town, most everyone knew each other and usually went back for several generations. There was always a connection. My mother took her role as "everyone's mom" seriously. Her goal was to single-handedly turn every student into a lady or a gentleman. Her motto, often preached to us in a sing-song voice accompanied by a stern look of authority, was, "Remember girls, Y.A.L.: You're a lady." If you were a boy, it was, of course, "You're a gentleman." No student graduated from Sycamore Middle School without hearing that over and over. Manners were as important as breathing.

"Anne? Are you nervous?" I asked, while we got into her swanky convertible. "You seem worried. Everything's going okay on the wedding plans, right? No cold feet? I already spent a fortune putting in the mister systems in the backyard. There's no backing out now. My yard will be as cool as bloody Disneyland." People always think they want an outdoor, summer wedding, but they weren't exactly lining up to spend August in the nine-one-six (apparently I'm a rapper now; nine-one-six is Sacramento's area code). Having an August, outdoor wedding in Sacramento equals sweating your buns off. We've already covered how I feel about sweating.

She thought about it while she took her ponytail holder out, smoothed her sandy blonde hair, and put it back into a cleaner ponytail. "I'm fine, Meg, and I appreciate the misters, even though I know our wedding was the excuse you used for permission to splurge." She was right about that. "I'm just sentimental these days. Were you like this before you got married?" She put the car in gear and pulled out onto the boulevard.

"Totally. I was so in love and excited that I was ultra sappy about everything. I cried all the time, especially over pop songs. And they were happy tears, but you know what Jayne says about that."

In unison we recited, "genetic defect." That was my mother's excuse for being overly sentimental and crying "happy tears" all the time. All four of us daughters inherited the same defect. It's lame.

When I was around eleven, my dad walked into the family room to all of us crying. His face went gray as he asked, "Who died?" We burst into laughter through our tears. When we explained that we were watching a sad episode of *Family Affair*, he threw his arms in the air in disgust and left the room, probably to go find some manly area of our bungalow style house. But I'm pretty sure no such area ever existed in our sorority house of a home.

We were at a stoplight when Anne looked over at me and interrupted my genetic defect memories. "Sometimes I wonder, though. I mean, I know I'm getting married for the right reasons, but not everybody is exactly supportive of this, and it kinda worries me. Just a little, and only when I'm feeling especially vulnerable. Do you know what I mean?"

"Oh Anne, if you're talking about Cindy, don't. Just put it out of your head. That's her problem, not yours."

Anne looked ahead then, focused on driving, but I knew where her mind was going.

Cindy Santini grew up with us. Other than having some narrow-minded (in our opinion) viewpoints on life, sprinkled with some right-wing attitudes that we didn't agree with, she was a great girl. When you came from a community like Gridley, your friendships were more fluid than people from larger places or places that weren't as tightly knit as ours. In Gridley, your friendships were ancestral, not just your own. So you learned to overlook political and religious differences. You learned to love unconditionally in a way that didn't exist as readily in a big city. Cindy was not a fan of this upcoming marriage, and while she hadn't said that straight to Anne, she felt it. Anne knew. I just didn't know she knew, until now.

"Regardless of whose problem it is, it still hurts. Part of me doesn't want her at the wedding if she can't accept it." Anne was still looking away from me as she drove onto my street. Then she changed the subject, which was my cue to drop it. "You blew off *The Virgin Diaries* earlier. I was serious when I asked to see them. Can we look at them when I drop you off? Do you have time?" She was being very polite and sentimental, neither of which I was used to.

"I wasn't blowing them off. I was trying to stay alive on that darn bike. We can get them if you have the time. You kind of have a lot going on right now."

"I can do it. Your little 'Diary of a Virgin' is the closest thing I have to a diary of my own from our childhood. I want to take a peek." We pulled into my circular driveway, headed for our little adventure down memory lane.

I unlocked the front door, and Anne went straight to a chaise in the living room. *This is serious. She's sitting in the living room. No one ever sits in the living room, unless they're opening Christmas presents.* "I'll go get them and be right back," I called from the stairs. "You want some water?"

"I'll get it. You want some too?" Anne yelled up from the living room.

"Yes, please. Thanks," I yelled back, while I got the diaries from a box in my office. "Here we goooo," I said. I hummed *Pomp and Circumstance* and marched down the stairs with my harvest gold mortarboard on my head and the diaries in my hand like they were my diploma. "I couldn't decide what to hum while I walked down the stairs: *The Wedding March*, since this is a bridal staircase, or *Pomp and Circumstance*. But then I found my mortarboard next to the diaries, so I'm all set." Forget about the fact that I was disgusting in my sweaty exercise clothes, which is precisely why I don't like to exercise in the first place.

"Okay," said Anne. "Now I want *my* little graduation cap. I feel left out," she whined as she snatched a diary out of my hands. "You know, all this sentimental talk reminded me of when we started high school. Do you remember that swimming party at my house, the day before the first day of school?" Anne asked as she laughed at me still marching in my grand processional to the chaise.

I took my cap off. "Remember? How could I forget? I'm scarred forever from that party. I get scared every time I see a large-breasted, old lady. Let's look that up in the handy dandy diary, if we may. Where's 1979?" This was not hard to find, as I'm a tad neurotic. Every diary was dated in puff paint and some had titles. It was a little nauseating—even for me. "There it is." I shouted, a little too excited. We were like Alice in Wonderland going through the looking glass. I looked at the first diary.

"Oh God." Anne groaned and fell back into the chaise like it was a fainting lounge. "Look at the puff paint. You are so out of hand. I think you may need help. Look at the titles: *The Diary of a Virgin, 78-79. The Virgin Diaries, 80-82.* What happened there? Why did you switch? I don't remember."

"*The Virgin Diaries* was more concise. Once I started taking journalism classes, I changed titles. I liked headlines." Anne rolled her eyes at me. I nodded in resignation. "I couldn't help myself. I know, I know."

"Outta hand. Totally outta hand." She shook her head. *Did she look a little frightened of my organizational skills? Proud?* I couldn't tell, but decided to go with proud since that made me feel better.

"Outta hand, maybe, but you're benefiting from my anal behavior, aren't you Missy?" I said in my best indignant Mom voice. I *liked* my puff paint and my precise-if-not-imaginatively titled diaries.

"Whatever," she said, with more sarcasm than enthusiasm. She held the diaries up with her thumbnail poised to scrape. "Now give me '78-'79 or I'll scrape some puff paint off."

"Not the puff paint! Here, take it." I shoved the '78-'79 diary at her, then watched over her shoulder at our first year of high school. It was so weird to think of it all right there in little journals. They had been missing for years, until my dad found them buried in the garage. Lost for over twenty years. It wasn't King Tut or anything, but it meant way more to us than some ole mummy.

Anne thumbed through the diary, looking at various entries. "Meg, when are you going to write books? Whatever happened to that? You were always going to be the next Judy Blume? And who's that lady your aunt wanted you to be?" She looked up, as if Erma Bombeck's name might fall out of the sky. "And then nothing."

"Erma Bombeck. My *mother* wanted me to be the next Judy Blume, and I wouldn't say *nothing* happened." I spread my arms toward my home like the lady on *The Price is Right* displaying a living room set. "I have a great career. I've got a crazy family. What more could a girl want?" I felt a bit defensive, since I knew she was right. Plus, there was the little matter of our big family secret. The hair on the back of my neck stood up. *Could she know?*

After years of unsuccessfully trying to relocate us away from the small market of Sacramento, my husband's Firm now wanted to move us to Minneapolis. This was a very big deal, as my kids are sixth generation Sacramentans. You can't go further back than that without being Mexican or Native American. We were so firmly entrenched in our valley roots, we might as well have been the very trees my family earned their way on originally. If I left town, it would be an upheaval not just in my family, as we all live within a seventy-mile radius of my parents, but also in my circle of friends who are all transplanted Gridleyans in Sacramento.

But The Firm was *The Firm*. John Grisham, without the murders and the mafia. What were we supposed to do? And moving across the country would give me the excuse to leave the career I loved, but which I would never be brave enough to leave on my own to write the books I'd dreamt about since eighth grade—a real life conundrum.

Nothing was final. We'd only been out to Minneapolis once to look at houses and to talk to other partners in The Firm. I lied to everyone at home and said we were on a Firm trip with clients. No one suspected, since we traveled so much with The Firm anyway. Eventually I was going to have to tell someone and get advice, but I just didn't know how. It was too huge of a decision to tell anyone and risk making it a reality. This was the only home my children had ever known. Our whole life was wrapped around our families and community here. I firmly believe in the "It takes a village" concept. How could I leave my village right as my kids were entering their teen years? That seemed insane to me.

Anne snapped me back into consciousness. "Meg, you know what I mean. That was your dream. What happened to it?" Gosh, the way she looked into my eyes was eerie. *Did she suspect?* She went back to leafing through the diary, lost in the pages of our youth, while I thought about my dreams.

I didn't know if she heard me, but I tried to explain and

keep her from becoming suspicious. "I don't know. I guess *life* happened." I thought out loud then. "I graduated from college, had school loans and had to find a career to pay off said school loans. *That* happened. I fell in love, got married and had two kids. *That* happened. I built up a big ole career. *That* happened." I sounded wistful, as if my whole life had *happened* to me, rather than being planned. "I don't have time to shower, let alone write books." I sat back on the couch, feeling like a failure. I knew my life had meaning and value. On an intellectual level, I knew I hadn't wasted my life, but why *didn't* I write the books I'd been talking about writing since eighth grade. Anne was right. I'd talked about it forever, but hadn't done anything about it. Gosh, I bet I was annoying to be around with all that talking and no action.

Could that be why this move seemed to be actually happening as opposed to the other moves The Firm had discussed? First it was San Francisco, then L.A., D.C., and Philly. But this Minneapolis thing seemed the most real of all. Was this some cosmic kick-in-the-butt for me to change my life? Well shit. That's all I had to say to that. Shit.

I looked over Anne's shoulder to confirm she was reading about our peer counseling session in 1979. With the mention of Cindy Santini's opinions on Anne's upcoming nuptials, I knew what Anne was thinking about. Neither of us needed to read about it in my diaries though. What happened that day in a small Gridley High classroom caused a domino effect of lies upon lies, betrayal, forgiveness, and more secrets that I hold to this day. It's a wonder any of our friendships have survived, let alone thrived.

We could be human iTunes and play back that session on demand, at any time. That day was burned into our memories forever.

This Kiss

Calvin Crest Camp
1978, Oakhurst, California
Michelle Radley Zearfoss, Valerie Smethers Harwell, Meredith Carlin First

"Gridley is a great place to be from."
~ Uncle George "Butter" Cole

1978

Like a Prius, I was raised a hybrid. There are bi-racial people, and there are bi-religious people like me. My father's family is Mormon (or LDS, The Church of Jesus Christ of Latter-Day Saints), and my mother's family went to the First Christian Church. You could say I'm half Mormon and half anti-Mormon. Sets things up for a very harmonious childhood.

My mother, while respectful of the Mormon Church and never badmouthing it to us, was very strong in her convictions that we would be raised in the Presbyterian Church, without getting baptized. The Presbyterian Church was our family's Switzerland—neutral in every way. My parents thought we could make our own decisions about what religion we wanted to belong to when we were adults. This was my mom's way of ensuring it was our decision and not the decision of our very Mormon, very persuasive, and very wonderful grandparents who lived across the street and doted on us. My Mormon grandparents couldn't help themselves in their passion for The Church. My grandpa's mother came to Utah in a covered wagon with the pioneers who fled the Midwest after the martyring of Joseph Smith. My grandma's father, George Cole, was the third president of BYU Idaho. The President of The Church (The Prophet) sent him, with a group of pioneers in more covered wagons, to start the LDS Church in northern California. The Prophet chose Gridley for the abundance of rich soiled farmland.

This whole pick-your-own-religion strategy worked fine for my sisters, but not for me. My friends were all different religions; they were baptized, had first communions, confirmations, Quinceañeras, and some later went on LDS church missions. Meanwhile, I felt like I had a pseudo-religion, never really belonging to any one church. I craved religion as much as I craved candy. Like Pinocchio, if only I could be baptized *something*, then I would feel like a real girl.

One of my very best friends was Jennifer Cone, single-handedly the nicest girl I've ever known and not just because she was Mormon. Jennifer was my hero growing up. She was that type of girl whom your parents loved because she never talked back, always did the right thing, and was just a deep down, to the core, nice girl. My mother always referred to those types of people as "salt of the earth." To me, Jennifer was more than salt of the earth. She was a future Betty from the *Archie* comic books. In my head, I compared everything to *Archie* comic books. And Betty was forever nice, just like Jennifer.

Jennifer's presence in my life made it tricky for my mom to manage my Mormon influences. It was natural for me to want to go to Primary (the Mormon version of youth group for primary school aged kids) with Jennifer during the week. I loved Primary. We would file into church like good little children with our arms folded, and it was cool to be reverent. I hadn't seen anything like that before my first trip to Primary. We sang songs and did crafts, and I liked feeling like I belonged.

At the Presbyterian Church they were very welcoming too, but I always felt like I didn't belong since I wasn't baptized. I couldn't take Communion because I wasn't baptized. It's not that my Presbyterian Church wasn't wonderful to me. They were. They gave me a Bible with my

Sunday School class, just like I belonged. They allowed my sisters and I every privilege of belonging without being a member, except for the important rituals, like Communion, that I craved.

At the Mormon Church, they didn't care that I wasn't baptized. They call Communion "Sacrament" and every one who's living the Gospel can take it—even me, the girl with no *real* religion. They looked at me as if I was born Mormon and just had the misfortune to have a non-member mother. It was almost as if they assumed I would be baptized eventually. To them, it was a matter of when, not if. That one fact that made me feel so safe is probably what scared my mom the most.

One day during fourth grade, Jennifer and I were walking home from school like we did every day, and she asked me to join her at Primary. It was convenient since we lived right behind the church. I was so excited. I forgot to tell anyone at my house that I was going with her. Fast forward two hours later when her mother brought me home and all hell had broken loose at my house. They had been frantically looking for me for hours. Sure, it was 1974 Gridley, so no one thought I was kidnapped. Except for my mother. This was worse than kidnapping. This was church-napping—an altogether different offense in Jayne Monahan's mind.

I had the major sit-down talk with my parents, where we discussed their reasons for not getting us baptized. I discussed the fact that I liked the Mormon Church better than the Presbyterian Church. I pretended not to notice the look of horror on my mother's face and the look of pride on my father's when I said that. My mother had her mole face on (my name for her stern, teacher look that could strike fear in anyone, not just children) for most of the conversation, while my father shook his head a lot. It was decided (my mother decided and my father complied) that I would not go to Primary for "quite some time," due to the fact that I did not tell anyone where I was. We all knew this was Mom's way of protecting me from too much Mormon influence. All I knew was that I didn't get to go sing at Primary with my friend Jennifer. As an adult, I get it. As an impressionable nine-year-old, I couldn't see why any mother could find fault in a religion that was practiced by half the family.

One of the great things about being Presbyterian (pseudo or not) was going to church camp. We went to Calvin Crest, several hours south of Gridley and down at the southern end of Yosemite. No shortage of natural beauty there. We didn't care much about natural beauty though. My main memory of camp, besides my faux-baptism, was my first real kiss. I'm pretty sure that's not what they had in mind when they created church camps, but I'm also pretty sure that I wasn't alone in getting my first kiss at church camp.

That year, I was lucky enough to go with Anne and Cindy. Like all my closest friends, Cindy Santini was Italian Catholic. I talked them into going with me just so I could have friends at camp. What parents say no to getting rid of their teenager for a week at a good church camp?

To outside eyes, Cindy and I, with our blond hair, blue eyes and skinny bodies, looked very much alike. The differences began when it came to boys. Cindy was never short on boyfriends, where I was the Queen of Unrequited Love. The difference between us, when it came to boys, was simple: I talk a mile a minute, and Cindy spends her time emitting pheromones and batting her bedroom eyes. While Cindy had a number of different cute boyfriends in the eighth grade—she even got a dozen red roses for her birthday from one—I pined, to no avail, for a boy from my Sunday school class. Pining that was, until summer camp.

Until summer camp and Lee.

Our first day at camp, we were walking from the mess hall to our cabin among those towering pine trees. To this day, I can smell a certain pine or redwood scent and say, "Mmm, smells like summer camp." We walked past a group of kids that looked nice enough, but seemed way older than us. This was junior high camp so no one was supposed to be older than tenth grade. That must have been what these kids were, since they all either had boobs or facial hair. Not on the same bodies though.

Right after we passed them, one of the girls called back, "Nice tennis shorts. Looking for a court?" and the other girls laughed. I realized they were referring to my white shorts. The last thing I needed was to get teased at church camp too. I couldn't get a break anywhere. Skinny girls have a hard time finding clothes to fit. Add to that, parents who never have enough money to go around—especially with four girls clamoring for clothes—and I was doomed. I thought those white shorts were cute on me.

I tried to convince myself that they weren't talking about me, when Anne said, "Meg, I think they're talking about your white shorts." I shot her a dirty look and tried to ignore the older group, but when I looked back I noticed a cute blond guy with an amazing body and a little blond moustache. It wasn't just the peach fuzz you would see on guys that age. It was actual hair. In my seventies lingo, I thought Lee was a total fox with a great bod, and he was looking back at me, smiling. He didn't seem to mind my little, white tennis shorts at all.

This was church camp, so we had lots of campfires and church singing. I loved it. We had crafts and clinics, and this gave me a chance to meet Lee. One night, as we sat down for campfire in a big set of bleachers in front of a huge fire where the counselors would perform skits and give talks, he came and sat next to me. I had butterflies in my stomach, and my heart was beating so fast. *Did he do this on purpose, or was it the only available seat? Or was he interested in Cindy?* That would just be my luck. He turned to me and said, "Hi." That was simple. I could handle "hi."

"Um, hi." *Try to act cool. Try to act cool.*

"I'm Lee Jackson."

"I'm Margaret Monahan. But everyone calls me Meg." So far, so good.

"Where ya from, Meg?" He was still talking to me. This couldn't have been a fluke.

"We're," I pointed to Cindy and Anne, "from Gridley." Wait for it: the perplexed look followed by the questions.

"Gridley. Is that in California?" I laughed. What else could I do? We got asked this all the time. No one knew where Gridley was...ever. "Yeah. Gridley is in northern California. Between Chico and Yuba City. Have you heard of those towns?"

"Uh. Nope, but I'm from Vegas so I don't know northern California." He was trying though. That was nice.

I became the self-appointed Ambassador to Gridley. You just couldn't shut me up. "It's sixty miles north of Sacramento. The state capitol? Ya gotta know that one."

"Okay. Yeah. How old are you?" It was vital statistics time. I may not have been properly kissed yet, but I did know how this "getting to know you stuff" went. I had three older sisters that I watched very carefully.

"Almost fourteen. I'm a freshman. How 'bout you?" I liked this whole talking-to-a-new-boy-thing. I didn't get this in Gridley because, again, there were no strangers in Gridley, and we rarely got "new boys."

"I'm gonna be a sophomore." It got quiet, and he whispered, "We have to listen now. Meet me after." With that, we turned to the counselors and got back to the service.

It was an amazing campfire, and not just because I got to meet Lee. It was great all around. I felt the spirit. I loved church camp. It was great to be with so many people the same age for church type stuff. You don't get that on Sundays in a small church.

That night, they asked us to accept Christ into our lives. We closed our eyes and prayed, and we had the choice to accept Christ as the center of our lives. It was very moving. I decided to make it like a baptism for myself. I called it my faux baptism. I figured if I left it up to my parents it would never happen, so why not consider *that* a baptism? I thought Jesus would be okay with that. It felt so good. It also felt great to consider myself baptized. I liked that idea. This could count as a religion, so I wouldn't feel like I had a pseudo-religion anymore.

Lee walked us back to our cabin after campfire. He *did* like me. It wasn't some fluke. I couldn't believe it. "So Meg, what do you do for fun in Gridley?" He was making an effort.

"Not much to do in Gridley. It's a really small town. Three thousand people's all. It's a farm town. We don't even have our own movie theater. Well, not in English anyway. It went Spanish years ago. We swim a lot." I rambled, and realized I didn't introduce my friends. "Oh, sorry. These are my friends Cindy Santini and Anne Calzaretta. I forgot to introduce them."

"Hi," Cindy and Anne said, almost in unison.

"Nice to meet you. Cindy Santini and Anne what? Those are big names. Are they Italian? You don't look Italian," Lee said to Cindy.

"Well, I am. One hundred percent. I'm from *northern* Italy. We have blond hair and light eyes up there." Here it came: "My real name is Cinzia, but Cindy is easier in America." This time, she said it with a little pity in her voice for us lame Americans. Cindy used to tell a new person that her real name was Cinzia within sixty seconds of meeting. She did it as fast as Anne would tell someone that people told her she looked like Kristy McNichol. Cindy became Cinzia full time by the time we were twenty-one.

"Cinzia," he said with almost a proper English accent, as he drew out the "chince" part. He looked over at Anne, and with the same predictability as Cindy telling someone her real name was Cinzia and she was northern Italian, we got to watch the Kristy McNichol thing again. "Has anyone ever told you that you look just like Kristy McNichol?"

Anne, with her usual modesty, said, "Oh yeah, all the time. My mom says I'm prettier than her though. Plus, check out my dimples." She flashed her thousand-watt smile, and the dimples seemed to sparkle.

And like every other boy, Lee was impressed. "So do you all swim just for fun, or are you on the swim team? I'm on the dive team."

"Cool," I said and smiled. "We don't have a dive team. No high dive in the town either. We've been on the swim team together since we were five." Gridley sounded awful the way I told it. That didn't seem nice. "It's a great town, you know, if you like small towns. It's really pretty, and we have lots of ranches and farms. If you like orchards, Gridley's the place for you." Okay. I sounded like a total dork. *Shut up, Monahan.* I had such a problem with that. Nervous talking. My mom called it diarrhea of the mouth. Pretty, I know.

We arrived at our cabin just in time to save me from my rambling. "Well, thanks for walking us back." I said, trying not to babble.

"Sure. Will you be swimming at free time tomorrow?" He asked like he *wanted* to see me.

I looked at Cindy and Anne as they nodded yes. "Looks like we will be," I said, smiling as he watched the two of them bob their heads. They thought he was a cute too. "Okay then. See you tomorrow. Nice to meet you Lee Jackson."

"Nice to meet you too, Meg Monahan." With a smile and a wave, he walked off to the boy's side of the camp.

"Come on Cinzia." I drew out the "chince" this time with my own version of an English accent. "Let's go to bed dah-link." We giggled on the way in, as she was as big a dork as me.

I mocked Cindy as I dressed. "I'm from northern Italy. We have blue eyes there," I said in my high-pitched, teasing voice.

"Shut up. It's true, you know," Cindy said, a bit defensively.

"Oh yeah, Cindy. We allllll know," Anne said, getting her two cents in.

"Oh you should talk, Kris-teee." Cindy threw a pillow at Anne, as she drew out the last syllable and laughed. Thank goodness we had each other.

We spent the rest of the week together swimming,

making God's eyes out of yarn and twigs, and doing other crafty camper things. We sat with Lee every night at campfire. That was the best part.

On the last night of camp, there was a musical show. Anyone who wanted could participate. Since we had all been in music our whole lives, we decided to do a little trio.

We practiced for hours but were still nervous. We didn't embarrass ourselves, but it was a relief to have it over with. Lee came right up to us after the show.

"You guys were great. I didn't know you could sing," he said with another fantastic smile.

"There's lots you don't know about me, Lee Jackson," I said with another smile that couldn't be compared to his. I had crooked teeth and was in desperate need of braces. Who did I think I was, acting coy like that?

He laughed and said, "Maybe we can write each other and solve that?"

"Absolutely. I'm the best pen pal ever. Ask Cindy. Aren't I, Cindy?" He was so grown-up, and I felt like such a dork.

"She is. There's nothing Meg's not good at." *That was nice of Cindy.* She was such a good friend.

Just then, Lee took my hand. *Oh my God. He was holding my hand. It was magical.* "Can I walk you back to your cabin?" he asked.

"Sure." I grinned from ear to ear. If that was what it felt like to be with boys as a high school girl, I could handle it. It was very nice indeed.

We walked back to my cabin talking about nothing. I don't remember, because I was too busy thinking how much I liked to hold hands. I held hands with Matt McDowell in the seventh grade, but it didn't feel like this at all. His hands were sweaty. Not like Lee's, all smooth and nice.

When we got back to our cabin, Anne and Cindy went in while Lee and I said good night.

Then it happened.

He leaned over and kissed me. Right on the lips. I considered this to be my first kiss, as it was way better than any other kiss I'd had up to that point. It was soft and tender and not too much tongue. He didn't try too hard. It was just nice. *Oh, why couldn't Las Vegas be right next to Gridley?* It was very bittersweet.

He stood back and looked down at me while still holding me around the waist. "See ya in the morning? Hey, wanna have breakfast together?" I melted. I was a pool of almost fourteen-year old butter.

"Yeah. Good night Lee Jackson. See you tomorrow." I *loved* saying his whole name. And I loved that he noticed and said my whole name too. I thought we were the cutest couple ever. I couldn't believe I had to leave him the next day and would probably never see him again. This was more tragic than Shakespeare. Romeo and Juliet had nothing on us. I didn't sleep well that night.

The worst was when we had to say good-bye. Anne and Cindy were totally watching like hawks. That was awkward. At least we weren't near the cars where Cindy's mom could see too.

Lee put his bag down and said, "I had a great time with you this week, Meg. I wish you lived in Vegas."

My stomach was so full of butterflies I thought I would burst. For the first time in my life, I couldn't find words. I stood there dumbfounded, gazing at him like he was Shaun Cassidy. Anne came to my rescue, as usual.

"When are you going to visit us in Gridley, Lee. We've got plenty of peaches and kiwi for you to try." *Oooh. She's even being funny. Thank you Jesus, for bringing me Anne.*

"Hey yeah." I had come to my senses. "Lee, when are you coming to Gridley?"

He laughed. We knew he wouldn't be making the, like, twelve-hour trip to Gridley. "I dunno. You're tempting me though. If I ever get my Camaro running, maybe my parents will let me drive up there."

Anne left, so I knew it was time for the real goodbye kiss. The forever-goodbye-kiss. No pressure there. How was I going to do it? I still didn't know how to kiss. *God this was awful.*

Lee walked closer to me and pulled me by the waist next to him. He seemed so manly the way he pulled me to him. I liked that very much. He gently put his hand under my chin and tipped it up to him. He whispered, "I'll miss you, Meg Monahan," and kissed me straight on the lips, even better than the night before. *I could really get used to this kissing stuff.*

This was church camp, so he pulled away quickly and said, "You're still going to write me, right?" We were standing so close I could feel the heat between us, and I liked it.

"Yup. Sure am. I'll miss you too, Lee." I tried not to cry, but it was so sad. This was just my luck: to finally meet an adorable boy who likes me back...and he lives like a thousand miles away. Geography was never my strong suit. Turns out it was only 650 miles away, but when you're a fourteen-year-old Gridley Girl, Las Vegas might as well be the moon.

His friends appeared then, out of nowhere. He gave

them a nod and reached over to hug me. I got a great, bear hug. I could say it was an "embrace," but that seems like too much. We said goodbye in unison, and off he went. I watched for a while but then felt like a dork and went to find Anne and Cindy. There it was: my first summer romance and my first real kiss. A bittersweet tragedy in my life already, and I hadn't yet turned fourteen.

That scared me.

Afri-Mex-Italians and Other Fake Ethnic Groups

Meredith's 12th Birthday Party
The Carlin Home, Hazel Street, Gridley, California
Back Row: Paula Quist Taylor, RoseMarie Curcuru, Melissa Costa Talbott,
Meredith Carlin First, Stacie Sormano Walker, Diane LaBarbera Symon
Front Row: Erika Wickman Dellamaggiore, Julia Haynes McConaughy

Having such a great little summer romance kept me going for a while, at least until I received my first letter from Lee. Before I show you the letter, you need to understand a few things:

a. Both of my parents are schoolteachers.

b. My mother taught English forever, so bad grammar and poor spelling was strictly forbidden in our house.

In our home, we were not allowed to be bigoted on any subject except proper grammar, with one exception: if the person's station in life did not allow him/her to receive a proper education. We should then ignore the aforementioned bad grammar because it was from ignorance rather than a bad choice to not pay attention to your English teacher (Gasp – the ultimate sin).

This was a typical conversation between my parents: Dad speaking to a daughter, "There's three reasons you can't go to the party tonight."

Mom, interrupting, "There are three reasons you can't go to the party tonight. Fred, subject and verb, subject and verb; they have to match."

Dad, "Oh God, Jayne."

Daughter, who just wants to go to the party, "Yeah, good, but can I go to the party now?"

Mom and Dad in unison, "NO."

No subject *or* verb in that.

Read between the lines here: no Monahan girl could ever have a boyfriend with bad grammar. This was never said, just understood. The worst/best part was that we never noticed this until we were grown, but we wouldn't have fathomed going out with someone who said, "I seen it," or a guy who couldn't pass a fifth grade spelling test.

It killed me that Lee seemed like both. My new Harlequin romance was dead before it got going.

Here's the first letter, in all its glory. I'll clarify like the newspapers. It's sic:

> Margaret,
>
> What a wherd name ha ha. You know you are one of the lucky ones, I haven't wrote in a long long time, but I gess your special.
>
> Well how are you doing I'm find but tird all this week I have gon to four hours of soccer pratice from 7:00-11:00 in the morning, my spelling is bad but if you can read it its all right.
>
> Yesterday there was a van that burned up on side of my nabors house it was pretty neet no one got hert.
>
> Well that's about all, theres not a lot going on around my house so I'll see you later.
>
> Love,
>
> Lee Jackson
>
> PS My birthday is Oct. 5

Admit it. You're shocked. I felt a bit guilty when I read the part where he apologized for his spelling to me, but come on. If I had given that to my mom she would have gone crazy with her red pen. It would look like a crime scene when she was done with it. And he's older than me. How can that be? How can you get to be a sophomore in high school and not know how to spell *guess*, or *tired*, or *weird*? Maybe it was the public schools in Nevada?

I was glad he spelled my name right. Even if he does think it's "wherd." Either way, I knew there was no future for me in this Harlequin Romance. It was good while it lasted. The great thing was that I was no longer the Queen of Unrequited Love. I could continue to be his pen pal and tell my friends about him, but I didn't have to pine away for the fact that I'd probably never see him again. Everybody won.

It didn't take long for me to find someone new to think about instead of Lee, even though I was as capricious a girl as you could find. Don't get me wrong, I still thought about Lee and that great kiss. I couldn't forget about that kiss so easily.

It was the week before the first year of high school when Anne told me about Dan Stone. Just writing his name made me smile. "Such a nice guy." That was what you heard anytime Dan Stone's name was mentioned.

We were at an end-of-summer swimming party at Anne's house. Everyone from The Group was there. My mother started calling us "The Group" when she was our teacher in middle school. We reminded her of some book she read in the olden days. Sadly, our group included Evil Sheila, our frienemy.

I use the modern term of frienemy, because if we had that term in the seventies it would have been in the dictionary with a picture of Sheila. Sheila wasn't always evil. Once upon a time she was a nice little girl, like the rest of us. She had a wonderful sense of humor, was the first girl to want to T.P. a house, and could talk about anything, anytime. Sheila was a fun girl. She even looked similar to some of us. With her sandy blond hair and blue eyes, I don't like to say she looked like us, as any comparison to Evil Sheila Scudmore would make my stomach turn.

As far as bullies go, she wasn't such a big deal, but it didn't seem that way then. In sixth grade—that's when they always turn—Sheila kicked my crutches out (from a skiing injury) and threw me in a darkened school closet. All I heard was her cackle, walking away with her minions. That's when Sheila became Evil Sheila and her followers became known as minions.

It's when Sheila and her minions first bullied unsuspecting girls with cruel phone pranks and even crueler dares to be admitted into The Group, even though they knew full well Sheila would never allow a new girl into The Group. Sheila always tried to be the self-appointed leader. More girls meant less attention on Sheila, and in Sheila's mind that was forbidden.

Sheila was so insecure that no one escaped her vicious tongue. The shrinking violet types ran away at the first glimpse of Sheila coming down the hallways of middle school. She was so horrible, we long dreamt she would get pregnant and be sent off to a home for unwed mothers. Lucky for us, she didn't have quite enough popularity to give her too much power.

Sheila's evil peaked just after eighth grade. She was convinced that Tami Costa was stuffing her bra, so she yanked Tami's bikini top off at the public pool to an audience full of teenage boys with their mouths agape. In a score for teenage girls everywhere, Sheila was banned from the pool for the entire summer, and Tami soared to popularity as "TaTa Tami," which may have seemed offensive to some, but Tami was fine with it since so many girls who witnessed the jaw-dropping scene kept telling her they'd never seen such pretty boobs.

The girl we were so close to in elementary school

entered the dark side at puberty. What is it about hormones that can make some girls so mean?

Our group doesn't remember life without each other. Our parents knew each other before we were born, and as far as we were concerned, everybody grew up like we did, with deep bonds that might as well have been familial. As long as I had those girls with me, and my bikini top firmly in place, I was safe around Evil Sheila. My flat chest was evidence I wasn't stuffing. Bullies are often big cowards, and Sheila was no exception. Anne had been protecting me and fighting my battles my whole life, and Sheila was plenty scared of her. No one messed with Anne.

The Group (evil members and all) was lounging in Anne's pool when Anne announced that not only did her next-door-neighbor, Bobby Hunt, like *her*, but his best friend, Dan Stone, liked *me*. She just announced this. Kind of like when a teacher announces what's for hot lunch: no-big-deal-oh-by-the-way. Remember, I had the body of a ten-year-old and the mouth of a snotty thirteen-year-old, so the boys weren't lining up for me. I couldn't have been more shocked if she had told me that John Travolta drove up in his flying *Grease* car to take me to a school dance.

This was 1978. *Grease* was the word, and I was going to marry John Travolta. I had no choice since Cindy Santini called dibs on Shaun Cassidy. There was no other way. I loved him when he was Vinny Barbarino, and I cried for him when he was *The Boy in the Plastic Bubble*. My goal was to look like Olivia Newton-John when my body came in, so that we would make the most fabulous couple and he would be mine. All mine.

Sheila looked at me with a mixture of pure jealousy and a fake happy-for-me expression. She ran her finger through her dirty blond hair, pulled down her bikini top from her non-existent chest and sneered, "Wow, Meg. Dan Stone. That's a big deal. He's *such* a nice guy." Did I tell you? That's what they always said.

"Oh Anne. You've got to be kidding. Dan Stone does not like *me*. He's way too old and way too...I don't know... way too *everything* for me. Besides, I only know him from church. Who picks up girls at church?" *Right? That was right, wasn't it?* My head spun at the thought that an older, super-cute, really nice boy liked me. I was so used to rejection and unrequited love that I didn't know how to process this news.

"Oh God, Meg, only everyone," said Tonya. "You're such a Presby...whatever. I always make sure I line up in communion so I'm right next to Marcus Williams. That boy is fine." She was over my news and dreaming of Marcus Williams. Everyone seemed to agree with her both on the meeting-boys-in-church-thing and that Marcus Williams was fine. Apparently, being underdeveloped meant you didn't know a thing about boys either 'cause this was news to me.

I was used to not knowing anything about boys or anything overly grown up really. I was always the Pollyanna of The Group: optimistic and called naïve often, especially by Tonya. She was much more wise to the world than I, and one of the few people who could boss me around regularly.

As a self-proclaimed "AfriMexItalian," Tonya Cena always referred to herself as the "ethnic one" of The Group. She's half African, half Mexican: raised by her Mexican mother and Italian stepfather. She didn't call herself African-American, because she thought that sounded like too much once you added the Mexican and Italian. She liked to say, "If you can't tell I'm American by my accent, then you're too stupid for me to be explain my ethnicity to anyway." So there you have it: AfriMexItalian. Don't try and tell her she's not Italian or she'll kick your ass. Or have your ass kicked by someone else.

Tonya likes to say that she didn't even know she was black until she went away to college. We had our share of rednecks in Gridley, but they left her alone. Our theory was that there were too few African-Americans for them to notice, plus maybe they were too busy going after Mexicans. She thought her mixed race bewildered the rednecks. There were too many slurs that applied to her, so they didn't know which racist comment to make and left her alone.

Tonya thinks that because she grew up around the Italian and Mexican sides of her family, she didn't notice anything else until she went to college and saw people who looked more like her. Her mom always called her "my little butterscotch baby," and that fit. Tonya had the flawless, mocha skin and movie star good looks that couldn't be matched. I doubt there were many people in college that *really* looked like her.

When we were in the second grade, Tonya was the only divorced kid I knew. She had to miss school one day to go to court to be adopted. That was the most exotic thing I'd ever heard. It sounded like an episode of Perry Mason to me. I pictured her on the witness stand telling the judge that she loved her stepdad, didn't know her bio-dad, and wanted to be adopted. My seven-year-old brain thought that was fantastic. She got to change her name and everything. She went from Tonya Harris to Tonya Cena. It sounded like one word, so she basically became Cher to me. After they formed this new family, they moved in next door to us. Our friendship was sealed forever when Tonya Cena became my next-door neighbor.

"Seriously Anne, how do you know that Dan likes Meg? He's such a fox. And she's such a...such a...well..."

Apparently, Sheila couldn't figure out what insult she was going to hurl at me as she eyed me up and down. "Chicken legs? Dan Stone likes chicken legs?"

There it was. This tired old reference from a girl who had cankles. While my legs might have looked like they wouldn't hold me up in a strong wind, and I had knobby knees, hers looked more like those dolls we used to make by stuffing old pantyhose and tying them together. Evil Sheila doubted the news, *and* she thought Dan was a fox. This was getting better by the minute. Especially since she called me chicken legs one more time. She needed new material. Her jealousy alone made me like Dan more.

"He told me. Swear to God. He was leaving Bobby's house next door, and I was out front. He stopped to talk to me and told me that he likes Meg and that Bobby likes me. Just like that." Anne was pretty excited about these tidbits of juicy gossip. She pulled herself out of the pool and sat on the diving board. "Is that how they do it in high school?" she asked. "'Cause that's not any different than eighth grade. I don't know. I thought things would seem more grown up in high school, but it seems the same, except they have moustaches and drive trucks."

We laughed at that thought. It made sense. They weren't that far out of eighth grade, and I heard my mom say once that boys' bodies developed faster than their brains, so it made sense. I laughed thinking how funny this all was. How was it possible that my dream of the perfect long-distance romance could be shattered in the same week that an older, super-cute guy liked me?

My dreamy thoughts didn't last long.

While I sat in the pool and dreamed of having a real boyfriend, my "friends" gathered around me, *outside* the pool. So deep in thought, I didn't even notice as they held me under my arms and whisked me out of the pool. Next thing I knew, Evil Sheila sat on my legs and a couple of her minions held my arms down while Tonya (traitor) put a giant pair of granny panties on me, and Anne (even bigger traitor) put the world's biggest granny bra on me. *Et tu Brute?* They picked me up and carried me to the front yard, over the ditch, straight next door to Bobby Hunt's house.

My mind raced. I squirmed and wiggled and did everything to get out of their clutches. They walked straight to Bobby's house. And what for? It wasn't Christmas and I certainly wasn't wrapped well. I struggled in vain. There were shouts like, "Hold on tighter, she's fighting hard," and "Move faster. I'm gonna drop her." That last one worried me since we were too close to the drainage ditch. At least the water in the ditch was low. I pictured myself falling out of their clutches and rolling into a ditch full of sludge.

Faster and faster, they sped to the Hunt's house like I was a little bag of manure for them to set afire. When did my friends become such hooligans?

Smack. Right there. That's when: the moment my bum dropped on the Hunt's doorstep. They had timed it so well, even having Cindy run ahead to ring the doorbell. They waited to dump me until they heard footsteps close to the door. There I was: eighty-five pounds of dripping granny panty and gi-normous bra, laying on the doorstep, looking up at Bobby Hunt and his dreamy best friend, Dan Stone, the boy I'd just been told liked me. It was a nightmare that I couldn't have dreamt up. I froze for a moment, looking into his beautiful green eyes, until I remembered that I was in Tonya's nana's underwear. I let loose a blood-curdling, glass-breaking, shrill, and unattractive scream, jumped up and ran. Ran faster than I'd ever run before. That is, until the granny panties dropped to my ankles in the middle of the

Hunt's yard. I fell to the ground, screamed some more, tore the panties off my ankles and left them in a heap in the yard. Throughout all of this, The Group was on Anne's doorstep wetting their pants with laughter. They were laughing so hard they were crying. I ran harder and even jumped the drainage ditch faster than The Bionic Woman herself. By that time, the bra fell off too. I moved it from around my bum and threw it at Anne when I passed her, racing straight into the house and falling, in a heap, into her dining room. I didn't know whether to laugh or cry.

Anne, Cindy, and Tonya fell on the ground with me, still laughing through tears. "Omigod. That was the funniest thing I've ever seen. I was dyin' when you tripped and fell 'cause the panties were around your ankles." Tonya was very proud.

Anne was impressed, "No way, the funniest part was the scream. You could go to Hollywood with that scream. Dang. I've *never* heard a scream like that."

Cindy tried to cheer me up, "I don't know. Did you see her jump the ditch? You might want to try out for track, Meg. That was cool."

"I would be *so* embarrassed. Don't you just want to die, Meg?" Sheila was a bitch. There. I said it. Someone needed to. That's when I first realized I needed some new friends, but I also realized this would have been a lot funnier if Sheila hadn't been involved. Sheila instilled her evil into things that could've been more innocent had she not put her stink on it. I looked at my real friends, Anne, Tonya, and Cindy, as they were sitting with me, laughing, and saw the difference in their eyes. They were searching my eyes for acceptance, "*Is she pissed? Will she laugh? What will we do if she's pissed?*" While in Sheila's eyes, all I saw was nothing. Her eyes were empty. That's when I knew that I had to laugh with them and play this off as their prank and not Sheila's. If I got whiney (not hard for me) then Sheila would win and get what she wanted. If I played it cool and laughed with them, Sheila would be the pissed one. Everybody won.

Tonya stared at me, searching my eyes for an answer. I looked down so she'd think I was serious and still mad. "I just want to know if your Nana is going bra and panty-less today?" I looked up and straight into her eyes trying to make her think I was mad. She was silent but kept eye contact. "Tonya?" Then I smiled, and everybody erupted into laughter. Everyone except Sheila. It worked. Why hadn't I thought of this in sixth grade? I could have saved myself such heartache.

"Omigod," said Tonya. "I was so afraid you'd be mad. I had to sneak into her bedroom and steal the bra and panties and then sneak them into my purse. I *knew* you'd know where they came from. Nobody has bigger boobs than *my* Nana." She was relieved and so were Anne and Cindy.

"I'm so glad you're not pissed, Meggie. I was scared too." Poor Cindy. She got sucked into Sheila's evil. They didn't call me Meggie that often. It softened the blow a bit. Sheila looked down, probably plotting her next move.

Anne tried to console me, "Dan Stone really does like you though, Meg. I didn't make that up."

"Well, I think *that's* over now. Add some blood to that and I was straight out of *Carrie*. Total horror movie. I didn't even know I could scream like that. And I have sisters who make me scream a lot."

The Kegger Kidnapping

Gridley High School

78 79

STUDENT CARD

4

NAME Meredith Cailin

The Group made it through the first day of high school unscathed. Sheila very much enjoyed the attention of the older boys. It was customary for the junior and senior jocks to stand along a row of windows in the main hallway and holler at the pretty girls. It was worse than a construction site. This area was the hub of the hallway system that most people passed through to get to classes, and it was directly across from long rows of gunmetal grey lockers. I had the misfortune of having my locker right across from these windows, and therefore straight across from the long line of older, testosterone-filled, hollering boys. Some of these tomcats could be described as men. This scared the crap out of me.

I was fine during class, but filled with terror during every in-between period. I'd have to walk back to my locker holding my books in front of my non-existent chest, open the locker (forget trying to remember the combination — my hands shook with the pressure), trade my books, re-position the new ones to hide my hopeless chest, avoid the spittle of the couple who made out next to my locker in between *every single period*, and walk to my next class. I perfected the art of slinking in between other people, hiding behind crowds, or my personal favorite, sliding over to Cindy's locker (further away from the watchful eyes) and angling myself so that I was on the locker side of her for the walk to the next class, just to avoid the "men."

Sheila was another story. Her locker was away from "jock row," but she would hurry to her locker after class, change books, scuttle to the area in front of the "row," and then saunter down that part of the hallway. On the days when she'd wear a dress her heels would click fast, then screech to a halt, and slowly clack down our part of the hallway, her shapeless calves working overtime trying to walk in her wooden platform heels. This went on in between every period. Sheila became easy to detect by sound, so I would watch from the corner of my eye while switching my books. My favorite part was when she'd stroll past the windows in her best female version of a John Travolta strut. Sometimes when she walked I could hear the soundtrack from *Saturday Night Fever* in my head. The only problem being I didn't want to *marry* Evil Sheila. Now, if John Travolta had been hanging out on the "row" at Gridley Union High School, I might have changed my whole low-key approach to the thing.

As soon as I heard clicking, I'd peek from behind my locker door to see Sheila with any combination of her minions practicing their row walks with fake smiles. If I looked carefully, I could see the fear behind the minions' smiles as they walked past the row. I realized the boys were mainly watching Sheila's better-looking minions and not Sheila. When the boys didn't notice any of the minions they were crushed. Where Sheila would dust herself off and move on, the minions were sad, hanging their heads all the way to their next class. I felt sorry for them in a way I never had before, and I worried more about my "friends" and where I fit in, in this new landscape.

On the first Friday of the school year, I left with the masses after the lunch bell. Gridley High had an open campus policy and the cafeteria food was horrible, so not many people stayed on campus to eat. As new freshmen without cars, this made lunchtime more stressful than the periods in between classes. I didn't have a routine down yet and hated the insecurity of it all. So I walked along with everyone else, like cattle heading for the barn. I was a little panicky when I didn't see any of my friends or even my sister Rowan.

At least if I found Ro, I could go home for lunch. Better than nothing, even if we never had any good food in the house. Right as I began to panic, one of Sheila's minions yelled over to me, "Hey Meg, want to go to lunch with us? Mark's giving us a ride." She motioned to a blue Oldsmobile parked in front of the school. My instincts told me to wait a bit longer for anyone else, but I didn't listen to my instincts and climbed into the car like the huge idiot that I was.

I slid into the back seat, the vinyl already scalding from the autumn valley heat. Many people think northern California is colder than southern California just because it's north. Those people have never spent a summer or fall in the Sacramento valley. If Sylvia Plath had grown up in Gridley, she wouldn't have dreamed of killing herself by putting her head in an oven. She would have felt like she lived in an oven already, so it would never have entered her mind.

I felt instantly better about my decision to jump in when I saw Anne waiting for me in the back seat. Thank God: a reliable face among the questionable minions. Then I looked forward and saw Evil Sheila wedged into the middle of the front seat, practically on the lap of our driver, Mark Grimes. My stomach fell again. I knew this couldn't end well, but we were already driving off at that point, and I wasn't a strong enough person to fake some excuse and ask to be dropped off at the cafeteria. "So where are we going?" I stammered, the fear dripping from my wimpy voice. "I'm starved." I tried to sound cool but failed.

Per Gridley requirements, I'd known Mark Grimes all my life. Our parents knew each other. Our grandparents knew each other. The familiarity was there except that he was three years older than me, and since I was in high school with him and Evil Sheila was in his lap, this familiarity had taken new shape: an alternate reality. I didn't know him at all *really*, but tried to act like I was as comfortable as Sheila, who now had her head on his shoulder. I almost gagged at the sight and hoped the restaurant was close so that I'd be able to walk back to school.

No such luck. Mark threw his head back in excitement and howled over the Van Halen blaring on his eight-track, "We're *drinkin'* our lunch today girls, 'cause it's Friday." He did his best catcall, like a cowboy would do. It was a common shout heard in Gridley: land of cowboys both fake and real. I thought Mark was a fake cowboy since he lived in town without cows or horses around him, and I had never seen him participate in any agricultural activity other than football (football counts in every category in Gridley), and now, I guessed, drinking for sport at lunchtime. But this was very attractive to Sheila, because she flipped her thin, dishwater hair—feathered in the front and curled under in the back—at me and cuddled up to him even closer. The minion on the other side of her laughed nervously as well. Both were very happy to be there.

I looked over to Anne and mouthed, "Shit. Is he serious?"

"I think so. It'll be okay," she whispered back. My heart raced with terror. I was starring in my own *After School Special* and by no effort of my own. If I was going to be an *After School Special*, I figured at least it should be by my own choice—like the pregnant girls who loved their boyfriends. Not because I chose to get in the wrong car at lunchtime.

My mind raced with possible scenarios of my demise.

What if Ro found out? As a popular senior in a small school, there wasn't much she wouldn't know. Then what? Monahan Girls don't go to keggers. Monahan Girls don't drink, do drugs, or have sex in high school. Monahan Girls don't bring shame upon their families. First and foremost, Monahan Girls are *nice girls*. I thought about opening the door and rolling out of the car like they do in the movies, but we were on Colusa Highway, going at least sixty-five. With my luck, I'd end up face down in a canal with some injury that would prevent me from lifting my head, so I'd drown in six inches of water. I could see the headlines in *The Gridley Herald*:

Monahan Girl Dies at Keg - Entire Family Shamed

My only option was to beg. "Oh please drop me off. I can't go to a keg. You know I'll get killed. You know it will get back to my family somehow. Please drop me off here and I'll walk back. *Please.*" I sounded like such a loser, but I didn't care. The wrath of Jayne and Fred Monahan was much worse than any teasing I could take from these people. The family goal of no drinking, drugs, or sex in high school was at stake so I shamelessly begged, and it didn't get me anywhere.

Mark Grimes laughed at me. He knew he was in control, and he enjoyed it. I could tell he liked the thought of taking a Monahan Girl to a keg. Football for sport, drinking for sport, now fallen Monahan Girls for sport—it made sense. Mark Grimes was also a little scary. He was at least 6'2", football-player-big, with a full, dark beard and moustache. He was eighteen or nineteen (who knows how long he'd been in high school?) and looked thirty-five. When God passed out testosterone, Mark must have gotten back in line a few dozen extra times. And this taking-me-hostage-thing made Sheila even *more* attracted to him. When he laughed at me she leaned over and kissed him. Open mouth, tongue kissed Daniel Boone right then while my life was ending. I was truly in an alternate universe, and if I didn't get out of that car quickly they were going to see me hurling all over them. The sight of a fourteen-year-old, evil or not, making out with a man that looked thirty-five terrified me. And she thought she was so cool as she rolled those blue eyes to the back seat to look at me while she was kissing him, her eyes glimmering with evil. *Holy Cow Batman, I've entered Hell,* was all I could think.

"Sorry Monahan. You're coming with us," Mark said with a laugh. Sheila turned around to give me another look of pride and put her head back on his shoulder. I sat back and dreamed. Dreamed of Sheila getting slutty, getting knocked up and being sent away to a home for unwed mothers. I knew it was a horrible thing to think, but it was a solution, and I'm all about solutions. Sheila was just smart enough to use protection though. For all I knew, she'd already been to the free clinic.

While I wistfully dreamed of Evil Sheila being sent far, far away, Anne nudged me and whispered, "All you have to do is come with me and find a ride home. They won't mind that you don't drink. It's more for them. Stick with me. I'll find us a ride back." She looked over at Sheila and Mark, making out again. "God," she said. "I can't stand watching them kiss anymore. It's so gross. He's hairier than my Uncle Mario." That made me smile. Anne's Uncle Mario was a swarthy, Italian man who really did look like he wore a sweater to the beach—a sweater of his own hair. Evil Sheila was basically making out with Anne's hairy Uncle Mario. Only he wasn't really old. And I'm pretty sure he wasn't Sicilian. But he looked like both.

My initial panic was over. If anyone could get us a ride back it would be Anne. She'd bat those giant brown eyes, and any guy would do whatever she asked. I wondered what that was like. Not just to bat your eyelashes and have men do whatever you pleased, but also to be so calm in a scene like this? To not have to worry about what your parents would say or how you'd shame your giant family? Anne was a Gridley transplant. All of her extended family was in San Jose. Safely three hours away where they couldn't stumble upon her say, at a kegger out in the country.

In Gridley, everything was defined either by being "in town" or "out in the country." Never mind that nothing was more than five minutes away. We thought things were so far away if they were "out in the country" because we lived "in town" and vice versa for the country kids.

Mark turned the car into a makeshift dirt driveway, which looked like it had been formed about fifteen minutes earlier. I smelled the faint scent of peaches. He drove down the road until there was a clearing where the farmer's burned their brush. My heart raced as I saw all the fruitless trees. I gasped as my mind raced and screamed at the same time. Yes, I am so neurotic that I can scream at myself, in my head. *Oh no. This can't be? We're in a peach orchard off Losser Road that I swear to God belongs to my uncle.* When I gasped, Anne looked around, realized where we were, and stared into my eyes, frozen. She knew what I was thinking: *We're at my uncle's orchard. My Mormon uncle.* Not that any non-Mormon uncle would be okay with a kegger happening in his orchard. It was like my screaming head was now inside hers, screaming at her as well. *The Gridley Herald* headlines flowing in my brain had just changed:

High School Keg Busted – Monahan Girl Jailed by Uncle Bill

Oh sure, *The Gridley Herald* had better things to report than the busting of a high school keg. Well, they didn't give *headlines* to the busting of high school kegs, but it made it no less serious to me. I thought this was the end of the world. Now, not only did I have to find a ride out of here, I had to find a way out without anyone in my family noticing I was here. That is no small feat when you're in the middle of your uncle's peach orchard, in a small town, where if you picked your nose on the way home from school, by the time you got home, your mama already heard about it and lectured you for your poor manners.

By the time I looked up from the haze of headlines and the screaming in my head, I was out of the car and leaning on it. I didn't even remember getting there. Sheila was already beer-in-hand with Mark's arm dangling over her shoulder. "Hey chicken legs, aren't ya gonna get a beer?" Sheila waved her red cup at me in a futile attempt at a dare. I rolled my eyes at her and went looking for Anne, who seemed to have disappeared.

The fragrant air stopped me for a moment. In Gridley, you only need your sense of smell to know the season. It's a much truer test than any obvious sense like sight or touch. This was the beginning of fall. That meant the air was warm but usually not blistering hot. And the air was delicious. It was the in between time when the prunes were ripe but not rotting in the ground from the heat causing the orchards to smell like your crisper drawer in the refrigerator when you've forgotten about your old fruit. Yes Virginia, a whole town can smell like a bad refrigerator drawer. The beginning of fall is the perfect time of year in most northern California farm towns, because the temperatures are mild, the air is sweet, and the summer crops are in which means people get to keep eating. When you live where food is grown, you learn to appreciate the simple act of eating. It's an awesome thing to help feed the world, and it's a serious subject in Gridley.

But where was Anne? I couldn't find her and started to panic. I searched the crowd for any signs of her. The male to female ratio here was easily four to one. I could see why Sheila and her minions were so eager to come to one of these. But were these really the boys one wanted to choose from when looking for dates? I was also surprised to see so many football players there. How did they play football after drinking beer all afternoon?

I snapped back to attention when I caught sight of Anne across the orchard. *Who was she with?* I moved. Some other people in front of me moved. I still couldn't see. I weaved through the trees, ducking in and out of branches, trying to keep steady feet on the rough dirt (the last thing I wanted now was to fall down, face first in the middle of this party) trying to get closer to Anne. Then I saw him: my Knight in Shining Armor. When I thought "Holy Cow Batman, I'm in Hell" earlier, I didn't expect Batman to actually send someone. It was better than the movies. Anne Calzaretta, my best friend, who promised to get me out of this mess, managed in less than five minutes to find Dan Stone and Bobby Hunt to take us home. I breathed a little easier then. I tried to fluff up my hair (Dan was a junior — I needed to look good) and walk across the party like I was very grown up and went to these things *all* the time.

So there I was trying to look grown up in my Dittos (size fourteen slim—I wasn't even in the ladies sizes yet) jeans and Sbicca sandals. I was torn now, between worrying about the outcome of this debacle and whether the mud and dirt from the peach orchard would ruin the jute wrapped heels of my sandals. Sbicca's were not cheap and I worked hard for every penny I spent on clothes. When babysitting paid an average of fifty cents an hour, it took a lot of bratty kids to come up with enough cash for shoes. Little did I know, I should have been more concerned with my ability to *walk* in said shoes in a peach orchard.

Anne looked up and saw me making my way across the orchard to the boys and her. She was holding a red cup (and not drinking it) and waving at me to come over. I waved back, trying my best to act cool. As I put my arm to my side, I stumbled on what seemed like the world's biggest dirt clod. Not some scary guy from the sophomore class, an *actual* dirt clod the size of a football. I stumbled, waved my arms trying to catch my balance, and looked more like a Weeble than the cool girl I was trying to impersonate. Determined not to fall, my arms flailed and my legs were like a bendy, Gumby toy as I grabbed a tree branch and did *not* hit the ground. I was so proud. Yes, I looked like an idiot, hanging onto that tree branch like it was a water ski rope and I was ready to get up on my skis for the best run of my life, but I did not fall. I let go of the branch and dusted myself off, tossed my head in what I thought was a coy move, planted another smile on my face to hide my fear, and pressed on. I was almost there. I would curse about my muddy Sbicca's later.

Right then all I could see was Dan Stone. Standing

there next to Anne, smiling down at me. *He was so tall.* He snickered a little when I stumbled (I refuse to call it a fall since I did *not* hit the ground), but in a nice way, not a condescending one. There he was: tall and lanky, his brown hair feathered back better than mine. Dan Stone was a fox. Period. He looked confident in that nice guy way in his jeans, t-shirt, and those tan, suede, high-top shoes that all the guys wore. I couldn't help but notice that he had managed to keep his shoes clean while my Sbicca's were now thrashed. And, that there was no beer in his hand. My hero would not have a buzz on while saving me. He totally scored extra points there.

"Meg, what are you doing? You almost took a header into a tree back there." Anne made a joke out of my *stumble* (not fall) and that put me a little bit at ease.

"Oh, you know, I didn't want all the drunks to feel out of place. Just trying to do my part to make this keg more fun." I punched the air sideways with a fist to show how enthusiastic I was about this party. Then, because I never know when to stop, I did a soft cheerleading yell and thrust my fist up in the air and said, "Yea kegs." Nervous sarcasm is the cornerstone of my personality. I've tried to overcome it, but it's like having blue eyes. You can cover them up with contacts, but eventually you have to take the contacts out and let the blue shine through.

Yea kegs? I thought to myself. *Who says that?* I had to get out of here fast. Lord only knew what I'd say next. I got caught up in Dan's cuteness instead of keeping my eye on the ball: *my escape.* I needed to remember that I was still in the middle of my Uncle Bill's peach orchard, and I had to find a way back to school…fast. The clock was ticking. Never mind the fact that I was starving, and the only nourishment in this place was made of barley and hops or the random piece of over-ripe fruit.

Just as I was getting lost in my thoughts of fear and panic again, Dan came over to me. It was very hard to focus since he was so cute and smelled so good. What was that scent? I'd spent enough time in the drugstore where my sisters worked to know it wasn't *Jovan Musk Oil for Men* or *Brut* (my Dad wore that). But what was it? I shook my head again so I could pay better attention to him. This must have startled him, "Meg, are you okay?" He looked down at me.

Great. Now he thought I was a freak with a tick. "I'm good. I'm great." I was nervous as hell and he could tell (sorry about the rhyme).

"It's okay that you don't want to be here. There isn't anyone here who didn't have your mom as a teacher. They know this isn't your thing. You're not gonna get some drunken reputation for being here for five minutes." As he said this he put his hand on my shoulder. *He put his hand on my shoulder.* He did. His actual hand was on my actual shoulder, all soft and warm. I didn't know what to do. He was trying to make me feel better but all that did was make my heart race and make me feel…. I didn't know how I felt. It was a cross between pleasure and terror.

"Thanks," I said. "That's really nice of you, but if you want to know the truth, I'm scared to death. I don't belong here. I'm lucky I didn't fall on my face back there. I'm losin' it. Fast." As usual, way too much talking.

"Then let's go. Do you want a ride back to school? Anne already asked if we could take you back. Is that okay with you? We can go right now and have you back in time for your next class. Come on." He motioned to an imaginary exit. Since this was the middle of my uncle's peach orchard, there weren't actual roads to walk down. Anne and Bobby joined us, and we made our way down several rows of trees until we hit a different path where Dan's truck was parked. Still under the romantic spell of it all, I saw that blue pickup as my chariot, my escape back to reality. Isn't it usually the other way around? Don't people usually want to escape *from* reality? I guess I've always been backwards.

Then I saw Evil Sheila and her minions.

Mark's car peeled out of the orchard, squealing when it hit the street. As they screeched away, Sheila hung out the window, waving and yelling, "See ya losers." She thought *she* was ditching *us*.

This was my new life in high school.

Anne put her arm around me. "What are you looking so sad about? Why do you let her get to you? She's a scuzz, and you care what she thinks about you." Then she whispered in my ear, so the guys wouldn't hear. "Look at yourself. You're leaving with Dan Stone, one of the nicest, cutest boys in the junior class." And then she pointed in the direction of the beater car Sheila had ridden off in. "And Evil Sheila is off making out with a hairy ape. Hell, at this rate, she'll be pregnant by sixth period, and you might be getting a real boyfriend. Think of *that*."

I did and it scared me more than anything. I didn't know any more about having a *real* boyfriend than I did about Evil Sheila getting pregnant. Oh, why was I so scared of everything?

When Dan took us back to school from the keg, we had to slide into his truck. This meant four people on one bench seat. This was a real source of stress for me. I had grown up watching high school girls sit all the way over in the cab of a pickup truck, so that they were right next to their boyfriends. It was to me the ultimate sign of an intimacy I did not understand. I thought that if I hadn't gotten my period, I couldn't possibly understand the nuances involved in knowing where to sit in a boy's pickup truck. Now, let's say it all together. "This scared me to death." Have you noticed a pattern yet? God, I was exhausting.

To me, the scariest part was figuring out which side to get in on. How did you know whether to get in on the passenger side or the driver's side? When a couple was a couple, the boy opened up the driver's side of the truck, and the girl slid in so that there was just enough room for the boy to get in and drive. Luckily for me, these were all questions that Anne had the answers to. "You follow the boy's lead. If he opens the passenger side door, you sit there. If he leads you to his side, then he wants you to sit next to him." She seemed quite authoritative on this, even though I knew for a fact that she had never done this.

"But how do you know if he's leading you to the driver's side? What if you walk straight to the passenger side? Then what?" Leave it to me to over analyze every… single…situation.

"Oh Meg. That's what you do if you don't want to sit by him. Don't think so much and just follow his lead." It was all too complicated.

So we got to the cab of Dan's truck and I didn't have to make any decisions, because Dan opened the passenger side door and we all got in from there. Well not Dan. He went around so he could drive. Of course, it occurred to me later, that in my over analyzing I hadn't accounted for the fact that there were four of us, so I would be sitting by him regardless of what door I'd taken. I still appreciated his manners and lack of assumption, but I wasn't prepared for how I'd feel sitting right next to him. I liked it. I liked it a lot.

So there we were, riding in the cab of a pickup like real high schoolers. It felt so strange. So grown up. And if I thought Dan smelled good in that peach orchard, being this close gave me an even better perspective. This was all a little overwhelming. Anne and I kept giving each other knowing smiles, hoping the guys wouldn't see that we were huge dorks and enjoying the ride too much. That's when I noticed it — the way Bobby looked at Anne. Soft is the only word that came to my mind. He gave her a look with such soft eyes. I'd never seen anyone look at anyone like that. And I could see Anne's face change when he looked at her like that. She didn't seem to be thinking of Rick Davis, a football star whom she had been in love with all our lives, at that moment.

I couldn't help but worry about how they lived next door to each other, so if this turned into a real relationship, their breakup would be such a drag. That's what I do though. Borrow trouble. My Grandma Alice always said, "Don't borrow trouble. You have enough of your own without borrowing more." As much sense as that made, it never stopped me. It was too easy to find.

Dan pulled up to the school and managed to find a front parking space. A real find since the actual school parking lot was a field away from school. All the prime parking was on Spruce Street in front of the school, so everyone got great parallel parking experience by the time they graduated from Gridley High. He expertly paralleled his truck into the spot. I was so impressed. When I jumped down from the cab, he was right there holding the door, so polite. "Meg, can you hang on a minute? I can walk you to class." Dan looked at

Bobby like they'd done this a million times, and Bobby led Anne away. My heart raced. I looked at Anne, not knowing what to do. She nodded her head like, "Go on," and walked away so fast that I had no choice but to stay.

"Sure." I got my purse from the cab of the truck, and he closed the door behind me. We walked together to the entrance of the school.

"Hey, are you going to the dance next week?" Dan looked down at his feet like he was nervous. *He was nervous. I wasn't the only one.*

"Um, yeah." *Duh. It's only my first high school dance. Of course I'm going.* I tried so hard to sound casual.

"I was wondering if you might want to go with me?" He barely looked at me then. *Holy Cow. I was getting asked out on a date.* My heart raced…until I remembered.

I wasn't allowed to date.

Monahan rules. I couldn't date until I was sixteen. A long held family rule that was unbreakable. This I knew. "Ohhhh," I sighed when I remembered the ridiculous rule. His face fell. Then I realized he thought I didn't like him. "No. It's not like that. I'd *love* to go to the dance with you." I talked in exclamation points my entire time in high school. Who am I kidding? I still do. He looked up at me and smiled, relieved, until I said, "But I can't."

That handsome face fell again. "I don't get it. Can you or can't you?" Gosh. He should have known right then to get out. Get out fast before he got too attached. This is when Tonya would have called me "PITA." She doesn't call me PITA for nothing. It stands for *Pain In The Ass.* That's me. I like to think that, most of the time, I'm worth it, but then there's the, let's say, ten percent of the other times. Well, PITA. That says it all.

"I can't. Monahan rules. I can't date until I'm sixteen, and my parents would definitely consider going to a dance with a boy that can drive, a date." I was still so nervous and talking too fast, until I noticed Dan's wheels turning in his brain. I didn't *see* the wheels, but I could tell he was thinking.

"So, it's your parents, not you?"

"Oh definitely. Not me. I'd love to go to the dance with you." I tried not to fidget. He made me very nervous.

"Then who will be taking you to the dance? Rowan?"

"Probably. Are you thinking what I'm thinking?"

"Let's meet at the dance." We said it in unison. I know, dorky, but so cute at the same time.

I walked toward the hall. "We should get to class."

"Cool. I'll see you later," he said as we turned in different directions.

"Yeah, thanks again for saving us today," I said, looking over my shoulder. He was so cute.

"Anytime, Meg."

My heart skipped a beat, maybe two.

Letters from the Front Lines of Bad Grammar

Freshman Cheerleading
1979, Farmer's Hall, Gridley, California
Stacie Sormano Walker, Meredith Carlin First,
Melissa Costa Talbott, Diane LaBarbera Symon

The morning air was crisp. The thick days of summer heat transitioned into early breezes, sweltering afternoons, and cool evenings, just enough of a respite to remind us why we lived in such a beautiful yet treacherous place. Autumn is the reward to all valley dwellers for a summer well-spent baking in the heat, just like the fruit on our trees.

"Did you really go to a keg at lunch yesterday?" Jennifer sat on my desk in my room, dangling her long legs where the chair was supposed to be. I was trying to do homework, but not getting much done.

"I did, but I didn't mean to." I believed in asking for forgiveness rather than permission.

"Oh, well, that's good. Is that going to be your answer when your mom asks you?" Was Jen getting sarcastic? I was becoming a bad influence on her.

"I won't have to have an answer 'cause hopefully she'll never ask. I told Ro about it and she understood. She gave me the standard talk, 'You're a Monahan Girl, which means you're a lady. Young ladies don't drink, do drugs, or have sex in high school. If you do anything bad, someone will find out and you'll always get caught. Save it for when you go away to college where they can't see it.' Sometimes I feel like there's a *Monahan Handbook* that we're not allowed to see. We have to figure it out as we go along, and when we blow it we have to pay for our mistakes; but learn from them at the same time. Why can't it be spelled out to us, so that we don't make the mistakes in the first place?" I was on my bed, on my belly, looking at *Teen Magazine*. I felt like I was on to something with the handbook theory though, so I threw the magazine down to think harder. Sometimes it was a chore to think hard.

Jen picked up the magazine and started flipping through. "Oh Meg, you crack me up. There's no magic handbook. You already know the rules. You just don't like the consequences when you break them. I think it's lucky that we have families that hold us to higher standards. I think it makes it easier. Look at Sheila, her family doesn't hold her to the same standards and now she's got a big, ole hairy boyfriend, and it's only the first week of high school." She laughed.

"Oh, Jennifer, he's so gross. And to watch her kiss him? Gag me. I've never seen anything so disgusting." We were laughing hard. That was the good thing about Evil Sheila: she made us laugh with her poor choices. "Do you really think we're lucky to have strict parents? I mean, look at you? You had a seven o'clock bedtime until the fifth grade. That's crazy."

"My parents are more strict with me 'cause I'm the oldest," she said. "Whenever I complain and compare my rules to yours, they always tell me the same thing, 'Margaret Monahan is the youngest. Her parents are worn out. You have to set the example for your brother and sisters.' I'm good with that." She sounded so responsible, so grown up, and so the opposite of how *I* would respond to that.

"I don't know," I said. "They're lucky to have you as the oldest. They'd hate having me as their daughter. I'd fight it every step of the way."

"That's the only real difference. I accept my parent's rules and you're still fighting yours. Once you accept them and see them as a good thing, life will be a lot easier for you. How'd you feel when you went to the keg? Was it scary or fun?" Jennifer was on a roll, and I was impressed with her wisdom.

"It was scary. I hated it. Nothing that makes you almost wet your pants can be considered fun." I moved over to my window seat, looking out at a cruiser on Hazel Street. We lived right on "The Cruise." It ran from the high school at the east end of town, down Hazel Street to our house. Then the cars flipped a U at the intersection of Hazel and Indiana and drove back to the high school to flip it again—an infinite loop of cruising. It sounds very retro and fifties like, but it was a long held tradition in Gridley, and we thought we were pretty lucky to live near the corner of Hazel and Indiana so we saw the whole procession of cruisers. It was also the town parade route, so all my parent's friends came over to watch the parades from our big front porch.

Norman Rockwell couldn't have painted more of an Americana picture than sitting on our front porch and watching a parade go by, especially if you were an adult and had a gin fizz in your hand. Dad was known for his gin fizzes, especially the year he mistook an empty limeade can full of bacon grease for an actual can of limeade. Twenty-five years later, people still talk about "Fred's secret ingredient" for bacon grease gin fizzes.

Jennifer was determined to teach me to accept my parental guidance. "See. That's proof that you're accepting their rules. You didn't *want* to be at the keg, and you found a way to get out of there without drinking. You didn't drink, did you?" She asked that last part quietly, as if afraid of the answer.

"Of course not." I was indignant that she would even ask. "It's actually your fault since I couldn't find you for lunch."

"Yeah, that's a good one. You don't have to get mad. I was just making sure you hadn't totally lost your mind. What's this?" Jennifer had been sitting on my desk, and she held up an envelope, addressed to me, in chicken scratch writing.

"Oh, man. That's another letter from Lee." I was still disappointed at his illiteracy.

"Gosh, Meg, you shouldn't be so hard on him. Does he know both your parents are teachers?"

I shrugged.

She kept going. "Does he know your mother is *General English*?"

I laughed at the title. I think my mom liked that title very much. She was referring to what Anne called me since my mom taught English and required all of us to speak it properly in her presence. My mom was *General English*, and I was the lower ranked *Captain English* since I was her daughter. "Nah," I said. "I don't think he knows any of it, but does it matter? How can I have my Harlequin Romance with a guy who can barely spell my name? Go ahead. Read that letter. You'll see." I was being a little smug, probably because the prospect was good with Dan Stone. Even so; those letters. The CIA wouldn't be able to crack some of that code. Jennifer read it out loud:

September 5, 1978

Dear Margaret,

How are you doing, I'm find. What a dum start.

We had a diving meet down here. I did good I got 1st (I dove really well). It was a nice trofy.

I just got my tooth caped to day boy did that hert, but its over now.

Sory I took so long to write but Ive been really busy. I trided out for one soccer teem that is really good and I made it, we play with the UNLV players there ruf.

I'm going to ELO it's going to be bad I can hardly wate its suppose to one of the best conserts in Vegas, I mit go to KISS

I don't even want school to start do you, but I ges its better than work.

Well that's about all write back you hear me.

Love,

Lee

"Ohhhhh," she whispered. Jennifer was the kind of girl who lived by the "if you can't say anything nice, don't say anything at all" rule. Lee, the cutest-boy-in-the-world-to-skip-English-like-all-his-life, had rendered Jennifer Cone speechless.

"Seeeeeeee. What'd I tell you?" I said. "It's horrifying. He's a sophomore in high school, and he can't spell 'trophy' or 'capped' or God help him, he can't even spell dumb. Seriously, I could not make this stuff up. You thought I was being all snooty before 'cause I'm the daughter of *General English*, but you get it now, huh?" I was fired up. I was being vindicated. I *knew* she thought I was being snotty when we'd talked about Lee's letters. Now I'd shown her.

"Well, yeah," she said. "I had no idea. I did think you were being snotty. You know. You have to admit, that was a possibility with you being *Captain English* and all." Jen stared at the letter as if it might get better if she kept looking at it. "I almost owe you an apology. I really thought you were exaggerating. Look how he wrote 'dove' instead of 'dived.' Your mom ruined us for that word. The whole rest of the world thinks 'dove' is the past tense of dive, when anyone who had her in English knows that it is only a dove. The bird. Never the past tense of dive." She finally laughed with me.

"I told you. *Jethro Bodine*. My first amazing kiss was with *Jethro Bodine*, in the body of the cutest, blond, surfer-looking guy ever." I grabbed the letter from her. "I'm still writing him though." Jennifer raised her eyebrows at me in confusion. "Why wouldn't I? He's still the most adorable boy *I've* ever kissed. I can't write that off so easily. Oooh, that was a bad pun." I chuckled at myself while Jennifer rolled her eyes. "Besides, I might need to use him for Evil

Sheila. She's still *so* jealous whenever she hears about him. I can't let that go so easily."

"Evil Sheila." Jennifer rolled her eyes at me again. "Sheila is the one you need to let go of easily. Why do you let her get to you?" She was right, but I never had the answer. Didn't matter how many times she asked the question. I sat there, silently. Evil Sheila did that to me. She could make even me go quiet.

I changed the subject and told her all about the ride back from the keg to school. How Anne and Bobby seemed to hit it off and how she seemed to like Bobby.

Anne had long been in love with Rick Davis, football star and all around hunk of Gridley High. She'd loved him as long as I'd known her, so that went back to at least kindergarten. Since Rick was three years older than us, Anne's love for him had never seemed to count before... until now.

Rick had been on the swim team with us our whole lives, and that summer he'd treated Anne like she was his age and not just some little girl. It's another one of those small-town things, where you've known someone your whole life and then, one day, they're different. They grew up or they're more attractive to you. Whatever it was, it was what happened to Anne and Rick.

Swim meets were organized so that each age group and gender had an area where they put all their stuff and laid around waiting for their events. Swimming is a whole lot of "hurry up and wait" just to swim a few minutes. That's what we loved though. It was all about the socializing and the snack bar. I was in it for the candy, because as my Grandpa used to tell me, I always won the endurance awards because I was in the pool the longest.

Uh huh. Took me years to figure out that was an insult. When I was little, I thought my Grandpa complimented me when he said that. Sometimes the elevator doesn't quite make it to the top of my brain.

The little things were what showed that Rick was interested in Anne in a new way. He'd hang around our area more. Our age group was the thirteen- to fourteen-year-old girls, and Rick was a fifteen- to eighteen-year-old boy, so although the areas were near each other, we didn't mingle much. I was scared of the fifteen to eighteen boys. They were so grown up and looked different in their Speedos than the thirteen to fourteen boys, if you know what I mean. I can remember my mother saying once, in a very prudish voice, "They really should put more clothes on when they get to be that age. They're so…so…*overdeveloped.*" Took me a minute to figure out what she was talking about.

When Anne would win her races, which she always did, Rick would congratulate her and ask her about her times. This didn't happen to the rest of us. Not that anyone would be interested in my times, slow as they were, but Tonya and Cindy were good, and he never checked on any of *their* times. When we won our relays, he'd pat her on the back in congratulations. He didn't touch the rest of us. Something was up, and Anne knew it. And Anne loved every minute of it.

Anne would talk about Rick all the time, but always in the abstract. "He's so gorgeous. I wonder what it would be like to kiss him? Do you think he'll ever break up with her?" Rick had had the same girlfriend forever. No one really knew how long. It was like they came out of the womb as a couple, holding hands and destined for marriage. No one bothered even looking twice at Rick Davis. And of course, his girlfriend was the female equivalent of him: pretty, perfect, and popular. This made him all the more attractive to Anne, as she considered diving into a love triangle right as we entered high school. Just hit it out of the park your first time up to bat. That was Anne.

I didn't understand this whole Bobby thing. If Anne was so in love with Rick Davis, why was she getting cozy with Bobby Hunt?

Trampy Sandy?

Gridley Invitational Basketball Tournament
1978, Farmer's Hall, Gridley, California
Meredith Carlin First

6

I managed to make it through the first week of high school without getting kidnapped and taken to any more keggers. And no one stripped me of my clothes and left me in the hall in old ladies underwear. All in all, it was a good beginning.

Early on in the second week of school, one of the cheerleaders from the senior class, who cheered with my sister Ro, asked me if I'd represent the freshman class in the rally that week for the first home game of the football season. "It's going to be a *Grease* Rally, and we'd like you to be Sandy in a contest among the classes. It's no big deal. You dress up and lip sync to a *Grease* song, and the audience votes on which class was the best. We're picking a Danny from each class too, and you'll perform with him. We thought you'd be good since you look a lot like Sandy, and you're a cheerleader so you're already good in front of audiences. What do you think? Will you do it?" She flipped her blonde hair and looked at me like I had just won an Academy Award and was thinking about *not* accepting.

I was stunned. My dream was to look like Olivia Newton-John and marry John Travolta. This would be the closest I'd probably come to that. "Please? Rowan said it was okay to ask you. Please?"

I had to shake my head clear. "I'm sorry. I'm just shocked to be asked. I'd love to help." Gosh. I felt honored. I didn't even care if I was picked just because I was Ro's sister.

"Great. Rowan will be able to help you with any questions and give you details on what you're doing and where you need to be. Just talk to her." She walked off, and I went to Spanish class feeling very important.

My third sister, Rowan, was a senior. Rowan is Gaelic for "little redhead." Our mother had gotten the genealogy bug before Ro was born, so when she popped out with a shock of red hair, Jayne the Genealogist had no choice but to give her the Gaelic name that was her birthright. Redheads are celebrated in our family. We make a big deal out of those recessive genes. The problem was Rowan would rather be anything but celebrated. I've never known anyone who hated red hair more than Rowan Monahan.

Ro was student body president, head varsity cheerleader, and editor of the yearbook. She was the total package—great body, smart, fun, and popular. You'd think that if you had a resume like Ro's, you'd have had an inkling of your fabulousness, but she couldn't see it. Her insecurity ran deeper than her natural red hair, and other than that, I wanted to be just like her.

I had never gone to school with Ro and was excited about it, even if she wasn't. She had to drive me around. Our mother thought of it as a rite of passage that the older sisters had to drive around the younger ones. That's the way it was.

After school, Ro and I were driving home and I asked her about the rally. "I'm so excited about being Sandy for my class," I said. "I know just what I'm going to wear. Remember that old angora sweater I found of Mom's? The one she wore in high school? It'll be perfect. It's even authentic 1955. This is gonna be so cool. I hope I get to lip sync to 'Summer Nights' since I know all the words to that one."

Ro cut me off as quickly as she could, even though I was jabbering a mile a minute. "*Whoa.* You don't need an angora sweater." Her green eyes danced as she realized my ignorance. "What did they tell you? This isn't nice-girl Sandy. This is trampy Sandy. You need to get some really tight black pants, a black tube top, and some red Candie's shoes. And where are you going to find any of that? I *knew* this was a bad idea, but they all think you're *so* cute." She said that last part in a mocking voice to ensure I knew that the other cheerleaders felt that way. Not her.

I ignored her. I was good at that. "Oh no," I said. "Please tell me you're not serious? I can't be *trampy* Sandy? Why did they pick me? There must be an *actual* tramp that can play this? I can think of a few," I said under my breath. That wasn't helping me any. We both knew that they weren't going to re-cast now. We had to figure this out.

As we pulled up to our house, we both came up with the solution at the same time. "Tonya," we shouted in unison.

"Perfect," I said. "She has the best wardrobe of anyone I know."

"And she might have something to fit you since you're both so thin." Ro was helping more now.

"Yeah, except *she* has a figure." Sad, but true.

"Well, there is *that*." Ro laughed. "Want me to come help you?"

"Yes, please. Thanks." Ro was being cool about this. She probably didn't want me to embarrass her.

I got out of my father's 1974 Mustang II Ghia that had become Ro's car, and then went next door and rang Tonya's bell while I prayed she was home and could help me.

"Hi." Tonya answered the door, happy to see us but puzzled that it was both of us. "What are you guys doing here? Hi Ro." I pushed my way past her, straight to her room for help.

Tonya's house was one of the oldest in town and had more character than any house I'd seen. It was built at the turn of the century (1900 that is) and had old, dark hardwood floors, mahogany banisters, and woodwork everywhere. Now that I live in a modern California suburb, I value the treasure that was that house.

It was all one story except for an upstairs room that was

like a princess tower. All windows on four sides, Tonya had no wall space for posters, and she had twenty-four shades to pull up and down every day, but it was worth it to live in *Rapunzel's* castle. She even had her own tiny bathroom in the corner—a little piece of teenage heaven. The rest of the house was filled with beautiful dark antiques, but the furniture in Tonya's room was dainty and white and added to the princess feel.

The windows on the east side of Tonya's house faced my bathroom window, so if my phone was busy (which, with five women in the house, it often was) she'd hang her head out her window and yell at my bathroom window to try and find me. She also kept a supply of little pebbles in a jar to throw at my window when I didn't hear her shouts. Tonya was one resourceful gal and not to be ignored.

I rushed up the mahogany staircase to her room, talking the entire time. "Tonya, you've got to help me. They asked me to be in the first rally of the year and I said yes."

"That's cool, Meg. Why do you sound panicked?" Tonya scurried behind me, trying to keep up. Ro was behind her, laughing.

"Because, when I said yes I thought I was entering the competition as nice Sandy from Grease. Instead, it's trampy Sandy, and I don't know what to do." I rummaged through her closet. "Since you have the best wardrobe of anyone I know, we thought you could save me." I pulled out some tiny black pants, held them up for size, and turned to show them to Tonya and Ro, who had plopped herself on the princess iron bed. "Will these fit me? Do you have any red *Candies*?"

"Slow down. You're making my head spin. *You* have to dress up as trampy Sandy? *You?* Seriously?" Tonya was two minutes behind and in as much shock as I had been.

"*I know*. I was so excited thinking I'd wear a fifties

wool skirt of my mom's and her angora sweater and a little headband." I looked in Tonya's antique mirror and stroked my hair, dreaming of my nice Sandy moment. Which was ruined now.

"Get over it, Meg," said Ro. "You're trampy Sandy now. Find some clothes." She got up from the bed, attempting, in her most sarcastic voice, to help.

"Those pants won't fit your bony ass." Tonya took the pants from me, shoved me out of the way, and went rifling through her closet. In a matter of moments, she came up with the perfect outfit—a tiny black top and some pants that actually fit me.

"You did it," I said. "You turned me into a tramp. How'd you do that?" I looked down at my boyish figure in the black outfit thinking maybe there was a future for me. She had *almost* made curves out of my pixy stick of a body.

"Well, we're going to have to pin this shirt a little, but otherwise I think it's believable. What do you think, Ro?" Tonya pinned the back of the shirt with a safety pin. It looked a little like real tailoring.

"Ro looked up in amazement. "Wow. You did it Tonya. Who knew? She looks like Olivia Newton-John's little sister." Ro smiled, and that was the best I was going to get unless I stuffed my bra.

I stuck my chest out and grinned. "Are you thinking what I'm thinking?"

They said it in unison. "No, Meg. You're not stuffing your bra."

"It was just a thought." I was a little sad. I kind of wanted to have boobs, even if it was just for an hour. "I'd rather look like trampy Sandy than her little sister. It's like being *Barbie's* little sister, *Skipper*, instead of *Barbie*. Nobody *aspires* to be *Skipper*."

"Yeah, except that nobody should be aspiring to be

Barbie either. Does that make you feel better?" Tonya was always thinking.

"Good point. Yeah, it does." I smiled. Leave it to Tonya to make me feel better about being Olivia Newton-John's gawky, younger sister.

"Wait though, I think I have one thing that might help." Tonya rifled through her panty drawer and came up with a padded bra with molded cups. "Ta daaa," she sang, "now you can be *Growing Up Skipper*."

Since I was bred to be a nice girl, I wasn't supposed to like dressing as trampy Sandy, but I was thrilled with that padded bra. "Oh Tonya. I'm *Growing Up Skipper* and trampy Sandy at the same time." I snatched the bra from her and put it on in a rush. "What do you think? Are they believable?" I asked as I stuck out my chest. That's the beauty of a padded bra. You don't have to have any boobs to fill it out. It does the work for you.

"I hate to admit it," said Ro, "but that does make a difference. Much better. Doesn't Mom have some *Candies*? I can't think of what color they are, but doesn't she have some?"

I gasped. "I think she does." I changed my clothes so we could run home and check. "Tonya, can I take these with me? We need to see if we can borrow my mom's shoes and maybe some earrings. Didn't Sandy wear big, red hoop earrings?" I put my *Dittos* on. Back to my boyish figure and my size fourteen girls clothes.

Tonya helped me gather up the outfit. "I think she did. Your mom will *definitely* have those." Mom was the queen of wild accessories. In the seventies, one minute she dressed like a normal mom and the next, she dressed like a cross between *Maude* and an African princess (minus the headdresses). For a few years, when she went through her *Roots* phase, *before* she met Alex Haley, she even had an afro.

"Come on, Ro, let's go check. Since you got me into this in the first place."

"Like you weren't thrilled to be asked," Ro said, dripping with sarcasm.

We were out the door. "Yeah, but that was when I thought I was getting to be nice Sandy. Thanks Tonya," I called, waving back.

"You're welcome." She waved out the door. "Can't wait to see how it turns out."

I barely made it through school that Friday, since I was so nervous about the rally. I'd never been to a high school pep rally. I didn't like the idea that I was *in* one before I'd ever *seen* one. I met up with Tonya and Anne outside the main school entrance, and we walked *en masse* from the main campus to the gym. Gridley didn't have a gym of its own. All of our gymnasium activities took place on the fairgrounds two streets across from the school; in a building called Farmer's Hall. That's right—only in Gridley.

We took the normal route past the weight rooms and the pool, then crossed Hazel street to Farmer's Hall. "Are you nervous, Meg? Or excited?" Anne asked.

"Are you kidding? Right about now she's ready to throw up, aren't you, Meg?" Oh, Tonya knew.

"Quit reminding me or I will throw up on both of you."

"Meg always wants to do this stuff," said Tonya, "then when it gets down to it she gets all nervous and wants to puke, then she pulls it together at the last minute. By the time she gets out there, we'll never know she was nervous. I don't know how you get over your nerves so easily. It's much easier to just be me and never get nervous in the first place." We laughed at the truth, but it didn't make me feel any better.

"Okay," I said. "Not what I need right now. Easy for

you to say. I wouldn't be nervous either if I had your talent. I'm barely keeping it together here, so help me out and tell me I'm gonna be great and you're gonna be proud of me, 'kay?" I was desperate.

"You're gonna be great. We're gonna be so proud of you," they said in unison, in fake, sing-song voices.

"Nice," I said. "With friends like these…"

We entered the gym to total bedlam. The basketball court was empty, because the whole school was in the bleachers, divided by classes. Posters lined the walls, celebrating the assumed victory for the Bulldogs that night. I began to sweat and must have looked pale, because Tonya cocked her head and looked at me, puzzled.

"Meg, are you okay? You just got white as a sheet. And that's pretty white for you." She and Anne laughed again. They were on a roll.

"I'm just totally nervous now," I said. "Look how many people are here. This is crazy. What was I thinking? I gotta go." I started for the door.

Tonya took my arm and said, "Whoa there, you're not going anywhere. I will not have you make the freshman class look bad at our first rally. Get back here." She pulled me back but still had a grip on my arm. "Anne, will you go sit down and save me a seat? I'm going to escort Miss Monahan to her sister so that she wins this stupid contest for our class and puts us on the map. Get it together, Margaret," she said in her best stern-mother voice. "You need to do this for the Class of '82. Show them what we're made of." She sounded like some Vince Lombardi style coach.

"What is this? You're all 'Miss Inspirational' on me now?" I said.

"It distracted you enough to get you to your sister," said Tonya. "Ro!" she yelled across the cafeteria. "Ro, can you come get Meg?"

Nice. Now all the cheerleaders looked at me, knowing I was so nervous.

Ro came over to us. "What's wrong? Why are you holding on to her?" She looked at Tonya's death grip on my arm.

"Oh, that." Tonya dropped my arm. "Just a little assistance. Meg was getting nervous and was ready to run out the door. You're gonna have to keep an eye on her or she'll bolt."

Rowan rolled her eyes at me. "Yeah, like that's what we need. Meg, these rallies are hard enough to put on without people no-showing for their parts. Suck it up and get ready. Tonya, can you help her get dressed and babysit her so she doesn't leave? Please?" Ro begged.

"Okay, probably a good idea anyway," said Tonya. "With all the work we've done to pull this outfit together I want to see this thing happen." She led me to a corner where she helped dress me behind a screen and turn me into trampy Sandy. It was a good thing she did too, because she made me trampier than I could've ever dreamed. It was shocking really, the transformation. She put makeup on me. She teased my hair. She adjusted every nuance of my/her outfit and managed to turn me into a cross between Olivia Newton-John's trampy little sister and an older version of a "Toddlers & Tiaras" pageant girl.

Tonya twirled me around so I could look at myself in the mirror. "What do you think?"

I gasped. "Wow. How'd you do that?" I turned each way to try and see myself from every angle. She'd pulled it off. I couldn't believe it. It gave me the confidence I needed to get my bum out there and lip sync like the trampy girl I needed to be.

Ro came over when she saw me dressed. "Wow, Tonya,

I gotta hand it to you. How did you *do* that?" She looked me up and down and shook her head.

"What?" I glared at Ro.

"I'm sorry. I just can't get over it. You're almost believable."

"Okay, Ro," said Tonya. "What now? Where should Meg be?" She was all business.

"Take her over to Kevin, and she can wait with him. I gotta go. Someone'll be over to tell you when she goes on." Ro left, and Tonya and I went to Kevin, my Danny Zuko.

Say it with me now, "I've known Kevin my entire life." And was the perfect Danny Zuko. He even had an old Gridley lettermen sweater on with his black t-shirt and black pants. His hair was slicked back with more Brylcreem than my Grandpa wore, and that was saying a lot. But Kevin's hair looked great on him. I knew he'd be good—but this was better than I had imagined. Kevin was adorable, a good dancer, and very animated, so I knew he'd be *way* better than me.

It was time. I wanted to get this over with. We were the freshmen, so we had to go first. One of the senior girls went over the process with us. "You'll go out to center stage, they'll put the record on, and you'll lip sync and dance until they take the record off." She flipped her shiny hair and continued. "You won't know where they'll turn it on or off. It's kinda like a cakewalk. You just dance until it stops. Get it?"

We nodded our heads while I stammered, "Got it."

It took her a second, but then she realized I was a well-trained Gridley High freshman girl, and she responded in kind. "Good," she said, with a smile.

One of the first things we learned as freshmen women in the Gridley High P.E. class was to respond properly and with military precision to our ambiguously gendered P.E.

teachers. Oh, they were married to men, because that's how it was done in the seventies. We just never understood *why* they were married to men, when they so clearly seemed to be in love with each other. Either way, when they instructed us on a new sport, they closed every subject with "get it?" The students would then answer "got it" and they would always reply "good." Get it, got it, good, is a great question to ask if you're ever looking to identify a true Gridley Girl.

"Now remember, above all else, just smile and act like you're having fun—even if you're not. Big smiles help a lot." She was very perky. "Are you ready?" We nodded again. "Okay, go. It's your turn. Go, go, go!" She yelled at us like she was the football coach. Holy cow, she was taking this *very* seriously.

Right as we were leaving the cafeteria, a cheerleader from the junior class threw a black leather jacket at me, "Hey Margaret, take this. We had an extra." I actually caught it. Not a normal occurrence for me. It was to be an omen of my performance that day—out of the ordinary, all the way around.

"Thanks. That's so nice of you." I hurried into the jacket, knowing that now I'd have something to take off, just like Olivia Newton-John. Things were looking up.

With a little shove from Tonya, Kevin and I rushed out to the floor. I held back the bile in my throat. That was just what I needed: to vomit on stage in front of the whole school. I took my place in the center of the basketball court and tried to breathe. Kevin came over as if to tell me something. I panicked. I couldn't handle any changes now. I was on the edge as it was. "Meg," he whispered and pulled something out of his pocket. *What was he doing? I couldn't handle this.* "Meg, look." He pulled out a cigarette from his pocket and showed just enough so I could see it. "I bummed it off a guy on smoker's corner. Isn't that cool?" I was shocked. Now

I was going to have to stomp out a cigarette too? First the jacket, then the cigarette, what next? I had to psych up and fast.

"Wow. That was totally smart." I took the cigarette and stashed it in the pocket of my newly acquired jacket. We put ourselves on our marks like we were real performers, and I scanned the crowd for Anne and Tonya, so I would have a safe place to look. I couldn't believe it. The gym was full. There were at least 300 people there (huge by Gridley standards). *How was I going to do this?* Then I saw Anne. Thank God. She was in the front row of the freshmen section. I would look at her and pretend no one else was there. Then I saw Cindy in the band section waving at me with her flute. I had a plan. I just had to hope it would work.

When Olivia Newton-John did the final dance number with John Travolta, she looked a bit awkward compared to him. I felt like we were going to be just like that, since I knew I'd be awkward compared to Kevin. Maybe that would help my believability? The music began, and I took a deep breath. I tried to shake my booty a little with the beat of the music, but I was really out of my element. It was all I could do to stay up on the heels I stole from my mom. No way would she have let me out of the house with this hooker outfit. I was, after all, "a lady." But who knew my school-marm mother would have high-heeled, red *Candies*? They sure didn't look hooker'ish on her, since I hadn't even remembered them.

Kevin, on the other hand, went right into the song with a bang. He sang his fool heart out. He stripped off his lettermen sweater and twirled it around like a real live stripper. I smiled so hard my cheeks hurt. He was the best. He made eyes at me, and I realized I was supposed to take my jacket off too and twirl it around like a stripper. So I did. And I did okay. I was relaxed—nothing like doing a strip tease to loosen a girl up. I twirled that jacket and threw it toward the crowd, and they went crazy. Crazy. I loved the cheering. I'd never had that feeling before.

There was no time to enjoy the applause though. Kevin continued with his professional dancing and lip-syncing. Seriously, if *he* had been Milli Vanilli, they never would have gotten caught. He was that good, shaking his booty like a real dancer. Kev was half Hawaiian, and I think he was channeling some of his hula blood, because I'd never seen anything like it before.

He drew the lyrics out at just the right moments and continued to shake those electric hips like he was Elvis. If he didn't become the most popular boy in freshman class after this rally, I would be shocked. He ran toward me, dropped to his knees and slid to my feet, just like John Travolta. The crowd roared, and not only could I not have been prouder of him, but I was so grateful that he distracted attention away from me, if only for a moment.

Then it was my part.

I had to compose myself pretty quickly. I was laughing at his great moves and so almost forgot about the cigarette. I had been standing there with it hanging out of my mouth like one of Marge Simpson's smoking sisters. I smashed it out with one of my mom's spiky shoes, all while he was still echoing his last lyric. The crowd roared again. This was too much.

I pretend-kicked Kevin away with my sexy heel, and he fell back like he'd done this a million times. I flipped my hair like I thought I was really cool, then put my nose in the air and strutted off. I turned around, gave my hair one more flip, then strutted back toward him and put one hand on his shoulder. He walked backwards with me like he was used to playing this every night on Broadway. It was like he was channeling John Travolta himself. I couldn't believe it. My heart was beating so fast.

I strutted more, put my hand on my heart, and pointed to him for the accompanying lyrics. I paced back and forth and Kev followed me like a puppy. I faced Kevin squarely and sang right into his eyes, while I shook my shoulders like I may have had a bosom. Thank goodness for the padded bra and the confidence it brought me. Then I laid it on and held the last note like I was really singing.

That was when I went a little crazy.

I turned and skipped toward the bleachers like when Olivia skips over to the fun house. I was like every other teenage girl and so had seen *Grease* at least three times at the movies. I wanted to be just like her. So I skipped to the bleachers, thinking I'd climb a few stairs like Olivia did in the movie. Kevin followed along just as he should have, lip-syncing the title of the song, "*You're the one that I want.*"

I went straight for the freshmen section, and Anne moved and the rows behind her cleared magically as well. I felt like Moses. Or was that Jesus? No, He walked on water. It was Moses who parted the Red Sea and Margaret Monahan who parted the first three rows of the pep rally. I stepped up the first step. Second step. Third step. The whole time, Kev was singing backup like a pro.

But I didn't think about getting *down* the bleachers before I climbed up them.

I got down one step, still lip syncing the "ooh oohs." One more step, three more "ooh oohs."

I shook and shimmied and otherwise behaved in no way, shape, or form like Margaret Monahan, because I was possessed by the spirit of Olivia Newton-John.

At first.

Uh huh.

I was on the last step belting out lyrics that I had to

hold for five beats. Then I crouched down, like Olivia, and with my finger crooked called Kevin toward me. I thought I was the coolest thing ever.

And I slipped right out of my mother's *Candies*. Slipped right out. I felt myself falling back. The whole thing was in slow motion. Complete with "mwa mwa mwa" *Charlie Brown* style sounds in my ear.

I fell in slow motion and landed in the bleachers right in between Anne and Tonya, where the sea had parted for me.

I know.

It wasn't how I planned it, and it wasn't at all graceful, but it was a dream come true for every insecure girl like me. I could have fallen and hurt myself in front of the whole school. Instead, right at the part where I almost blew the coolest moment of my life, I landed on my bum amongst my friends. And like any other good cheerleader, I jumped back up to try and save it. I turned around to face the crowd and threw out my right arm with my hand in a fist. I went into total cheerleading mode with a raised knee and the opposite hand on my hip—the classic ending to use when you are trying to rev up the crowd. And the whole time I was drawing out the lyric "neeeeeeeeeed." It was just instinct, but the crowd loved it.

The whole thing was very unlike me. It was all much more "beautiful swan" behavior than my normal "ugly duckling" style. The crowd went crazy. When the record player screeched we took little bows like we did this every day. I shook so hard. I was done with the nausea though.

The emcee shouted into the microphone, "Ladies and Gentlemen, Meg Monahan and Kevin Tipton from the Class of '82." He drew out the number two like he was a real announcer, and the crowd roared again.

The sophomore class "Sandy and Danny" came out,

and Kevin and I were whisked back to the cafeteria again. I was still trying to catch my breath when they told us to run back onstage for the voting, just a few minutes later.

Oh, yeah. The voting. Everything was a freakin' popularity contest. All well and good, as long as you were the winner.

Kev pulled on his letterman sweater, and I put the leather jacket on. I still couldn't believe what luck it was that they had an extra jacket at the last minute. People didn't have extra leather jackets laying around in modest, 1978 Gridley.

The emcee announced us all one by one again, and Kev and I ran out to the stage, holding hands like real pros. I still couldn't believe his composure. I followed his every move and gained my confidence from him. "From the freshman class: Meg Monahan and Kevin Tipton." We took our places in front of our class and took more bows.

The emcee stood next to each set of "Sandys and Dannys" and asked the crowd to scream and clap for their favorites. I figured it would end up split evenly down the classes. Made sense, right? Who wouldn't vote for their own class?

When he stood by us, the crowd went wild. I was near tears at this point. Partly because I was so relieved that the whole thing was over and I'd survived, and partly because I couldn't believe how well we'd done.

The emcee went to the sophomores, juniors, and seniors. The crowd didn't go crazy again until they got to the junior class. Made sense. Their Sandy looked like the real Olivia Newton-John. She was one hot number, and I always wished I looked like her. The seniors didn't get a whole lot of applause — probably because most of their class was out getting stoned.

It was a tiebreaker between the Classes of '80 and '82.

The sophomore and senior Sandys and Dannys went to sit down, and the emcee pulled Kevin and I over next to the juniors.

"Okay, Bulldogs. It's down to the lowly freshmen and the Class of '80. Show us your Bulldog spirit when I announce your favorite Sandy and Danny. Are you ready?" The crowd cheered. "All right then. Meg Monahan and Kevin Tipton." He dragged out Tip-tonnnn like it was a boxing match in Vegas.

Three out of four classes were on their feet, hooting and hollering. This was Gridley: land of cowboys who knew how to hoot and holler. It was the best.

Seriously.

Then the whole school was on their feet, screaming and clapping for us. Okay, so probably it was mainly for Kevin, but I didn't mind riding the wave of his stardom. We waved to the crowd, and Kevin pumped his arms up and down to get them to cheer more. Kevin was a better cheerleader than me and probably should have reconsidered his basketball career and joined the squad.

The emcee was so overwhelmed he didn't even have the audience vote for the juniors. He just announced us the Sandy and Danny of Gridley High. The songleaders came out to do the final dance number, and we scurried away to sit and watch the rest of the rally. Anne and Tonya saved us spots at the front of the freshmen section. We sat down and people patted us on the back and told us what a great job we did. Kids yelled, "Eight-y-two. Eight-y-two. Eight-y-two." I felt like a freakin' Homecoming Queen.

Closest I'd get too.

Family Period

The Carlin Family
1979, Grandma's House, Dobbins, California
Lori Carlin Proctor, Larry Carlin, Joan Carnahan Carlin,
Meredith Carlin First, Melissa Carlin

As if falling in front of the whole school wasn't enough for me, I still had the game and dance that night. Cindy had called after school to make a wardrobe check. We never wanted to be over or under-dressed. As a grown woman, I still call to check on what we're wearing before we go out. "Meg, what are you wearing tonight? I can't decide." She sounded a bit frantic.

"I'm going to wear that plaid peasant top and my white Dittos. You have plenty of great clothes. What's the problem?" Being the "after thought" child, Cindy always had great clothes. Her sisters were six and nine years older, so she never had to wear hand-me-downs.

"Okay," Cindy answered, "plaid top and Dittos. I can do something like that."

"I'll meet you in the bleachers. Look for Anne and Tonya. I don't want to have to sit by Sheila."

"Totally. Got it."

I hung up the phone and went to find my clothes, then into the bathroom to check my makeup and hair.

What I'd been hoping for my whole life was upon me. Okay, maybe I'd just been hoping for three years.

I got my period. I was finally living my own Judy Blume dream. I was a woman, and it was about darn time.

I did what any good Monahan girl would do. "*Mommmm,*" I screamed.

Nothing.

I sat there, a prisoner of the toilet. In my naïve mind, it didn't occur to me to just wipe, wash my hands, and go looking for my mother. For all I knew, a flood could have arrived. I thought I was trapped on this toilet until someone found me. So I screamed some more. "*Mommmm?*"

Nothing. "*Is anyone there?*" I looked around for something to read. Might as well hunker down and wait.

Nothing. "*Rowannnn?*" I looked down and noticed that the floor needed to be mopped.

Nothing. *"Katieeee?"* I looked out the window and noticed we could see the Buttes from our toilet. Huh. Never knew that before. The smallest mountain range in the world and I could see them from my toilet. Go figure.

Was I going to live my life on this toilet? Graduate from high school on this toilet? Get married, have children, and die on this toilet?

I sat longer. I didn't want to holler for my dad, even though it would be just like him to hear me screaming for everyone else and not wonder what I needed. How could he help me right now? He may have lived in a sorority, and he may have been known to buy tampons without batting an eyelash, but he was not who I needed right now.

I was suddenly a castaway on Gilligan's Island without Ginger and Marianne to entertain me. I was not going to die on this toilet. I was a woman now, and I needed to yell more. *"Is annnny-onnnne hommmme? Hellllp!"*

Then I heard stomping on the stairs. Someone was bounding up them. I must have put the right inflection in my voice that time, because they were running. My mom burst into the bathroom. My mother had actually run somewhere—an absolute first. My viewpoint on running and sweating came from my mother. She normally never even came upstairs, and now she'd actually run.

I was caught off guard with her bursting into the bathroom. "MeggieMac, are you okay?" She was winded and had worry all over her face.

I was embarrassed and sheepish. I had dreamt of this for so long, but I never imagined what I would do when it happened. "I got my period."

"Ohhhhhhhhhh. My baby." She was sappy and full-on into another "my baby" milestone. "My baby got her first period. All my girls are women now." By this time, Ro had joined us in the bathroom. It turned into a regular party.

Where were they all ten minutes ago? "Ro, Meggie just got her period."

"Congratulations, Margaret. Now you'll know why we were telling you to wait for it. Welcome to the world of cramps and tampons." This time her sarcasm was warranted. Ro had the worst menstrual cramps of anyone I had ever known. Her periods really were *The Curse.*

"Now Ro, they may not be that way for Meggie." She looked back over at me, still stuck on the pot. "You'll be fine, Meggie. Don't worry."

Mom always called me Meggie when it was a "my baby" milestone or if she wanted something. Like, "Meggie, will you get me another Tab with lots of ice?" while she held her giant, plastic cup and jiggled it for me to take it from her for a refill. Or, "Meggie, will you please go to the store for me?" When she wanted something bad, she'd call me "Meggie Mac" to shorten part of my middle name. As in, "Meggie Mac, I'm really craving a giant Nestle's Crunch bar. Would you run to the store and buy one for me? Please?" She'd have her money all ready and folded lengthwise. Always proper, right down to how she folded her money for the cashier. For some odd reason, her propriety never extended to her housekeeping skills, as we had one of the messiest houses of anyone I knew.

Katie was home for the weekend and joined the party in the bathroom. "What's going on?" she asked Ro.

"Meg just got her first period," Ro answered, bored already.

"Oh." They stood together staring at me, both bored. "Why are we all here staring at her?" Katie laughed at Ro.

"I don't know. I think we're supposed to gaze at her for another passage for mom. You know. The whole, 'my baby just got her first period' thing?"

"Oh. Okay." Katie leaned against the doorway and folded her arms. They all stared some more.

"Um. So what do I do now? I'm still sitting on the pot here, and I have a big football game to go to tonight." I was talking in my snottiest tone, but in my defense, I was just sitting there with my jeans around my ankles, waiting for some instruction.

"Don't worry, Meggie," said Mom. "We'll get you fixed up." She turned to Katie and Ro and gave orders like the drill-sergeant-eighth-grade-teacher that she was. "Katie, get some money from my purse and go across the street and get some junior tampons. Is that right, Rowan? Do we have any junior tampons in the house?"

Ro laughed at her since Ro would love to need junior tampons. "No, Mom, we only have the super duper kind for girls with periods from Hell."

Mom gave Ro the mole face for saying Hell. "That's what I thought. Okay Katie, off you go." She shooed Katie out of the bathroom. "Margaret, are you going to just sit on the pot and wait for Katie? You can get off there. I'm sure it won't be so bad. Your grandmother didn't even have sanitary napkins in her day. They just used rags."

"Ughhh. Mommmm. That's so gross," said Ro. She couldn't imagine using rags with heavy periods.

"It is gross, but you girls need to remember how lucky you are to have tampons. When I was a girl, we couldn't even swim when we had our periods. You girls get to do everything, and life goes on like nothing's happened. You're very lucky." Mom loved to remind us how lucky and ungrateful we were all at the same time.

Ro groaned again. "Yeah mom, that's what I am. Lucky."

"Well okay, Rowan, you're not lucky but yours is the exception. Most women don't have to go through what you do. It is sad." Mom sighed for Ro, patted her on the back, and looked her up and down like maybe Ro *did* something to get such horrible periods. Ro rolled her eyes. In her opinion, no one understood her pain.

I worried I'd be stuck on this pot forever discussing menstruation history and horror stories. Talk about periods from Hell, I was living one.

No. It got worse. My dad came upstairs.

"What's going on up here?" What was next? Would my grandparents drop in? Or any number of my parent's teacher friends who would stop by for a "quick drink" on any given day, but especially on Fridays?

"We're having a party, Dad, right here in the bathroom. It's a party in my honor. Did you know you can see the Buttes from the toilet? Come on in and join me on the pot." My silly father walked over until he realized the trap. He rolled his eyes at my sarcasm, noticed I really was on the toilet, and immediately turned around.

"Oh geez, I was just wondering what all the ruckus was. I don't need to see *this*." He started to leave but Mom grabbed his arm.

"Fred, our baby just got her first period. She's a woman now." Mom was gushing again. This time to the only person who was supposed to share in her sappy moment: the man who made "my baby" with her.

"She is *not* a woman. She's just bleeding. This does *not* make her a woman." He leaned in without looking at me, to make sure I heard him. "And you remember that, this does *not* make you a woman." He stepped away and looked at mom. "I'll be downstairs finishing dinner. Do you have someone out buying stuff for her? You're not thinking of sending me are you?" Even though he bought tampons for us, it didn't mean he liked it, and it was much better for him when he could quickly throw them in the basket and cover them up with things like cereal and bread. He would never want to go buy them on their own. He had a man card to protect, and that was hard to do with so much estrogen surrounding him.

"Fred, you know she's not bleeding." Mom was always the teacher—even to Dad. She turned to me to make sure I knew. "It's not blood. You know that, right?" I nodded yes, and she turned back to Dad and called out at his back, halfway down the stairs by then. "But don't worry. Katie is out buying them now. You're off the hook. This time." We all laughed. We loved that Dad lived in a sorority. We always told him it was his own fault, once we found out that it's the man's sperm that determines what sex a baby's going to be. We figured he *wanted* to live in a sorority. His standard answer was always, "If I wanted to live in a sorority, it would not have been like *this* one."

Ro lost interest and went to get her cheerleading outfit on for the big game. Mom went downstairs to check on Katie. I just sat there…on the pot…nowhere to go…nothing to do. I knew she said I should get off, but I didn't want to risk it. What if it was different than in the olden days when she got her period? I felt like I should at least have a copy of *Are You There God, It's Me, Margaret?* to read while I was waiting. It only seemed right.

Just when I was thinking of running into my room to get a book, Katie and Mom came into the bathroom. "I got the tampons," Katie said, all out of breath. She passed them off to Mom and left. It was like an Olympic relay with a box of junior sized tampons for the baton. All I needed was a coach to yell at me for not doing it right, or maybe an East German judge to give me a bad score for "technique." Thank God. I thought for a minute there that we'd have to have a family teaching session on "proper tampon insertion techniques." I didn't have time for that. I had a real football game to go to. And my first high school dance to attend. And a cute boy to see. I was a very busy girl with more important things on her mind than the Junior Tampax.

"Meggie?" Female bonding moment: I would always be called by my endearing name, Meggie, and never the more formal, Margaret, in a bonding situation such as this. And never Meg. Not once has she ever called me Meg. She didn't even like it when my friends called me Meg. God only knows why. It's just a shortened version of Meggie. What's the difference? Always with the propriety, that's Jayne.

"Do you need some help getting the tampon in, honey, or have you practiced already?"

Screeeeeeech. The mental record player went off in my head. Loud. It happens whenever someone says anything shocking, surprising, or off-putting. It's just like the needle on my portable, ladybug record player: it scratches off and gives me a wakeup call. "What?" I sat up straight on the toilet. Why I felt the need to have good posture in this very undignified scene was beyond me, but I was startled. "Practiced? Mom, that is *so* gross. How would I practice?" I was freaked out at that point. I couldn't imagine putting one of those things up me, let alone practicing without a period. Who did she think I was?

"Honey, I remember how much you loved that Judy Blume book, and Margaret's character practiced with a sanitary belt so I thought maybe you did too." That was a little too much like life imitating art for me. She was defensive and didn't like that I was grossed out by her.

"Moth – errrr." I drew out in my snottiest teenage voice. "A sanitary belt is very different from a tampon. Did you think that since we had the same name that I had to do what she did? Ugh. I have not practiced. That's just plain gross. I think I'll try it myself before I ask for help though, K? You can just wait outside. But don't go away." I said that part with some desperation. I still needed her.

Okay, so now you're horrified at the graphic nature of this story, but you should know: it went in fine. Hooray. All those horror stories I heard did not apply to me. Woohoo. I got my first period and did not need my mother's help with the tampon. Thank you, Jesus. I felt like quite a woman at that point. Mom was clapping from the hallway, still misty at the thought that "her baby was a woman now."

She went downstairs and left me to get ready for the game. Not without another teary hug first though, and a shout up the stairs, "Don't forget to wash your hands." Nice. I'm sure she had to regale my father with all the grisly details. She was probably going to get on the phone to all her friends too. They had to mark these "life passages" with her as well.

I took one last look in the mirror before I went downstairs. Did I *look* different? Did I look like a woman? I didn't feel any different. Other than the fact that I worried about how many tampons I needed to put in my purse and how often to change them. I was feeling good. I was very happy to finally be a woman. Why was I in such a hurry to grow up but deathly afraid of it at the same time?

I put my sandals on—it was still ninety degrees outside—and went downstairs. My parents were waiting for me in the living room and watched me as I hit the last few stairs. Mom gasped, "White pants? Margaret, you're going to wear white pants? Tonight? Are you sure?" She seemed so worried. And even after her lecture about how lucky we were to have such great tampons these days. What sense did that make?

"Mom. I've had this outfit picked out for weeks. I can't change it now. It's not like I have that extensive of a wardrobe. This is what I'm wearing—first period or not." I snapped my head to show that my mind was made up, and she looked at me, worried again.

"Okaaay, but that would worry me." Her voice lilted

at the end to show me that she did not agree with me and could not guarantee that she wouldn't say "I told you so" tonight when I came home with stained pants.

"I'll be fine, Mother. Are we leaving now?" I looked toward Ro like "Get me out of here," and we tried to hurry out the back door.

We didn't get far though. "Girls." Mom yelled from the family room. "Remember?"

We yelled back to her in unison, "Y.A.L." We drew out the "L" to give her the emphasis she required, slammed the door behind us, and hurried off to the football stadium. And I was a woman. Didn't get any better than that.

We got into the car, and I could finally breathe. "Hooray. I'm so excited. My first high school football game and dance. I can't wait."

"Calm down. You won't seem cool if you appear too excited." Ro patted my leg like I was five.

"Got it. Must be calm."

We walked into the stadium — if you could call it that, it was Gridley after all — and Ro, in her cute little cheerleading uniform, joined the cheerleader gang, and I looked for The Group.

Luckily, Cindy and Anne were sitting as far away as they could from Evil Sheila while still sitting with The Group. I sat down next to Cindy. "Where have you been?" she asked, a little worried.

I leaned over and whispered in her ear, "I was busy getting my period." I was grinning from ear to ear.

"What?" She jumped up and whispered into Anne's ear. Anne whispered into Tonya's ear. Tonya whispered into her cousin's ear, who whispered into…okay, you get the point. We then paraded down out of the stands and all the way around the stadium to the bathrooms. We were a spectacle. We were a train of freshman girls. We did not care.

Cindy and Anne squealed as soon as we hit the bathroom doors. They were as excited as I was. That was so sweet. Even Evil Sheila was nice. It was pretty weird actually. Tonya seemed proud. They grilled me with all the usual questions and were impressed that I used tampons immediately. Even Sheila seemed impressed with that fact. They were as grossed out as I was that my mom asked me if I practiced.

The dance was the best part of the night though; my first high school dance. It was a lot of firsts that day: first rally, first performance at a rally, first fall at a rally, first recovery at a rally, first class win at a rally, first period, first high school football game, first high school dance, first kiss from Dan. Screech. Did your mental record player just scratch in *your* head?

Mine did too.

Jennifer came over Sunday morning to hear all about the night before since she couldn't go. We were each sitting on a twin bed in the room I shared with Ro, and I got to re-live the whole glorious night for her.

"Did you hear that I'm a woman?" I was gloating now, and I didn't care.

"I did. Woohoo. Meg Monahan is a woman. Did you really kiss Dan? I want to hear it all." She rolled over onto her belly on Ro's bed.

"Oh Jen, it was the greatest. Made me totally forget about Lee. That was cool. I was missing him so much before. Kept thinking he was the only guy I'd ever meet who liked me back." I got comfortable on my bed then, knowing I was going to have to tell her everything—not that I minded.

"Okay, okay. Let's hear it. Enough about Lee. I thought

we already decided he wasn't quite smart enough for you." Ooooh, she was getting snippy now. Not like her.

"Okay, so Dan, Anne and Bobby and I were standing in the front of the bleachers just watching people dance. Evil Sheila was hanging all over Mark Grimes and making out in the bleachers. They were disgusting. That is—while they were there. They left pretty early. If I'm lucky, she'll be pregnant by Christmas and shipped off to a home for unwed mothers by New Year's. Wow. What a dream that would be." I stared off at the thought of school without Evil Sheila. That *was* a dream school.

"That's mean but, ugh. He is so gross," said Jennifer. You know you're bad if Jennifer thinks you're gross.

I nodded my head in agreement. "You won't get an argument from me on that. So anyway, we're just standing by the bleachers and checking it all out. So far, it seemed a lot like everything else about high school: the same as eighth grade only with facial hair. The dancing was the same. The social scene was the same. There were more people, and there were bleachers for people to make out in. And there was a lot of making out. I've never seen anything like it. And it was a lot darker. I guess that's why they could make out so much. Oh yeah, way less chaperones than eighth grade too." I rolled on my back then and stared at the ceiling. I did my best thinking while staring at that ceiling.

"Yeah, yeah," said Jen. "Making out. Good enough. Are you going to get to the kiss or not?" She was sitting up and staring at me now. It was very funny to see how anxious she was to hear this story.

"Do you know what the song *Brick House* is about?" She shook her head but looked frustrated, like she didn't care either. This was too much fun.

"Well, we were standing by the bleachers checking the scene out, and this guy from the junior class comes up and tells us what the song is all about. It's about a woman with huge boobs. They say she's built 'like a brick shit house.' Makes no sense to me, and I think I may never like that song as much as I did before. I loved that song. Plus, when the guy was talking to us he kept looking at mine and Anne's boobs, and I swear he was thinking that the song was not about any of us since our boobs weren't huge. Ugh." I was sitting up at that point too, 'cause I was a little mad, all over again. "He even pointed to a girl from the sophomore class and said, 'That song was written about a girl like *her*.' Ugh. He was so gross."

"Okay, enough about the song. Get to the kiss. Where is Dan at this point?" She was getting snippy again, and I was still enjoying it.

"Well, as luck would have it, he came along right as the guy was telling us about *Brick House*, and he asked me to dance. He even held his hand out for me to take it. It was *so* cute. I was totally melting. I still can't believe he likes me." Jen was sighing then and getting antsy again for more details. "Okay, so we got to dance to a slow song. It was *Come Sail Away*. It was *so* great. This is the totally cool thing about high school: you have *so* many more boys to choose from. I *love* that." I rolled over on my bed again, laying on my back looking at the ceiling. It was amazing. It was like maybe the ugly duckling really could turn into a swan. There was hope for me yet.

"Earth to Meggie. We haven't gotten to the kiss yet." Jennifer was snippy, snippy.

"The kiss. Ooh. The kiss. So, *Come Sail Away* goes fast after a few minutes. It's one of those confusing dance songs where you go back and forth between slow and fast, so it was a little scary for me. I don't think I embarrassed myself though, and he was a pretty good dancer. I liked it. Then we danced again to *Best of My Love*. That was much easier to dance to. All they would've had to do is put *Stairway to Heaven* on, and it would've been like every other eighth grade dance I'd been to, except for all that making out. Have you seen people make out at school too?" She nodded yes. I was talking so fast now I don't know how she kept up. "Gross, huh? I know. It's horrifying. There are these two that have a locker near me, and they make out right in front of me in between every single class. It's so gross. I can see their tongues. I hate it when I forget to look the other way and there they are. Right in front of my face with their tongues down their throats. I will never be that way. *Ever. So* gross."

"Now you're just plain making me mad," said Jen. "I don't care about other people making out. I want to hear about the kiss."

I needed to get to it, or she was going to explode. "So at the end of *I Honestly Love You*, he leaned in and kissed me. No tongue, just polite and sweet. It was a nice kiss, nicer even than Lee's kisses. I'm glad that's possible in other boys, and that it wasn't a one-time deal. Can you believe they played Olivia Newton-John at a high school dance? That shocked me. I thought they'd be way cooler than that. Not that I don't love that song, but it's so old. I guess they figured that they played enough Lynyrd Skynyrd and Pink Floyd to make up for it." Jennifer was glaring at me. "Sorry. Sorry. Back to it. When the dance was over he walked me out. He offered me a ride, but Ro said I better go back with her. Didn't want to get in trouble on my first high school dance, and my parents are seeming to stick with this whole 'can't date until you're sixteen thing.' I hate that."

"You don't have to tell *me* that," she said. Wasn't that the truth? I was talking to the most sheltered girl *ever*.

"So, he walked me out, and just outside the building where we were away from others, especially Ro, he said 'I'm really glad those girls dumped you on Bobby's doorstep.

Even if you *were* in those grandma panties.' He laughed then, and I was mortified. I didn't know what to do at first, so I laughed with him, and it was good to break the ice and at least have that subject mentioned and hopefully over with."

"That's cool. I wouldn't want to talk about that one if I were you either. I still can't believe they did that to you." Jennifer shook her head and I didn't blame her.

"Then he leaned over and kissed me. A gentle, slow kiss with a little tongue but not too much. I liked that. I'm a little scared of the tongue. I don't know what to do with it and what to do with mine. It's very confusing, this whole kissing thing. And how do you learn? It's not like you can practice. I guess you could. That just seems weird. Anyway, Ro took me home and made fun of me the whole way. I didn't care though. I was on cloud nine." Just then the phone rang. We both sat straight up. Jennifer looked at me, a little scared. I was scared too. We were thinking the same thing: Dan. I pounced on the phone to get it before my sisters or, God forbid, my parents answered.

"Hello." Sound cool. Try to sound cool.

"Hello, Meg?"

"It's Dan," I mouthed to Jennifer.

"Hi." I didn't know what to say. *Be casual. Act like cool, cute, older boys call you every day.*

"Yeah. I just wanted to call and tell you I had a great time Friday night. I went to church today and didn't see you. Which was a bummer since I only went to see you." *Oh man. Why did I have to work in the nursery today? I didn't think he'd be there. Well, that's it. It's church for me, every Sunday.*

"I was there. I babysat in the nursery today. Didn't stay for fellowship. I didn't think you'd be there. That's such a drag." I fell back on my bed. My face was hot. Was I blushing? Jennifer was laughing at me.

"Yeah. My mom was pretty shocked when I said I was going with them. I think she suspected something though when she saw me looking around the sanctuary." He was laughing then, and I liked the idea of his mom knowing about me.

"Well, no more babysitting for me then. If you're coming to church now, I'm there every Sunday." *Don't be too eager. Remember, you're cool.*

"Good. I was hoping you'd say that." Silence. *Don't talk, Margaret.* No nervous chatter. "It's such a drag that you can't date." Thank God he spoke, or who knows what I would have said. He sounded genuinely disappointed.

"Tell me about it. My parents don't seem to want to buck thousands of years of tradition. I don't think Mom has us traced back thousands of years, but as she's the Genealogy Queen, I guess I wouldn't be surprised if she did." *Okay. Don't bore him.*

"No kidding. Your mom's funny. I liked having her as a teacher." Well, *that's* a first. Either that or he likes me and is trying to score points. I guess there are plenty of people who love my mom. It's just the bad seeds — like Evil Sheila — that think she's mean. Mom always claims they're the ones who need mean. "Well, I've got to go help my dad now. We're getting ready for harvest. I'll see you tomorrow at school, okay?"

"Sure. See you tomorrow." I hung up the phone and resumed my position on my bed, looking dreamily at the ceiling. Dan worked hard farming rice with his family. My parents liked that about him. Whatever. Now that I knew he was a good kisser, I didn't care how hard he worked. Somehow I was going to have to find out about his writing skills. I'd had enough surprises, and if he was illiterate then I was going to have to bag this whole boyfriend thing altogether.

Homecoming with Lucy and Ethel

Freshman Cheerleading
1979, Farmer's Hall, Gridley, California
Melissa Costa Talbott, Diane LaBarbera Symon,
Stacie Sormano Walker, Meredith Carlin First

It was all I could do to keep up with school in October with all the extra activities that came with Homecoming in high school. All my extra time went to Homecoming festivities and dreaming about Dan. He would come by my locker in between classes just to say hi. Sometimes he and Bobby would take Anne and me out to lunch. Those lunches felt like dates, which of course, made me even sadder that I had to wait two more years before I could go on an actual date. The whole thing was ludicrous to me. What did they think I was going to do on a real date? I wasn't Evil Sheila. I didn't even kiss at school, let alone practically make babies at the dance like Sheila and Mark. I was still a nice, wholesome girl who happened to spark the attention of a boy who was sixteen.

Well, when I put it that way, I could see, a teensy bit, how that might make them nervous. Especially since one of the nicest things about my mother was the fact that every year she was the one who counseled the eighth grade girls who found out right before graduation they were pregnant. Like the flowers that popped up out of nowhere, it happened every spring, and every spring it depressed her. It was a cycle where she went straight from pregnancy counseling, to her search for graduation dresses for the girls who otherwise wouldn't go through the ceremony because they couldn't afford a dress.

There was a reason the Mexican community in Gridley called my mom "La Señora Monahan." It wasn't just her name. She was the champion of all underdogs, and it was her goal that every minority in Gridley would receive every advantage that the non-minorities got. She was tireless in that effort, and they loved her for it.

But I had to get this dating situation changed. The rule was outdated. I even found out from my aunt that my mom dated when she was fifteen. So I didn't know if this whole sixteen thing was from the Mormon side of the family or what, but I needed to have it abolished. I didn't know how I was going to do it. I just knew I would. I was on my own personal civil rights mission for dating. I'm pretty sure Martin Luther King wouldn't have helped me but it seemed super important at the time.

Anne and Bobby seemed to be hitting it off. It was almost like double dating without the real dating part — unless you counted the lunches. Which I kinda did. It made me feel like I was on a date, even if it was daytime. Bobby would meet Anne at her locker and walk her to her next class if it was near his. There were times when I saw Rick watching over them. Anne noticed it too, and whenever Rick was watching she'd toss her head back with a laugh like Bobby was the funniest guy in the world — which, by the way, he was not. I wasn't sure what she was up to, but I have to say, I didn't mind that she was making Rick jealous. He needed to stay with his own girlfriend and leave Anne alone.

The leaves turned and the morning air became crisp and cool. The evenings were smoky from the burning rice fields, and the rotting prune scent in the air was gone. That meant only one thing: Homecoming was upon us. If it smelled like smoke, then it must be Halloween, and if it was Halloween, then it must be Homecoming. In this year of firsts, Homecoming was even more exciting than anything else we'd experienced in high school. In a small town like Gridley, Homecoming was a big deal. Alumni would come home (even though most of the town was already alumni), and we'd have the biggest attendance of the year at the football games. Each class would work tirelessly on their Homecoming float. The week would culminate with a parade down Hazel Street of all the floats and then a rally at the park in the center of town. Americana at its best. We were a Rockwellian town, and we knew it. Thrived on it, even.

This Homecoming wasn't just exciting because we were in high school. This Homecoming was exciting because none other than our own Anne Calzaretta was elected as Homecoming Princess of the freshman class. That's right. We were going to have to curtsy in her presence and call her HRH Anne. She was officially Homecoming royalty. Anne knew she didn't stand a chance to win against the junior or senior princesses, but that didn't stop her from giving every other freshman a hard time and telling them they had to vote for her out of "class loyalty." She was determined to make this the year a freshman was elected Homecoming Queen.

Homecoming week was a blur. We had different theme days where we dressed up for school. There was cowboy day (a natural for Gridley), alien day (lots of painted green faces and pipe cleaner antennae), clown day, and of course, on Friday everyone had to wear their blue & gold to show their Bulldog pride. As a prissy Monahan girl, a devoted cheerleader, and an overall dork, I *lived* for dressing up on these days. Blue and gold spirit ran through the blood of all good Monahans (after four generations, how could it not?), and I was no exception.

We worked every day the week of Homecoming to get our float finished. As freshmen, we were determined to have a good showing and try to win the prize for the best float. The Homecoming theme was Star Wars. It didn't matter that the movie was a year and a half old. Star Wars fever was still going strong in Gridley.

Our float starred a Bulldog kicking a Husky onto a giant rocket into space. All of this was built on a semi-truck bed with chicken wire, cardboard, papier mache, and tons and tons of blue and gold napkins. The whole thing was done with military precision, and I was pretty impressed. The parents bossed us around a lot, but they knew what they were doing and left the work up to us. I could not have had more fun. I had the prospect of a cute boyfriend, one of my best friends was Homecoming Princess, I got to build a cool float, and it was our first year to play in Football Follies. This was heaven to a dork like me.

Each class formed teams of girls to play in the Football Follies. We practiced flag football for a few weeks and then had the actual event the night before Homecoming. I, of course, sucked at flag football and was worthless to my team. Good thing I had devoted friends who weren't too competitive, or I would have been thrown off that team for my level of suckage. It wasn't a huge event, but it was fun.

We even had Princes and a Football Follies King. Jock Santos was the Prince from our class, and Anne was his escort. Jock's parents were my parent's best friends. Of course, Jock's parents both grew up with my dad. Not my mom though as she grew up in Marysville, the town next to Gridley. I warned you about Gridley.

And his name really is Jock. And he lives up to it. On occasion, there would be someone stupid enough to say something like, "Hey Jock, where's Miss Ellie?" That rarely happened more than once. Even as a freshman, Jock Santos was feared. He was crazy smart without much effort.

Ever since Jock and I were in middle school, he'd called me "Lep." I'd say it was a pet name, but since it was short for leper, I'm not sure there was any real affection there. In private, Jock Santos was the nicest friend in the world. When we were not alone though, he had a reputation to maintain and part of that was tormenting me and treating me like I was his sister.

All through high school, his favorite question to me was, "Hey Lep, what are the wholesome people doing tonight?" Our worlds divided at times between wholesome and partying, but the friendship never wavered. I will forever be his "Lep," and he will forever be my "Jock." Scratch that. It does not sound nice at all.

On Homecoming day, we got out of school early for the parade and rally. Ro and her friends were in charge of everything since the pep squad ran all the rallies. They got to ride three-wheeled motorcycles to lead the parade from the high school and into downtown. Everyone else either walked or drove behind the parade and then went to the gazebo for the rally. Everyone except the Homecoming royalty. They rode, parade style, in convertibles and waved to the crowd.

So there was our own AnneMarie Calzaretta in a red Mustang convertible, riding down Hazel Street giving us her best royal wave. She had the whole elbow, elbow, wrist, wrist thing down. We had practiced for days. There was no way I was going to let her go down Hazel Street waving a peace sign at the crowd like she wanted to. I can't believe she listened to me and waved like a queen. I kept saying, "If you want to be the queen, you have to act like the queen. Come on. You can do it."

Anne sat atop that car like she was born on that perch. She was having a good hair day and couldn't have looked better. I felt like her mom, watching with pride. The convertible was inching up to us in front of the gazebo when she caught my eye. She ruined her good waving streak when she saw us and stood up and raised both her arms in the air. She yelled, "*Woohoo – Class of '82*," with both her hands in peace signs, which coincidentally also were the number two for '82—very convenient for us. I couldn't decide if she looked spirited and funny, or if she reminded me of Richard Nixon. Either way, she got a good response from the freshmen in the crowd as they screamed when she stood up. Tonya mimicked her moves and screamed right back at her. I was laughing so hard that I didn't even realize I didn't yell back at her. *This might happen for her. She might pull this off and be one of the few freshman Homecoming Queens of Gridley High.* Stranger things had happened.

The convertibles stopped in front of the gazebo, and the escorts of the princesses got out of the front seats to help their princesses out. Jock didn't look like he enjoyed the job — he was very robotic and methodical — but he did well. I had never seen him so chivalrous before. But then again, I was the girl who was like his sister, who he called "Lep," so I didn't get nice behavior out of him. Jock walked Anne to the gazebo with their arms linked. The princesses sat on a bench with their escorts behind them to watch the rally from a place of honor.

Anne went back to her royal wave when they announced her name, but as she sat down again she flashed one last peace sign, and the hoots and hollers from the crowd started all over. Once the crowd screamed for her, Jock joined them with both his hands in peace signs and the crowd went crazy. *Great. Now we have two Richard Nixons in the crowd.* I looked at the people around me and noticed there were more freshmen at the rally than any other class. Would that translate to more freshmen voting for Homecoming Queen and therefore a win for Anne? We voted during the last period of class, the day before, which would automatically rule out a lot of juniors and seniors since that was normally when they left early to go get drunk or stoned. This was getting exciting. Very exciting.

It got even more interesting when they did the contest between the classes. The princess for the senior class was Rick's longtime girlfriend. Talk about awkward: Rick had to stand behind his girlfriend and watch Anne, as the freshman princess, with Bobby in the audience cheering her on. Rick's girlfriend kept an eagle eye on Anne the whole time. High school drama at its best. Tonya and I were watching it all like a tennis match. Each princess had to spray whipped cream on their escorts' heads. The princess with the tallest mountain of whipped cream won.

They had sixty seconds to spray without the foam falling over. With the freshman class we had super-competitive Anne and Jock opposite equally as competitive Rick and his suspicious girlfriend. The clock began. Anne was slow and methodical and made circles on Jock's head. Jock was a statue. The crowd, as always, was divided by class with everyone cheering on their own classmates. Rick sat frozen in his spot as well, but his eyes were on Jock the whole time. So much so that he looked cross-eyed. His girlfriend noticed too and kept looking back and forth between Anne and Rick. You didn't have to be a rocket scientist to figure out there was some tension in this group.

Anne acted like she was oblivious to it all, systematically building quite a mountain of whipped cream on Jock's surprisingly willing scalp. Rick's pile of cream was building as well. It was getting close. The princesses kept spraying and kept building. They were neck and neck until right as the buzzer went off, Rick looked over at Jock and his entire mountain of whipped cream spilled onto his face. The crowd for the senior class melted into a huge gasp. The place was silent for a moment, as the cheerleaders took the whipped cream cans away from each princess and measured the mountains of foam on each escort. Ro, standing between Anne and Jock, held their hands up as the big winners. The freshman class went wild. The seniors were still silent. Anne was making her peace signs again, and Jock was patting her on the back and smiling at Rick. Jock was the only person onstage who didn't know the real drama going on. He was hooting and hollering for "eight-y-two, eight-y-two."

Tonya elbowed me and pointed to a spot right off stage where Rick was getting a talking-to from his girlfriend. He looked like he was defending himself pretty well, but we knew this wasn't over.

Anne and Jock ceremoniously walked down the stairs from the stage to meet their people. "Eight-y-two. Eight-y-two." They were yelling in our faces now as we hugged them.

"You guys were the best," I said. "Jock, I've never seen you hold so still. I was so proud."

"Yeah you have, Lep. You don't notice cuz you're too busy running the wrong cheer in football." He looked away and laughed. So proud of himself. Jock had the laugh of Will Farrell as George W. Bush.

Tonya pushed me a little. "You *do* do that, Meg. You've never known the difference between offense and defense."

Jock laughed again and muttered, "She said doo doo."

"Okay, why are we talking about me?" I rolled my eyes at all of them. "You guys were great."

I had my arm around both of them, and Anne leaned over and whispered, "Did you see them?" She nodded her head in Rick and his girlfriend's direction.

"How could I not?" I looked over and they were still deep in discussion.

"He loves me, and she doesn't know what to do about it." She shrugged her shoulders and grinned like a little Cheshire.

"Knock it off. You shouldn't be happy about that. You have a boyfriend."

"What are you, my mother? I can enjoy this if I want. I'm not married. He's not married. There's nothing *wrong* with this."

Jock look confused as he listened to us. Tonya didn't want to have to explain it. "Anne, you should be careful.

You could get hurt in this one." With that, Tonya asked Jock to come with her so she could get him away from us. No need in him knowing what was going on.

As soon as Tonya and Jock left, Rick looked over at us. Well, Anne was the only thing he was looking at. It was a quick glance but Rick's girlfriend saw. She saw and stormed off to some waiting cheerleaders. My sister Ro was one of them. Anne threw her head back and laughed. I had to admit, she was pretty cute. And Rick fell for it. He walked right over to us, not caring at all that his girlfriend was staring daggers at him.

"You freshman think you were pretty cool today winning that pie contest." He didn't look at me for a second. It was all directed at Anne. He was looking her up and down, and she was doing the same thing to him. At once, I felt like a voyeur.

I tried to bring them back to reality. "We didn't have to think. Thanks to you, we won, and we'll do the same thing tonight when Annie here becomes Homecoming Queen. Right, Annie?" I put my arm around her so I could look Rick squarely in the eye and whispered right to him, "Look, I don't know what you have going on here." I waved my hand between him and Anne. "But you have a perfectly good girlfriend over there waiting for you, and Anne has a perfectly good boyfriend..." I looked around for Bobby. Why don't you go back to her and leave Anne alone? She doesn't need your drama." I stood there. Still with one arm around Anne and the other on my hip, and still trying to get my face in front of Rick's so he'd look me in the eye.

He wasn't having anything to do with it. He had his eyes missile-locked on Anne's. Nothing anyone could do about it. "Is that how you feel, Anne?" If Matthew McConaughey had been an actor then, I would have said that this guy could do a dead-on impression. Instead, he was being a playboy and trying to involve my friend in his love triangle.

But my friend was more than willing.

Anne was already shaking her head with a wicked smile on her face. Their eyes were still locked, and it was as if I no longer existed—except as a chaperone. "Come on, Meg." She took my hand and pulled me away from her crazy love triangle without ever taking her eyes off Rick.

Next thing I knew, we were walking fast out of the park and into Rick's truck. I looked back and saw all the cheerleaders, including his girlfriend with her hand on her hips, and my sister, watching us. Rick looked back too and grinned the same wicked grin that Anne had earlier. No, this was a shit-eating grin. He was proud. He was trying to get back at his girlfriend, and Anne was his method. *What were we doing?*

"Hurry up, Monahan. Get in." I was always called by my last name when I was of no importance: a mere pawn in his quest to make his girlfriend jealous and Anne's chaperone to debauchery. Holy cow, I knew I'd hear about this when I got home.

I slid into the truck and sat by the passenger window after Anne slid in next to Rick. He had his palm resting on the vinyl seat, patting it for her to come closer. That wicked grin was back, and I had to admit, he was sexy. Flat out hot, if we had had that word then. By our standards, he was a stone cold fox. And she was done. This was not good. It was like she was star-struck. I was worried that if we were in this truck with him any longer our panties would fly right off of us. At least Anne's would. She was not thinking of Bobby at that moment.

I didn't know where we were going or what we were doing. I worried and tried to figure out what I was going to do to make sure I didn't get in any trouble. We drove down Hazel Street and out to Highway 99, Gridley's main artery.

A couple of turns later and we were sitting in front of Anne's house. "Can I come in?" Rick asked in the sweetest tone I'd ever heard come out of him. I'd known this guy my whole life, and I'd never seen this side of him. He was downright charming. No wonder his girlfriend was so heartbroken. He was amazing, sweet, and wonderful. Poor Anne. My heart broke for her. She didn't stand a chance.

He turned the engine off, took his keys and opened the door. I had to do something quick. "No Rick, that's not a good idea. We need to get Anne ready for the game tonight and don't you have, I don't know, football things to do?" I was babbling. Not that it mattered. Their eyes were still locked. I babbled again, "You know, prep work? Plays to memorize? I don't know…" I trailed off and looked over as he rushed her like he was on the football field. They were kissing so intensely I couldn't have separated them with a garden hose. The only place I'd seen anything like it was on Showtime. I only thought people kissed like that in the movies. I didn't think it happened in real life.

He had his hands on her face, on her back, running through her hair. And she didn't seem to mind. He was messing up her hair, and she didn't care. And she was doing it back. She ran her hands through his thick hair and rubbed her hands up and down his back. I was fascinated. I sat there, with my head cocked like a puppy, not sure what to do. Slowly and almost slyly, he caressed her breast as her hand reached down between his legs. He let out a soft moan, and I almost fell out of my seat.

I woke up from my partial catatonic state and screamed, "Oh my God. I have to go now." I bolted from that truck and ran down the driveway to Anne's house in complete mortification. I hadn't realized I had sat there long enough to witness *that*. It was embarrassment on so many levels: that I sat there long enough to see how they were kissing, and that I sat there long enough to witness that action. Holy Cow, if I were Catholic I would have gone straight to confession.

I stood on the doorstep and shook my head, trying to get those mental pictures out of it. It didn't work. I rang the doorbell hoping there would be someone home.

Nothing. I rang again.

Nothing. This time I thought, *the hell with it. Desperate times call for desperate measures.* I checked the front door and it was unlocked. *Salvation.* I let myself in and plopped my stuff down on the family room couch. I had spent enough time there that I knew my way around. I turned the TV on and went to the kitchen to look for some food. If my friend was going to ditch me to make out with the star of the football team — who had a girlfriend — and leave me here to be a fake chaperone, then I deserved a snack. I said that out loud, "That's right, gosh darn it. I deserve a snack."

And wow, the snack food in the Calzaretta pantry was way better than mine. I got some Pringles and Oreos and sat down to watch *Dinah Shore*. Not much else going on at that point. Then I heard them. At first it was the front door and muffled voices and kissing noises. I was smart enough to not go out there and, God forbid, witness more R-rated images. I was scarred enough.

Then I heard Anne's voice, whispering, "My room's this way," and soft footsteps.

More whispering. I tried to concentrate on Dinah Shore interviewing Burt Reynolds. "What about Meg?" Rick asked. "Where is she?" Oh yeah, like he cared.

"Meg knows her way around. She's probably watching

TV. Hurry though. My mom could be home in an hour." The footsteps sped up and then a door slammed.

I plopped back in the couch, more relaxed now that I wasn't using my Miracle Ear. I closed my eyes and thought about how easy eighth grade was. *How did we get here?* My friend might be losing her virginity, and I was watching *Dinah Shore*. How did that happen? It wasn't that I wanted to change places with her. Part of me wanted to go rescue her from any choices she might regret, but the other part of me knew it was none of my business. Way too challenging for a naïve fourteen-year-old.

God stepped in and took care of it for me. Being religiously confused doesn't mean you miss signs of God when they are thrown at you.

I heard a car crunch up the gravel driveway and looked out the dining room window. It was Tony Calzaretta, Anne's ultra conservative, hot-blooded, Sicilian father. This wasn't going to be pretty. Tony Calzaretta could scare Tony Soprano.

"Anne. Anne. Rick. Quick. Get him out of here." I screamed and sprinted back to her bedroom as fast as I could. This time, I didn't care about what I might walk in on. I burst into her room, *"Your Dad's home. Hurry. Get him out of here."*

Rick's shirt was off. *Damn. He was handsome.* Anne's shirt was off. *Tramp.* He was on top of her, but they both had their pants on and she still had her bra on. *Thank you, Jesus.* She shoved him off her like he was on fire. Anne Calzaretta did not mess with Tony Calzaretta and win. Not ever.

"Get up. Get out of here!" she whisper-screamed and shoved his shirt at him. "Go out through the slider in my parent's room while I stall my Dad. Then you can hop the fence to Bobby's house. Oh no. Bobby."

I knew she hadn't thought about Bobby.

She said it again, this time softer and sadder. Well, at least she felt bad. I knew she'd been in love with Rick all of our lives, but Bobby loved *her*. I wasn't sure we could say that about Rick. I'm not sure he loved anything more than himself…except maybe his crotch.

Anne re-grouped fast. "Okay, go out the back door and jump the ditch, and then come back and act like you left your truck in our driveway and went to see Bobby after you gave us a ride home. He'll be so excited to talk to you about the game tonight, that he won't even notice. But go now. Or he'll chop your thing off, for sure."

I was wondering why she had to give him the strategy. If he was such a great football player, he should have been able to figure this out on his own. And maybe he wasn't the man-whore I thought he was if he was this inexperienced at running from angry dads.

Either way, he already had his shirt back on (damn). He ran to the Calzaretta's master bedroom and out their slider door. We watched from their bedroom window as he sprinted across the lawn, around the swimming pool, and then damned if he didn't jump that drainage ditch and make it across. I nodded my head, realizing why he was such a great football player.

"Boy, Anne, if we lose tonight we'll know who to blame." I walked out of her parent's room nonchalantly, like these sorts of things happened to me all the time.

"Shut up. If we win, it will be because he warmed up over here, and I will take all the credit." She smiled her million-dollar smile. "Right after I become the first freshman Homecoming Queen." She flipped her hair at that statement, and I thought about another of my mom's favorite clichés. "From your mouth to God's ears."

We laughed until we heard the front door open. Anne's dad was home early from work.

"Anyone home? Whose truck is that in the driveway?"

"Hi Daddy." She was as sweet as pie. She gave him a hug, and he kissed her on the cheek. "That's Rick Davis' truck. He brought us home from the rally. He probably went to see Bobby for a minute. How was your day?"

Mr. Calzareta looked at her funny. *Ruh roh.* Was she being too nice? "It was good." He gave her another funny look and went into the kitchen. "Who's eating my Pringles?" *Ah crap.*

"Uh, that was me, Mr. Calzaretta. I'm sorry. I was starving, and Anne said I could have some." I shot her a look to back me up on that.

"You don't mind, do you Daddy? It's *Margaret.* You know how she needs food since she has no meat on her bones." She drew my name out like I was a poster child for hunger.

"Well, you have a point there. Chicken legs needs food wherever she can get it. Do your parent's *feed* you Margaret?"

I wanted to say, *"Okay, do you know where your daughter's hand has been and you want to talk about my feeding schedules?"* This was my life.

Then we heard the doorbell. No one moved. Anne looked at me. I looked at Anne. Tony looked at both of us. "What? Why are you girls acting so funny? What? The royal Princess of the freshman class can't answer the door?" He stomped over to answer it, and we ran to follow him.

It was Rick. *Gosh darn it.*

"Oh hi, Coach, how are you?" *Nice manners.* Mr. Calzaretta was a Pop Warner football coach, so he was forever "Coach" to the football players. No matter their age.

"Hello, Rick. Are you all ready for the game today?" Anne called it right.

"All ready. We should win."

"That's good son, real good. You've been playing real good." He was patting him on the back then. Suddenly I thought, *ugh, what would he think if he'd known his daughter had just touched this guy's crotch?* I shook that mental image out of my head and decided to watch the show.

Rick looked at me then. *Me? Don't involve me in anymore of your shenanigans.* "Um, Meg, I think you may have some of my homework in Anne's room. Can I get it from you?" He nodded toward Anne's room. I saw the puzzled look on Anne's face. Glad I wasn't alone.

"Homework?" I was not catching on, and he was getting frustrated. Mr. Calzaretta was watching everything. "I don't know what you're talking about."

"Can we just check your books?" He was still nodding toward her bedroom. "I'm pretty sure you have my Spanish notes." Spanish? He was a senior and I was a freshman. He wasn't in my Spanish class. "Come on." He nodded toward Anne's room again, so we followed him back there.

Mr. Calzaretta followed us too. That worried everyone. While we walked, Rick whispered without leaning too close, "My keys fell out of my pocket when we were..." He trailed off and I did not need any more details. I was pretty sure I would soon be blinded for seeing more than enough.

"Ohhhh," I said, probably too loudly. "Your Spanish homework. Yeah. I have that. I totally forgot. Fridays do that to me." I was a little too enthusiastic.

Rick got to the room first, scooped up his keys and put them in his pocket. I was right behind him and gave him a page of notes. "Here you go, Rick. Glad you remembered or you wouldn't have been ready for that test on Monday." I was getting into my role now.

"Thanks Margaret. See you all at the dance tonight." He looked at Anne then. "Are you all going?"

Anne smiled a tender smile that broke my heart.

"Yeah we'll *all* be there," I said. "Dan, me, Anne, and *Bobby*." I emphasized the last name.

His face fell. "Okay. Well, see you tonight."

As he opened the front door to leave, Anne said wistfully, "Bye Rick, good luck tonight. Not that you need it." She waved him goodbye. Their eyes locked again in that stare, and I felt so bad for both of them.

Mr. Calzaretta watched. He looked at Anne. He looked at Rick. By the time he got around to looking at me, he scratched his head.

Yeah, Mr. Calzaretta, I know what you mean. Welcome to the confusion.

He touched my elbow as Anne and I headed back to her room. "Margaret." At least it wasn't "chicken legs." "What was that? Are you going out with Rick?" He pointed to the front yard, where Rick was. "I thought he had a girlfriend."

"Ugh. I'm not going out with him. I can't even date. You know that." I kept walking, but he took Anne's elbow.

"Is he sniffing around you, Anne?" His eyes bored into her as if he had injected her with truth serum. I thought he worked for the highway department, but at that moment, Mr. Calzaretta seemed like he might be with the CIA.

"Daddy, what are you talking about?" Her voice shook. That wasn't good. "You know I'm going with Bobby. What would I be doing with Rick? Besides, he has a girlfriend." She unhooked her arm from his hand and walked off.

He leaned in and spoke softly in her ear. Not too softly for my Miracle Ear though. "Good. He's too old and too…" he stammered for the right words. "Too grown up. I don't want him sniffing around you. You're too young." I think he was trying to say that Rick was too white-hot sexy for his young daughter, and that he was afraid Anne's panties would fly off at his mere presence. And I could voyeuristically agree with that statement. Mr. Calzaretta was one smart cookie.

We made it back into Anne's room without any more questions. She shut the door and leaned back on it. "Shit. I'm exhausted. How am I going to get through this night?"

"Well, slutty Suzy, I don't know. How will you?" I flopped down on her bed. I wasn't even the one practically losing my virginity and I was exhausted.

"I'm not a slut, Meg," she said softly and made me feel bad. "That's not fair. I didn't do anything you wouldn't do if the boy you've always loved swept you off your feet and took you away." She flopped down next to me and looked wistful. She sat up and rested on her elbows. "Do you see now why I love him? Do you see how great he is?"

I had to admit, I did. But I also saw the heartbreak. "I do, Anne, but he's one kiss away from breaking your heart. He's never leaving his girlfriend, and I'm pretty sure he's only out for himself." She shook her head. I knew she didn't want to hear what I had to say. "No," I said. "Don't defend him. Think about it. He's a guy who always gets what he wants, but he always ends up back with his girlfriend. I think he likes you a lot, but not enough. I think he just wants to sleep with you and then move on and go back to her. And I think another girl will come along that he'll feel that way about, and it will just keep happening."

She cocked her head at me. Now *she* was the puppy. "Wow. How do you know that? Since when did you get so wise?"

I smiled. "I'm not wise. Ro told me that last week,

when she saw him talking to you between classes. You're not the first freshman he's done this too. Ro is friends with Rick and his girlfriend, so she's seen the cycle. Dang, that *would* be amazing if I was that wise." We laughed at my lack of experience and her lack of judgment. Until I saw her sit up with tears in her eyes. "Oh, Anne. I'm sorry. Should I not have told you?" I patted her back.

"No. No." She shook her head and cried. "I needed to know. It's just so wrong. Bobby likes me, and I just did that to him. I feel awful. I just did to Bobby what Rick does to his girlfriend all the time. I'm not any better than Rick. I'm awful." She fell back again and this time buried her face in her pillow. I could barely understand her through it. "I don't deserve Bobby." She continued crying, but softer then.

I moved over to the side of the bed she was on and patted her back some more. "It'll be okay. You'll see. Maybe Bobby doesn't even know?" She popped up at that.

"You think?" She looked hopeful again. "I didn't even think of that. He may not know." She got up, straightened her clothes, and fixed her hair. "He might not know at all, and we can just go back to things the way they were. He's a junior and Rick's a senior, so maybe he's not heard at all. Oh thank you, Margaret. You made me feel so much better."

"Well good, 'cause we need to make you beautiful. Do you want to get ready here, or do you want to go to my house and have Ro and Katie help us?" I thought it would be best to keep her distracted at this point and away from Bobby next door and potentially knowing everything.

"Great idea. Let's go to your house. I'll go get my dad to take us." I sat on the bed while Anne went to get her dad, thinking about how we dodged a huge bullet today.

Love is Thicker Than Water

*Sycamore School Eighth Grade Graduation
1978, Butte County Fairgrounds, Gridley, California
Back Row: Paula Quist Taylor, Valerie Smethers Harwell
Front Row: Diane LaBarbera Symon, Stacie Sormano Walker,
Meredith Carlin First, RoseMarie Curcuru*

Anne's dad dropped us off at my house, and there were a bunch of cars in front. I gasped as I remembered, "Oh no. We totally forgot that my mom was having a birthday party for Ro today. We are so busted." I got Anne's bag and rushed out of the car, when Anne pulled me back.

"Meg, isn't that Rick's girlfriend's car?" Anne looked as scared as I've ever seen her.

"Dang. Dang. Dang. What now? We can't not go in. It's my house. I always wanted two staircases, but I never knew I'd need one to hide you upstairs for being a man-stealer." I pushed her and she pushed me back, while we got her garment bag with the dress in it and walked up the front walk.

"What are we doing?" Anne looked nauseous now.

"This is my house, Anne, and you are one of my best friends. You are going to march in there and act like my best friend. You are going to pretend that you did not just have your hand near her boyfriend's crotch." I sounded so much like my mother. It was weird.

"He put it there," she yelled. "I didn't know what to do."

She looked sad, but I didn't flinch as I continued in my best Mrs. Monahan voice. "You are going to pretend that you are not getting ready to steal her Homecoming Queen title away from her. You are going to act like nothing happened and that you are madly in love with Bobby." I gasped when I said Bobby's name. "Bobby. That's it." I was so excited. I knew this would work.

"Bobby? What about Bobby?"

"Come on." I pulled her toward Tonya's house. "We're going to Tonya's house to use her phone. We're calling Bobby to come to Ro's party. That way you two can act all lovey-dovey and throw off Rick's girlfriend and all the senior cheerleaders. It's genius. Man, I should be paid to think this stuff up. This will eliminate all the gossip about you two, because while people were thinking you were off doing God knows what with Rick, all the most popular senior girls will know that the truth was that you were at Ro's birthday party with your boyfriend." I flashed her a smile that was the closest I could get to sparkly like hers.

"You *are* a genius. That's perfect." The color had come back to her face by the time we banged on Tonya's door.

Tonya answered after a few seconds that felt like a half hour and said, "Damn, girls, where's the fire?" We pushed our way through without explanation, and I ran for the phone.

I picked it up and handed it to Anne. "Can we use your phone?" I didn't wait for her to answer. "Dial his number, quick," I said to Anne and looked back at Tonya. "Thanks. We have to save ourselves from Slutty Suzy here. Did you already hear?"

Tonya didn't look happy. "Yeah, but it's not good. Guess who made a special phone call to tell me?" Oh God. I knew.

"Are you serious? Ooooooh, she is such a bitch."

Anne hadn't caught up yet. "Who? Who is such a bitch?"

Tonya and I said it in unison, "Evil Sheila."

Anne's face fell. "Oh, God. Oooh, shh he's answering." Her voice changed to pure honey. "Hi Bobby. It's Anne." Her face fell again. It was like the acting comedy and tragedy faces: happy, sad, happy, sad. It was very hard for me to keep up emotionally. "Is something wrong?" She didn't look happy. I wished I could hear the other end. "No.

That's what I wanted to talk to you about, Bobby. Nothing happened. Don't believe Sheila. She's an evil bitch. Everyone who knows her well knows that. What are you doing right now?" She was nodding and looking better. The color came back in her face again. "We're going over to Meg's for Ro's birthday party, and I was hoping you could meet me over there so we could talk about this." She was running her hands through her hair and things looked hopeful. Tonya and I held our breath until we heard her say, "Oh good. Thanks Bobby. We'll see you in a few. Okay. Bye." The sing-song was back in her voice, and she seemed happy again.

"Well?" Tonya and I were ready for an explanation.

The venom was in Anne's voice. "That bitch, Sheila, called Bobby. She called him and told him that I went off with Rick, and she was pretty sure I was going to lose my virginity today in preparation for winning Homecoming Queen. Can you believe that? That girl is unbelievable, and she needs to be stopped. I swear to God." Anne was pee-issed. That's a technical term: pissed with two syllables, which is *much* madder than with one syllable.

"Okay, I think we're all agreed that Evil Sheila is a vile bitch, but we have to keep our eye on the ball here. We have a show to put on for those senior girls, and you need to look pretty to do it." I was guiding her to the front door.

"And we also have to get you gorgeous tonight so you can win Homecoming Queen," Tonya said back at us. She had the right attitude.

"That's right. Tonya, do you want to come with us to Ro's party and watch the show? I think you should. Then you can help get our future Queen ready for tonight?" I needed to keep the mood up so Anne didn't melt down and lose it.

"Absolutely. Wouldn't miss it." Tonya turned some lights out and left with us.

As we crossed the lawns to my house, I tried to psych Anne up one more time. "Okay, are you all set? All you have to do is be honest and charming, and Bobby will do the rest. He's totally in love with you."

"And he is *such* a nice guy." Anne tried to convince herself.

Tonya joined in on the pep talk. "That's right. He's totally nice. And he's crazy about you."

Anne looked at Tonya for more encouragement. "He is, isn't he? I'm really lucky." She seemed more convinced.

"Atta girl. That's the attitude." I sounded like my mom. It was a little frightening. I reached for the doorknob, to our old house, built before my father was born, which made it ancient in my opinion. Anne leaned against the mailbox with her eyes closed. I grabbed her by both shoulders. "You can do this. Buck up." Oh God. That was it. I had just said "buck up." It was official. I was fourteen and had already become my mother. If I started saying "jolly well" it was all over.

I opened the door and tried to be perky. I didn't like the word, but it was the right way to behave at that moment. We walked in with all eyes on us. The room went silent at the sight of us, and thirteen pairs of senior girl eyes were laser set on Anne.

Ro broke the silence. "Hi you guys. Anne, is that your dress for tonight? Let me see it." She went to Anne, and several others followed suit. Except for Rick's girlfriend. She stayed by the fireplace with a few cheerleaders and didn't move a muscle except for her eyes, which stayed on Anne's every move. "Oh Anne, it's beautiful. Look at her

Gunne Sax dress you guys." Ro did a pretty good job trying to deflect attention and ease the thick tension in the room. "You're going to look so pretty. Too bad you're not going to win." She winked at Anne at that statement and looked over at Rick's girlfriend to smile and show her senior solidarity.

Tonya piped up like the smart-ass that she was, "We'll have to just wait and see about that. Did you hear the crowd roaring for her at today's rally? If they all showed up to vote and your stoner class didn't, then we could have the next Homecoming Queen right *here*." Tonya put her arm proudly around Anne.

One of the other cheerleaders got in on it then and put her arm around Rick's girlfriend. She said, "Of course, we have our future Homecoming Queen right here." She squeezed her in such an awkward way that Rick's girlfriend looked like maybe the other cheerleader was infected.

Just when I thought a fight was going to break out, we were saved by the bell. Literally. I hurried to the door to find Bobby on the porch looking very sad. I stepped outside and closed the door behind me, so I could give Bobby the same pep talk I had given Anne. "Hi Bobby. I'm so glad you came." I was a little too perky so I toned it down a bit. "Anne's going to be really happy to see you. Don't give her too hard of a time. She really likes you and doesn't care about Rick. He just won't leave her alone. I swear. I was there the whole time." I pulled him into the house. "But Anne can tell you all that. I'll stay out of it. Come on." Yeah. Like *that* was going to happen. I was officially Ethel Mertz to Anne's Lucy Ricardo. This was not supposed to be my role. I was supposed to be Mary Tyler Moore to her Rhoda.

We walked into the lion's den, I mean living room, and Bobby was a little surprised to see that he was the only guy there. "Uh, hi." He shoved his hands in his pockets and looked at his feet.

Ro came to the rescue. Again. "Hi, Bobby. I didn't know you were coming." She shot me a look that said, "what the hell?" and then went back to being a lady and good hostess, just as we were raised. "Can I get you something to drink?"

Bobby looked around and decided he wanted what everyone else was having. "I'll have a Coke. Thanks." Ro went to get Bobby his drink, and he made his way over to Anne and Tonya.

He sort of hugged Anne and that looked hopeful. Of course, Rick's girlfriend didn't miss a thing. She even moved away from the fireplace so she'd have a better view.

Ro was turning seventeen the next day, and her boyfriend, Tom, was coming up from Fresno for it and Homecoming. Ro was a camp counselor and got a full-fledged boyfriend at church camp. She didn't get just any old boyfriend. Ro scored an Andy Gibb lookalike. And this was at a time when every girl *loved* Andy Gibb. Her boyfriend was every inch as adorable as Andy Gibb and—this was too good to be true—he drove a yellow convertible MG, so Ro was the envy of all her friends, even the bitchy ones.

All of Ro's perfect, little, beautiful, senior friends were waiting for Tom to drive up from Fresno, which was four hours directly south of Gridley, so it was a big deal that he was coming to visit for Homecoming weekend. The girls were milling around the living room with my parents, eating a little and talking in hushed voices, waiting for the arrival of "Andy Gibb." When we first heard the sound of a car, a few of them peeked out the window to gasp at the sight of him. It was like they thought he was Andy Gibb and not just Tom Sanders, Presbyterian Camp Counselor and sophomore at Fresno State. I mean, Tom *did* play the guitar well (of course he did, he was Andy Gibb). Every good Christian camp has to have some good guitar players as counselors, but he wasn't part of the Bee Gees family.

That didn't stop these groupies though. Tom drove up with the top down and his longish blond hair blowing in the autumn breeze, and—here's the best part—his guitar was in the back seat. Just resting there, propped up on the seat. Like a real, live rock star.

Only not.

And I thought *my* summer camp romance was a Harlequin Romance. Ro's was the real deal. He was adorable, and these girls were green with envy. It was hilarious. As the girls went crazy over Tom, I motioned for Anne, Bobby, and Tonya to come upstairs with me so we could watch from my bedroom windows.

As soon as he got out of the car, Ro greeted him with a gaggle of girls surrounding her and staring. We ran back downstairs as soon as they came inside so we wouldn't miss a minute of this scene. Bobby didn't run. In fact, he was still pretty off balance.

We entered the living room like the Andy Gibb lookalike came to our house every day. We were Andy Gibb's best friends. This was no big deal to us. Ro's friends were trying to act casual but were still whispering to each other.

Even Rick's girlfriend, who at times was Ro's version of Evil Sheila, was caught up in the Andy Gibb hype. All of a sudden she became Ro's new best friend. Wasn't it Shakespeare who said, "Keep your friends close and your enemies closer?" That must have been our motto since I couldn't seem to shake Evil Sheila, and Ro had her own version here too.

After Rick's girlfriend had seen Tom drive up in his cute little MG, she said to him, "I saw that car at the gas station earlier, and I *wondered* who you were." Then she flashed him her beautiful smile, so dripping with false sweetness I almost had a diabetic attack. Someone, quick, fetch me some insulin. Stat! As Tonya liked to say about her, "Saccharin—complete saccharin—spare me." The fact that she noticed his car immediately (even before he made it to our house) spoke volumes of her emptiness, but it also confirmed that nobody missed a beat in Gridley. Nobody.

It kept getting better though. Tom regaled us with a few songs. I swear to God. We didn't have a campfire, and we didn't sing "Kumbaya," but he sang. And those girls? Oh, those girls. They sat around him and hung on his every word. Anne and Tonya and I could not have enjoyed this scene more. Ro's popularity soared that night. Not that she needed any help in that department.

Bobby seemed to wonder why he was there. As soon as Ro opened the presents, he asked Anne as much. "Why am I here? Can we go talk somewhere?" Anne looked at me for permission.

"Go in my room. I want to stay for the presents." Anne took his hand and led him upstairs.

It was like any other party where the guest of honor was dating an Andy Gibb lookalike—until the presents. All the presents from the girls were garden variety: the newest Van Halen album, a few eight-track tapes, some *Love's Baby Soft* and *Charlie* cologne.

Then came the gift from Tom. Ro opened it slowly, and I could tell that was difficult. She was trying to be so polite rather than just rip the wrapping to shreds. She pulled out a fourteen-karat gold cross necklace. The girls oohed and aahed like they were on "The Price is Right." Tonya and I worked hard not to sputter and burst out laughing at the idolatry. They really did think he *was* Andy Gibb.

Until it came crashing down harder than the drunk guy who passed out at the dinner table.

There was one more gift from Andy/Tom, and he was very ceremonious as he handed it to her. It was a scroll of parchment paper tied in a bow. No one could figure out what it was, but the worshipping girls all moved in closer, encircling Ro like she had a newborn baby. Ro was uncomfortable with all the attention, but Andy/Tom stood smiling down at her with his rock-star golden hair glistening in the light and his perfect teeth almost blinding us. She untied the pink satin ribbon and opened the scroll to read it. Andy/Tom asked her to read it aloud. He was a little too excited and proud of himself. There it was, in all its horrifying glory.

A Certificate of Marriage.

Seriously.

The girls hooted and hollered. They had now gone from game show hostesses to the game show audience. They were so excited. One of them took it from Ro so they could admire the calligraphy. He even got her middle name right. They didn't bother looking at Ro's face, which by the way, had gone ashen. She was stunned and not in a good way. I took one look at her and knew we wouldn't be seeing Andy Gibb 'round these parts anymore. Ro was seventeen and hadn't had a lot of boyfriends. She wasn't looking for a husband. If he smothered her now, she'd bolt. When Ro read "Certificate of Marriage" aloud, our mother choked on her drink. Dad just left the room, and no wonder.

The girls swarmed around her and read the certificate, while poor ole Andy/Tom beamed at them all, so very proud of himself. He didn't notice that Ro still hadn't gotten any color back in her face or that her hands shook while holding the scroll. She was scared witless, and he probably thought she was shaking because she was overcome with emotion. If only the real Andy Gibb had written some good breakup songs. Maybe Andy/Tom would write them now, because I could guarantee that very soon he'd be strumming that guitar to a good breakup song and crying over his marriage certificate that I knew Ro would give back to him. What a little heartbreaker my fireball sister Ro was.

That brought the party to a screeching halt. The girls fawned over Andy/Tom until they had to go home and get ready for the big game. Anne stayed with us so that my sisters could help her get ready for her big night as Homecoming Princess. We left Andy/Tom to watch some TV with our very uncomfortable dad.

Anne was going to wear her eighth grade graduation dress for Homecoming, which would be a crazy thing to do by today's standards, but we were much more frugal in 1978 Gridley. Besides, Anne's graduation dress was all the rage. She had a cream colored, tiered skirt, long Gunne Sax dress, with spaghetti straps and a matching lace jacket. It was stunning against her still tanned-from-swim-team, flawless skin. Katie curled Anne's hair into a perfectly feathered, shorter version of Farrah Fawcett's. Anne was even prettier than Kristy McNichol tonight, and nervous as hell. I'd never seen her nervous, and it was a little disarming. She was fussing with her hair and makeup like never before.

Ro was looking through our jewelry to see about a different necklace for Anne when she asked, "Okay, Anne, spill. What happened today? I thought Rick's girlfriend was going to kill you. What were you thinking?" She kept sifting through our jewelry box and looking up every few seconds to see if Anne was going to answer.

"Oh, God. I knew you'd ask eventually. It was nothing, I swear. What's that they say when they want to get away with murder?" Anne searched for her words.

"Temporary insanity," Katie shouted, like she was on a game show.

"That's it. Ro, I had temporary insanity. But I'm fine now. I even got to talk to Bobby thanks to your sister." She smiled over at me.

"Yeah, what was *that* about? I was so surprised to see Bobby Hunt at our door." Ro was looking back and forth between Anne and me.

"That was your sister's idea. She had me call Bobby to have him come over and distract Rick's girlfriend from thinking I was a slut. And it worked." Anne smiled.

I smiled. I was very proud.

"Nice move, Meggie. You're awfully sneaky." Ro wagged her finger at me. "So did you get to talk to Bobby?" she asked Anne. "Is he okay now, or is your Homecoming dance ruined?"

I waited for the answer since I didn't even know this one.

"Yeah," she said. "We talked and we're good. I told him how I'd had a little girl crush on Rick since I joined the swim team in kindergarten, and that Rick took advantage of that to make his girlfriend jealous. I basically told him I was an idiot, but that if he gave me another chance, I'd be a good girlfriend." Anne smiled proudly.

"And? Did he buy that?" I needed to ask. You never know.

"Of course he bought it, Meg. Because it's true." Anne was indignant.

"Okay. I needed to check." I was glad our night was not going to be ruined.

Katie walked in dangling a necklace from her hand. "I found it. Stop looking, Ro. I found the perfect necklace. I knew I had a Black Hill's gold necklace I wanted to lend you, Anne, but I wasn't sure where it was. I just found it. So here you go." She put it around Anne's neck while we all backed up to see how she looked. Anne got up from the chair in front of my vanity and twirled. She looked amazing.

Our mom came in then. "Oh, Anne. You look beautiful. That dress is perfect with your coloring. We need to go downstairs and get the camera." Mom asked Anne to back up some more and twirl for her so she could get a better look. "Oh honey, you're going to make me cry. It just seems like yesterday that you were a little girl in pigtails and running around in your swim team suit twenty-four hours a day." Mom dabbed at the corners of her eyes.

"Oh Mom, you'll be okay." I said and rolled my eyes at her.

Then we all rolled our eyes and said in unison, "Genetic defect." That made her cry a little harder and laugh at the same time.

"Come on girls, let's go take pictures." Mom was waving her hands, teacher style, to get us to follow her. Thankfully, she didn't ask us to walk single-file down the stairs.

As we were going down the stairs, Anne asked me, "Margaret, did you vote for me? I swear to God, Meg, if you didn't vote for me…" She trailed off like she was going to punch me if I didn't answer correctly.

"Of course I voted for you." Holy cow. I didn't want to get beaten up right before Homecoming.

Anne took a breath and was calmer now. "Okay. I was worried 'cause you said freshmen never win, and you didn't want to waste your vote."

I squirmed a little then, because I did say that and it sounded so mean now hearing it back from her voice. "I know. I'm sorry. I shouldn't have said that. I guess I just listen to my parent's political discussions too much. I definitely voted for you, and I don't think it was a waste of a vote."

Thank God I was telling the truth. When I voted I did think about it for a minute, because I didn't want to waste my vote, and if Anne didn't win then I wanted the junior class princess to win over the senior class princess.

Who knew Homecoming could be so political?

Homecoming Queenie

Gridley Union High School Homecoming, 1978
Gridley Union High Stadium, Gridley, California
RoseMarie Curcuru, Jerd Soares

Anne's parents came over and had drinks with my parents before we left for the game, sitting in the only red, white and blue living room that I've ever seen. Mom took her patriotism very seriously. She had red, white and blue plaid carpet in the master bedroom. In the living room, there was red carpet, white walls and a big blue sectional that she was moving around the house in different configurations all the time. The words, "I'm rearranging the furniture" struck fear in the hearts of our whole family as it meant we had to drop everything to help.

Mom took tons of pictures, promising to give them copies. We posed in every way imaginable. Mom was merciless with the camera. Ro left earlier to cheer, and Katie stayed with Anne, Tonya, and me in case we had any wardrobe emergencies.

Wanting to stay "cool," we made sure we rode to school with Katie and not our parents. Katie and I were going to stay with Anne in the library, where all the princesses gathered before half time, so Katie packed a little sewing kit and makeup bag in her purse. Always the backup mother, the one thing Katie didn't do was tell us "Y.A.L." She left that to Mom who made sure she sang it to each of us when we left. Sometimes I thought it was her good girl mantra; one last reminder that we were not to do anything to embarrass her or ourselves, like a moral insurance policy where we all paid the premiums and we all got the benefits.

Rick's girlfriend was already in the library when we arrived. She gave us an awkward smile. No real warmth there, but she was too much of a nice girl to be blatantly rude. Not that Anne deserved any warmth from her. She had, after all, just had her hands on her boyfriend's crotch. That didn't warrant an enthusiastic greeting. We went to a different corner, and the whole scene reminded me of professional fights I'd seen on TV with my Grandpa. Each class was divided up into corners in the library with their own entourages. We were the last ones there, so we took the last remaining corner. Once we settled in and Katie unpacked our stuff, the advisor told us how things would go down.

"May I have everyone's attention please? Everyone?" She shot me a look for continuing to talk to Anne. Story of my life: always caught talking. Some get caught with their pants down—I always get caught with my mouth open. "This is how things will work tonight," she continued. She gave instructions on how each princess would ride around the track in their respective convertibles, and the escorts would help them out of the car and to their marks where they would stand for the queen announcement.

"Now to the most important part. The current Homecoming Queen will get out of her car last. She will stand in the middle of the four princesses with her escort. When the winner is announced, *please* stay in your place. *She* will come to *you*. I repeat. *She* will come to *you*. Do not move. This is very important for the photographers who will be snapping away furiously for the newspapers and yearbooks. Does everyone understand their part in this? If we all do our part, this will be smooth sailing." She looked around the room and studied the face of each princess and her escort. Anne nodded nervously. "Okay then everyone, smile wide and have fun. Good luck." With that, she took her clipboard and left the library, probably to check the time.

"I think that's our cue to leave so we can watch the show from the stands. Cindy is saving us seats. Will you be all right from here?" I was looking at Anne to make sure she wanted us to go.

"Go on, Lep," said Jock. "She's a big girl and can take care of herself. Besides, I'm here. I'm more help than you guys." He smoothed the lapels of his suit—which looked surprisingly great on him—and stood up tall like he was the man of the hour.

"Yeah, that's what I'm afraid of," I said. "You don't have a flask in your pocket, do you?" I frisked his jacket.

He batted my hands away as quick as they touched his jacket, but I managed to determine there was no hidden booze. "Knock it off, Lep. I'm good. No hooch here." He leaned over to whisper in Anne's ear, making sure it was loud enough for us to hear. "Don't worry, Anne, I have it stashed under one of the library tables. Heh heh." He always had the laugh of a cartoon dog. A raspy, sneaky laugh of a character up to no good.

"Very funny," I said. "The last thing she needs is to get suspended right before she makes Gridley High history." My hands were on my hips, and I was a super-dork, but I didn't care. Jock couldn't be trusted in this situation. He was a good football player, which put him in training to add "drinking for sport" to his resume.

My sister, Ro, broke up the stupid banter. "Okay girls, let's go." She gave Anne a big hug and said, "Good luck, Anne. Make history for us tonight. Do it for all the Monahan girls who never get to be Homecoming Queens." Katie laughed at herself.

"Hey, wait a minute," I said. "There's still hope for me. I'm only a freshman." They all nodded as if to say, *Oh, poor Meggie. She's in such denial.* "Seriously? Not a chance?" Well that was just plain sad. Why can't bossy, skinny ugly ducklings have a chance? Once I put it that way, it made more sense. I shrugged and started to leave. "Make us proud, Annie, and don't fall." I turned to Jock. "And don't embarrass us." He scowled.

We got out of the library and saw three minutes left on the clock. "Let's jet so we can find our seats." I didn't want to miss a moment, so we ran/walked in a hurry to our seats. When we got to the bleachers, Katie went to sit with her own friends, and Tonya and I found our seats with Cindy and Jen.

"Well, how is she?" asked Cindy. "I'm bummed I had to save seats. I wanted to hang with you too."

"I'm sorry. How bad was it with Evil Sheila?" I whispered the last part and pointed in the direction of Sheila sitting a few people down.

"Surprisingly good. She's been obsessing over her ape playing football." We rolled our eyes at her. I needed to get a life and quit worrying about her.

Then the clock ran out. "Oh. Oh. This is it." I clapped my hands like a two year old. I was so excited.

The songleaders did their dance routine and ran off the field during the processional. It was hard to focus and get excited about it like any other game, when we just wanted to find out who would win Homecoming Queen. The freshman float was first so we all got up and screamed our heads off as it approached. We worked so hard on that float and were dying to win the float-building contest. Like anything else, freshmen never won.

The rest of the floats went through the track past us and stopped, two each, near each goal post. Then the convertibles came out with the princesses. Anne was first, and she did her best parade wave and remembered to smile even if she seemed a bit nervous. Jock didn't wave until he got right in front of the crowd. Then he stood up a bit and did his best royal wave. A bunch of us laughed and jumped up to hoot and holler at him. Then the whole crowd stood up to clap for all of the princesses. All due to Jock's parade wave.

Jock got out of the car and helped Anne out. He was so chivalrous. It was like he was a different guy. They walked to their spots and did everything as they were told. We were so proud of her. The rest of the princesses came in, one by one, without any tripping. Rick's girlfriend was beautiful in her dress. I crossed my fingers that she wouldn't beat Anne out for Homecoming Queen. Anyone but her.

The previous year's queen came out last, was helped out of her car by her escort, and stepped in the middle of the group of princesses. Newspaper reporters took pictures along with the yearbook staff. Then the announcer began.

"Before we announce the Homecoming Queen, we need to announce the winners of the float contest. It was a *Star Wars* theme this year, and the winning float goes to *Rocket Husky* by the Class of 1982. The freshman class wins!" Our side of the bleachers went crazy. We were jumping around and hugging each other like we had just won Publishers Clearinghouse. Determined to make our mark on Gridley High, we were on our way. Not just "punky freshman" anymore.

I looked down to see Anne and Jock waving peace signs in the air to us. Our symbol for "eight-y-two," and we all chanted back. "Eight-y-two. Eight-y-two." It was the most fun I'd ever had.

The announcer tried to quiet us down. "Okay, ladies and gentlemen, time to announce the 1978 Homecoming

Queen of Gridley Union High School." The crowd erupted again, at least the high school age portion of the crowd did. "Representing the freshman class is Miss AnneMarie Calzaretta and her escort Mr. Jock Santos." We went crazy again. Hooting, hollering, and every other verb that describes teenage enthusiasm. The announcer barely got to the sophomore class, which was fine with us. He announced each princess in class order, with their escorts, and then the 1977 Homecoming Queen and her escort.

And then it was time for announcing the new Homecoming Queen.

"Ladies and gentlemen, the 1978 Homecoming Queen for Gridley Union High School is…" he stopped. We looked up at the booth to see what was wrong. Nothing seemed wrong. Anne looked at Jock. Then she looked up at us. Jock looked up at us. We shrugged our shoulders. The crowd murmured, and just before it got loud he came back on. "The 1978 Homecoming Queen is AnneMarie Calzaretta."

Going crazy barely describes it. Anne jumped like I'd never seen her. She hugged Jock and then they both jumped. They jumped so much you would have thought it was two girls hugging and jumping and not one big football player and one girl. The freshman section of the bleachers was insane. We were so proud of ourselves. We won the float and Homecoming Queen. We were leaving our mark on Gridley High now.

Anne walked over to last year's Homecoming Queen and looked so excited that I thought she was going to yank that crown right off of her head. Jock pulled her back, and we could see him telling her to stay where she was. Tonya and I laughed and yelled, "Let her come to you. Let her come to you," and that's what she did.

The crown bearers and flower girls walked over to Anne and Jock with the former Homecoming Queen. She stood in front of Anne and took off her winter white fur cape and put it on Anne. We jumped and screamed again. She took the crown from the pillow the little boy carried and placed it on Anne's head. The flower girl handed her a large bouquet, and Anne knelt down to give her a hug.

Jock escorted Anne to the stage where the princesses sat in their "court" on little benches. Jock and Anne were downright elegant as she sat on a white, wrought iron garden chair. Two little loveseats for the three princesses and the former queen, and one chair for the new Homecoming Queen. Once the escorts sat their princess or queen, they stood behind them as if they were their personal security detail.

Then the photographers went wild. Anne had to sit in her full-length dress, and now the fur cape and the heavy crown, carry two bouquets, and paste a smile on for picture after picture. It was surreal. Our little tomboy, our little athlete, our little heartbreaker, Anne Calzaretta was the Homecoming Queen.

I couldn't believe we pulled it off. We had mimeographed fliers and shamelessly passed them out before school, after school, and in between classes. We'd rallied the freshman class to make sure every single one of them voted. We harped about class unity and showing those older kids that we were "more than just little freshman." We used every method we could think of to make sure Anne got every vote she could.

And it worked.

I couldn't remember a time when I smiled harder or

more. This was great. It couldn't have been better if I was the one on the stage with the crown on my head.

No. Scratch that. But that would be the *only* thing that would have been better.

The photographers finished and the football game resumed. That was when we all got to rush the track and give our congratulations. "Come on," I whisper-screamed to Tonya and Cindy. "Let's go see her."

We ran down the bleacher stairs and through the gate by the snack bar to get onto the track. Then we ran as fast as we could down the track to the stage. We threw our arms in the air as only cheerleaders can do well and yelled, "Woo-hoo! Eight-y-two!" Again, very convenient that two is a peace sign and rhymes with "woo-hoo." We swung around the back of the stage to hug Anne sitting in the fancy chairs with the princesses.

"Oh my God, Meg, did you see? Can you believe it?" Anne gave us all big hugs, and even Jock gave us hugs. Lame hugs where he barely held us and then gave us three token pats on the back, but for Jock that was tantamount to marriage. That was downright intimate for him. He was not a hugger.

"This is the greatest night ever," I yelled. We had to yell to hear each other.

"I *know*. It's the best." Anne was as excited as we expected. "And what about the float? I can't believe we won the float too. All our hard work paid off."

"It's the coolest," Tonya said. Then Rick's girlfriend shot Tonya a look.

"Okay freshmen, we get it. You're excited. Can you please let us watch the game? Some of us have boyfriends playing." She shot an evil look over at Anne. I so wasn't going to let that one go.

"Um, yeah. She's right Anne. How is Bobby playing tonight?" I shot a wicked look right back at that mean girl. I didn't care if Anne just had her hand on that girl's boyfriend's crotch that afternoon. She was not going to ruin this night for her.

Anne figured out what I was doing right away. Thank goodness. "He's doing great, Meg. He threw that last pass that Rick caught for the touchdown." Then she looked at the girlfriend as if to say, "Your boyfriend wouldn't *be* a star without *my* boyfriend's brilliant passes," then smiled her best saccharin-sweet smile.

Bobby came over after we won the game to congratulate Anne. I didn't move so I could turn my Miracle Ear up and listen. I saw my future, fifty years from then, as Anne Calzaretta's Gladys Kravitz. *Abner, come quick. Anne and Bobby are kissing. Hurry Abner.* I shuddered, but it didn't stop me from listening. He had his helmet in one hand, and on the other side he leaned down and whispered in her ear. "Congratulations. I hear my girlfriend is the Homecoming Queen," and he smiled the sweetest smile. I so hoped she didn't break his heart.

Anne whipped her head around. "Girlfriend? I'm your girlfriend?"

"Well I thought you were? Aren't you?"

Anne smiled back at him as sweetly as he had. "I guess I am. Nice passes tonight, Mr. Quarterback. You were great. I don't know who I'm more proud of tonight."

He laughed. "I think you should be more proud of me since I got most of the football team to vote for you."

Anne looked surprised. I wasn't. "You did? You did

that for me? That's the sweetest thing anyone's ever done for me, Bobby. Come here." He leaned down again, and she gave him a soft kiss, on the lips, in front of everyone. I turned away then, because it felt like that afternoon with Rick and I was a voyeur in Anne's life and didn't have one of my own anymore. *Where is Dan? When do I get to kiss someone? I can't spend the rest of my life as Gladys Kravitz with my Miracle Ear on.*

What timing. Dan came up behind me and pounded Bobby on the back for doing such a great job. He shot Anne a million dollar smile while slowly putting his arm around my waist. My whole spine tingled at his touch. "Look at you, Miss Freshman Homecoming Queen. Are we going to be able to stand you at the dance tonight, or will you be too busy with your courtiers?" He still had his arm on my waist and used a fancy word like "courtier." I wasn't even sure what that meant, but I knew that smart was sexy.

"Shit Dan, I don't even know what a courtier is. I was planning on hanging with you three tonight." Anne never missed a beat.

Bobby and Dan laughed out loud. "Now that's the AnneMarie Calzaretta we know and love. Thank God." Dan patted Anne on the back. I knew she wouldn't let Homecoming Queen go to her head. She was so darn competitive that she had to make it happen. Anne Calzaretta couldn't imagine going into any competition and not trying to win. What was the point of that? Homecoming court was not any different to her than a soccer game or a swim team race.

"Are you still coming to the dance with me?" Dan leaned over to whisper to me. "Are you done being Anne's lady-in-waiting?"

I turned around and smiled up at him. "I think my shift is over. We should go now." He smiled back, and my stomach fluttered like I had just done a flip dive into a pool.

Anne leaned over the chair she'd been stuck in for over an hour so she could whisper to the three of us, "Do you think I can get out of here now? The game is over, and if I have to smile anymore, I think I might throw up on these girls. I'm not sure that's very Queenie."

"Gosh Anne, you're the Queen. I'm pretty sure you can do what you want. Let's go." I took her flowers so she could get up wearing the long, fur cape.

"Thank goodness," the sophomore princess said. "I was dying to leave and get out of this dress. I was just waiting for someone else to go first." She hopped up and hurried off the stage.

Anne looked at Rick's girlfriend and the junior princess as she left the stage. "Bye girls, it's been real. Have fun at the dance tonight." She swung her royal cape around, took Bobby's sweaty arm, and sauntered off like she was Queen of the World. I couldn't resist. I took Dan's arm and walked behind her like I was her lady-in-waiting.

Talk of the Grope

Dinner with Grandma Alice and Grandpa Clif
1979, The Wiser Home, Gridley, California
Meredith Carlin First, Alice Cole Carlin, Clifford Carlin, Melissa Cole Carlin,
Lori Carlin Proctor

I was exhausted all weekend, but still excited about everything that happened — the best night of my life at that point. I couldn't wait to talk to Jennifer about it. She was able to go to the game, but not the dance, so I had a ton to catch her up on.

She came over after church on Sunday, looking as cute as ever with her hair long and straight down her back. I seemed to be in a perpetual state of growing my hair out. I had all my Farrah Fawcett layers, but Jennifer had pristine seventies straight hair. My dream. She looked fresh and crisp, with her adorable skirt and freshly pressed blouse. Jennifer was always dressed perfectly. Perfect describes her well, as long as it's the non-assuming perfect and not the perfect that you love to hate.

"Wasn't Anne beautiful last night?" said Jennifer. "And Jock? I couldn't believe Jock in his suit. He looked like such a gentleman. I kept waiting for him to spit some chewing tobacco, and he didn't. He was really cool." She was as excited as I was. It was a proud night for all freshmen.

"They both looked great. The dance was so fun." I laid down on my bed, looking at the ceiling. I couldn't believe how great and scary life could be all at once. "I get butterflies in my stomach every time I think of Dan, but I get scared at the same time. I hate that."

"Why do you get scared? What happened?" Jennifer looked worried.

I sat up. I didn't want her to worry about me. "Nothing bad. After Anne got out of her fur cape and changed into jeans, we all went over to the dance together. I talked her into keeping her crown on. She was so cute." Jennifer laughed "We danced to every song. They even played *Stairway to Heaven* again. I don't care how old that song is, I never get tired of it."

Jennifer laughed again. "I don't think anyone could get tired of *Stairway to Heaven*."

"When we slow danced, he held me and I melted. He's the sweetest. He kissed me a lot. A lot more than I expected, and he's a good kisser." I laid back down on my bed. "A *really* good kisser." I sat up again, getting restless. "I could kiss him all day."

"Wow. Where's the scary part?" Jennifer still looked worried.

"I don't know. I feel like such a dork. Bobby and Anne were so cute, and it seemed so easy for them." *Gosh, it seemed so easy for Anne and Rick too.* "I feel kind of forced. Kind of like it's just not right. I don't know. Does that make sense?" I laid back down on my bed and covered my face with my pillow. That felt safe.

"I don't know what makes sense," she said. "I think you can only go by what feels right to *you*. If it doesn't feel right, then why would you do it? Doesn't God give us instincts for a reason? Aren't we supposed to listen to them?"

That made me sit up on the bed again and look at her. I decided to just blurt it out. "He touched my boob."

Then *she* sat up. *Shot* up was more like it. "What? Are you serious?"

"Yeah. It was weird. I didn't know what to do or how to feel. Other than scared. I *know* I felt scared. It seemed awkward since I feel like I don't *have* boobs. At least I better not, 'cause if these are the boobs I'm stuck with for my whole life then I'm gonna be *so* pissed." I shuddered at that thought. "You don't think these are all that I'm stuck with, do you?" I waved a hand past my chest like I was Vanna White waving the newly solved puzzle.

Jennifer shook her head. "I have no idea, but I don't think that's the point. If it made you feel bad or wrong, you shouldn't be doing it. Back up and tell me everything. What happened? He didn't touch your boob on the dance floor, did he?"

I laughed at the thought. I didn't know how I would have handled *that*. "No. We had nothing but fun on the dance floor. It was like a double date with Bobby and Anne. Even though I can't date. We hung out all night, dancing only when we liked the songs, and talking and kissing the rest of the time. It was great." I went to the window seat and sat down to look out. "When the dance was over, Ro said Dan could drive me home as long as I promised to come straight home. I was so excited. When we went out to his truck, he went around and opened *his* door for me, not mine. Cue number one that I was supposed to sit by him and not by the passenger door. Also, the first point at which I got kind of scared. Though I liked sitting by him and feeling him next to me."

I thought I saw Dan's truck going past the house, and my heart stopped. I looked again, but it wasn't him. I remembered that I was in the middle of the story and continued. "We drove home and talked about what a fun time we had. He parked right down there." I pointed to the curb in front of the house. "We kissed good night. I'm never sure of what to do with my hands, so I did stuff I've seen in the movies and stuff I've seen Anne do." I shuddered when I thought about Anne's hand on Rick's crotch and thought, *well, not everything I've seen Anne do.*

"I ran my fingers through his hair. He seemed to like that. Sometimes I touched his face and he touched mine. But then his hand slid down and rested on my chest. He squeezed it a bit, but honestly there's not much to squeeze." We laughed, because at that point I squeezed my own breasts. "Seriously, we're laughing, but look." I held each boob with each hand and got barely a handful. "I'm so lame. How can I let a guy grope me when I'm not yet fully formed?" My laughter changed to tears quickly. "What am I supposed to do?"

Jennifer sat next to me on the window seat, her eyes full of concern. *I'm so lucky to have a friend like her that I can tell anything to. Knowing she won't tell anyone. Ever.* "I don't think you have to do anything. That's the whole point. Maybe if he does it again, and what are the odds he won't, you can ask him not to."

"Yeah, how do I do that? I can't even imagine saying that." I went back to my bed and flopped down, this time on my belly. I wanted to shut it all out.

"What's your alternative?" She came around and sat on Ro's bed and looked at me.

I sat up. "Breaking up with him? That's always an alternative." Made sense to me.

"Seriously? You think you should break up with him? Is that how you feel?" I was surprised that she was surprised.

"Why not? It would alleviate the problem. Wouldn't it? He can't grope me if I'm no longer making out with him." I laughed but I felt like crying again. Why was this so easy for Anne? She was juggling two guys and it was no problem. I wonder if both of them were groping *her* boobs and she just didn't care. Could that be? Could it be she liked having her boobs groped? Maybe this was my problem 'cause I didn't like my boobs? Ohhhh. This was so complicated.

"Would you be able to break up with him? This being your big 'high school romance' and all? You seem to like the idea of it." There it was. She came up with the root of it.

"Maybe that's it. It's the *idea* of the romance I like. When it comes right down to it, I'm not so cool with having a boyfriend."

"You were quick to give up on the dream of Lee from summer camp. I mean, Margaret, who breaks up with someone over their grammar and punctuation?" We laughed again and that was nice.

"It was spelling too," I said, kind of sulking like a pouty baby. "And I did *not* break up with him. He has no idea I feel that way." There. That made me more grown up.

"That's even worse. But I think you're right. You like the idea of a boyfriend, but it all needs to be on your terms. Maybe there's nothing wrong with that. I know there's nothing wrong with not wanting someone to grope your boobs." She had a point. *Oh God, was my mom right?* Well, I know I would never tell *her*. That's for sure.

"What are you doing tonight?" I changed the subject.

"Nothing, but speaking of that, I need to get home for dinner. What about you? Any big plans?"

"Going to my Grandma Alice's for dinner. Yum." My Grandma Alice was the coolest lady ever. She and Grandpa lived in a little pink house across the street. It was the ideal childhood: having the greatest grandparents ever live right across the street. Grandma's food could cheer anyone up— even the newly groped teenage girl.

"I'll talk to you tomorrow then?" Jennifer picked up her purse to go.

"You got it. See ya." I got my shoes on to leave.

I was jogging down the stairs, yelling at the same time. It was a gift. "Mom, are we going to Grandma's now?"

She looked up from her knitting, "Oh gosh, is it six already?"

"Yup, let's go. I'm hungry."

"Okay, go get your Dad. Rowan is meeting us there after work."

"Dad, let's go," I screamed down the hall.

"Thank you, Margaret," she said with too much sarcasm. "If I wanted to holler, I could have done that myself. Go get him from the backyard." I smirked and went out for my Dad.

I got as far as the back door and yelled some more. "Dad. Time to go to Grandma's." There. That was done. I walked back to the family room. "Mom, I'm going to go without you, okay?"

"Sure, honey. Go on. Tell your grandma we'll be there in a bit." A bit. Everything is in a bit. Could be five minutes. Could be an hour. Could be five hours. But it's always a bit with my Mom.

"Got it." I left through the front door, passed Tonya's house, and crossed the street. That's all it took. I knocked as I walked in the always unlocked front door. No one locked their doors in Gridley back then.

I called out, "Grandma. Grandpa. You here?"

"In here, Meggie," she called back. "Come help me with the biscuits, honey."

"Yum. I'll always help with biscuits." I ran into the kitchen, the quicker to eat them.

Grandma was done with the dough and put them on the cookie sheet, but she still managed to stop what she was doing and hold my face with the back of her hands to smother me with kisses while saying, "How's Grandma's girl today?"

I wiped flour off my cheeks. "I'm good Grandma. What do you need me to do?"

"Here dear, you finish putting them on the cookie sheet so I can check the roast." I plopped the biscuits onto the cookie sheet. She wasn't rolling them out with flour and shaping them with a glass. These were the dropped biscuits and they were my favorites. They seemed more real and less Pillsbury-like when they were dropped.

I kept working on the biscuits but Grandma wanted to talk. I should have known. "So Meggie, your Mom tells me you have a boyfriend. Is that true? The Stone boy?" Why is it that all old people refer to kids as "the Stone boy" or "the Calzaretta girl"? Is it their memory, or can they only identify kids in their family groups and never anything more specific than that?

"Well, yeah, but I don't know for how long. I think I'm breaking up with him." I spoke quickly and looked down. It was too weird discussing this with Grandma. Especially when I wasn't even comfortable with the whole thing myself.

"Put this in the ice box, will you?" She handed me the milk. "Why is that, honey?" She was working it hard.

I never heard my grandmother say "refrigerator." It was always the "ice box" to her. I used to think it was funny. Now I miss it.

"I don't know, Grandma. It's weird. The whole *boyfriend* thing." Maybe that would change the subject.

"What's that mean? The boyfriend thing? You know you shouldn't even be dating. Maybe this is a sign that it's too much too soon?" Even though I tried my best to look at the biscuits and not catch her eyes, she made sure she looked in mine.

"You're probably right, Grandma. It's all so hard. Can we change the subject? What's for dessert? Did you make angel pie?" That'd do it. Grandma Alice liked dessert better than anything. My dad said that when she was younger, she ate dessert first. She had to give it up after she became a diabetic, but she kept on making it for all of us. That seemed unfair.

"Okay, Meggie, but I'm here if you want to talk about it. I know it's hard for you to imagine, but I was a young girl once too. I know a thing or two about boys."

I stared at her for a minute. I thought of the pictures I'd seen of her as a young girl and how everyone thinks I look like her. I tried to imagine her kissing a boy, but I couldn't do it. I couldn't imagine her as anything other than my sweet, old grandma. In my mind, she was never a girl. Not possible.

"Yeah, I don't see it, Grandma." I smiled at her, and she laughed out loud and hugged me. I hugged her back with my wrists cocked so I didn't get dough on her. Then she smothered me with "Grandma Alice kisses." A staccato of five different kisses, all over the face, and always in the same rhythm. Grandma was a gifted concert pianist. A musician first and foremost—even with her kisses.

"You're so funny, my Meggie. You're Grandma's girl."

I didn't know why I was Grandma's girl. Or why I was funny. I felt pretty stupid about everything, but I took the kisses and hugs. She tilted my chin up and said, "It's okay that you can't see me as a girl. I couldn't imagine my grandmother as a girl either, but know that I'm always here, okay?"

She looked so serious that she kind of scared me. It felt ominous and confusing. "Okay, Grandma. I promise. I'll remember."

The dinner was great, as usual: a roast, mashed potatoes, biscuits, and for dessert my dad's favorite angel pie; a pineapple-banana pie that he loved and she was proud of since he didn't eat any sweets except for this one. Grandma Alice did it all. Thankfully, no one brought up Dan at dinner. I thought I was off the hook—until we left.

We were at the front door and my Grandpa said, "Your

grandma tells me you have a sweetheart, Meggie Mac."
Man, I was going to have to talk about this to *everyone*. Next,
they'd have their bishop over there to interview me to make
sure I was still chaste. This was too much pressure. I was
definitely going to break up with him on Monday. I couldn't
take this.

"Uh, yeah, but not really. I'm probably breaking up
with him so I don't want to talk about it." Oh well, there
you go. The floodgates opened. My mom looked at my
dad who shrugged. Then she looked at Ro who shrugged.
Then I walked out the door because somebody had to start
the leaving process or we'd be there all night discussing
"Meggie Mac's boyfriend."

My mother sped up to walk next to me on the fifty yard
trek to our house. "Margaret, you're breaking up with Dan?
How can you break up if you can't date?" She smirked.

Well, that's a good question.

"I don't know, Mom, but it's over. Isn't that good
enough for you?" God. I was so sick of talking about this.

"Well, it is. Is there anything you want to talk about?"
She sounded genuinely concerned, but I was not in the
mood.

"No. You were right. Are you happy? I'm too young.
It's too weird, and I'm breaking up with him. Satisfied?"
I ran off, probably too dramatically, into the house and
slammed the door because a girl could only take so much.

"Are you okay?" Ro asked as she looked down at me
while I laid on my bed, staring at the ceiling. It seemed like
that was all I did anymore: stare and think way too much
about my love life, or lack thereof. That couldn't be right.
This can't be how it's supposed to be.

"Yeah. I just didn't want to talk about it a million

times. And not with Grandpa." I hated the whole situation, and was seriously thinking life may have been better when I lived in unrequited love land and dreamt of Jeff Fisher. Nobody was groping me then, and I didn't have to feel guilty and stupid.

"What happened? Did something happen to cause this?" Ro could tell. She wasn't stupid. For all I knew, my mom had called Katie, and Katie talked to Ro and told her what to ask. As my second mother, Katie was inclined to know everything. Everything seemed to flow through her even though she didn't live here. Katie probably told Mom that she saw me sitting next to Dan in his truck. Oh this was *too* much of a pain. Why did people bother?

"Yes," I said. "You know it did. Just come out and ask. He felt me up and totally freaked me out. There. I said it. I'm a freak and don't want to be groped."

Ro laughed out loud at this. She sat on my bed, where she was supposed to be comforting me, and laughed at me instead. This was the sister I was blessed with. Laughing at me in my frigid humiliation.

"You're not a freak, Meg. I'm sorry I'm laughing, but it's funny." She continued to laugh through her apology. Ro spat her words out since she was laughing so hard. I couldn't help it. I laughed too.

"You mean, I'm not frigid? I'm not a freak for not wanting to be groped. Dang, Ro. I barely have boobs. Why does he want to *touch* them? It's creepy." I started to cry, because it wasn't funny anymore. I was tired of it all.

"Oh, don't cry. You're totally normal. You just turned fourteen, and he's almost seventeen. That's not a good match to start with. And you're right, you barely have boobs." I punched her in the shoulder. *I* could say it. She, with her perfect body, could not. "No, I'm serious. My point is that you don't even have your boobs yet, so that's a sign that you're not ready to be groped. I know that sounds weird, but do you know what I mean?" I think I did.

"You mean that since I've just turned fourteen, and just gotten my period, and am not even close to being fully developed, hopefully, that it's perfectly normal for me to not want to be groped? To just be kissed? This is normal for a person at my level, but not normal for a guy of his age?" It was starting to make sense. I was the luckiest girl in the world to have such a smart sister.

"That's exactly what I mean. If you were my age, you still might not want to be groped, or you might like it. Either way, it's okay. Either way, you're not frigid. It's not possible to be frigid at our age. Why do you think they teach us to not have sex until we're married? This whole thing is too complicated for us. We need to wait until we're ready. I still wonder if it will make sense then. I'm doubtful." Dang but she was wise. Where did she learn this stuff? Maybe Katie was teaching her, although I didn't know where Katie was learning it. I didn't hear my parents talking about this. We only talked about other people having sex. That wasn't "Monahan Approved Behavior." No sex for us until marriage. Period. "Maybe you should talk to Dan about this. He's such a nice guy. Maybe he'd be fine with not groping you." She laughed again. It was hard to say the word grope and not laugh.

I cracked up too. "Oh, yeah. That's what I'm gonna do. 'Hey Dan, would you mind not touching my boobies. You're freaking me out.' Sorry. Not happening. I'll die first. Breaking up is the only answer." At least I could laugh about it now. "Thanks Ro. You made me feel so much better. I appreciate it."

"No problem. Just keep those boobies in your shirt," she said, cracking herself up. Again.

I threw a pillow at her as she walked out of my room, no doubt on her way to report to Mom that all was well. One more Monahan safe in her Virgindom, just as it should be in Jayne Monahan's world.

But I still had no idea what to do.

So I did nothing. For a few days. And days turned into weeks. I couldn't date, so it wasn't like I was alone with Dan enough for him to try and cop a feel again. It was just random encounters between classes, and occasional lunches and rides home from school. There were no more school dances after Homecoming, so I was spared that.

The only difficult part was hanging around Bobby and Anne. They were hot and heavy. Not hand-on-his-crotch hot and heavy, thank God. Whenever the four of us were in Dan's truck, they'd make out. That prompted Dan to kiss me. What else were we supposed to do? Watch them? I'd had enough of *that*, thank you very much.

One day, after Thanksgiving break, Dan offered me a ride home, and of course, Anne and Bobby were coming too as he took them home most days. I'd been walking on pins and needles around him since Homecoming, so I was nervous to get into the car with them knowing what could potentially happen. As usual, he walked me around to his side of the truck and opened the door for me, still the gentleman. I looked up into his beautiful green eyes and said thank you. My heart fluttered a bit as he was *so* cute. *How could I resist this guy? Why was I?* More confusion. It was endless.

I got in the car and slid over on the vinyl seat next to Anne. There we were again, two happy couples. Was I going to have to break this little love-fest up, just because I couldn't handle a little groping? I laughed out loud without realizing it, because I couldn't even *think* of the word grope without laughing. Dan looked down at me and flashed his perfect teeth. He said, "What's funny?"

I realized that I'd laughed out loud at myself and tried to cover. "Oh, nothing. I was thinking about Spanish class today. That's all." I smiled over at Anne who was looking at me funny. Dan nodded and started the truck. I turned the radio up, and we listened to Van Halen for the two-minute drive straight down Hazel Street to my house.

We parked in front, and Anne and Bobby immediately started making out. *God. What was their problem. No, I meant that to God: what was their problem?* They couldn't keep their hands off each other. Dan put his arm around me and we kissed. Only I was so paranoid that I couldn't even enjoy kissing anymore. Forget the fact that I was still not sure if I was good at it. It took so much thinking and creativity. How did people do it? You had to think about how to use your tongue and when. You didn't want too much or too often. And then there was the whole what-to-do-with-your-hands thing. Where did they go? How much did you move them? It was exhausting. I was beginning to think I wasn't up for the whole thing.

That's when it happened.

As soon as I let my guard down, his hand crept over and rested on my boob. It sat there, still as the night. Not squeezing. Not groping. I tried not to laugh again at the word grope. What was he going to do with it? Was he breaking me in? Did he think if he left it there for a certain amount of time it would be okay to squeeze, or God forbid, move over to the other one? Or (gasp!), move downstairs? At that thought I panicked and blurted, "I need to break up with you."

He sat up straight and looked down at me like I was crazy and he hadn't heard me right. I shrugged my shoulders as if to say, "Yeah, you're right. I'm as loony as they come." But I said, "We should probably go talk." Bobby and Anne pulled themselves apart for three seconds to stare at us and promptly resumed making out the second we got out of the car.

Dan took my hand when I got out of the truck and held it as we walked to the front porch and sat down on the hanging swing. Great. I chose the most romantic place in our house to break up with the sweetest guy in the world. I was as loony as they came.

Thank God, he talked first. "What's the matter? What was that all about?" He looked heartbroken. *He deserves so much better than me.*

I didn't know where to begin, so I talked. Typical of me: engage mouth before brain. "I don't know. I think I'm not ready for this. Not ready for you. I think you should find a girl who deserves you more. I just know I'm not the one." I looked down at my hands, unable to look in his eyes. If I did, I'd fall back in his arms again, and that wasn't right.

"Don't I have any say in this? Can't I decide who's right for me?" He was half laughing, as if he couldn't believe I was saying any of this.

"Yeah. You'd think you would, but you don't know me well enough." I laughed with him.

"That's the whole point. I want to get to know you better. Breaking up would make that a lot harder." He was making sense, but I was pretty sure I was doing the right thing. Mainly because the second I said it, I felt a thousand pounds lighter.

"I know, but I'm so stressed out. All I do is think about you and worry what will happen next and if I'm doing the right thing. It's crazy. I'm crazy. I think you're better off without me. It's not you. It's me." There it was. The first time I ever said some of the cruelest words in the English language.

Dan cocked his head like a puppy. I patted his hand to try and make him feel better. He recoiled from me and glared. My first real break-up experience, and I never got any better at it, and I never learned to enjoy it.

"That doesn't make any sense at all. What the hell does that even mean? 'It's not you. It's me.' What is that?" His voice wasn't rising, but it was very stern.

I felt childlike in response to his tone and wasn't sure what to say. "It means don't try to understand it. It's crazy. I'm crazy. I don't want you to think I don't like you. I like you a lot. I can't do this." I raised both hands up in an effort to demonstrate.

"Do what? What is *this*?" He raised his hands up too.

"I don't know, the whole relationship thing. I'm not ready for a boyfriend. Does that make sense?" I looked down again, fearing his answer.

"No." He was very curt. "None of it makes sense. But girls have never made any sense to me, so I don't know why I'm surprised. I guess I thought you were different. You seemed so smart, and you're a Monahan so that practically guaranteed that you're nice." We smiled at each other at that, even though I was disappointed to hear that I "seemed" smart to him. I was no longer smart, since I just broke up with him.

"I'm sorry. I am. I think this is best though." I gave a sheepish smile.

"Yeah. Okay. Whatever." I bristled and he noticed. "I mean, okay. I didn't mean to sound mad. This is confusing.

I thought you liked me as much as I liked you. I thought this was good." He motioned between us.

"It was. It is." I tried to reassure him, but I didn't want to talk about it anymore. I had to stay strong or I would cave. He was so darn cute. "It's not the right time for me. I can't even date. You deserve a girl who can go on proper dates with you." I raised my eyebrows in an effort to sell this theory to him, proud that I thought of it.

"Yeah, you're right." Ouch. Truth or not, that hurt.

Dan got up and gave me his hand to help me out of the swing, gentleman to the end. I was a total crackpot for breaking up with this guy.

"Thanks. And thanks for being so nice about it. I am sorry." I was still trying to smile nicely.

"No you're not."

My face fell.

He saw this and realized what he said. "No, I mean you can't be sorry or you wouldn't break up with me. I get that you don't want to hurt my feelings though. I do, but it's impossible to break up with me and not hurt my feelings. That's the nature of it. The only way to not hurt my feelings is for me to never have cared, or for you to not break up with me. Know what I mean? You're new at this. I get that."

I smiled up at him and felt worse than I had in years. *How could I do this?* "Yeah. I get that. I don't want to hurt your feelings, and I do care about you as much as you care about me." My eyes filled with tears. His face went soft and sweet. He smiled the nicest smile I'd ever seen, and he seemed misty. I wanted to touch his face and make it all better, but I knew I couldn't.

It was like he was a mind reader. How did he do that? He held me so tight. I didn't want him to ever let go. I hugged him back, holding on for dear life. *What was I doing?*

How could this feel like such a weight off my shoulders, but feel so wrong at the same time? How could I feel so good and sure about this, and so bad and scared all at the same time?

He pushed me back, but we still held on to each other as he looked in my eyes. Tears fell down my face, and he brushed a few away. I'd never had a non-family member do that to me. It hurt. His eyes were glassy, but he kept it together. "If I'm crazy about you, and you're crazy about me, why are we doing this? Why don't you take some time and I'll leave you alone. Can we do that? Just don't say we're broken up. We don't know each other well enough to be broken up. What do you think?" He wiped a few more tears, and I prayed that snot wasn't pouring out of my nose. Not a good time for that.

"What does that mean?" This kind of sounded like a good idea.

"It means that I'll leave you alone. We won't be 'together,' but we won't be broken up. You can have some time to figure out whatever it is that's scaring you. I see that you're scared. I don't know what you're scared of, and I think you don't know either. Am I right?"

Dang, he was good. "Yeah. That's exactly right." I knew I should tell him that I was scared of the boob grabbage, but how would I say *that*? This could at least take the heat off of me and stop my obsessing.

He looked down at me, pleading with his eyes. "Well?"

I smiled up at him. "I can do that. You're right. I am scared. I just don't know what to do about it."

"Well, hopefully we can figure that out. Just don't go getting another boyfriend. We can do this." He waved his index finger between the two of us, making me feel like we were a couple.

And for the first time, it felt good and not scary.

Confession

*Meredith's Surprise 9th Birthday Party
1973, Straw Hat Pizza, Yuba City, California
Jennifer Lynn Cone, Stacie Sormano Walker, Meredith Carlin First,
Diane LaBarbera Symon*

Northern California winter arrived. The orchards were bare. Smoke from the burning of the rice fields was replaced with tule fog; clean fog that made it smell like the whole area just got out of a long shower, not the salty smelling fog they got by the coast. This was ground fog reserved exclusively for California's great central valley, of which we lived in the northern part. Tule fog has even made national news (a big deal for us in sleepy northern California). Not only for the oddity, but also, sadly, because of the traffic pile-ups it causes. Driving in tule fog is like trying to drive in a glass of milk. You can't see anything. It can sneak up on you fast. When that happens on the freeways the pile-ups can be huge. Tule fog is the leading cause of weather related deaths in California. Public service announcement courtesy of Margaret Monahan. You're welcome.

Since I wasn't driving yet, fog was still my favorite. I loved it when it seemed to magically roll in, as if Walt Disney himself ordered it for dramatic effect. It only came in winter, so if it was foggy that meant it wasn't raining, which was a good thing for me. It was also the closest thing we got to a white Christmas. When you were a kid waiting for Santa and you woke up to fog and squinted a bit, it looked like a snowy landscape. It was a stretch and a bit pathetic, but it was all we had. Plus, it almost always burnt off by the afternoon so we had crisp, beautiful days later, which was always better than rain.

Things were going well with my time apart from Dan. We only saw each other at school and on occasional rides home. I even kissed him the other day for the first time in ages. It was a nice, slow, warm kiss. No stressing about tongues or groping, just light and lovely. I still hadn't figured out what I was going to do, and I hoped he'd be patient. I'd noticed another freshman girl sniffing around him and it worried me, but I wasn't sure what to do about it so I pretended it was nothing.

The morning I had my first hard-core peer counseling session there was a classic glass-of-milk fog. Like most California schools, ours was outdoors. The lockers were inside the main hall, and we exited through outside corridors to different wings, usually divided by subjects. It was so foggy that day that when I went out the hall door to a wing it was like walking into a cloud. I should have seen it as an omen, but I missed it. I got a peer counseling notice in algebra to report for the next period when I was supposed to be in PE. Not a real fan of PE, I was excited to get to see someone for peer counseling instead. Not a fan of Evil Sheila, I was a bit anxious when I saw that the request was from her lead minion. This was sign number two that I missed that morning.

A few weeks into the school year, we had received mimeographed forms from our first period teachers. Hot off the press, the forms still smelled strong and purple ink came off on our fingers. Little did I know, these would be my future ticket out of class and into real-life teenage drama. High drama. The form asked us to write down the names of three students in whom we confided. It didn't give further explanation, and I never thought any more of it.

A few weeks after that, I was part of a group of twenty-five students summoned for a meeting. Ro was there with a bunch of other students from all grades. It was a diverse cross section of the student body. Not that I noticed that at the time. I was just worried about why we were all gathered in the library and missing class.

My math teacher, Mr. Osbourne, who was the new

peer-counseling advisor, explained to us that we were chosen by our peers as students in whom others confided. If we were willing, the school wanted to train us as peer counselors. It would be considered a fully sanctioned club for the high school, and we would listen to the problems of other students and try and help them without giving advice. He told us this was a great honor that we should take very seriously.

Our parents told us it would look good on our college applications. Here was the clincher though: we'd get to miss three days of school for training, and all peer counseling sessions would be done during class. Uh huh. We'd get to miss a lot of class. Everybody who was chosen accepted the job. It was a no-brainer.

The next week, we headed off to the local Methodist Church for our training. As planned, we missed school for three days. We did more role-playing than I've ever done in my life (even up until now, and I've been to plenty of feel-good team building sessions) and learned the power of an "I" statement. "So Sue, *I* understand that *you* feel frustrated when your boyfriend gets mad at *you* because *you* won't go all the way." Or, "So Sheila, *I* understand that *you* get angry when all the attention isn't directed toward *you*." Like that. Even in peer counseling I could obsess about Evil Sheila.

We were not allowed to give advice. Basically, we were there to listen and paraphrase like little mockingbirds. I didn't mind. I liked anything that got me out of class. At times though, class would have been more interesting than paraphrasing people's fictional problems all day long. But at other times, it was fun. I did feel good about being chosen. Ro was chosen for the senior class, and our mom was so proud that both her daughters were peer counselors. She was always much more impressed with any activity that involved brain usage than popularity or looks. Mom even became the peer counseling advisor for her middle school. We could never escape her.

That milk-glass-foggy day, I opened my locker still wondering why on earth Evil Sheila's minion wanted to talk to me. Was it a scheme? Would Sheila pop out of the corner of the room and yell at me? Were they testing me so they could see if I could really keep a secret and then try and get me kicked out of the program?

I was so anxious as I put my books in my locker. *Why me?* I wondered if I could pawn it off on someone else. Maybe Ro? She was a senior, so if they set her up she would be less likely to get in trouble. Plus, she could probably help them more since she was older and wiser. These girls were getting into things I knew nothing about. Sleeping around at fourteen was not exactly my expertise. Not to mention that I was flat out scared to death of every single one of them: Evil Sheila and all her minions. They were straight out of the Wizard of Oz to me. Total flying monkeys with their wicked witch as a leader. I was sure I didn't have a house to drop on her so avoidance was my only tactic.

I stood staring at my locker pondering ways to get out of this when Anne came by. "Whatcha staring at? Are you coming to PE?" Anne loved PE and loved to make fun of me when I bumbled it. Lucky for her, I was a constant source of amusement.

"Sorry. You'll have to make fun of someone else today. I have a peer counseling session right now." I slammed my locker door shut and said, "Hah!"

"Who ya seein'?" she said in a singsong voice with a sneaky grin on her face. She was dying to know.

"I don't know if I can tell you or not so don't ask." I fidgeted as we walked away from the lockers.

"If you don't tell me, I'll wait by the hall to see who goes in." Well, she had me there. Everyone could see who went in and out of the room. That didn't seem very confidential, but how else would we get into the rooms?

"Oh. You have a point there. Okay. I'm seeing one of the Minions."

"Whoa," Anne gasped and stopped in her tracks. She was afraid for me too. No good could come from this. "No shit?"

"Well, shit is right. It's weird. Why would she want to see me? What do I do?" I was scared all over again now.

"Do what you were taught, all those 'I statements' and stuff. 'I hear you feel controlled and scuzzy since you hang around Sheila.'" Anne was trying to imitate my voice and thought she was hilarious, but she was right. I would stick to the training and keep it all business.

"Good. I can do that. Take myself out of it and follow the training. I can do that." I tried to convince myself by saying it over and over.

"Oh, you're screwed. You're nuts. I wish I could be a fly on the wall in there to hear what you have to say. Hah!" She imitated my voice again with her "hah!" and walked off laughing toward P.E.

I turned the other way and walked to the peer counseling room. My shoulders slumped and my head hung low like I was off to the gallows. I was scared to death to face one of Sheila's flying monkeys.

I opened the door and she was already there, sitting nicely, waiting for me in one of the chairs that was old and clearly donated by somebody's dead grandma. The room was a little cold and damp from the foggy day outside. Our high school was built circa 1952, so the heating was not sophisticated and air conditioning was non-existent. We spent most of our time at Gridley High being either hot or cold. Not a whole lot in between.

I wanted to turn back and bolt. It was a classic fight or flight situation that we learned about in eighth grade science. Could I get away with it? Would she notice? She smiled at me then. It was a warm smile. That puzzled me. I was taken back to third grade when we were so tight. Practically best friends. I pictured her with her huge brown eyes, jumping rope to *Ruby Red Dress* playing on the phonograph. We used to have so much fun then. I thought we'd be friends forever.

But then Sheila turned evil and none of us looked back.

She waved at me to come over and sit down. She even patted the chair next to her and smiled again. She was being so nice.

I looked at the chairs. They were beautiful, actually. Silky fabric that needed to be replaced, but they were great chairs from the sixties. Slipper chairs, low to the ground, probably once lovely in some old lady's living room. I looked at her again. She was even more beautiful than when we were little. Unlike me, she was fully developed with soft brown hair, warm brown eyes, flawless olive skin, and of course, the perfect body. She was everything I was not: darker, prettier, and worldlier. All that and big boobs too. She was easy to hate in that way. Why did she hang around Sheila? What was wrong with her that she became a minion; a flying monkey for a wicked witch? Did she wake up one day in middle school and just decide to be a minion and do the bidding of an evil girl?

To make it all more confusing, she was Cindy's cousin. Only in a town like Gridley is there a population so small that everyone is related. We were very close once, but no longer. Separated by Evil Sheila. And here she was asking for my help. This was very strange indeed.

I shook my head to clear my busy head. I'd been doing that forever and still do it and it still never works. They say the definition of insanity is doing the same thing over and over with the same results. But I'm no quitter.

She seemed a bit startled by my headshake, but smiled again to put me at ease. I realized that she was as nervous as me, so I sat down on the slipper chair, low to the ground. I ran my fingers through my hair. Nervous habit. I was a habitual hair flipper too. Part of my neuroses.

"Hi." I tried to break the tension.

"Hi."

Was that it? She called me here and all she had to say was "hi?" I fidgeted some more thinking that she really should know that she came here to do the talking. Not me.

I gave up. The silence was killing me—another horrid habit of mine. "Um, so, how can I help you today?" Great. I sounded like I was going to get her prescription at the drug store. It didn't matter how I sounded. She went right into it with a bang.

"I took someone to get an abortion, and now I'm afraid that I'm going to go to hell for being an accomplice in the murder of a baby." When she said "murder," she whispered and put her hand to her lips, then closed it in a fist as if the words were so vile they needed to be captured and immediately thrown in the trash. She lowered her fist to her lap where she settled her hands. Her eyes were wide, and her horrified expression was as if she couldn't believe she just said that out loud, to a live person. She looked down at her folded hands and sat in shame as if hearing the words out of her mouth was worse than the original alleged sin. She sat. Waiting for me to react.

I sat with my mouth agape. Seriously. Any longer and I may have drooled.

How was I supposed to react? Whenever I heard scary things like that I would hear radio fuzz in my head. It started out loud and static-y, it was never a song I recognized, and it wouldn't go away until I calmed myself. It was mental white noise, the equivalent of putting your hands over your ears and humming because you didn't want to hear something. By the time the mental radio softened in my head, I noticed that my mouth was still wide open and I was slipping in the chair. With my mind racing, I thought how funny it was that I was slipping on a slipper chair and I had to suppress a laugh. Not a good time to laugh, but I was glad the mental radio stopped.

There I was: a religiously confused, neurotic bundle of hormones, on the cusp of adulthood, trying to keep afloat in a new semi-adult world, and now faced with teenage abortion. I thought my grandma might have had it right when she said the world was going to end in 1983. At this rate, maybe sooner.

I tried to sit myself upright again, but I kept slipping on the slipper chair. I wondered if that was why they were named slipper chairs. The fabric of my Dittos jeans against the silky fabric of the old chairs was not giving me any friction. Nothing but a little static electricity was going on down there. Like a polished up old metal slide on the school ground and swoosh. I fell off that slipper chair at the thought of dealing with teenage abortion.

With a big thud, my bony buns landed right at the feet of the minion who'd just confessed her biggest sin to me as if I were her priest. My skinny legs dangled in the air around her head. This was no time to laugh. But how did these things keep happening to me?

She didn't laugh either. She burst into a huge case of giggles. I thought she was crying at first and couldn't think of what to do. I think my fall actually helped break the ice for her. So I laughed with her. As I brushed myself off and sat back down in the silky chair, I laughed so hard I cried. I thought that was happening to her too, until I realized that her laughter had turned into real tears. She sobbed. Her shoulders shook and it was getting ugly with the blotchy face and snotty nose.

I looked for the box of tissues we kept on hand for just these occasions, while she sat sobbing. All I could see from behind were her shoulders shaking. I felt so awful for her. *How was I supposed to help?* I was a fourteen-year-old virgin with two months of peer counseling training. I had zero world experience. My only experience with boys was my own relationship where I was scared to death of his every move—and for precisely that reason. No good seemed to come out of having a boyfriend. It seemed to me everyone either ended up pregnant or heartbroken. How could those be happy endings?

I handed her the tissue from behind and patted her on the back. I figured that the least amount of direct eye contact was best. She was probably pretty embarrassed. Though it seemed impossible to be more embarrassed than I, since I had just fallen out of my chair and had my legs dangling in her face.

I cooed to her while I patted her back, like she was a baby. I didn't know what else to do. This was my first crier. She raised her hand to mine, patted it gently, and looked up at me with those huge brown eyes. Her lashes were damp with tears. She said so softly that I almost didn't hear her, "Thank you, Margaret." My heart broke for her. She wasn't just a minion of Sheila's. It was like she was my friend again. *How did that happen?*

I took her hand and walked around the chair, leaving it in her lap. I knelt down in front of her so I could see her eyes. "I'm sorry. I'm so sorry." I tried to compose myself and think of how to handle this. I thought of Ro and what she would do. Ro would have handled this with aplomb. So would Mom. She wouldn't have even had to think hard. She would have had the right words there, on the tip of her tongue, ready for just that moment. Mom and Ro weren't there for me though. I had to come up with those words on my own.

"Tell me about it. Why are you crying?" There we go. I was so proud of myself for remembering to take myself out of it. It was all about her. Find out what was bothering her and get her to deal with it on her own. *Phew.*

I sat back in the other chair and moved it around so we could face each other. Boy, did she open up then. "She came to me a month ago and told me she was pregnant, by that *guy*. Ugh." I assumed she was talking about Sheila, but I didn't know for sure. I was surprised she said "guy" like it was a disgusting thing. I thought they all loved Sheila's boyfriend.

"Anyway, she asked me to go with her to Chico for an abortion. He could only drive her there, not stay with her. So I drove her instead of him. What a loser only being able to go one way. What could I do? I was torn between what I believed and what I was supposed to do as a friend. How could I leave her to go through that by herself?"

"She got into the mess by herself, or with him," I blurted. "Why couldn't she get out of it with *him*?" We both gasped. I shouldn't have said that. This was exactly what I was afraid of. My sharp tongue was engaging before my brain. But I hated how boys seemed to get off so easily. I did it myself by calling Sheila a slut, because rarely did I call her dudes sluts. More importantly, I was assuming it was Sheila when I had no idea who it was. I snapped to attention and tried to save myself. "I'm sorry. That wasn't fair."

"No it wasn't, Margaret," she said, spitting my name out like it was bitter medicine. "Maybe I shouldn't have come." She didn't move though. Instead, she glared at me. "Do you know why I chose to talk to you?"

I was so mad at myself. I half hoped that she wouldn't tell me and she'd just leave in a huff. I didn't want to make this any worse. I didn't look up. "No. Why?"

"Because of all the peer counselors I thought you would understand the most." I looked at her funny and she explained. "You may not like us anymore, but you did once. We used to be close and I miss that."

"You do?" She could have knocked me over with a feather. Good thing she didn't since I had already fallen once.

"Yeah, I do. We know how you all feel about us. We're not blind." More bitterness. "You think you're better than us. Sheila likes it that you're afraid of her, but I don't. I miss how we all used to be."

I sat in shock, not saying anything for fear of putting my foot back in my mouth.

"I went with this friend because I didn't want her to be alone," she continued. "The problem was, I didn't think about how I'd feel about it until afterwards. And I didn't think about God. And church. And confession." She looked out the window as she trailed on about all the things she *didn't* think about, and her eyes glazed over. New tears streamed down her cheeks. "Did you know I was confirmed in seventh grade?" I shook my head. Certainly I would remember that, since I lived such an ambiguous religious life and coveted other peoples rituals.

She got up to throw away her snotty tissues. As she walked back to her chair, she explained that when she was confirmed she became accountable for *her* actions. "So I sat in mass the Sunday after her abortion and realized that I was accountable for her actions by going with her. By taking her there and driving her home, I condoned her sin. I should have talked her out of the abortion rather than being there with her. She could have gone to some home for unwed mothers and given the baby up for adoption. Or gone somewhere to live with relatives and then given it up." She was looking for solutions that could never happen now. "Basically, I was an accomplice to killing a baby."

When she said the word "killing" I flinched, and she burst into tears again. Since I'd already lost all credibility by my last remark, I didn't know what to do, as usual.

So I let her cry.

I looked out the window. I thought about how if this was Sheila and she *had* married the hairy ape, her name would have been Sheila Scudmore Grimes. I felt guilty for thinking that was funny, and that made me feel horrible. I thought about how many times I had dreamed of Evil Sheila having to go to a home for unwed mothers, and I felt guilty that if she *was* talking about Sheila, then it had almost happened. Occasionally I looked at her to make sure she was okay. I didn't want to stare and make her uncomfortable, but I also didn't want to look like I felt like I needed to be somewhere else. My mind raced with possibilities, ideas, and things *to do* to help. I had to remember that I wasn't there *to do* anything but listen.

This went on for at least three minutes. Three minutes of crying without talking is long in any world and eternal in girl world. Even longer in mine, but I stayed strong and shut my mouth which was the ultimate challenge.

I couldn't stand it any longer. I had to say something. "So have you talked to your priest about this? Have you gone to confession?" That seemed safe, right? Didn't Catholics go to confession weekly? I didn't know the rules, like whether or not they confessed the big sins, or if they just confessed the little ones like, "I hit my brother three times this week and I talked back to my mom twenty-seven times this week." How many Hail Marys did a priest give you if you led with, "I held my fourteen-year-old friend's hand while she had an abortion this week?" Wow, when I put it that way, I certainly wouldn't go to my priest. Why was I asking her if *she* did?

Too late.

Apparently she agreed with my thought process. "Oh my God, Margaret! Are you serious? Yeah, that's the first thing I did was confess to my priest so he could figure out who I was and tell on me to my parents." She sneered so hard that her face contorted. She shook her head. "God, Margaret, are you high?" This came with more sneering and head shaking. "Of course you're not. Saint Margaret the Perfect wouldn't be high at school." I flinched hard and she noticed. "I'm sorry. I didn't mean that. You just piss me off."

"No, *I'm* sorry." We became Chip and Dale then with

our, *I'm sorry. No I'm sorry. You're right. No, you're right*, back and forth.

I pushed the Chip and Dale thoughts out of my head and continued. "I don't know a whole lot about how Catholics work, but I thought if you went to confession it was confidential. I thought the whole point was to tell your priest and give the sin up to Jesus. Then I thought the priest told you what to do, prayers and stuff, and then you were supposed to feel better after that. I didn't think it was supposed to get back to your parents. Do they really find out?"

She listened. "No, you're right Meg." She hadn't called me that in years. Her voice softened. "That's how it works. It's just so scary. It was hard enough telling *you*. I couldn't imagine telling Father Brady." She was thinking hard about it as she wiped her nose with her now very nasty tissue. I got her another when I realized I hadn't done any "I" statements yet. This was the time so I wouldn't be a complete failure for the session.

I tried to move into action. Otherwise I'd have no hope of making it to Spanish, and I had to do an oral presentation that day that I wanted to get over with. "So, I'm feeling like you're scared about confession and worried about being caught." I sat back in the chair, pleased with myself.

"Yeah?" She sat back too with a "what gives?" look on her face.

"Yeah," I repeated. *Why didn't that work?*

"Well *then* what?" She looked pissed. I was sweating.

"What do you mean *then what*?"

"*What do I mean?* What do I *do*? I'm here for advice, Margaret. Tell me what to do. *What to do!*" she screamed. I was worried about the class next to us. My mind wandered, picturing them in Spanish, conjugating a verb and suddenly hearing a desperate girl screaming for help.

"*Well?*" She had calmed down some but was still adamant that I answer.

"I'm sorry. I can't tell you what to do." I slumped down in my chair a little. I knew this wasn't going well. For years she had been a follower. Even when we were friends, she followed. She wasn't used to making decisions for herself, and my news that I couldn't tell her what to do was not going to thrill her.

"Why can't you tell me what to do? Your whole life you've been telling people what to do, Margaret Monahan, why would you stop now?" She was just getting going. "Why do you think we put you in this *peer counseling* thing?" she said with venom. "'Cause you're decent and good, and most important, *you're good at telling people what to do, you bossy girl.*"

I said she was a follower, I didn't say that she couldn't defend herself. At that, she sat back in her seat just as I had after the "I" statement. She was proud of herself. Smiling even.

It was my turn to cry. I burst into tears. I couldn't help it. It was all too much. I tried to cry softly since she had most likely scared the class next to us already. Then our roles reversed. She went to the tissue box, and smarter than I, brought the whole thing to me and dropped it in my lap. *Why didn't I think of that?*

She sat back down. "I'm sorry, Meg. I didn't mean to make you cry. I know this is hard. Believe me, I know. I didn't know you couldn't give advice. You've been telling me what to do since kindergarten. Why would you stop now? Shit, I don't know how you do it. How can a bossy girl like you, who has opinions on *everything*, sit here every day and listen to people bitch without giving advice or telling them what to do? That's totally against your nature." She sat back but didn't look at me. She looked out the window and shook her head.

My tears stopped. I blew my nose and thought about how, while I was glad she understood my dilemma, I still didn't know what to say. I felt like I had failed her. I felt like I was wholly unprepared both as a girl and as a peer counselor. How was I going to survive the rest of high school, let alone college, if I couldn't survive peer counseling?

The minion started back up. "Okay, so if all you can do is tell me what you think I'm feeling then I'm going to have to figure this out myself." She got up and paced. She walked over to the standard issue 1950's steel desk in the corner used by the teachers' aides when we weren't in sessions, and picked up their tape dispenser. She took a piece of tape and rolled it in her finger while she looked at a family picture on the desk. She picked the picture up and showed it to me. It was a cute family picture: mom, dad, a toddler and a baby. "See Meg, this could have been someone with her baby. That baby could have made a family instead of dying. I feel responsible for taking a baby from a family." She slammed the picture frame back down on the desk and came back to the chair.

I looked up for a moment. I couldn't give advice, but I could tell her the other side of an issue. "When we fight at my house, sometimes my mom makes us discuss both sides of the issue so we see that there are always two sides. Maybe you're not looking at the other side of the issue?" I sat back, satisfied with my assistance and knowledge that I didn't give any advice.

"What the hell does that mean?" She sneered.

Dang. I thought that was so good. "Both sides?" I repeated. She shook her head. "If someone has an abortion, there are two sides to that too. On the one hand, they can go to a home for unwed mothers and give their baby up for adoption. If they do that, they have to leave town for nine months, and in a place like Gridley *everybody* knows where they've gone. Then they have to live the rest of their lives knowing that they have a baby *out there*. Somewhere. With that option, you don't have to worry about God as much as you have to worry about your parents and the whole town knowing you had a kid out of wedlock."

"Okay?" She sat up straighter, really listening to me.

"I don't know much about abortions, but what I do know is that when you have one, you don't have to tell your parents, you don't have to even tell the guy, right?" She nodded. "It's purely between you and your God, so maybe your friend made the best decision about herself that she could at the time because she was so afraid?" I couldn't believe this was coming out of my mouth. All I knew was that no one I knew would ever make a decision like that lightly, and the minion didn't deserve to go to hell for being a good friend. Someone had to say that to her, even if I didn't say it outright.

She sat thinking while I finished my thought. "Sometimes, seeing both sides can help you figure out what you want to do. That's why I asked if you talked to your Priest. You might be worrying when this may not have been a sin for you at all." I took a breath hoping that didn't count as giving advice.

She took a huge breath. "You're right. God, I can't believe I'm saying that to you." She sneered a little as she laughed at her own joke. "I need to go to confession. It's my only choice." She stared at me as if she was willing me to agree with her. I looked down at my feet like they were the first feet I'd ever seen. "I know. You can't tell me what to do. How about this, if you agree that I should go to confession—which I already know you do since you asked if I went—then look up at me and quit staring at your stupid feet. Okay?"

I kept looking at my stupid feet. I felt like a caged animal. The only way I was going to get to give my presentation in Spanish was to agree with her and get this session over with. I was emotionally drained, and this had to end. Plus, it wasn't like I was telling her what to do since I was just looking up and not giving advice.

I looked up. And I threw a smile in for good measure, because I did think it was the brave thing to do. I'm all for people following whatever religious practices they hold.

She laughed out loud. "Hah! I knew it. Margaret Monahan always chooses the right thing to do. I knew you wouldn't let me down." I smiled with her, but didn't laugh because I didn't want to encourage her thinking I gave her advice.

I spoke then because, let's face it, I just can't not speak. "And for the record, I don't always choose the right thing to do. You know that."

"No. I know. But you try really hard Meg, and I like that. I still know you care. That's why I'm here." The bell rang for the end of class, so she got up and I followed her. She dangled her arm over my shoulder and whispered in my ear, "Now, this is all just between us, right? I don't have to tell you the hell that would be your life if you told anyone about this, right?"

My blood went as cold as her eyes. "Yup. Totally confidential," I promised. She smiled, sweet and threatening at the same time. I've remembered that smile and try to use it on my children now, but it's still not as good as hers.

"So, I'm off to confession after school today, because it's the right thing to do. Then I can pretend this never happened and sleep again. God, I hate this. Why can't I be more like Sheila and not have a conscience?"

I laughed at that in my head, but was smart enough not to say a word.

With that, she shot me another icy look and left the room. I stayed behind to write down my time in the journal. It was how we kept track of our sessions. I took a deep breath and was so glad it was over. What had I gotten myself into, and what if she really was talking about Sheila?

Like Jack Tripper?

Sycamore School Eighth Grade Graduation
June, 1978, Butte County Fairgrounds, Gridley, California
Meredith Carlin First, RoseMarie Curcuru

It was the last day of school before Christmas vacation and I made it to Spanish and got through my presentation well. At the end of class an aide from the front office came in with a message and handed it to Señor Felipe. He thanked the aide, looked at the note, and then looked at me. My first instinct was to be afraid. I was not used to being a peer counselor, so I wasn't used to getting messages and being pulled from class.

"Señorita Margarita, ven aqui, por favor."

"Si Señor." Thank God it was a "si o no" answer; I was still trying to adjust to Spanish. I pretty much heard my Spanish name and "please," so I went to the front of the class to collect my message. It was a pass directing me to go to the peer counseling room rather than English class. We normally only had one session a day. Even more unusual was the student requesting my time: Anne Calzaretta.

What? Why would Anne book a peer counseling session with me, one of her best friends? Was this a joke? Was she just trying to get out of class? Whatever it was, I didn't mind. My next class was with the meanest English teacher in the history of Gridley High, so one less class with him was fine by me.

I left Spanish with my books pressed against my chest, as always, and made my way to my locker. Dan was waiting there, leaning against my locker and looking adorable. He shot me a big smile when he saw me. I got shivers down my spine every time I saw him, yet I was still afraid of being in a "relationship" with him. *What was my problem?* I secretly hoped he would fall in love with Amber and let me off the hook. But he was too darn cute. What on earth did he see in me? I still couldn't believe it. Amber had been sniffing around him for months, so I knew I'd have to decide quick or the decision would be made for me. Meanwhile, I had this mysterious peer-counseling request to attend to.

"Hey. How was Spanish?" He backed away while I unlocked my locker.

"It was good. How 'bout you? How was English?" Small talk. I was still distracted over the impending "session" with Anne.

"Boring as always. What's up with you? You seem distracted?" His eyebrows were raised. *So cute.* I pulled my English books and folders out of my locker and tried to concentrate on what I needed rather than his dimples.

"Oh, nothing. I got a peer counseling notice to meet Anne in the next period, so I'm worried. I'm sure it's fine." Then I wondered if I should have even said that. I didn't think the sessions were secret, since students could see the other students as they left class and as they went into the room where the peer counseling sessions took place. I was worried anyway, since worrying seemed to be the best thing I did then.

"Come on, it's *Anne*. She probably just wants to get out of class. You don't need to worry. I've got to get to history though. I'll see you later." Dan went off toward the history wing.

"Okay, bye." I smiled at him and tried to look cute and worthy of his affections, but I was still unconvinced, both of my worthiness of Dan, and of Anne's intentions for a session today. I had a weird feeling, but I didn't know why.

I shut my locker, spun the dial to clear it, and left toward the peer counseling room, saying hi to several people along the way and trying to act normal. The door to the classroom was unlocked, and I let myself in. Thankfully, I got there first. I put my stuff down and sat on the slipper chair and tried to clear my thoughts. Those chairs weren't the same to me ever since I fell out of one during the session with Sheila's minion. But my weird feeling was bearing down on me so that no chair was going to be comfortable at that moment. *What could she possibly need to discuss with me?* I realized that I had English that period but not Anne. Anne had typing this period. She would never try to get out of typing. It was the only class she liked next to PE. She was the Queen of PE since she was a star athlete.

Anne came in right as I was thinking up ways I could get out of PE. She threw her stuff down on the ground by the door and sat across from me on the other slipper chair. "Oh good. You're already here."

"Yeah. But I don't understand. Why would you want a peer counseling session with me? Don't I already know all of your problems and secrets? Don't we already discuss everything? What could I not know? Omigosh. Are your parents getting a divorce?" Now I was scared, but Anne seemed fine.

"No. My parents are fine. Well, as fine as parents can be. It's not that." She seemed so calm.

"Oh God, you're pregnant? Who's the father?" I was outta hand.

She laughed at me — very much *at* me and not with me. "God, stop. I'm not pregnant. Far from it."

"Well, then what is it? At first I thought you wanted to get out of English, but then I remembered that you have typing right now. What's so important that you'd want to miss typing?"

She laughed again. "I was being nice. I didn't want to miss typing, but I thought you could handle missing English."

My eyebrows raised, and I smiled. "That was very nice of you. But come on. I'm dying here. What's the problem?

I've had this weird feeling in my stomach ever since I got the notice while I was in Spanish." I leaned forward hoping that would make her spill it faster.

She leaned forward too but didn't say a word.

"Well?" I was snippy and that was very un-peer counselor'ish of me, so I sat back on the couch to look more relaxed and helpful.

"You have to take a solemn oath first." Anne sat upright and was dead serious.

"An oath? Are you kidding?"

"Yeah. Raise your right hand." She motioned for me to raise my right hand, then she looked around and pulled out her Spanish book.

"Seriously? Your Spanish book? I'm taking an oath on your Spanish book? I hope it's not an oath to swear allegiance to Spain or to only speak Spanish, 'cause I'm not that good yet. I'm not taking that oath." I laughed and she didn't. That's never a good sign.

"It's all I had. I forgot to bring a bible. Pretend these are your diaries. Treat this as sacred as the secrets in your diaries. Raise your right hand back up and put your left hand on the book. That's how they do it in court, right?" She was so nervous and serious.

"I think so." I stared straight at her but did exactly as she asked.

"Do you, Margaret MacGregor Monahan, swear to keep secret everything we discuss in this peer counseling session?"

"Yes."

Anne shook her head. "No, that's not right. You have to repeat after me. That's how they do it in court, right?"

"I think so." I was still puzzled.

"Okay, do your hands again." I had taken them off the

all-important Spanish book. I returned them and looked up. "I, state your name."

"I, state your name." I repeated. She was not amused.

"You're not funny. I'm serious. I, state your name."

"I, Margaret Monahan."

"Do solemnly swear on my own Virgindom."

I burst out laughing. "My Virgindom? What is that, like my Kingdom of Chastity?" I laughed more.

She scowled. "Just say it. I solemnly swear on my Virgindom."

"I solemnly swear on my Virgindom." I tried to keep a straight face

"On the secrecy of my Virgin Diaries. There. Is that better?" Anne continued, and I nodded as I realized how very serious she was. I worried again that maybe she was pregnant.

"On the secrecy of my Virgin Diaries," I repeated, trying to match her seriousness.

"That I will keep all things said today a total secret, not telling *anyone*." Her face was so serious.

"That I will keep all things said today a total secret, not telling anyone. So help me God." I added the last part so we could get this done.

"Good. That's good. You knew the last part." She sat down and threw her Spanish book on the ground, so much for the sanctity of the Holy Bible.

Then she said it, with no warning and no foretelling.

"I think I'm gay."

She said it with such nonchalance, like you might say the color of your hair or how you'd tell someone it was her turn in a game.

My internal record player scratched in my head. I didn't know what to say. "Gay? Like happy? Like how old people talk?" She shook her head. "Gay like the first name of that girl in the senior class? You're changing your name to Gay?" She nodded her head no, and I gasped. "Or gay like Jack Tripper?" I watched too much TV, and we loved *Three's Company*.

Anne seemed disappointed that I didn't understand immediately. "No, not gay like Gay Anderson, and no, not gay like Jack Tripper. Jack Tripper isn't even gay. He just *pretends* to be gay."

"He only pretends to be gay for Mr. Roper," I said. "The rest of the time he's normal." She flinched when I said "normal." "Are you saying you're *pretending* to be gay, 'cause that doesn't make any sense either." I didn't understand why she flinched when I said "normal."

"No, Meg, I'm not pretending to be gay. Why would anyone do that?"

Well, how the hell would I know? This whole thing was confusing. I shook my head. "So, does that mean you like girls instead of boys? Like me? Do you like me? Is that what this is about?" Total confusion. She'd blindsided me. I was ill equipped to handle this. I seemed to say that a lot. My peer counseling techniques pretty much ended with an "I" statement and strict instructions not to give advice. There was never any role-playing about what to do when your best friend tells you she thinks she's gay.

Anne laughed hard at this. "No. I don't like you, Meg. I mean, I *like* you but I don't like you like *that*. I don't *like* you, like you, like you. You know what I mean?"

"No actually, I don't. I'm totally confused and kinda scared. What do you mean?"

"You *know* what I mean, Meg." She gave me a knowing look like I should have figured this all out by now. Her eyes bored into me, and I was feeling very air-headed. *What am I supposed to know?*

I stared at my hands and tried hard to comprehend what she was saying. It was worse than my first day in Spanish, when I thought for sure I'd struggle forever with the language. Then the light bulb turned on in my feeble mind. With Spanish, it took a few months to kick in. At least with Anne, I figured this out after a few minutes. I was improving. I looked up and she saw the recognition in my face and smiled. Those perfect dimples. *Were those lesbian dimples? Could I say that word? Was it mean, like fag or queer?*

"Are you saying you think *you're* a lesbian?" There it was. I said it. The "L" word and I didn't mean love. Prior to that moment, that word had been a joke. People said "Lez be friends" a lot as a joke. Or they'd refer to certain girls, usually the ones built like boys, who really liked PE, as "lezzies." But I had never referred to a real, live girl as a lesbian, and never a girl like Anne Calzaretta. *Hey, Anne really likes PE? But she doesn't act like a boy. Don't lesbians act like boys?* Sure, she was good at every sport she played. She *did* swim faster than a lot of guys on the swim team. But she didn't *look* like a boy. Don't you have to look like a boy to be a lesbian? Or at least look like a PE teacher? Our PE teachers were ladies with really short haircuts, and everyone always said they were gay, even though one was married and none of the rumors were ever substantiated. *Anne doesn't have really short hair. Anne doesn't look like a PE teacher.*

I tried to shake the thoughts out of my head again. It was a wonder I had any brains left with all the thought-shaking I did. "I'm sorry. I don't know what to say. As your peer counselor, I'm supposed to follow certain rules and I don't know how to do that now. Can I ask a question?"

"You said it," she winced and looked like I slapped her.

"I can't believe you said that word. I can't say it. It sounds dirty to me. Don't call me that, okay?" Anne looked down at her hands. She seemed ashamed. This was wrong. She shouldn't be ashamed.

"I'm sorry. I didn't know what else to say. I don't want you to be ashamed." I tried to make eye contact with her so she would know that I didn't want her to feel bad.

"Yeah, I know what you mean. I'm confused too. That's why I'm here. I've wanted to tell you for a while but didn't know how. Then when peer counseling came to school, I thought that was the perfect way to tell you without you feeling too bad. This way you *have* to keep the secret." She looked up at me again and made eye contact. "What's the question?" She seemed as confused as I felt.

I had forgotten that I had a question. "Oh. Well. You don't *look* like a le-, gay person." Not the quickest recovery.

She smiled at my not saying the L word. "Is that it? That was the question?"

"Sorry, but yeah, I mean, you don't look like our PE teachers. And they're the only le-, gay people I know, besides Jack Tripper, and I don't know Jack Tripper, and well, I don't even know if the PE teachers *are* le-, gay and Jack Tripper wouldn't be a le-, gay guy since he's a guy, and he's *not* gay. He pretends to be gay, which I guess *does* make him a le-, gay, dammit. 'Cause he does like girls, but it's a television show and not real life. Aaaaagh." I was talking so fast and was so confused, I screamed. Loud.

"Holy Cow, Meg. Quit screaming. You're going to get us in trouble. And God, you started to say that word like, five more times." Anne looked around and at the door as if the Gay Police might bust in any minute and blow her cover.

That's when I remembered rule number one in peer

counseling: it's not about you. It's about them. "I'm sorry, Anne. My head is spinning and I'm not sure how to help you. I think this is why they'd rather people don't go to their closest friends for peer counseling. Sometimes it's too hard. But I understand why you came to me. Who else could you tell? Does anyone else know?"

"Nope. Just you. And I want it to stay that way. Okay?"

"Absolutely. I understand." I went back into peer counselor mode. "It sounds like you're feeling confused because you think you're a le-, gay. Did I get that right?"

"Oh God, Meg, not the 'I' statements. You don't have to do that." She lowered her voice then and said, "Take a breath. You've almost said the L word so much you've invented a new word, 'le-gay.' If I weren't so paranoid and scared, I might like it."

I laughed a nervous laugh and then sighed. I was relieved but wasn't sure why. I was in no position to offer any help on a subject I knew less about than she. I felt helpless, and I didn't like that a bit. "Okay, if I don't have to do the 'I' statements, then what?"

"I don't know. Then nothing, I guess. I just wanted to tell you. I felt like you should know. You're my best friend, Meg. And you're my only friend who's a peer counselor, so that made you the safest. You drew the short straw." She smiled and seemed satisfied with her decision, but her voice trailed off at the end, like she was far away. When her voice did that I realized she didn't need anything from me. She wanted to tell me her secret. She wanted to unburden herself and make sure I'd still be her friend, even if she liked girls.

I was relieved. Like I didn't have to solve any problems anymore. I just had to listen, which was the whole point of peer counseling in the first place. I never understood that before. I thought all problems needed to be solved. All I needed to do was be there for her.

"So. Now I know. Now what? Are you going to date girls? 'Cause I don't see how *that's* gonna work out around *here*." We laughed, but I was scared again. I'd always had a fear of the unknown, and this was way too unknown for me.

"No. I don't think Gridley's ready for girls dating girls yet. I don't have a plan beyond telling you." She seemed distant again.

"Okay. Well, anything else?" I was suddenly uncomfortable. It was all so much to process.

"No, you want to go back to English?" Anne *seemed* okay.

"Only if you're ready?" I asked.

"Sure. I'm ready." She got up and I went to hug her. I wanted to make sure she knew that it didn't change anything between us, that I would always be her friend. She hugged me like normal. It didn't seem to be a different "lesbian" hug. But I didn't say the word.

I pulled back. "You're not going to kiss me now, are you?" I asked, with an uncomfortable laugh.

"Nah, you're not my type."

We walked out of class. I thought about that and was a little indignant. "Not your type? I still look like a boy, doesn't that qualify me as *something*?"

"I guess that qualifies you as *not* my type." She laughed and thought she was hilarious. It felt the same between us, but not. We went into that class as two fourteen-year-old girls, and we left it as, well, still two fourteen-year-old girls. Only one was a lesbian. And one was not. But neither was normal. And both were scared.

We left that classroom with a secret neither one of us really wanted to *have*, let alone *keep*.

And keep a secret is exactly what we did. For the next twelve years, we never spoke of that day in peer counseling. Sometimes I wondered if she wanted to. Wouldn't you want someone to talk to? But I decided that it was too personal and I had to follow her lead.

I moved away for college and we weren't as close during those years. But after we all graduated and settled around Sacramento, Anne was brave enough to share her truth with her friends and family. While it was a shock to some, Anne was accepted and loved, regardless of who she loved.

There was one thing Anne said to me the night she came out to The Group that I'll always remember. She asked, "What will your mom say?" I looked at her, puzzled, forgetting that my mom was everybody's mom.

"Absolutely she'll be fine," I said. "She's not a bleeding heart liberal for nothing."

"But, Meg, you know? Y.A.L. Will she still think I'm a lady?" Bless her sweet, little lesbian heart. She was dead serious. AnneMarie Calzaretta, tough girl that she was, really wanted to make sure that my mom would still think she was a lady. I got misty. That genetic defect again. My mom would have loved that Anne even *remembered* about Y.A.L., let alone cared.

"Well, I personally think that Y.A.L. can now stand for 'You're a Lesbian.' Don'tcha think?" She laughed with me but her eyes were pleading for a serious answer.

"You'll *always* be a lady." I smiled when I said it and she believed me.

A lady, indeed.

What Would Jesus Do?

Church of Jesus Christ of Latter Day Saints,
400 Spruce Street, Gridley, California
1948, Clifford Paul Carlin Artwork

1979

Christmas vacation was tough, to say the least. Peer counseling turned out to be much more of a commitment than I ever expected. In one week, I had to counsel a friend on abortion and then listen to my best friend tell me she thought she was gay. I rang in 1979 worrying that my friends were going to burn in hell.

With Anne's confession happening on the last day of school before Christmas vacation, that gave me two and a half weeks of break to stew; until I ran into Mr. Osbourne, my algebra teacher and peer counseling advisor, at the grocery store. That's where you run into everyone in Gridley, at a store.

I was getting a few things for my dad for dinner, and there he was in the checkout line. We said hello to each other and asked about our Christmases when I realized that he might be the perfect person to tell me more about homosexuality. All I knew was from *Three's Company*, and Anne had made it painfully clear that *Three's Company* was not real life. I had heard people say that homosexuality was an abomination to God, and that gay people would go to Hell. That terrified me. How could Anne go to Hell for being born different? That made no sense to me. I'd seen Anne with plenty of boys. More than I wanted to see. She tried really hard to be straight. How could this be a choice?

As we were both leaving the checkout lines, I held my bag of groceries and fidgeted a bit before getting the nerve to ask him. "Mr. Osbourne, as a peer counseling advisor, would I be able to come to you with questions from sessions I've had with students?" I looked down at my feet. I was so nervous.

"Of course, Margaret, always. Just come in when we get back from Christmas break."

"Okay. Thanks." But I still stood there. I didn't want to wait until Christmas break was over. He could tell something was wrong.

"Is it something serious? Are you alright?" He looked worried, and I didn't know what to say, so I nodded yes. I was fighting back tears and didn't know where they came from. "Do you need to talk now? Are you okay?"

I didn't want to make a scene. I knew I had to get out of there fast. "I'm fine. Thanks Mr. Osbourne." I was talking fast and rushing away from him at the same time. "I'll see you when we get back from break. Thanks." I waved and ran out of the store. When all else fails, leave.

I walked down the street when I heard a car pull up alongside me. I turned to look, although I knew it was Mr. Osbourne. He leaned all the way across his front seat and rolled the passenger side window down to talk to me. "Margaret, I know you're not okay. I saw the tears in your eyes. Get in and I'll give you a ride home."

I was still afraid to talk about it but very relieved at the same time. I hesitated a moment before opening the door. I slid in and put the groceries on my lap.

"Thanks, Mr. Osbourne. I appreciate it. I've been so worried."

"Would you like to go to my office at the church to discuss this? You could call your parents from there?"

That seemed like a good idea. I needed a little more time to form my words anyway. How do you say all the things that had happened in the last few weeks. "I'd like that, Mr. Osbourne. Thanks."

We drove down the street and into the parking lot of

the Mormon Church. He got out the keys to his office, and we went in. He was the Stake President, which meant he was responsible for all the Mormon Churches in our area. It also meant I could talk to him in confidence. Even though, technically, I was not a Mormon. Between that and the fact that he was a peer counseling advisor, I felt comfortable telling him everything.

"Have a seat, Margaret. The phone is right there so you can call home." He sat behind his desk, and I called my mom to let her know that I ran into Mr. Osbourne and needed to talk about a peer counseling thing. She sounded worried but knew enough not to ask questions. The benefit of having educators for parents: they understood school stuff more than most.

I hung up the phone and looked around. I'd never been in this office before — or any Mormon Church office for that matter. It had the classic Jesus picture above his desk — the same one that was in every sanctuary of every Mormon Church. It was my favorite picture of Jesus. On the opposite wall was a picture of the current Prophet or President of the Mormon Church. Other than that, it was a typical office with a generic wooden desk and industrial style chairs.

"So, what's bothering you?" he asked. "What can I do to help you?" Mr. Osbourne was one of the nicest, most caring men I'd ever known. He could just look at you when you were troubled and make you burst into tears. Not in a bad way, but because he cared. He was my algebra teacher at the time, and he approached math in the same way he did everything else in life: methodically and logically, but with real compassion. Mr. Osbourne cared about everything he did.

"I don't know where to start, so I'll just say that I had

two peer counseling sessions before Christmas and they were big." I told him everything, without any names, of course. I tried to speak slowly, but it was a challenge. I've found that when I discuss uncomfortable things I speak even faster to get them out of the way. This doesn't work when your speech is already at a faster rate than the rest of humankind. I finished with the abortion story and burst into tears. Hearing it from my mouth made it more real and ten times scarier.

Mr. Osbourne looked surprised at first, and then composed himself with a straight face. I noticed and wailed, "See. Even you're shocked. I can't handle this."

He straightened his glasses on his nose. I hiccupped again and continued, "I tried hard to follow all the rules. I didn't give any advice. I remembered to use 'I' statements, but Mr. Osbourne, what do I do? Since the first girl was worried about her soul, that got me to thinking about both of them and their souls. Is the first girl in trouble with God now because she drove a girl for an abortion?" He handed me a tissue, and I tried to clean myself up while he talked.

"You don't need to worry about that, Margaret. As a peer counselor, your concern is being there for her and listening to her, not worrying about the state of her soul. Since she's Catholic, she can talk to her priest about it, and that is what you should focus on. As a peer counselor, you're going to hear all sorts of problems that may trouble you. It's important for you not to take these problems on as your own. Do you understand that?" His eyes bored into me. He sat back in his chair, crossed his legs, and studied my face for answers. Sometimes I thought he could read our minds the way he studied our faces when we talked.

"I guess so. That makes sense." I cleaned my face and

was no longer dripping snot. He did make sense, and I had never looked at it that way. "I can't imagine girls my age having sex, let alone, having abortions. It's all so weird. It scares me."

"What about it scares you?" He leaned forward then, and put his elbows on the desk and his chin on his hand to really look into my eyes — always the teacher.

I thought about it for a second. I had never thought about *why* it scared me before. "I guess just growing up and getting older scares me. I don't like the unknown. I like to know what's going to happen and that we're all safe. Ever since I started high school, I feel like we're not safe. It seems like bad stuff happens so quickly, like the pregnant girl. That wasn't her plan. It just happened, and she had to make a huge, adult decision. How do you do that at fourteen?"

"Exactly." His face lit up with a smile, like I was getting the point. Even though I didn't feel at all like I was getting the point. "She had to make a huge, adult decision, because she had already made a huge, adult *choice* by having sex. When you make one adult *choice*, like having sex, that often leads to having to make other adult *decisions*, like choosing birth control or the consequences of getting pregnant. You can't pick and choose which adult decisions you want to make. You have to deal with the consequences of *all* your actions. That's why our Heavenly Father tells us to wait until marriage to have sex. It's a very *adult* decision with very *adult* consequences. It should only be done under the sacred covenants of marriage. He gives us these rules so we don't have to be put in circumstances like the girl in your session. Does that make sense?" Again, with the caring look that made me cry.

"That makes perfect sense." My head was swimming

now with too much information. I was sleepy from all the crying.

"What about the session about homosexuality? How did you handle that?"

"Oh." My voice was soft. This was the hard one. Even though I was young, I had already had many serious theological discussions with my grandfather. I knew the answers I was going to get from Mr. Osbourne, and as a bi-religious girl I knew about the struggle between my family's two religions. I wasn't always good at walking the tightrope between the two, but I tried just the same.

This was one of my best friends, and I needed to sound very generic like it was just another person. Even though he was an advisor, I didn't want him to have any idea about whom I was talking. "That's very confusing for me. Since the first girl was worried about her soul for being involved in an abortion, that reminded me that I heard that being gay is an abomination to God, and that all gay people would burn in Hell. Is that true? 'Cause that doesn't seem right. This person that came to me thinks that they were *born* gay. Do you think that's possible?" I was talking fast again. I figured the faster I got it out of my mouth, the faster the problems would go away.

"It's true that some people think they are born gay, but there is no scientific evidence to tell us that you can be born gay. I can tell you that we believe behaving in a homosexual manner is a sin. So, even if people think they are born gay, the homosexual act is what is a sin, not the fact that they are gay. Does that make sense?"

"So you're saying that being gay is not a sin, but having gay sex with someone is what the sin is? That is so confusing."

He seemed a bit uncomfortable at my take on it, so thought for a moment as he smoothed out the hair he had left on his receding hairline. "That's right. Having sex outside of marriage is a sin. Therefore, all gay sex is a sin since it is having sex without being married." He moved into teaching mode again and was a cross between a math teacher and the Stake President. Either way, he was methodical and understanding, and it helped take the emotion out of it for me.

"If that's the case, then why can't gay people get married so it won't be a sin?" This seemed to make perfect sense to *me*. "That way, they wouldn't be sinning anymore."

"Because, Margaret, God tells us that marriage is to be only between a man and a woman." Again, he said this in his same methodical manner.

"He actually *said* that?"

Mr. Osbourne smiled at my confusion. "Yes, Margaret, He said that."

"Then what are gay people supposed to do? If God made them gay, but then tells them they can't act upon what He made them, how are they supposed to live? That doesn't make any sense to me."

"Margaret, we believe that Heavenly Father put us on this earth to learn and serve and work on His behalf. Do you believe that?"

"Absolutely." He was going somewhere with this, but I didn't know where.

"So sometimes, Heavenly Father gives us challenges that we don't understand. Sometimes, we don't understand them for years and then we are made to understand. Other times, we go our whole lives with challenges that we never understand. Why are some people handicapped or blind?

They don't know. They know that they are born with or receive these challenges, and they are to do their very best to live a Christ-centered life, regardless of their handicaps. We don't know why people are homosexual, but we do know that they are expected to live a Christ-centered life in spite of their challenge of being homosexual. They are expected to follow Heavenly Father's rules regardless of their sexual preferences. Do you understand?"

"So you're saying that being gay is a *challenge*, like being handicapped or blind? It's one of their challenges in life? And the challenge is that they have to fight their instinct to want to marry someone of their same sex?" I was desperately trying to understand this and make sure my friend would be okay all at the same time.

"Yes." He didn't say another word. It was as if he knew I needed a minute to process all this information. And I did. We sat in silence. My mind was still racing. It didn't make sense. How could God make Anne gay and expect her to fight that her whole life? That couldn't be the same as being handicapped or being blind.

"So for their whole lives," I continued, "they are supposed to ignore the fact that they like people of their same sex and watch everyone around them get married, have children, and go along living their lives without being challenged in that way? Even the handicapped and the blind get to live their lives with acceptance of what they are, but gay people are supposed to fight nature? That doesn't make sense to me, Mr. Osbourne. I may not be a religious scholar, or any kind of scholar, but one thing I've noticed when I talk to Grandpa Clif about religion is that God usually makes sense to me." He didn't say anything, and I sat there and thought more. The clock on his desk ticked. The wind was blowing outside. None of it made any sense.

"Mr. Osbourne?"

"Yes, Margaret?"

"What if we have this wrong?"

"What do you mean?" He sat back, studying my face.

"Well, everything is open for interpretation. The Bible, the Book of Mormon, they were all interpreted, right?"

"Yes?" He raised his eyebrows, curious where I was going with this.

"And Heavenly Father has always made it clear that we'd have challenges in life, but above all, Jesus taught that we should 'love one another.' Right? Especially our enemies? Jesus said to love our enemies, right?"

"Yes."

"Well then, what if we have this all wrong? What if the challenge is not for gay people at all? What if the challenge is for the rest of the world?" I was talking faster then, because I thought I had come up with the answer. "What if the challenge is for the rest of the world to be accepting of homosexual people? Didn't Jesus say, 'love your enemy, for if you only love your friends, what is the challenge in that?' or something like that?"

"Yes, Jesus said that in the book of Matthew, but I still don't understand what you're saying."

"What I'm saying is, isn't it possible that the challenge is not for gay people to fight how God made them? Isn't it possible that the challenge is for every non-gay person to accept that gay people are different from us only in who they want to love? In all other ways they are the same as us, and we need to love them regardless of who they want to love? Like Jesus said? 'Love one another.' Jesus didn't say, 'love only non-sinners.' He didn't say, 'love everyone except gay people.' He said 'love one another.' Period."

His eyebrows rose again. We sat for a minute, thinking in silence. The portable clock on his deck ticked some more. The wind kept howling outside.

More silence.

It didn't matter what he said after that. A light bulb had gone off in my head. I had wrapped my brain around this in a way that made me feel safe in the world. A way that made Anne safe in my head. Anne was going to be fine. Jesus loved her regardless of who she loved.

"You've raised an interesting point, Margaret. I'm going to have to think on that, but in the meantime, what did you tell the person that came to you with this issue?"

"I didn't, really. I just used 'I' statements and tried to make them feel better. I was just so shocked that I didn't know what to say. I think I can handle it better now though. Now that I'm not worried about their souls."

"You shouldn't worry about their souls as a peer counselor anyway, but you should pray for them. That would make you feel better as well. Give the troubles over to Heavenly Father, and you won't carry the burden yourself. He wouldn't want that." Mr. Osbourne stood up and got our jackets off the hook by the door.

"That makes sense. Thanks for talking to me, Mr. Osbourne. I feel so much better. Even if you don't agree with my theory, it still makes me feel better to think it. I don't think that Heavenly Father would make someone the way they are and expect them to fight that." He smiled, and we walked outside the office to the car.

"Please remember though, the scriptures do not support your theories. Do you understand?" He started the car and drove away while looking at me with intensity and warmth at the same time.

I nodded my head but couldn't give up hope. I needed a safe place in my head for Anne and her soul.

"I knew you were inquisitive when you joined my class," he said. "And even though I don't agree with your theories, I'm going to pray on it, and I think you should too." We sat quietly until we got to my house. Nothing in Gridley was more than a two to five minute drive, and nobody walked anywhere if they could get a ride, especially in what we thought were very cold winters.

"Thanks, Mr. Osbourne. I don't know how inquisitive I am. I just know I need to stop worrying about my friends, and I feel better about it now. I'll definitely pray for them, but that's the thing, I don't think it's a choice. This person who told me they were gay wants nothing more than to be not gay. The two cases I'm dealing with are different. A person chooses to have an abortion, but how can they choose to be gay?"

The man I admired so much sat thinking, really thinking about what I said, but I didn't need him to answer. I had the answer that made me feel better.

"Thanks for the ride, for the talk, for everything."

"You're very welcome, Margaret. I'm happy I could help."

I shut the door and smiled as he drove off.

Things were looking up. Evil Sheila's minion wasn't going to Hell for being an accessory to an abortion, and I was convinced that Anne wouldn't burn in Hell either. Life was good again.

Everybody Knows Lesbian Parties are the Best Parties

15

Debbie's 50th Birthday Party
2009, Curcuru Home, Gridley North
Meredith Carlin First, RoseMarie Curcuru

2008

I sipped on my lemon drop, prepared for me by the prettiest lipstick lesbian bartender ever. Anne's parties were a favorite of ours. Not just because we got to sound like we were a hundred years old when we referred to them as "Anne's Lesbian Parties," and not just because my husband was the envy of all his guy friends for getting to go to awesome lesbian parties. They were my favorite because I think if every anti-gay person in the world had just one close gay friend, gay hatred would no longer exist. I have been long convinced that gay hatred is just ignorance (it's the Jayne Monahan in me) and not really hatred at all. I just haven't figured out how to spread the word on this newfound intelligence of mine.

This party was Anne's last birthday party as a single woman and was in a downtown loft owned by a friend of hers who also owned the restaurant below. Catered by the restaurant, the party felt more like *Sex and the City* girls than *Gridley Girls* all grown up. It was the usual bunch: the lesbian crowd, the friends from Gridley, and the parents. No real in between. Even though our society had progressed tremendously over the last twenty years, Anne and Kelly were not flag-bearing, parade-going gay. Anne still didn't tell anyone she worked with that she was gay. She thought it complicated her professional life. She no longer lied about it. She just didn't offer it up for the world to judge.

This was when I got philosophical and sentimental at the same time. I looked out the window at Sacramento's small but lovely skyline. Then looked back in at the loft filled with beautiful people and thought about how more than half of the people at this party were treated like second-class citizens. They didn't have the same rights as the rest of us, and it made me so sad. How can a girl who has been my friend my entire life, who shared the same upbringing and education as me, who has contributed to society in so many ways, who has paid so very much in taxes, be denied the right to legally marry? How is that possible when we are supposed to have separation of church and state?

One of my favorite John Mayer songs came on. *Dreaming With a Broken Heart.* I watched Anne and Kelly talking privately in the corner of the room. They were at that warm and fuzzy stage of alcohol consumption where you love everyone. In two chairs facing each other, with the lights of Sacramento as their backdrop, they were so beautiful. I ran to get my camera so I could sneak a photo for them. I didn't want them to know, because they looked so close and intimate. If they turned and smiled it would have ruined the moment.

John Mayer kept singing, and he reminded me of what gay people go through just to love each other. He was singing about heartache, but to me it should have been an anthem for gays everywhere. Dreaming With a Broken Heart was exactly what they did when they thought of marriage, because it was just a dream to them. Anne leaned over and smoothed Kelly's blonde hair behind her ear. Kelly reached up and put her hand on Anne's. I snapped the picture. I knew that would be a good one for the wedding book

My gay friends didn't want to change religion. They were not trying to get anyone to accept their lives as morally correct for anyone else. They were only asking to be treated as individuals in the same manner as everyone else. When the civil rights movement was going on, no racist ever told an African-American person, "Quit being black and we'll let you get married." At some point, we as a people will realize that gays are not trying to ruin society as we know it. They just want the same rights as every other American.

I looked around the room at the contemporary furnishings; the large mural on the two-story great room wall, the leather sofas and chic lighting, and wished someone would make the movie *A Day Without the Gays*, like they made *A Day Without the Mexicans*. It made sense in cities with large gay populations, and I think that film would be just as profound. Especially if they showed the non-stereotypical influence gays have on our culture. They're not just flaming hair stylists, florists, and interior designers.

That depressed me. The night had started out great. Catching up with old friends and Anne and Kelly's crowd. Lesbian parties were way more fun than the suburbs, or breeder land as Anne called the 'burbs. I even got to dance with the Bruce Vilanche lookalike woman who was going to marry Anne and Kelly later in the month.

We danced to old eighties music and celebrated happy times. I was feeling really accepted and not like one of the few straight girls on the dance floor, until I heard the Vilanche lookalike whisper-scream to the girl next to her, "Hey, look at me, I'm dancing with the straight girl." She danced around me like I was the anomaly.

"Straight girl?" I asked. "That's all I am now? The straight girl? What am I supposed to call you? I have a name." I was being too sensitive and she noticed.

"I know you have a name, Meg. I'm sorry. I've never danced with a straight girl before, and I wanted my friends to see." I realized I shouldn't have been so sensitive since she's probably referred to as the "lesbian" or the "gay girl" all the time. A tough job since I was still depressed and way too sensitive. I finished the dance and went to look for my husband, Colin.

I knew I shouldn't have gotten defensive. Anne and I hadn't discussed Cindy Santini yet, and whether or not Anne was prepared if Cindy didn't show up for the wedding. Being a minority, or the different one, was never easy. Depressed, I went to sit by Anne's parents and Colin so I could change my mood. Anne's parents could brighten any mood. Anne's dad, Tony Calzaretta was as much a piece of work now as he was in the seventies trying to keep us all in line. He was not a tall man. Not much taller than me. Strong as an ox, both in mind and spirit, his beefy hands were gripping a glass of scotch, and he was deep in conversation with Colin and Anne when I come up. "Hey Margaret, I hear you're quitting your job to write books about my Annie. Is that true?"

I didn't know who to glare at first: Anne or Colin. "I don't know what you're talking about Tony." I smiled my best fake smile and kept on. "I love my job. Apple Computer is my life." They all laughed. The jig was up. No one believed me. I had some big-mouthed friends.

"Okay," I said, "I can't say for sure on the job thing, but I am going to write a book. Not about your Annie though. It's going to be about a group of forty-somethings who grew up in Gridley. And one of them will be gay." More laughter. "Aw, shit. Okay. I'm writing a book, but it's fiction so don't go getting any ideas."

He patted me on the back like a proud father. "That's good, Meggie. That's real good. Tell the lesbian story. Someone needs to."

Jan, his wife of forty-five years, pushed him in his seat. "Stop it, Tony. It's not like that." She looked indignant.

"What? It's not like what? They *are* lesbians. Why can't I say that? Hell, half the girls in this room are lesbians. If you don't watch it, you may be next." Everyone laughed.

Jan Calzaretta was the antithesis of her Sicilian husband. She was soft-spoken, blonde with striking blue eyes, and a petite thing that you just wanted to pick up and put in your pocket to keep forever. The one thing they had in common: iron wills. Never mess with a soft-spoken mom. They're the worst kind. Just when you let your guard down, when you thought you could disagree (or disobey, in our case), down came the hammer. She pointed to his highball glass. "How many of those have you had tonight? You're *not* funny."

"I think he's hilarious." Great, Colin had to get in on the fun. I kicked him under the table. He shot me an innocent look. "What?"

I whispered back. "Stay out of it."

Jan wasn't done with Tony. "You act like it's contagious. Don't perpetuate that."

Tony put his arm around her and squeezed her close to him. "I'm sorry honey. I was just making a little joke. I thought I could since we're in a crowd of...Annie what do you call people like us? People who like the gays?"

Jan visibly flinched. "Oh, God. He's digging deeper."

"We call it gay friendly when people like 'the gays,'" Anne said. "And right now, you're not so much." She laughed to try and make him feel better, but she'd really emphasized "the gays," like when a racist says "you people."

"Gay friendly. That's right. This is a gay friendly crowd, Jan, so I can make jokes. Right, Meg?" He looked at me for encouragement. Of which, I had none to give. "Meg's a writer now so she knows these things."

Colin elbowed me at this. "Did you hear that? He called you a writer and said *you know things*."

We *all* laughed at that. "I don't know what I know, Tony," I said, "but Annie does call me gay friendly. And I'm with you. I think this crowd can handle your jokes." Then I gasped and swatted his arm like there was a fly on it. "Oops. Oh no. I think you caught it. I think you're gay now." Then I slapped his arm. Everyone laughed. At any lesbian party there was bound to be a militant lesbian or two, and I didn't want to risk Tony having a run-in with one. Those were battles he was not prepared for.

"Nice move, Meg. Daddy, that's your cue to shut-up. Meggie just saved you." Anne locked her lips and threw the key away for her dad. "Shhh. No more."

Thank you Jesus, Tony made the same gesture and threw his key away. Jan put her head in her hands.

"Wait!" Tony yelled as everyone groaned. "Can I ask just one more question?"

"It depends on who it's for. Who do you want to ask?" Anne was in charge now.

"Margaret. I want to ask Margaret one very important question." Tony sat up straight and looked like the class clown who now wanted to be taken seriously. I worried since he used my proper name.

"Okay, Tony. Shoot." I was scared.

"What's my name going to be in the book, and who's playing me in the movie?"

More laughter. I could see Jan was relieved. "I think I need to see all manuscripts and sign off on them before anything is done," Tony said and everyone laughed again.

I shuddered at the thought of having to write my first novel with Tony Calzaretta's editorial approval.

"I don't have a name for you yet, since sadly, you will not be in the book, but I was thinking of Agassi for a last name. Do you like that?" I waited while he thought about it.

He rubbed his chin with his thumb and index finger like he was a great literary critic. "Hmm. Nah. I don't think I like it. I'm not sure it's Sicilian. Is it Sicilian?"

"I don't know. I just liked the ring of it. I heard the tennis player's name the other day and thought it was a good idea. You know, Andre Agassi?" Why was I getting insecure about an unwritten book?

"*That's* where I heard it. He's that long-haired boy, right?"

We all nodded.

"I don't like that at all," he said. "Nope, that won't do. He's definitely not Sicilian. I'm definitely going to need to read this manuscript."

Colin leaned over to me and whispered, "Just say yes. It will make him happy and he'll never remember later."

I smiled and whispered back, "You're a genius."

"Remember that pool party?" asked Anne. "Years ago at that house in College Greens?" She changed the subject to save Tony.

Colin groaned. "How could I forget? That was my first gay party, and we had only been married a few months."

Anne told the story of a pool party during the Clinton administration of "don't ask, don't tell."

This party had been predominantly gay men with a smattering of lesbians and straight people, probably not the best combination for the Colin's first gay party since he was a sheltered, Midwestern boy. There were a lot of gay military men from Beale Air Force Base, and it was very difficult to tell who was gay and who was straight. Just how they wanted it.

I was on the diving board getting ready to dive into the pool when a guy told me my bikini looked great. Colin, not realizing who was gay and who was straight, shot him a "hands off" look. The men all laughed and said, "Don't worry, we're not looking at *her*, we're looking at *you*."

Anne teared up from laughing so hard, so Colin finished the story. "And then they all looked me up and down like I was a piece of meat. It was so degrading." He said the last part like he was imitating me. I socked him. "Seriously, though. I'm much more careful how I look at women now that it's been done to me." Lots of murmuring and "Oh sures."

Marci, Anne's ex-girlfriend of many years, moved a little closer to the conversation and said, "Well, if we're going down gay party memory lane, what about the time Meg called me Anne Heche?" The room fell silent. No one said a word, but I got a lot of glares from a lot of angry looking women. Lesbians don't mess around about Anne Heche. To them, she is the enemy who pretended to be gay to have an affair with Ellen DeGeneres to further her acting career. There is no negotiation about this fact. Nobody, including Anne, sent me that memo before my previous blunder.

And then a shout out from a girl I couldn't see through the crowd. "What the hell, Meg? Why'd you say that?" The entire party gathered around our table. What had been an intimate conversation between childhood friends and their spouses and parents, was now a gay sociology lesson with thirty of Anne's closest friends.

Shit.

Marci had been Anne's partner for eight years before she decided to leave Anne. For a man.

I know. They should be on *my* side for that one reason alone. Why were they defending a girl who played for both teams? It just wasn't right.

From the first moment I met Marci, I knew she wasn't born a lesbian. It was 1991 and right after Anne came out, so I didn't have a whole lot of gay knowledge, but I did know that a lot of lesbians were fake lesbians. They were only lesbians because they were man-haters, or worse, because they had been molested as children. Marci had all the indicators of a man-hater. She had been abandoned by her father at an early age, molested as a child, and was very hostile toward straight guys. She was no longer hostile, and I loved her to death, but she was not born gay. Just my opinion. One very important note here: this was just my opinion to Anne. I did not walk around discussing my opinion on men-haters and whether or not they were really gay or not.

Problem was, when a couple breaks up, sometimes one party will lash out at the other and discuss things their best friends said to them, just as a way to hurt the other party. Yikes. I was in trouble.

When Marci left Anne for a man what was I supposed to do? Take Marci's side? Help plan her wedding? She left Anne for the express purpose of getting pregnant with her old boyfriend. Anne didn't want kids, and Marci's biological clock had overtaken her life. She did not get pregnant. Didn't marry the guy. Decided she really preferred being a lesbian. Broke up with the guy and re-joined her lesbian community. She was still friendly with everyone, including Anne and Kelly.

This was the thing about lesbians: when they broke

up they often stayed friends. So when you went to a lesbian party you met all sorts of couples and former couples. It really was an amazing study of sociology and the strong spirit of females. Anyone who wanted to trash talk females should spend time in a lesbian community to see the true spirit of female camaraderie. Happily married women would understand wanting to "join the other team."

There were all sorts of benefits to having two wives in a marriage: two cooks, two caretakers, two chauffeurs for the kids, two social planners (that could get tricky), two party throwers (also kind of sticky), and two periods a month. Yes, there were negatives too, but the most appealing advantage was that a lesbian marriage offered the one thing every hetero mom wanted most in the world: a wife.

I knew happily married women who would kill for a wife. We all needed a little help. That led me to what I thought would save me from my Anne Heche comment and distract the lesbians from their mounting rage toward me. A straight girl may never make a comment about Anne Heche unless it is to express her dislike of the woman. I know that *now*.

"So what's everyone think about gay marriage?" I asked. "Do you think it's going to be repealed or legalized?" They all groaned…loud. Then I felt something bop me on the head. Someone had thrown a carrot at me. I leaned over to Anne and whispered, "This is all your fault. You and your big mouth. Do something to fix this before this crowd has me stoned."

"Ooooh stoned. Remember that movie in seventh grade?" She sounded like we'd just seen that awful movie where the adulteress was stoned at the end.

I girl-slapped her. "Do something."

Anne piped up, finally, but only after laughing at me. "You hit like such a *girl*." Not a compliment. Then she moved into action and raised her voice. "Okay. Okay. Don't throw any more food at her. We paid a lot of money for that food. Don't waste it by throwing it at the breeder." She slurred through her laughter. They laughed back and glared at me.

I glared back. I was not going to be public enemy number one. *They used to call me "gay friendly" damn it.* Why couldn't they see that now?

"No, seriously," Anne continued. "It wasn't like that. It's actually all my fault." More murmurs and "yeah right's" from the crowd.

"Yes, her fault," I yelled. Colin kicked me under the table this time. "Ow! But it was her fault," I yelled again in defense of myself.

He held his index finger to his lips and whispered, "Let her help you. You're digging yourself deeper here."

Anne got up on a barstool. Not a smart move for what I could now see was a drunk girl. *When did that happen? She was fine ten minutes ago.* That came on fast. Colin steadied her so she could stay up. "Okay, listen," she slurred. "Listen to me. I'm the birthday girl so listen to me." People quit talking and throwing produce at me. "Everyone remembers my…my…my…Marci. Right?" She pointed at Marci, and everyone looked at her and nodded in agreement.

She kept on, now and then wobbling with Colin steadying her. "And you all know that Marci left me for a…a…a…ma-an." Two syllables for man; an important distinction. She spit out the word "man," and everyone groaned but nodded their heads yes. Then they glared at Marci. *Maybe they'd throw a carrot at her?* No such luck. Anne pressed on. "Well, I was devastated. It's bad enough to be left, but to be left for a *man*?" She slurred and looked down at my husband and felt bad. She patted his thick hair. "Oh, I'm sorry Colin. I didn't mean you. You're great." She looked back up at the crowd. "For a man." Even he had to laugh at that. "But seriously? A man? What could a man give her that I couldn't?" *Much* more laughter then as one of the girls yelled, "A penis!" Everyone laughed but Anne. She didn't get it at first.

Then she laughed the sweet, kind of spitty laugh of a drunk girl. She sounded like a cliché of a drunk in a movie. You couldn't help but love her and this crowd definitely did. They were murmuring things like, "Poor baby," and "Oh, Anne," and "That bitch." I was pretty sure the "bitch" comments were from the militants that I knew would kick my ass if we didn't get this thing turned around fast.

Then someone yelled, "But what did that have to do with Anne Heche?"

"I'm getting to that," Anne yelled back. "Be patient." She wobbled again.

By that time I had drunk at least four lemon drops made by that cute lipstick lesbian I told you about earlier. She could have made an evangelical woman switch teams. I was probably drinking so much because Colin thought she was so cute. He kept saying, "Let's go get you another drink, honey, and see that hot bartender." Colin *loved* to fantasize about his threesome that would never happen, especially at the lesbian parties. They were a teenage boy's dream come true.

Anyway, those lemon drops gave me a little too much liquid courage, so I decided it was time to defend myself. And Annie wasn't doing too well at that point. She was kind of looking green. "Anne, why don't you sit down? I can take it from here. And I'm sure Marci will help me, since she's the one who got us into this." I glared at Marci, and she smiled sweetly back. Colin helped Anne down onto a chair. Anne's mother cooed at her to drink water and told her that she had way too much to drink and should be more careful. Tony sat and laughed at her.

I got up on that stool and was met by boos. It was horrifying. "Okay, hear me out. I know you think I'm awful. Just hear my side." They went silent. "After the breakup and after they had healed and become friends again, we were all together at a party. Anne said to me in passing, and way too casually, 'Oh yeah, Meg, Marci is going to be here in a few minutes and she might still be pissed at you for calling her Anne Heche.'" I looked around the room to see if they were still listening, and someone, I couldn't tell who, shouted, "Damn right."

I waited for the shouts to stop and continued. "Well, I was shocked. I got mad at Anne and said, 'What the hell? Why did you tell her I said that? You're not supposed to share what your friends say to you during a breakup. Everyone knows that rule.' Doesn't everyone know that rule?" The women agreed with me then. Things were looking up.

I was turning this around until some chick in the back—my heckler—said, "Yeah, but you haven't told us *why* you called her Anne Heche. *Why* would you do that?" What I didn't know until that night with Marci was that the worst thing you could call a lesbian was Anne Heche. They hated her with a passion reserved only for terrorists. They hated her at the level of hatred for guys like Osama bin Laden and Sadam Hussein. Yeah. I know. Serious hatred. Who knew? I certainly did not know this at the time I went flapping my gums.

I held my hand up for quiet. I had seen my mom do this to control a classroom, and the two fingers up worked quite well at Boy Scouts, so I thought I'd try that too.

It worked.

"So when Anne was all sad about the breakup, I told her she didn't need to feel so bad since Marci was like Anne Heche." Uproar. They screamed again. Anne climbed up next to me on her barstool, and there we were: The Lesbian and Her Breeder. It sounded like bad gay porn.

"Stop it. She's trying to explain," Anne slurred, loudly and spitting on several people. Colin was having a hard time keeping her on the barstool this time, as she had continued to drink while I was talking rather than switching to water as her mother had requested. The crowd quieted as they listened to their leader.

"Okay," I continued, "so I did not know how everyone hated Anne Heche." More groans. Apparently I should have known this. Everyone knew this just like they knew that night comes after day. I held my hand up again. "I didn't know. I thought Anne Heche was awful for using Ellen that way." More cheering. This was an enthusiastic bunch.

"I love Ellen as much as the next person, and what Anne did was wrong, but I don't *hate* Anne Heche. I don't even *know* Anne Heche. I didn't know I was insulting Marci. I'll tell you what I told her that night after Marci came for my throat when she saw me."

People cheered again at the thought of Marci coming for my throat. It was turning into some angry Shakespearean tragedy. Then people asked Marci questions like, "Did you kick her ass? What'd you do to her, Marci?" Their eyes were gleaming. They wanted my blood. I will never say Anne Heche's name again.

After I finish telling you this story.

So Marci got up on a barstool. I thought Colin was going to have a panic attack trying to keep all three of us on barstools. "Hi. Hi." Marci was acting like she was getting ready to sing us some Karaoke. All she needed at that point was a hairbrush for a microphone. "I'm Marci. In case you didn't know." Cheers went up then. Great. She was the victor, and I was the villain. I threw my hands in the air and sat back down. At least that would be easier on my husband.

"Meg isn't as bad as you think," Marci said, not at all in a flattering way. They groaned. "No seriously. I was pissed at her at the time. I even called her a bitch." More cheers and Marci laughed since she had fans.

I looked up at her, hurt. "You did?" I was glad it wasn't to my face.

"Yeah. I'm sorry." They sighed. This was a tough crowd. I didn't know when to love them or hate them. Marci pulled on my hand, and I stood back up with her. Luckily for Colin, Anne sat down again. She needed another drink.

Marci continued, only she had her arm around me for the rest of the story.

"When I saw Meg that night, I did go for her throat. First I was polite, but then I saw her go into the bathroom and I followed her." Laughter. "I asked her why she said that, and she told me what I think she already told you. Meg, you tell them." They booed again.

"I told her I was sorry if I hurt her feelings, but that I didn't say Anne Heche as an insult." They laughed at me. Emphasis on at me and not with me.

Marci was laughing too. "Yeah, that's what *I* said."

I wanted to get this over with, so I didn't wait for the laughter to die down. "I told her that I didn't have a problem with Anne Heche as a person." They roared again. "I know." I was trying to calm them down so we could be done with this endless story once and for all. "I know. I didn't understand it until Marci taught me."

Marci interrupted and shouted, "Yeah. I taught her. I told her *I* did have a problem with Anne Heche as a person, 'cause she was a bitch." They went crazy. Absolutely crazy; laughing and cheering at Marci. I thought maybe Marci was going to get a new girlfriend that night—fake lesbian or not.

"Okay. Okay," Marci continued, holding up her hand. I'd started a trend. "I shocked Meg when I said that. She really didn't understand the level of our hatred toward Anne Heche, so she tried to explain it to me—the best way she could as a straight girl." Marci rolled her eyes and they all rolled theirs with her.

I chipped in again. "I told Marci that all I meant was that Anne should have felt better about the fact that she got dumped by Anne Heche." They groaned again. "Please. Hear me out. I thought it would be easier to be dumped by a woman who wasn't really a lesbian than by a real lesbian. Then it becomes less about Marci not loving Anne and more about Marci's capacity to love a woman. Does that make sense?" Murmurs. The tone of the room changed as they thought about what I meant, so I continued. "Anne has always taught me that there are two kinds of lesbians: those born a lesbian and those, well, those *made* a lesbian by men." More murmurs and nods of agreement. I wanted to hurry and get this done. "I thought if I reminded Anne that I didn't think Marci was not born a lesbian, that would soften the blow of the breakup, and it did. It did, huh Anne?" I looked over at Anne, whose eyes were glassy. She was hammered.

She didn't even try to get up at this point. She just

yelled and slurred, "That's true. She made me feel lots better. That's why I immediately told Marci. I wanted to hurt Marci in the worst way, and the best way to do that was to call her Anne Heche." Anne struggled to get up on her barstool again, and Colin had to go into overdrive holding all three of us up.

Anne was getting excited then. "No. The very best way to hurt her was to tell her that my oldest, dearest friend, the beautiful *Meggie*, called her Anne Heche. Everybody knows you can't hurt a lesbian worse than that." She looked out at her friends then and shot her fist in the air and yelled, "Am I right ladies?" They hooted and hollered and pumped their fists back at her. I was not getting my ass kicked. Thank you Jesus. Or, thank you AnneMarie Calzaretta.

Anne's party was a huge success, even if she did have to be carried away from the bathroom and up the stairs to the bedroom of the apartment, by Colin and Jock. Yes, Jock is still our brother from another mother. I told my husband that if I ever caught him passed out in the bathroom, on his birthday, with his head in the lap of his ex and her patting his hair and cooing at him, that I would absolutely kick his lily-white ass. No exceptions. He told me that if he was ever that stupid, he would expect to have his ass kicked. That sparked a ten-minute conversation on lesbian sociology, whereby Colin kept marveling at how they all stay friends. "How do they *do* that? They *stay* friends? I don't even want my ex in the same *state* as me, and they stay friends?" He shook his head so long it had to hurt.

Drunken Pigs

Freshman Cheerleading
1979, Farmer's Hall, Gridley, California
Melissa Costa Talbott, Stacie Sormano Walker,
Meredith Carlin First, Diane LaBarbera Symon

1979

What's that they say about "preachers kids" and "teachers kids"? They're often the wild ones? It's some version of that, but either way, that was how I felt after the first basketball game of the season.

After school and before our basketball game, Anne, Tonya, and Cindy were hanging out at my house. They decided we should have a cocktail before the game. I was hesitant at first, but against my better judgment, not only did I drink, I played bartender and made bourbon and cokes for them and a bourbon and soda for me—highballs for everyone. At one point, just to be cool, I put my head back and looked up and said, "Why is the ceiling spinning?" This got great laughs. The ceiling wasn't really spinning. I had only had a few sips, and I made the drinks purposely very weak. I was just trying to be cool. No good ever comes from a story that ends with "I was just trying to be cool."

One thing led to the next and we actually drank our drinks before it was time to go the basketball game and cheer. I thought nothing of this and was convinced that I was not impaired. We now know that everyone who's impaired is convinced they are not, but at fourteen, we really thought we were fine.

Ro took us to the game and she didn't notice anything, so we thought that was a good sign. We had a good game. We won. The cheering was good. We even did the cheers where Cindy and I had to jump on Anne and Tonya's backs. We jumped. We landed. No one fell. There was a close call where Cindy almost fell off Tonya's back. Someone from the yearbook team actually caught a picture of it. Her arms were akimbo but she landed the jump eventually. We cheered really well considering we were a bunch of lightweights on highballs.

At half time, I decided to talk to my favorite math teacher, Mr. Osbourne. In hindsight, I realized, this was a really stupid move. I was super friendly. I thought I was sparkling. But my friends watched me in horror. Mr. Osbourne was nice enough, but I later knew he was embarrassed for me. I wanted to die when I woke up the next morning and realized that I was drunk and a little too happy to be talking to my math teacher.

When I returned to my squad, they all yelled at me, "Margaret, what are you thinking? You dumbshit!" That was Anne. She doesn't mince words. "You don't go talking to adults when you've been drinking."

Then Tonya. "Yeah, Meg, get a clue." I was mortified. If it's possible, I was scared sober and got through the rest of the game fine. I avoided all adults and prayed to God that no one ratted us out. We would have all been kicked off the squad and God only knew what else.

Thankfully, that didn't happen. Ro brought the annual pictures home for me and never said a word. I think if she had noticed she would have said something. There was one picture of me, leaning over Cindy, with a real goofy smile on my face. Since that one didn't turn up in the yearbook I've always wondered if she knew and protected me. The only one that did go in was the one of Cindy almost falling off Tonya's back. It pays to have your sister as the editor of the yearbook.

After the game, Jock reveled in my newfound fallen angel status. "Hey Leper, nice work out there. What happened to you? Are you joining the ranks of the partiers and leaving the wholesome girls behind? What will happen to them without their fearless leader?" Jock was convinced I was "Queen of the Wholesome Girls."

"Shut up, jerk. I'm fine. I don't know what you're talking about." I thought I was very clever when I changed his name from Jock to jerk. I was indignant and tried very hard to sound sober.

"Lep, you look and sound like you did in kindergarten when we were the Drunken Pigs." He snickered his dastardly-cartoon-character laugh.

"I remember. It was all your idea. I wish you'd quit including me in that." Calling all emotional, drunk, teenage girls. Please report to the gym. I was too defensive and knew I needed to leave. So I did.

As I walked to Ro's car I did laugh at the Drunken Pigs. They *were* funny. When we were in kindergarten we were supposed to do a skit on The Three Little Pigs. Jock, Anne, and I were the three pigs. Right as we were going to the stage (which was the front of the classroom, but all the parents were there for this production) Jock and I acted like drunken pigs and changed every pig reference to drunken pig. Anne followed along as soon as she figured out what we were doing, and we stood up there and said, "I want whiskey!" to the Big Bad Wolf. The Big Bad Wolf would threaten to "huff and puff and blow our house down" (while looking at us like we were insane) and we'd yell back, "We want whiskey." We staggered around and slurred our words. "We're the drunken piiiiiiiggggggs." We made the most of our big time on the stage.

In the seventies, three martini lunches were normal, just not for school teachers. School teachers saved their drinking for after school, usually at my house. Jock and I had seen our dads slur and stumble on more than one occasion and thought it was so funny that apparently we needed to spice up The Three Little Pigs. We were, after all, the children who were taught to make highballs as soon as we were tall enough to reach the counter.

The kindergarten teacher was mortified. Our parents were in the back laughing their heads off. My mom was embarrassed (nothing about this was ladylike), but the rest of the parents laughed. Jock's mom had a diabolical sense of humor (the apple doesn't fall far from the tree), so it didn't surprise me that she laughed and was not as embarrassed as my mom. We didn't get in trouble. Our teacher talked to our parents about it and decided that they didn't know what to say to us. That it was better off left alone. No one has left it alone. They all tell that story at least once a year.

"Hey Jennifer, what's up? Did you have fun at the game last night?" We were in my room on Saturday morning after the big drinking night and she had a funny look on her face. "What's the matter? Is something wrong?"

"You know what's wrong, Margaret. You drank last night. What's going on?" She imitated my question and continued, "Are you crazy? You got drunk and then went to cheer at a basketball game. You all could have been kicked off the squad if you had gotten caught. And then you go talking to Mr. Osbourne? He totally knew you'd been drinking." She acted like Ro would have if she had found out. Oh God. I hoped Ro hadn't found out too.

"You could tell I'd been drinking?" I was scared.

"Anyone could if they knew you. Do your parents know?"

"God, I hope not." Jennifer scowled at me. "Gosh, I hope not. I don't know what my problem is. I've been so frazzled. High school is hard and peer counseling is hard. At first I thought I was just faking drinking with them so they'd leave me alone, and then I realized I'd had a whole drink without even noticing. I know that's not an excuse, but it's the truth." She kept scowling, more out of concern than judgment and I appreciated that.

"Margaret, that's lame. Don't you think that's what all the other drinkers and druggies say? It's no big deal until they flunked out of school, or got pregnant and had to transfer to Esperanza." Jennifer wasn't painting a pretty picture. Every good girl feared Esperanza. It was the continuation high school where people went to finish after having to leave Gridley High. It was good that it was there but it was not a destination goal for a college bound student.

"Oh God. Oh God."

"Margaret!"

"Oh Gosh. Oh Gosh. You know what? I think it might be okay to say *God* in this case since I need *His* help! *Gosh* isn't really going to help me now, is he?" I was getting a little rebellious because I was scared.

"Okay," she said. "What's wrong? This is weird. What's *wrong* with you?" She sat down on the bed next to me. "What's wrong? You can tell me."

Tears streamed down my face. I couldn't do it. I couldn't keep that secret. It hurt too much. I worried too much. Even though I was pretty sure Anne wasn't going to hell, it was too big a burden for any fourteen-year-old. "I can't telllllll yooooooou." I hiccupped in the crybaby, melodramatic way of any teenager with a huge burden.

"Yes you can. You can tell me anything. I'll help you." Jennifer sounded scared. I didn't know what to do. It was all swirling around in my head, which wasn't doing so well after the previous night as it was. On the one hand, I wanted to tell her because she probably *could* help me. On the other hand, I had sworn on my Virgindom to keep the secret as long as Anne wanted me to. What were the rules for sacred oaths like that? Were there any exceptions? Was there a statute of limitations on secrets? My head was going to explode.

"Anne thinks she's gay." I said it super-fast, so that it wouldn't count.

"What?" Jennifer looked pale. She scooted away from me a bit, so she could look me straight in the eyes. "What did you say?"

"Anne Calzaretta is a lesbian; a girl who likes other girls. You know. *Gay*," I whispered. Jennifer took notice.

"I know what a lesbian is, but how do you know Anne is one?" she whispered back, more worried than she was a few minutes ago when she thought I was a drunk.

"She told me in peer counseling, which is why you have to swear you won't tell a single soul. Do you swear?"

Jennifer raised her right hand. "I swear. I won't tell anyone. Who would I tell? Gosh, Meg. I guess you weren't exaggerating when you said you were stressed. How long have you known this?"

"A couple of weeks. It keeps getting so complicated. At first, I didn't think it was such a big deal. I thought about *Three's Company* and stuff like that. People make jokes all the time like it's no big deal, but now I've been paying attention and asking a few questions here and there. Did you know that some people think it's an abomination to God?"

She nodded, and I kept on rambling. "Some people think it's such a bad sin that you'll go straight to Hell for it." I was talking fast now. I wanted to get it all off my chest. "I don't believe that though. Anne didn't wake up one morning and *decide* to be gay. I don't think it works that way. She says she's felt this way since kindergarten. She thinks she was born this way. Do you think you can be born this way?"

I didn't give her a chance to answer. I kept on rambling. "I think so. I think you're born this way, and you have no choice in the matter. I don't know how you live your life that way though. I mean, I know it's almost the eighties and all, but she can't even tell her parents, and she totally can't go find a girlfriend. What's she gonna do? Bring some girl to the prom? Yeah. That'll happen. And how would she do that in Gridley? We're not exactly progressive here. We just got cable TV. We still don't even have pushbutton phones yet. If we don't have pushbutton phones, we can't have lesbians." I talked so fast I had to gasp for air. I fell back on my bed. "And that's not all. One of Evil Sheila's minions came to me worried that she was going to go to Hell for driving a girl to Chico for an abortion. Can you believe that? An abortion. It's no wonder I had a little drink. If anyone deserved to drink, it's me."

Then I heard my mom's voice. "Margaret? Anne? Are you hungry?" I sat up straight and looked at Jennifer. She whipped her head around to me with a shocked look on her face. I wanted to throw up and die, in that order.

I ran to the top of the stairs where I could see my mom. "Did you just call Anne, Mom? 'Cause Anne's not here."

"Sure she is, honey. I let her in a few minutes ago. She went up to your room. What do you mean? Where did she go?" Great. Anne overheard me and bolted out, and now Mom was going to be worried, and I was going to have to explain myself. My mind raced, and I thought it might explode. *Aaaaaaaagghhh.*

I tried to sound calm. "I don't know, Mom. Maybe she came upstairs and then remembered that she had to be home at a certain time and left?" Mom seemed to buy that.

"Okay honey, your dad says lunch is in a half hour. He just went to the store."

"Okay, thanks."

I ran back to my room, slammed the door, and threw myself on the bed. "My life is over. My life is over." Then the tears came. I couldn't cry loud because Mom would ask questions, so I cried into my pillow and gasped for breath while Jennifer sat over me, staring into space.

"Your life isn't over," she said. "You don't even know if she heard you. You might have just told your Mom the truth; maybe Anne *did* have to go back home without saying anything."

"Do you think so?" I popped up and wiped snot from my nose with my sleeve. "I guess it's possible. Oh, man. I'm not going to sleep tonight. I don't even think I can breathe until I see her in school and see if she acts normal. Maybe I should call her. Should I call her?" I was talking way too fast again. I wanted to throw up.

"It will be okay, Meg. I have to go though. Try not to make yourself crazy." Jennifer was leaving, and I was going to be all alone with my thoughts. That was the last place I needed to be, my thoughts and I, alone in a room together. This was going to be one long weekend.

By Sunday evening I couldn't stand it anymore and called Tonya. "Hi. It's me. Whatcha doin'?"

"Nothin'. How 'bout you?"

"Nothin'." Silence.

"Meg? Did you call for a reason or did you just want to sit on the phone and listen to me breathe?"

"Oh, sorry. I don't know what to do." I sighed and rolled over on my bed.

"Do about what?" Pause. "Ohhhh. I know. Is this about some secret you told that has Anne all upset?" *Aaaaaaagh. She knew. I knew she knew.* My life was over.

I tried to keep my cool. "Oh, man. I was afraid of that. It's not what she thinks. What did she say to you?"

"Nothing, really. She said that she confided in you, and you told someone else. She doesn't know who, and she's pissed. If you ask me, she seemed more hurt than pissed, Meg. What did you do?" Tonya sounded worried.

"It's not like that, Tonya. It's just a misunderstanding. I don't know how to talk to her." What was I going to do now? I was laying on my bed, wondering what homes for unwed mothers were like. *Maybe a year there would get me out of this?* I wondered how long it took to get pregnant. I shook my head to get rid of my crazy thoughts. That usually worked, but not this time.

"It's weird, Meg. Anne was so serious about this that I didn't even *ask* her what the secret was. Even though I'm *dying* to know. I didn't dare since she was so upset. You better call her."

"Yeah. I will as soon as I figure out what to say. Thanks for telling me. Sorry you had to be in the middle."

"No problem. I know you'd do it for me." She laughed at that as if it might not be long, since that was life with girls. Always rumors, misunderstandings, drama, and then making up. I tried to will it away. Who knew I would ever have thought that life was simpler in sixth grade? I always thought that was the worst year of my life, and Evil Sheila was the worst thing to happen. I had no idea growing up was going to be *this* hard.

I took a deep breath and picked up my turquoise phone to dial Anne's number. It rang a few times. I got more nervous, as I didn't know what I was going to say. Her mom answered, and that bought me more time.

"Hi Mrs. Calzaretta. Is Anne there?"

"Oh hi, Margaret. Sure. Just a second." Mrs. Calzaretta seemed nice so at least she didn't know that her daughter hated me. But that made sense. What would Anne tell her? "I hate Margaret. She told someone that I'm a lesbian. Because I am." Yeah.

I heard Anne coming to the phone, a little rustling and

she came on the line. "Margaret Monahan? I am *not* speaking to you." Click. Line dead. Nobody home.

So, it was back to stewing. Once again, my dramatic life seemed over.

I had an endless, sleepless night. I tossed and turned and begged God to help me with this. *Help me make Anne understand.* I wouldn't understand if the roles were reversed. I'd be mad as hell.

The school day dragged on. Anne wouldn't even make eye contact with me. Dan was sweet and asked what was up. I told him I couldn't talk about it. I went home for lunch with Ro and tried to hang on for the rest of the day. By the time I got home from school, Anne hadn't made eye contact with me once.

Since the only person I could discuss this with was the source of my trouble in the first place, I had Jennifer over. She always had the answers. "Jennifer, I don't know what I'm going to do. Anne hates me. She hates me and won't talk to me. I can't even get her to *look* at me. It's awful."

I threw myself back on my bed. I seemed to be doing that a lot lately. It was getting kind of old. I felt like one of those dramatic girls that I didn't want to become. The type who always had some tragedy in her life, and after a while you couldn't remember the last time you saw her happy.

"It can't be *that* bad, Meg. I saw her in school today and she seemed fine." I could tell Jennifer was totally exaggerating.

"Oh, Jennifer. You're just trying to make me feel better. Was I around her when you saw her?"

Jennifer looked sheepish.

"Exactly. It's hopeless. I swear, I'm going to have to move. I feel bad 'cause it was always my dream for Evil

Sheila to get pregnant and have to move to a home for unwed mothers, and now that's sounding kinda good to *me*." I laughed at myself, even though I really had nothing to laugh about.

"That's helpful," she said. There was that sarcasm again. "I don't know what to tell you," she said, "other than the fact that things always work out in the end. That's what my mom always told me." She looked kind of far away.

This whole thing was so confusing. I rolled over and buried my face in my pillow and didn't hear my mom come in.

"Margaret, who are you talking to up here?" I shot up on my bed and looked around in a panic. The room was empty except for Mom and me.

"I wasn't talking, Mom. Why do you ask?" I didn't sound convincing.

"You were very clearly talking to someone. Who's here?" She proceeded to check both my closets. No one was in there. She went into my bathroom. No one was there either. I knew she wouldn't find anyone but didn't know what to say. What *could* I say?

Mom sat next to me on my bed. I sat there, staring ahead. I didn't dare look her in the eye. "Margaret, you're scaring me. I know I heard you talking, and I would swear I heard you say Jennifer. Who do you know named Jennifer?"

Oh, this was not what I needed right now. What could I say? I didn't understand it myself, and at fourteen I was hardly able to articulate it to my mom. Not to mention the fact that I was completely stressed out about Anne. This was the *last* thing I needed at that moment. I already felt like I had lost Anne, so was she going to take *this* away from me too?

I decided to keep the lie going. What did I have to

lose? Seriously. As far as I was concerned, life was pretty much over anyway. "Oh, Mom. You know I don't have any friends named Jennifer. Anymore." I looked down then, hoping she'd get the hint that I was sad and didn't want to talk about it.

"No, Margaret. I can't let this go. This isn't the first time I've heard you up here talking to yourself. Your father has heard it too and so have your sisters. We've let it go for a while, but it seems like you're carrying on full-blown conversations with yourself, and I want you to tell me right now what's going on. Right now, Margaret." Her voice was stern but shaky at the same time. Her lip quivered, and I thought she was going to cry at any moment.

Like any other kid, I hated to see my mom cry—especially if I was the one making her do it. I didn't know what to do. If I told her, she'd think I was crazy. If I didn't tell her, she'd know I was lying. What was up with me being put on the spot like this so much at once? I sat there. Frozen. I seriously could not move and could not speak. I probably looked like I was in a catatonic state, and I know now that I was almost going into shock. I was mentally and physically breaking down.

My mom got really scared. She ran downstairs, yelling for my dad. Mom didn't run anywhere, and now she was running for my dad. I sat frozen in my bizarre, catatonic-like state. "Fred. Fred. Come up here, please. Quickly." I heard my dad taking the stairs hard and two at a time. This rarely happened as my parents purposely put us all upstairs so they could be as far from us as possible.

I heard them murmuring by the stairs, but couldn't make out what they were saying. They came into my room together. Both looking stunned. Not quite like deer in headlights, but almost. I didn't like seeing them look at me that way. I didn't like being examined in this way. I wanted things to go back to the way they were before. Before... when Anne still liked boys and wasn't a lesbian. Before... when I could talk to Jennifer whenever I wanted and no one questioned me. Before...when we weren't in high school and people weren't drinking, doing drugs, having sex, and then abortions. Before...when things weren't so complicated and life made sense.

Just before.

Dad sat down on the bed next to me. Mom stood right in front of me, I assumed so she could get a better look. When I didn't move, she bent down in front of me. Eye to eye. "Margaret, can you hear me?"

I nodded my head.

"Were you talking to Jennifer Cone?"

I nodded my head again.

My dad looked shocked. They gave each other knowing, scared looks. "Margaret," he asked, "does Jennifer talk back to you?"

I froze for a moment, not sure what to do. I nodded again. They looked at each other again. This time they seemed really scared.

"Do you *see* Jennifer when you talk to her?" he asked. I shrugged my shoulders in confusion. They still looked scared.

My mom sat down on the other side of me and took my hand. *Here it comes.* Deep down I must have known it had to happen someday. I never really thought about it though. Mom squeezed my hand and dad put his arm around me. I just sat, staring ahead.

"Honey, do you remember that Jennifer passed away?"

The Dream

Meredith's Surprise 9th Birthday Party
September 4, 1973, Straw Hat Pizza, Gridley, California
Jennifer Lynn Cone

2008

My heart raced as I shot straight up in my bed. Sweat dripped between my breasts and down my back. I felt both scared and calm. I tried to remember my dream. It was the only way I'd be able to get back to sleep, and I needed sleep much more now that I was stressing over a potential cross-country move and what it would do to my kids, career, and life in general. My drapes were open, and the moon was shining over the lake, streaming light onto the bed. It created a calming effect that took my fear away.

All I could remember about the dream was a teenage girl with straight, blonde hair parted in the middle. She was talking to me in a familiar voice, but I couldn't place her. Was it me? Was I dreaming about my younger self? That didn't make any sense unless my younger self was visiting me to tell me not to move. I smiled and tried to shake the thoughts out of my head. I'd been doing that forever and it never worked, yet I kept trying — a sure sign of insanity.

I could hear the blonde girl's laughter, as if she was in my head and knew I was making fun of myself. I felt like I was still dreaming. All I knew was I felt peaceful when I heard her voice. I wanted to stay with her, because she felt like a friend I'd known forever.

Then it hit me. It was Jennifer. I didn't recognize her at first, because she never lived to be a teenager. Tears streamed down my face as I saw how lovely she'd become. It was just a dream, but it felt so real. *She* felt so real.

More than thirty years had passed since her death, and Jennifer was visiting me in a dream. *Why now?*

Reality

Halloween Parade
1973, Hazel Street, Gridley, California
Meredith Carlin First, Melissa Costa Talbott,
Jennifer Cone, Lori Albright Silva

1979

I yanked Dad's arm off of me and threw Mom's hand back at her like they were both infected, and buried my face in my pillow.

"Get out of here. Both of you. Leave me alone."

Like little soldiers, in unison, they bent down to look me in the eyes. My mother first, her voice soft, not stern like I expected since I had been yelling at her. "We will not get out of here until we know you are okay. Do you remember, Margaret? Do you remember? Jennifer passed away, honey. Just after fourth grade, on Father's Day? Honey, please look at me." She was crying. I so didn't want to see her cry. "Please look at me."

I turned and looked at my dad first. He was kneeling with tears in his eyes. I quickly turned to my mom. She looked even worse. Her face was blotchy, and the tears came hard. "Oh, honey." She held me tight. I collapsed into her. I didn't know what else to do. I didn't want to hear it. I didn't want to talk about it, but as usual, I had no choice. If Jayne Monahan wanted to talk about something, you talked, but this was different. My mom was scared, and that scared me even more.

We sat on the bed again, with them on each side of me. We kept wiping our noses with our sleeves. "I remember, Mom." I could barely get the words out. You can use all the clichés you want to describe it, and none of them are significant enough. Watershed moments. The day I got my sanity back, or the day my utopian bubble burst. My fantasy life ended. Or the worst of all and the most apt: the day one of my best friends died all over again.

"Honey, I know this is hard, but I need you to tell us

what you remember. All of it." My mother with her peer counseling training, she was going to fix me…immediately.

I couldn't talk about it. What if she never came back? If I admitted that I'd been talking to her all these years, then who would I have to discuss this crazy high school life with? Who would I have to tell all this weirdness? When girls were off drinking, having sex, and then abortions, to whom could I tell *that*? No one could hear that without freaking out. Jennifer was all I had, and if I shared this with my parents, I would lose her all over again. So I sat there. I figured they might get bored and leave.

I waited.

I lay down.

I looked at the ceiling.

I played with my hair a little.

I waited some more.

They were still there. I still wouldn't look at them.

They waited.

My dad cleared his throat. He gave funny looks to my mom like, *What the hell? Why aren't you making her talk?*

She gave him looks back like, *I have this.* And we all sat, stubbornly waiting for the other to talk, with my mother's eyes never leaving me. My every twitch and move was recorded in her brain. I twisted my hair, she watched. I rolled over on the bed, she watched. I was uncomfortable, she watched. I pet the cat and tried to pretend no one else was there, she watched.

Finally, she broke the silence. "Honey, do you remember the last day you saw Jennifer, the last day of fourth grade?" I rolled over on the bed and looked out the window. She came around the bed and knelt in front of me again. "Do you remember walking home from school with her? Meggie?" Her voice got a little more frantic as she followed me around the bed, questioning me. "Meggie, do you remember?"

I remembered it all, every second of every part of my last day with Jennifer. I remembered us walking home from school on the last day of fourth grade. We were so excited, because we were going to have our favorite teacher—our second grade teacher—again in the fifth grade. It was like manna from heaven for us. We were going to be "Kings of the School," since we were finally the oldest in our K-5 school. Jennifer talked about how awful it would have been if we had to have a mean teacher twice. "Think about it, Margaret, if we had to have Mr. D twice?"

Mr. D was a notoriously strict teacher that we never had to have even once, let alone twice. "That would be awful," she said. "We get to have Mrs. Harp *again*. We're the luckiest kids in the whole world."

She looked into our future, and all she saw was good. How come she didn't know? How could she not have known that fifth grade was never going to include her? I remembered how we talked the whole way home and made plans for our summer. Jennifer was turning ten the next month, and we were so excited to be in "double digits." Her parents were finally going to move her bedtime up from the crazy seven-thirty that it was then. We walked home on clouds that day. That thought always freaked me out even more.

We got to our normal dividing spot and said our goodbyes. I'd love to say that we hugged each other or had some memorable, sentimental goodbye, but we didn't. We talked about when we'd see each other over the summer. I had swim team and she didn't. She had all her church activities, and I didn't. She told me to come to church with my grandparents, and maybe we'd be able to talk my mom into letting me go to church with her sometime. A normal goodbye, where she walked east to her house, and I continued north to mine, cutting through the church parking lot and Mr. John's backyard. No profound looking back at her with a cute wave, or climactic music warning us that something bad was going to happen. Nothing like you'd imagine in the movies. A normal goodbye — except that I never saw her again. Just like that.

"Meggie?" My mom was still kneeling in front of me. She wasn't giving up. My dad was sitting next to me, but I hadn't even noticed he was still there. "Meggie, do you remember how excited you girls were that you were going to have Mrs. Harp again?"

I nodded.

This seemed to help her a bit. She came and sat down on the other side of me. "Meggie, you need to talk about it. Tell me what you're thinking."

"I can't, Mom. Leave me alone." She looked shocked. Shocked and hurt, but what could I do? They were treating me like I was Sarah Seaver and all messed up or something. I thought I was adjusting fine to this. So I was carrying on full-blown conversations with a girl who happened to be dead. What was the big deal? Really? I could have done a lot worse.

After Jennifer died, Sarah Seaver, another of our lifelong friends, didn't cry. Her parents worried about her and took her to the funeral home for the viewing. I felt bad for her. I didn't want to see Jennifer like that. I liked that my last memories of her were happy. Sarah said Jennifer looked really pretty. She had a beautiful pink dress on, and her hair was in ringlets. Jennifer had the same blonde hair I did, and I liked the idea of her in Shirley Temple style ringlets, but I didn't want to see them. Sarah cried after that. Her parents felt better, but it didn't make Sarah feel any better. Sarah was stuck with her last memories of Jennifer in a casket. No kid wanted that.

This freaked me out. I realized how awful it would be to not have Jennifer to talk to. I wanted to take her with me. What was wrong with that? Thinking of all this made me really *feel* crazy. *What if they were right? What if I was losing my mind?* That single thought shut my brain down. It was like my mind went into shock but my body was fine – a quasi-catatonic state.

I laid down without looking at them. Mom rushed to the side of my bed to stay close to me. Dad followed her so they were flanking me like lion statues guarding a mansion, only I wasn't a mansion. I was a broken girl who thought she had lost her mind at the delicate age of fourteen.

The rest was a blur. Mom tried to get me to talk. Dad followed her instructions. They were kind of ethereal to me, like an out of body experience. Much more like I was watching a movie of my life rather than living my life. I just laid still in bed, like Sleeping Beauty — without the beauty or the sleeping — looking at the ceiling like I'd done thousands of times before, only this time it lasted for two days.

Ro checked on me even more. She has a very strong spirit and a very delicate soul. I'm not sure what that means, but it's how I think of her. She's one of the strongest people I know, yet at the same time she has the most fragile heart and temperament. She can't stand to see anyone in emotional or physical pain. Since I'm the only little sister she has, she takes her role as my protector *very* seriously. Suffice to say, this freaked her the hell out.

"Meggie?" I ignored her. "Dad sent up another tray of food for you?" I ignored her as I had all weekend. "It's your favorite—two mustard dogs and a Coke. He steamed the buns just the way you like them." She pushed the hot dog toward me but I didn't move. "You don't want to eat? Okay, how 'bout some Coke?" She pushed a glass of Coke toward me, made just the way we Monahan women take it: tons of ice so it's always cold, even on the hottest of valley summer days. It could be thirty degrees or a hundred and five out, but we'd still take our Coke like it was fresh out of frozen Lake Minnetonka in January.

I stared at the ceiling.

"Meggie, please," she pleaded as she put the tray down and laid next to me on the bed. I don't know how long she was with me, crying and petting my hair like I was our cat. I just know that after that she had a brilliant moment of clarity.

Ro went downstairs and announced, "Margaret needs Grandma Alice, stat!" I told you we watched too much TV in our house. She walked across the street, told Grandma what was going on, and of course, Grandma dropped everything and came back with her.

Grandma Alice, the matriarch of the Monahan Family, and the rock on which we all relied. Mom was just nineteen and Dad was twenty when they married, so Grandma Alice was like a second mother to Mom and all of us—not just a Grandma. In our eyes, she was Heaven-sent and could do no wrong. She was the model of the perfect mother to us, and we still aspire to be like her today.

Being raised by the first president of the first Mormon

Church in the area wasn't easy for Grandma as a girl. When Grandma started school in Gridley, she was teased for "following the devil's religion". They even checked her head for devil horns. And Grandma was born in Gridley, which anyone who's ever lived in Gridley can tell you, is a big deal. It's like there's a secret, card-carrying society of Gridleyans who know who's "from there" and who's not. You can live in Gridley for thirty years and be perfectly accepted and welcomed, but you always know you're "not from around here".

Rather than read books to us as kids, she regaled us with stories from her childhood. Grandma Alice was a master storyteller. We grew up on her lap, hearing the old stories passed down from her mother about their dealings with Indians back in Idaho. Native American was not a term yet, and Grandma had a deep-seated fear of Indians from hearing the stories as a child from her family.

My favorite was the one about a cunning and beautiful fox. I don't remember the specifics, just the message: it's nice to be pretty, more important to be smart, and most important to use both for good and not vanity. How could you not want to be just like any woman who taught little girls that message from the moment they were old enough to sit on her lap?

I smelled my grandma's White Shoulders perfume before I felt her sit on my bed in the exact spot my parents had been in thirty-six hours earlier. I felt better just having her there, feeling her warmth and love without any words. She petted my hair just like Ro had earlier.

No words. Just love. Tears fell from my cheeks, but I didn't make eye contact. I could see her out of the corner of my eye in her lovely church dress with matching shoes. Her hair was freshly done at the Beauty Boutique just as it was every week of my life. They had gotten the color right and it was less pink, more back to her natural blond. She had tried for years to have red hair like Lucille Ball, but I liked it when she stayed blond like me. I always heard how much I "looked like a Cole, just like your grandma."

When I started to bawl like a baby she held me tight, murmuring over and over, "Oh MeggieMac, you're Grandma's girl. It's okay. Let it out, honey. Grandma's here."

"I can't Grandma. I can't," was all I could get out through my stifling tears.

"It's okay, honey. It's okay," she kept murmuring while holding me tight.

I don't know how long we sat there holding each other. Sometimes I look back and it feels like it was forever. Other times it seems like it was just a few moments. That's how memories work. Depending on our mood, they change in intensity so that we can learn from them.

The tears slowed and Grandma asked, "Why are you so worried about talking to Jennifer?"

I didn't speak at first. I didn't have the answer right away. "Because that makes me crazy," I blurted out without looking up. I couldn't. I didn't want to see disappointment in her eyes.

"You're not crazy," she said in her most stern voice, as she tipped my face up to look her in the eyes.

I was startled, but I let her talk.

"There is nothing wrong with talking to your good friend on the other side. Don't let anyone ever make you feel ashamed about that. Your mother means well and she's a wonderful mother to you, but she doesn't understand the way we do. She's still hurting from the passing of her own father so death really scares her. Everybody mourns differently. She thinks of things on a more intellectual level where you and I..." she pointed between the two of us. "We look at things on a God level. You and I, we know that death is just a transition. We know it's not scary because we know we'll be together forever. Do you know that, Meggie?"

I nodded since I was crying again and I couldn't speak. She made me feel like I was part of the club. I may not have had a religion of my own, but she didn't care. She knew I would be with her in Heaven regardless. At that moment, I realized that it didn't matter what you called Heaven. It could be the Celestial Kingdom or it could be Joe's Bar and Grill. She knew we'd be together regardless of the sign on the door. It didn't matter that Jennifer was Mormon and I was not. I would see her again. Grandma never doubted that for a moment, and after that, neither did I.

"Heavenly Father doesn't think you're crazy for talking to Jennifer. Why should you?"

I was so relieved that I cried harder. Even if my parents didn't agree with Grandma Alice, at least there was one person in the world who didn't think I was crazy.

I should have known Grandma would put it into perspective for me. We were raised on stories of her dreams, or visions, as she called them. And we heard about the visions of our ancestors too. Mormons believe very strongly in family history, so they keep journals and we're lucky to have journals dating back several generations.

That didn't keep me from worrying about my mother though. Above all, my mother's opinion of me was most important.

Rebirth Through Death

Visiting after Pop Warner Cheeleading Tryouts
1977, Gridley, California
Alice Cole Carlin, Meredith Carlin First, Melissa Cole Carlin

Grandma left me in my room to think about everything we discussed. She told me to be open to my parents and what they wanted but not to borrow trouble. We smiled at that because Grandma said that to all of us as often as possible.

She must have reported back to my parents because they were back in my room, ready to talk, within a half hour.

"I don't want to quit talking to her, Mom." I figured I might as well get that out right away. I still wanted to hold onto my friend.

Mom looked back and forth from Dad to me, as if she was unsure how to answer. "Okay, honey. Um, you don't have to quit talking to her, but what else do you remember? Do you remember how you found out she passed away?"

Oh yeah, like I was going to forget that. Now who was the crazy one? "Are you serious, Mom?" She didn't look amused.

"Humor me, Margaret," she said in a dry tone to tell me she didn't appreciate my sarcasm, my defense mechanism during stressful times. "Tell me what you remember." She had been pacing and came back to sit down by Dad and me.

"It was like *now you see her, now you don't*. One day we walked home from school, and a week and a half later she was dead. Just like that." I was staring into space again. They looked at each other again.

"What else do you remember, honey? What happened after that?" She kept trying to make eye contact with me. I didn't know it at the time.

So I talked. I figured I had to. I listened to my mother, and I told them everything, as I remembered it, surrounding Jennifer's passing.

It was Father's Day, 1974. As his Father's Day present, Dad was playing golf with my oldest sister, and the rest of us were home doing nothing. Mom was in the backyard sunbathing.

The phone rang. Ro answered and said it was Sarah Seaver for me. Sarah's grandma and Jennifer's grandma were good friends. She sounded funny, but I didn't know why. She blurted it out. "Margaret, Jennifer passed away."

"What?"

She repeated it. "Jennifer died."

I got mad. "Sarah, that's not funny. You should never joke like that."

Sarah burst into tears and said, "I'm not joking. She died last night."

I don't clearly remember what I did after that. All I remember is running out to the backyard to find Mom. I only knew I was yelling because that's why Ro followed me to the backyard. She had heard the phone conversation and was scared. I knew I was crying, and I told mom that Jennifer died, and she said, "Oh, Margaret, it's only a soap opera, honey. You don't need to cry."

It took me a second to understand what mom was saying. Ro understood first and said, "No, Mom. Not Jennifer Hughes. Not *As the World Turns*." We watched *As the World Turns* on school breaks, and there was a Jennifer Hughes character on the show that had recently died. Mom thought I was talking about her. Ro corrected our mom. "Jennifer *Cone* died last night, Mom. Sarah Seaver just called Margaret to tell her. You should call Grandma."

I looked up at Ro and smiled through my shock. She was able to figure out what I hadn't in a split second and come up with a solution. I like solutions, even if they're small. Having a plan gives me comfort. Calling Grandma Alice was a plan: the Relief Society hook-up. That's what

I call it. Relief Society is kind of like Sunday School for married women. If you needed any information you went to your nearest Relief Society lady and they'd be able to hook you up. If you were new in town and needed a good plumber, Relief Society hook-up to the rescue. Same for any need you had. Women, in general, try to be there for each other. But Mormon women are there for each other always.

I thought maybe we could call Grandma Alice, and she could tell us the whole thing was a misunderstanding, and that Jennifer was resting peacefully in a hospital in Chico and would be back home tomorrow. That was the kind of Relief Society hook-up I was looking for.

Mom jumped up, her body glistening with baby oil and iodine. The scent of baby oil still reminds me of that day. She hurried us all into the house. The first call was to Grandma Alice. Mom was standing in our 1960s kitchen in her black one-piece with a towel around her waist. With her big Jackie-O sunglasses still in one hand and the phone in the other, I watched as she talked to Grandma. "Hello, Alice. Yes. It's me." Pause. No expression on her face. "Yes. We heard. So it's true?" Her face fell. My heart sank and felt like it was sitting in the pit of my stomach. Ro slumped in her seat like a rag doll. I stood there frozen, wondering, *if I throw up right now, would I be able to see my heart? Would I know what it was so that maybe I could put it somewhere for safekeeping, so I would never have to feel this way again?*

Next thing I knew, Ro and I were shuttled into the car and driving off. I didn't know where we were going. We went to Sprouse-Reitz first and couldn't even get into the store without people coming up to us and talking to Mom in the parking lot. They looked at me, talked to mom and shook their heads. Occasionally, they patted me on the head or on the back. I didn't know what to do or say. And I didn't like that feeling. We got whatever it was Mom needed from the store and just drove. The next thing I knew we were at my mom's favorite cousin Barbie's house in Honcut. She and her husband, Bill, lived on a giant ranch in the only town I knew that made Gridley look big. Honcut was ten miles from Gridley, and back then it was all rice.

"I've never known why you took us there other than the fact that you wanted to get us out of town and away from all those sad looks. That was probably a good idea, but I got a fair amount of those looks from Barbie and Bill." My mom and I smiled at each other. I wiped my nose on my sleeve again, and she handed me some toilet paper. Kleenex was always on short supply in our house. I don't remember how she got the tissue for me though. It just appeared.

"That was exactly what I was trying to do, honey. I was going to take you to Grandma Alice's, but I figured her phone would be ringing off the hook with Relief Society ladies making funeral plans, so our best bet was to get out of town. Seeing Barbie seemed like the best idea. Who would find us in Honcut?" We all laughed at that. Honcut, indeed.

"I don't remember much after that until the funeral," I said. "Oh, except for Sarah Seaver. I remember that her parents were worried about her because she wasn't crying. They thought she didn't believe that Jennifer was really dead." They gave me knowing looks at that. They could relate to *that*.

The day of the funeral I left swim practice early. When we left we got those same looks from the people who didn't go. Those sad looks people give when they don't know what to say. I just gave the same look back. Made sense at the time.

While we were in the car in between the funeral service and the burial, Mom was mad and talking to Dad about it. "Do you remember that?" I asked, and my mom smiled. I guess she was glad that I had these memories. She thought maybe I was losing my mind, and she wanted me to relay as much as possible in the hope that she could bring me back to reality.

"I do." She looked at my dad. "Do you remember Ida Garrison crying and carrying on?" My Dad nodded that he remembered, but she continued anyway. "One of the best things about the Mormon religion is their celebration of life. They know that death is a transition, and that when they cry they're crying for themselves and not the loved one who passed. Ida Garrison was wailing and carrying on like a scene from a movie. I thought it was inappropriate and very un-Mormon-like of her, especially with all those children there who had just lost a good friend."

Even now, almost five years later, you could tell Mom was still disappointed—that made me smile again. I was glad to have a reason to smile, 'cause I was still feeling like a crazy person.

"I remember now," I said. "You were upset because I was sitting right next to Ida, and you're right, she did scare me. Do you remember after the burial? You made me go and hug Mr. and Mrs. Cone? I was really scared. I just wanted to go home and go to bed. Kinda like what I want to do right now." They laughed but didn't move a muscle. They weren't going anywhere until they got me to the present day. "So, I went to hug Mrs. Cone and she cried softly. I tried really hard not to cry. I knew it was okay to cry, but I didn't want to get into that hiccuppy cry that you can't stop. Mrs. Cone hugged me so tight. Kind of like how you did just now when you were trying to get me to talk.

"Mrs. Cone pulled me back and looked at me all sternly and scared me again. She's the nicest person, but she was so strict that I was always a little scared of her. She stared into my eyes and said, 'Margaret Monahan, don't ever forget her.' I think I looked startled, because her face softened and the stern tone went away. She said it again, this time softly. "Don't forget Jennifer, Margaret. Please. Promise that you'll always remember her.' I nodded my head through my tears. I remember thinking she was crazy. How would I ever forget Jennifer? Gosh, I didn't even know how I was going to get home from school without her? Jennifer was the most grown-up, responsible girl I knew. She taught me how to clean a toilet. I know that's weird, but how do you forget that?"

My parents laughed through their tears. Partially because that was an odd thing for a fourth grader to say about their best friend, and partially because they knew they should have taught me how to clean a toilet. Mom asked, "Do you remember how she died, honey?"

I looked up, knowing that she saw the fear in my eyes and shook my head. I didn't want to talk about that. But as usual, Jayne Monahan would get her way.

"Do you remember that she died of an aneurism? What do you remember?" She patted my leg to reassure me that it was okay to remember.

"I don't, Mom. I remember that she missed a lot of school because she had such bad headaches. I know she had an aneurism. I thought it burst in her sleep and she never woke up. Is that right?"

"No, honey, she woke up in the middle of the night with the worst headache she'd ever had. Her parents woke up hearing her cries. Her father took her straight to the hospital in Gridley where they diagnosed the aneurism. She was rushed, by ambulance, to Chico and she passed away in surgery to repair the blood clot." We sat there, completely still, with tears covering our faces. It was wrong on so many levels but talking about it was unbearable. Why couldn't I just go back to pretending she was alive? That was so much better.

Breaking the silence, my mom asked, "How long have you been talking to her?"

I thought about it for a minute. "I don't know. I guess forever. I don't remember not talking to her. People talk about loved ones being in our hearts forever when they pass away, so it seemed okay to talk to her. Then it turned into full-blown conversations, and she was really helpful. She grew with me." The magnitude of everything I was saying hit me. I realized how nuts I sounded. "Man, Mom, am I crazy?" I asked in a voice that I barely recognized. It was so soft, almost a baby voice.

The voice of fear.

They looked at each other again. Why did they keep doing that? They were really scaring me. "I don't think you're *crazy*, Margaret. I think you're a young girl who lost one of her very best friends at a very young age. I can't imagine what that's like. I think we have to help you get through this and understand it. Your father and I don't really have any experience with this, so it's new to us too. Can you look back some more and try to remember the very first time you talked to Jennifer after she was dead? Try to remember when that was, maybe a time frame? What season was it? Was it hot or cold outside?" I had no idea why she was talking about the weather, but I tried to imagine it. "Close your eyes and see if you can picture it," she said.

I did as I was told, although I was beginning to think she was the crazy one. So there I was, sitting on the edge of my bed, with my eyes closed, fourteen years old, with my parents staring at me and looking for answers. Answers they expected to come from me. I tried to pretend they weren't there. I tried to pretend I was talking and listening to Jennifer. Different memories flashed in my mind. All the different discussions of the mean things Evil Sheila did over the years. I laughed to myself at the thought that when Jennifer was alive, Evil Sheila was just Sheila. She wasn't evil then. Did Jennifer's dying make Sheila evil? Nah, they weren't that close, but now I wonder if Jennifer's dying made me more vulnerable to Sheila's evil ways? That was probably more accurate.

The different crushes I had on various boys flashed through my mind. I always talked about them with Jennifer. Different songs I listened to in my room when I talked to her. It really felt like I always talked to her. Then I heard a song that snapped something in my brain. It felt electrical, like the popping sound when a light bulb goes dead. I couldn't tell at first what the song was, but then it continued and I knew for sure, precisely to the day, when I first started talking to Jennifer. I couldn't remember all the lyrics to the song, but it talked about a guy who never wanted to make you cry, he just wanted to keep you with him.

I gasped once I figured it out.

Both my parents snapped to attention. "What? What is it?" My mom had such hope in her eyes. She was determined to get to the bottom of this, and I didn't want to let her down. But I thought I was going to seem as crazy as ever.

"It was David, Mom. That's when I started talking to Jennifer. After David died."

Really God, We Haven't Been Through Enough?

The Sparkling Bluebirds
1974, First Presbyterian Church, Gridley, California
Back: Melissa Costa Talbott, Gail Haury Ernstam, Jeanne Tull Harriman,
Paula Quist Taylor, Heidi McCracken Wright, Jennifer Lynn Cone
Front: RoseMarie Curcuru, Meredith Carlin First

I looked up at Mom and saw the tears streaming down her face. I think she fully realized my need to reinvent Jennifer, to be able to talk to her even if just in my head.

In July of 1974, a month after Jennifer died, the suffocating heat made it a typical summer afternoon in Gridley. The peaches were fragrant but not the prunes, so the air was sweet and not putrid. Colleen was at her summer job, and Katie, Ro, and I were watching TV at home.

We lived in the little house on East Sheldon Avenue then and only had air conditioners in the living room and my parents' room, so we stayed in the living room all summer so we could breathe. The phone rang and my mother went to answer it. We didn't think anything of it until we heard gasps, followed by tears. Tears followed by methodical tones and the sound of note taking. I knew to worry when my dad put his paper down. It took a lot to get him to put his paper down. He could tune out the biggest catfights happening around him and still read the paper. At the sound of her first gasp, he slowly lowered his paper and stared into the kitchen, still holding it in his lap.

As the youngest and the one least likely to have any patience, I ran into the kitchen. Mom was sitting at the kitchen table with the ten-foot phone cord wrapped around her. She obviously had had a hard time finding paper and a pen. Dishes, books, and various junk were scattered across the table where she was trying to write. Tears were streaming down her face, and she was still taking notes. I knocked a stack of newspapers off the chair across from her and sat down. I didn't know what to do, but I didn't want to leave either.

"Okay." Pause. "Okay. Good." Another pause. "Yes. We'll be there. See you then. And Barbie, please let us know if there is anything we can do." Another pause. "Goodbye." She hung up the phone, with the cord still wrapped around her, and put her face in her hands, resting her elbows on a dirty dish. "Oh shit." Her favorite curse word. She wiped her elbow with a dish towel and yelled into the other room, "Fred!"

Dad came into the kitchen immediately. "What's going on?" He stood next to me, still holding his newspaper, looking down at her.

"Margaret, will you go get your sisters please?"

I was getting kicked out. I huffed out of the room and went to get Katie and Ro.

The whispering began. We tried to get close enough to hear, but the house was small and Mother's wrath was very large. We waited until it was our turn to hear. "Meggie, who was on the phone?" Katie whispered.

"Cousin Barbie. Sounds like someone died. Probably one of the old aunts we barely know," I whispered back, sure it was no big deal. Instincts like a cat.

"But I heard her crying," whispered Katie. "If it was some old aunt that nobody knew, she wouldn't have burst into tears like that." She was always the voice of reason. It came with being the perfect one.

"Oh. Well. Maybe it's an old aunt that *she* knew and liked?" Sharp as a tack. In my defense, I was nine and didn't like to think about death much. I thought I'd had my share of it to last a lifetime. Ro watched the exchange like a tennis match. Luckily, the guessing didn't have to last long.

"Girls, I know you're trying to hear." We quickly backed away and tried to look innocent. "That was Cousin Barbie on the phone. Please come in here."

We walked into the kitchen like the Von Trapp family, as obedient as we could muster. "There's been an accident."

Uh oh. That didn't sound good. When you came from a family as big as ours, you got used to lots of weddings and funerals, but you only liked the former.

"Your cousin David drowned yesterday on the American River."

A collective gasp. All three of us put our hands to our mouths in unison. David was not an old cousin. He was twenty-one. David was adorable and full of life, with dimples and, I swear to God, twinkling eyes. There was always mischief in them, in a good way. I was nine and never had older brothers, so I loved to go to our cousin's ranch in Honcut when the whole family was there. Most of mom's family lived in Sacramento, and we mainly saw them out at Barbie and Bill's ranch in Honcut. David and his younger brother Ronny always made it so fun. The good side of a huge family: great cousins to play with.

"How? Was he tubing?" Katie was going into survival mode. She needed details to process it. Ro and I still had our hands on our mouths in shock.

"I don't think so," Mom said. I think he was whitewater rafting on the north fork of the American River. We don't know all the details yet." Mom and Dad looked at each other then. "The funeral is on Wednesday, at the Cathedral in Sacramento." With that they walked down the hall to their bedroom. *That was it? Nothing more?*

"Katie, what was that look about?" I asked. "Why did they leave so quickly?" I didn't understand what was going on.

"When college boys go tubing on the rivers," she said, "they usually bring coolers of beer. I bet Mom and Dad were looking at each other that way 'cause they're wondering if beer was involved and they don't want us to know." She looked distant. Ro still looked stunned.

"Ohhhhhh," I said. "But she said he wasn't tubing. And he was a strong swimmer, right?" This didn't make a whole lot of sense to me. "I thought the only people who died in the river were people who didn't know how to swim and so the current takes them?"

"No. Not at all," she said. "The river currents can be so powerful that they can take really strong swimmers. And you don't have to be drunk to drown in the river. Rivers are scary. That's why they always harp about life jackets."

What *didn't* she know? This was why she was my second mother.

Finally Ro spoke. "I'm never water-skiing again." I didn't have to worry about water-skiing. I was already deathly afraid and had never tried it. I was a certified flag bearer in the boat. I didn't like water where you couldn't see the bottom, and this wasn't doing anything to help that fear.

"I don't blame you, Ro," I said. "This is exactly why I don't water ski. Look what happens. Remember that guy with the hook for an arm? That's 'cause he got run over by a boat while water-skiing and lost his arm." Ro shook her head, as I got totally worked up.

"Stop it. Both of you," Katie said. "We ski in lakes not rivers, and Margaret quit scaring Rowan. He probably didn't have a life jacket on, or maybe he was on the north fork and the rapids took him. We don't know yet but quit overreacting." Katie scowled and gave us Mom's mole face.

"Oh, okay, *Mom*," I said in my best snotty, na-na-na voice. "Whatever you say." *I'm still not water skiing, and I'm certainly not going on the north fork of the American River, whatever that is.* Smart aleck reporting for duty.

"Grow up, Margaret. Your cousin died. Show some respect." Katie stalked off to her room. Okay. That hurt. As usual, she was right. Just like a mom.

Ro and I went back to the living room. "Ro, do you know what the north fork of the American River is?" I was afraid to ask Katie, since I had just been so snotty to her and our parents were still locked in their room. Mom was on the phone getting more details.

"Uh, uh," she said, shaking her head. "But Mom said maybe he was whitewater rafting and maybe the rapids took him, so I guess that's a scarier part of the river. I've seen it on TV before, and it sure looks scary. Now I know why."

Turns out, Ro was right. Our cousin had been on a whitewater rafting trip on the north fork of the American River. He was thrown from his raft while on a class five rapid. There are only six classes of rapids, and on the north fork of the American River, most of the tours have fours and fives. David was an experienced whitewater rafter though. There was nothing anyone could have done to prevent this. When David was thrown from the raft he hit his head on a rock and died instantly.

That next Wednesday, we loaded up the whole family into our baby blue station wagon to make the hour and half drive to downtown Sacramento. Dad played the radio the whole time, and no one talked much. It was AM radio and KFRC; a station out of San Francisco that everyone in northern California listened to in the seventies. It was my only source of pop music.

As we drove up to the cathedral I saw so many people dressed in dark clothes (an unusual sight in the summer valley heat). Young people, old people, and everyone in between all with the same looks on their faces. The same look I'd gotten when I had to leave swim team practice early for Jennifer Cone's funeral. That same look I got from people in the Sprouse-Reitz parking lot before we got out of town the day Jennifer died. That look that says, *I'm so sorry for what you're going through, but I'm completely helpless to do or say anything to make you feel better.* That's usually followed up with a hug that makes you cry or old people tousling your hair.

As I was looking around at all these faces, I saw David's mom with her tear-stained face. I noticed that she had the same blank expression that Jennifer's mom had, like the lights were out. It was then that the Bo Donaldson song came on the radio, "Who Do You Think You Are." From that moment on, I thought of David whenever I heard that song. And parts of the song really applied to losing Jennifer and David, both at such a young age. Often, when I hear a song I only hear certain lyrics that apply to my life at a certain time. I've always been notoriously bad at determining song lyrics anyway. I sang them wrong, and I just heard snippets of this song that applied to the loss of these two young people.

"Meggie? Meggie?" My mom shook my shoulders, and my dad looked at me with a panicked face. "Meggie? What did you say about David?"

I had been sitting still just staring at my parents while I remembered David. "Oh, Mom. I *am* crazy. I started talking to Jennifer after David died. That makes me crazy, doesn't it? Plus, I just remembered it because of that song that came on as we drove up to the cathedral. Isn't that like *Sybil*? I'm a nut job." The hiccuppy crying came back so I could barely breathe.

Mom put her arms around me again, which made me cry even harder. "Honey, you're not a nut job. You've been through a lot. I never thought about the connection between the two passings. You weren't very close to David since he was so much older than you."

"I know, Mom, but don't you see?" She shook her head. Dad sat in silence with the deer-in-headlight look. "I wasn't that close to him, but it didn't mean I didn't love him. It didn't mean I didn't freak out when I saw his family. Don't you remember, Mom? Seeing his parent's faces?"

Both my parents sat up straight, staring ahead. Remembering. Their faces were faraway and sad.

"And that song? Mom, that's why I talked to Jennifer. The song said, *if you want me there, you gotta care*. The only way I knew to *care* was to talk to her. I figured if I talked to her, she'd stay with me forever."

I could see my parent's minds were still in 1974

Sacramento. I look back now and have no idea how I would have reacted if I were in their shoes. What do you say to your teenager when you find out she's been talking to her dead best friend for four years just so she can make sense of the sudden losses in her life?

As any funeral of a twenty-one-year-old would be, David's was tragic, sad, and huge. His mom's side of the family was Italian Catholic, and David was a great guy who was taken too early, so the cathedral was full of young and old—all with the same stunned looks that only came when someone passed at a young age.

"Do you remember, Mom? How sad it was? Everyone's face looked just like the Cone's did weeks before. That freaked me out. I guess I didn't realize how much until now. Don't you think it's weird though?" My parents nodded. They really did figure that since I was so much younger than David it hadn't affected me. It made sense. I cried again. "I'm sorry. I'm sorry I'm such a freak. I don't know what's wrong with me. I don't want people dying. At least not young people." I sat there, hunched over and sobbing, with my parent's arms around me. I could tell they were looking at each other over my head. Probably thinking about what a nut job their daughter was and wondering if they had a spare straight jacket for me.

"Honey, you're not a freak." Mom held my shoulders so she could force me to look her in the eye. "You're just…" She trailed off and apparently couldn't find the words. She and Dad looked at each other over my head again and nodded as if to say, *yeah, good job, Jayne. Good choice of words.* I didn't buy it for a second.

"How could you *not* be confused?" she said. "That was a lot to handle for a nine-year-old. This is your way of coping with it." She paused again. "I do think we should find someone for you to talk to though, to make sure you don't have any more questions or anything."

"A shrink? No way. I'm not going to a shrink. I'm fine. I promise I'll quit talking to Jennifer. I promise." I panicked. The most I knew about any kind of shrink was from *The Bob Newhart Show*, so I had no idea why I was so against "talking," as she called it. But it sounded scary, and I wanted nothing to do with it.

"Honey, there's nothing for you to worry about. We'll find someone for you to talk to. It won't be a 'shrink.' You'll be fine."

In Memoriam
David Warren Breese
August 19, 1952 – July 28, 1974

Brothers: Bobby Breese and David Breese

Reunited

Jennifer Cone's Eighth Birthday Party
July, 1972
Back: Paula Quist Taylor, Pam Stewart McMullin, Meredith Carlin First,
Stacie Sormano Walker
Front: RoseMarie Curcuru, Andrea Cone, Abshere, Jennifer Lynn Cone,
Lisa Christensen

1979

Spring of my freshman year in high school was crazy. It felt like I was living in a movie plot rather than my own life. Anne wouldn't talk to me. Tonya and Cindy were rattled about that and I couldn't tell anyone what was happening. I went to class, ate lunch, did homework, and went to Chico twice a week for counseling. My parents swore I wasn't a crazy freak who talked to dead people, but if they were so sure of that then why was I seeing a shrink twice a week?

The counseling was not as bad as I thought it'd be. She asked a few questions and tried to draw me out. It was a lot like extended peer counseling sessions. The first time she used an "I" statement on me I laughed at her. "Seriously?" I asked. "You use 'I' statements like we do in peer counseling? They don't teach you anything better than that in college?"

She laughed with me and went on for five minutes about the power of the "I" statement. Yawn. The only good part was when I got to talk about Jennifer. Before these counseling sessions I never realized that as soon as I talked *to* Jennifer, I couldn't talk *about* her, as if I had a secret from the rest of the world and it might get out.

A few weeks into the sessions I had a dream so vivid that it felt real. It was a little scary. In the dream, Jennifer and I were walking home from school on that last day of fourth grade. All my senses were heightened in the dream. The sky was bluer than normal, the air sweeter. I felt deliriously happy. Happy beyond anything I could understand. It was strange.

We walked home from school just as we did in real life. Picking the honeysuckle plants and stopping in amazement to watch the milk pour out. They smelled sweeter in my dream. We laughed and talked about our summer and how excited we were to get our favorite teacher again for fifth grade.

I realized that we both had beautiful teeth. In real life, Jennifer and I both had crooked teeth. The only time you saw our teeth in pictures was when we forgot. In my dream, we had beautiful smiles with perfect teeth.

We stopped to pet the neighbor's cat, and it was nicer to us, purring and rubbing against our legs. It was a sweltering hot June day, but we weren't hot. There was a gentle breeze and it felt like a perfect eighty degrees, which rarely happened in the valley in June.

By the time we got to the church where we normally separated, we were laughing so hard we had tears in our eyes. I don't know why we were laughing, but we were so happy. As we said goodbye to each other, Jennifer's body started to inflate like a balloon and she floated slowly away. She looked like the blueberry girl in *Willie Wonka* without turning blue. As if she was a helium balloon released to Heaven.

I screamed in terror. I tried to reach her but there was no string. I reached everywhere and jumped and jumped but I couldn't catch her. Her balloon-like body kept floating away, and I kept yelling, "Jennifer. Jennifer. Come back. Come back. Come back to me."

Nothing worked. The helium balloon in the shape of a pretty nine-year-old girl with a perfect smile and perfect blonde hair and blue eyes could not hear me. That's when I realized — when I saw her eyes — that she looked so happy. I stopped screaming and jumping and stared at her. She was fading away slowly with the most beatific smile on her face.

She waved to me and said in a quiet voice, probably because she was so far off, "See ya, Margaret. See ya later."

And that was it. Nothing profound. No secrets of the universe, cures for cancer, or winning lottery numbers. Just "See ya, Margaret." The weird thing was, I didn't mind or feel cheated. I was content. Just like that look on her face. Complete serenity. The emptiness from missing her was gone. I've never felt better than I did in that dream. It was the closest thing to Heaven that I have ever felt.

After that, I didn't care anymore who knew that I talked to dead people. I knew I had to talk to Anne. I knew I didn't need to go to counseling sessions anymore. I knew I wasn't crazy. And I felt closer than ever to Jennifer. I felt like she had visited me in my dream, like she was giving me permission, maybe even forcing me, to go on with my life. But I knew I had to do one thing to make sure of this first.

I needed to go see her mom right away, before I lost the nerve. No one but Jennifer's mom would understand this.

So after school on the day of the dream, I walked to her house on my way home. I rang the doorbell and fidgeted, worried that she wouldn't be home. She answered right away. *Thank you Jesus.*

She was surprised to see me. "Well, Margaret Monahan, how are you?" She gave me a hug and asked me in. "It's so nice to see you. What brings you by?"

I was so relieved that she asked me in right away. I didn't want to waste a minute. I felt like my sanity was resting on her shoulders. We sat down. She asked me if I wanted anything to drink. I told her no, and then I told her everything.

How I'd been talking to Jennifer since her passing. How my cousin had David passed away a month later.

How my life was crashing down around me now since my parents thought I was crazy, and Anne thought I betrayed her confidence because she overheard me telling a secret to Jennifer. I didn't tell her about what the secret was though. I told her about the counseling sessions, and how my sisters were being so nice to me that it was creepy. Everyone tiptoed around me like I might break like an egg at any moment. I told her how much I hated myself and couldn't believe that I turned out to be such a Judas to my best friend.

And then I told her about the dream, the whole vivid dream.

When I got to the part where Jennifer floated away peacefully with a serene smile on her face, tears streamed down her face. She had been misty for the whole talk, but when she heard that she burst into tears. I went to sit next to her and gave her a hug. We sat there on the couch—the same couch I used to sit on with Jennifer—and she cried on my shoulder in a bizarre, role-reversal way. The child was comforting the mother. But it felt good. It felt right. I knew I did the right thing in coming to her. I should have done it sooner. Maybe I would have avoided that counseling. Or maybe the counseling is why I had the dream? I didn't know and I didn't care. All I knew was that I was exactly where I was supposed to be.

She sat up and wiped her nose with a tissue. "Oh Margaret, I am so glad you came by. I'm so glad you trusted me enough to tell me all of this. How awful this must have been for you." It was my turn to cry. I nodded while I cried. She handed me a tissue. "Are you still seeing the counselor?"

I nodded and got enough composure to speak. "I am, but I don't want to. I think I'm okay now. It's as if Jennifer's visit made me realize I'm not crazy."

"Of course you're not crazy. And I'm sure your parents don't think you're crazy. They just want to help you. You know, you're not the only one to go to counseling. Jennifer's little sister had to see a counselor too. She was only three when Jennifer passed, and all she remembers is that her daddy left the house with Jennifer in his arms and Jennifer never came back. That was really scary for her. She had difficulty processing that, and it came back as she got older. She's doing much better now."

I had never thought about that. Whenever I thought about Jennifer's family, I only thought about her parents. Her brother and sisters seemed so young that I thought they'd be unaffected. Of course it would be weird for them. Jennifer passed away three days before Mark's eighth birthday, her sister Danielle (we always called her Dani) was three, and the baby, Heather, was nine months old. She had two more sisters that were born after she passed. I figured they were all too young to be traumatized by it, but that's not really possible. They lived with a ghost in the house that nobody talked about. Some of them remembering her and some never having known her, but nevertheless, she was always there.

"Wow. I had no idea. I'm glad she's doing better. I would have thought she was too young to be affected by it."

Mrs. Cone nodded. "I know. I know. And Margaret, I talk to Jennifer all the time. There is nothing wrong with that."

I sat up a little straighter. "Really? You do? Do you see her too?"

"No honey, I don't, but I wish I did. I think it's great that you feel like you watched her grow up with you. Did your counselor ask you if you felt like it was really *her*?

Did she ask you if you felt like she was still alive, or if you identified with the fact that she was gone?"

"Yeah, she did. Apparently that was the big point to tell if I really was crazy. If I thought she was still alive we'd have big problems, but since I was picturing her and talking to her and still knowing that she was dead, that made me okay. Something about unconscious manifestations or maybe conscious ones. I don't remember."

Mrs. Cone laughed. "I'm so glad you came to me. It means so much. I know this has been difficult, but it means a lot to me that you tried so hard to keep Jennifer with you. That you still remember her."

"Are you kidding? Of course I remember her. How could I not? You made me promise, remember? I felt like I took a solemn oath. I couldn't let you down." I smiled because I knew I sounded ridiculous.

"A solemn oath? I like that." Mrs. Cone patted my knee. "How do you feel now? Do you feel like she's still with you?"

"I think so. I'm not sure. I don't think I've had enough time to think about it yet. Right now, I'm grateful to know I'm not a total freak. You know?"

She laughed. "Yeah Margaret, I do know. I've thought I was going crazy hundreds of times since Jennifer passed away. When a mother loses a child people don't like to discuss it. It's too scary for them, so I've had to deal with this privately with my husband. Thank goodness we have each other."

We sat in silence for a minute. Each of us processing what we'd discussed. "Well, I should be going," I said. "Thanks so much for talking to me; for letting me dump all this on you. It probably wasn't easy for you, and I try to not talk too much about Jennifer to you. I never want to upset you." I got up, and she pulled my hand to sit me right back down.

"Margaret, don't *ever* do that. Please *always* talk about Jennifer to me. I appreciate it. I need it. I *want* to talk about her. I *need* to talk about her. I don't want to pretend that she was never here. That's why I made you promise to remember her. I can't stand the idea that she was never here." She was so animated. I'd never seen her talk about Jennifer this way, but it seemed right to me.

"Well, there's another promise then," I said. "I won't hold back. I'll always talk about her to you. Mrs. Cone, do you think you could do something for me?"

"Well sure, honey. What is it?" She looked worried again.

"The last time I talked to Jennifer, I talked about Anne. I told Jennifer a very important secret of Anne's, and she walked in while I was telling Jennifer. Anne didn't see anyone and thought I was blabbing on the phone about her. Now she won't speak to me. She's so mad and thinks I can't keep a secret. And I'm a peer counselor now, Mrs. Cone, I have to keep secrets or I'll get kicked out of the program. But more importantly, I feel like a horrible friend. I feel like I betrayed her." I sounded desperate because I was.

"So how can I help? Do you want me to talk to Anne?"

I was so relieved, my voice squeaked. "Oh could you please? It would mean so much."

"Absolutely. Why don't you bring her by tomorrow, after school?"

"Hopefully, you won't regret telling me to come by any time, since I may be here every day now."

We both laughed.

"I'll never regret that." She smiled a beautiful smile that made me think about Jennifer's smile in my dream. It was that perfect smile.

"*That* was the smile!" I pointed to her mouth like I was a witness in a murder trial and needed to identify the perp. "Sorry for yelling," I said as I put my hand over my mouth, "but that was the smile that Jennifer had in the dream."

She kept smiling and put her arms around me to give me a big hug. "That was the smile? She had my smile?"

I hugged her back—hard. Then I pulled back to see her smile again. "Yep. That was the smile. That's so cool. She had your perfect smile in the dream." We cried again. We both missed Jennifer terribly, but these were happy tears that we got to share in a relationship with a great girl—who now had a perfect smile.

Just like she always wanted.

The next day, I saw Anne in PE and didn't look at her. I expected to keep getting the silent treatment and decided to wait until the end of the day to see if I could get her to walk home with me. I even asked Ro to drive us in case Anne fought me. I figured that Anne would come if Ro asked her.

"Hey."

I looked up and it was Anne talking to me. "Hi. You're talking to me now?" I grinned 'cause I couldn't believe it.

"I got the weirdest phone call last night. Mrs. Cone called and asked me if I'd walk home from school with you so we could talk to her. She wouldn't tell me why. She just asked if I'd please do it. Isn't that weird?" I could tell Anne didn't know what to think. But like me, she'd do anything for Mrs. Cone. We all would have. It was like being in some strange, depressing club that nobody wanted to join, but we had no choice but to be bound together for the rest of our lives through the love of the same lost person.

I stood there frozen but smiling. *She called her. She knew how much this meant to me, and she called her. I was so lucky.*

"Margaret, why do you have that weird smile on your face? What's going on? Why does she want to see us?" Anne called me by my full name so I knew she was still mad.

"I think we should talk about it after school." I looked at Evil Sheila lurking nearby.

Anne saw Sheila and shot her a dirty look. Sheila moved farther away from us. "Okay, she's gone. Please tell me what's going on. I'm so pissed at you. I want to hate you. I want to get you kicked out of peer counseling, but then I don't. At the same time, I still want to be friends with you. I miss you so much, but how could you do this to me? How?" Her eyes were glassy, and I didn't know what to say.

We were supposed to be going over to the pool for sailing practice. Yes, we sailed boats in the Olympic-sized swimming pool. Whatever it took to get a well-rounded physical education. "Come on, we can talk while we walk across the street to the pool," I said.

We left the locker room, and I tried to keep watch for Sheila. The *last* thing I needed was that girl and her miracle ear eavesdropping on us. "Anne, I did not tell your secret. I was talking to Jennifer Cone when you came into my room."

Anne was stunned. I'd never seen a look like this. There was compassion, shock, love, and fear on her face all at once. Great. One more person to add to the list that thought I was crazy.

"I know," I said. "It's crazy. My parents have taken me to a counselor in Chico for a month now. I'm not totally crazy though, because I know that Jennifer is dead. I just liked to talk to her. Especially when things scared me. And you scared me, Anne. You scared me to death. I didn't know what to do. I was afraid you would burn in Hell. I even talked to Mr. Osbourne about it." She gasped like I had told him about her. "No. Not about *you*, about the *idea* of it, and about another session I had right before yours. I've had a lot to deal with, and I couldn't handle it."

Anne still shook her head. "Wow. Never in a million years would I have guessed this. I was trying to figure out why you would tell someone when you seemed to like peer counseling so much. And you *always* keep my secrets. I couldn't figure out how you could be *this* low." The whole idea washed over her, "Oh wow, you're talking to dead people." She said, louder than I liked.

Anne was still shaking her head when Sheila ran up behind us yelling, "What? Margaret Monahan talks to dead people? What the hell, Margaret? Are ya crazy now?" She danced off toward the pool with her minions, laughing at us.

All of a sudden, like the flash of a superhero, Anne flew up behind Sheila and put her in a headlock. It was like some ninja wrestling move, only to my knowledge Anne has no known ninja experience. Sheila was trying to walk with Anne's arm wrapped around her neck. I went running up to…well, not to help 'cause I liked seeing Sheila in a headlock. I guess I went running up so I could hear every word. And that was a good thing.

Anne talked in a soft, low voice. A voice that would have made me shake if I heard it in a dark alley. "Sheila Scudmore," she hissed, "if I wouldn't get suspended and kicked out of cheerleading, I would kick your ass all the way to the ocean. You will not say a word about this to *anyone*.

You will get your slutty ass over to the pool, and we will never speak of this again. Do you understand me, Sheila? I *know* things about you. Things that would be worse than the ass-kicking I'll give you if you don't leave us alone." Anne still had Sheila in a headlock. People were staring, but they were too afraid to do anything so they kept walking to the pool.

Sheila's face went grey, and she nodded while her neck was still in Anne's grip. Anne confirmed, "Do we understand each other?" Sheila nodded again, and Anne let go of her.

"Freaks," Sheila shouted at us, and Anne was back on her immediately, putting her neck in a second headlock.

"Seriously, Sheila, do you *want* me to get suspended, because I swear to God I will do it. I will sit home and watch TV for three days, and I will think about the public service I performed. I will kick your ass right here in front of half the freshman class. And I will like it. I will like it a lot. Do you hear me Sheila? They will cheer me on. I will become a…what's that called?" She looked at me. I shrugged in confusion.

"Like Jesus? What's that called?" she asked with Sheila's head still in her clutches.

"A martyr!" I yelled, like I was on a game show.

"Yes. A martyr. I will kick your ass, get suspended, sit home watching game shows and soap operas, and be a hero and martyr of Gridley High, and I…will…*like*…it. There is a reason the whole freshman class calls you Evil Sheila." She stopped for a moment, proud of her speech and to let that sink in on Sheila. "Now, are you going to shut the hell up? Is this over? It's your choice. Make it right now."

Sheila's eyes were getting glassy. Omigod. Did Evil

Sheila actually have a heart? Not possible since there was no Oz in Gridley, and she was no Tin Man.

"All right. All right. I won't tell. Get your hands off of me, you beast."

Anne let go of her, but Sheila wasn't done. She walked over to me and hissed in my ear. "Evil Sheila huh? I'm sure *you* thought of that, Monahan." There was way too much hissing happening. "No way your goon here was clever enough to think of that." She had her thumb out, pointing to Anne.

At that, Anne stomped her foot and stuck her neck out to flinch toward Sheila. Scared the crap out of her. I think maybe this was the best day of my life. Sheila jumped away from Anne and hissed one more time at me, "I won't forget this, Monahan."

I sneered back. I didn't care about her anymore. What I had been through in the last few months had helped give me strength I never knew I had. Evil Sheila couldn't hurt me anymore. "Whatever, Sheila. I'm not scared of you. Go to the pool and find someone to slut around with. It's apparently all you're good for anymore." I gasped as I said it, not sure whether to feel good or guilty. None of this was good, and I was sick to my stomach, sure that I was going to Hell for saying that.

"Nice one, Meggie." Anne patted me on the back. "Hey, Sheila," Anne yelled at Sheila's back. "I may not be as clever as Meggie, but I sure can laugh when *she's* funny. Hahaha!" Anne kept doing an exaggerated laugh as Sheila and her minions walked to the pool shaking their heads.

"*Ding dong, the witch is dead.*" Anne sang the song from *The Wizard of Oz* as loudly as she could. I joined in. We were free from the reign of Evil Sheila. Oh, I knew she wouldn't quit being evil, but we could handle it now.

We still went to the Cone's house after school. We had cookies and milk like we were still in fourth grade and maybe Jennifer was just in the other room. We told Mrs. Cone that we discussed it at school and Anne was no longer mad at me. Mrs. Cone explained more about it to Anne, and said she didn't think I was crazy. That was such a relief.

Mrs. Cone was ready for us that afternoon. I think she was really looking forward to it. We watched old movies of Jennifer. We even got to see movies of us with Jennifer from Bluebirds. We all did a square dancing routine for Father-Daughter Night in skirts that we made ourselves. I remember thinking that Jennifer was a much better seamstress than me. I hadn't remembered that before seeing the movies.

It was a great afternoon. Anne and I were friends again, and I got to help Mrs. Cone that day. I believed my craziness actually mattered to someone. I knew I wasn't *really* crazy. My crazy-talking-to-dead-people was actually a *good* thing to Mrs. Cone. It reminded her that we all remembered Jennifer. She would be with us always. Mrs. Cone was convinced of that now. And all because I was the crazy girl who talked to dead people.

Well, just the one dead person.

Face Your Fears and Move On

We couldn't celebrate our 30th High School Reunion
without bringing Jennifer along.
June 16, 2012. The 38th Anniversary of Jennifer's passing.
Gridley Cemetery (the old part), Gridley, California
Back: Paula Quist Taylor, RoseMarie Curcuru
Front: Gail Haury Ernstam, Melissa Costa Talbott, Meredith Carlin First

2008

The redwoods and pines towered above, shading me from the heat that had started in the morning. Sometimes it felt like we went from winter straight to summer in the Sacramento Valley. The only way you could tell it was spring was if you followed the crops or the different blossoms on the trees, because it could go from fifty to ninety in a matter of days.

The flowers were in bloom and the air sweet with their fragrance. The cemetery was quiet. Not a big surprise since there weren't burials on the weekends. Only the odd visitor like me was around. I told Colin that I needed to go to Gridley and think. He had no idea that meant sitting in the cemetery talking to dead people he never knew, but he also didn't ask any questions since he knew this was the biggest decision of our lives. He knew it hinged upon me. I could have negotiated whatever my heart desired at that point, and he would have given it to me. He knew he was asking the unthinkable by taking me away from my home, family, and roots. I couldn't believe I even entertained the idea.

I didn't discuss the dream about Jennifer with anyone. I didn't understand it enough to try and articulate it. I wasn't sure if I ever would. Some small voice, deep down in me, always wondered if I was crazy to talk to Jennifer in the first place. I was scared of what could happen if all those feelings bubbled back to the surface. Too many people depended on me to have a nervous breakdown. There just wasn't enough time in the day for crazy.

I stopped at Safeway to buy some flowers once I knew where I was going. At first, I really did just get in the car and drive north toward Gridley. I didn't have a plan. I did some of my best thinking while driving so it seemed logical.

I walked past the graves of three generations of ancestors: the Mormon pioneers, their families, and all their dead babies. I wondered how it was back then, losing babies all the time. Like it wasn't bad enough for them to be burned out of their villages and have to go further west just to practice their religion. How did they survive grief after grief, losing babies while crossing the country in covered wagons? Did I even have a right to grieve a friend I'd lost over thirty years ago? Did I have a right to not want to move to Minneapolis, when I lived in a time where I could just jump on a plane and come back to visit whenever I wanted?

But what if someone else dropped dead? How would I live with myself if I wasn't there for my family, if I wasn't part of my family's local life anymore? On an intellectual level, I knew I'd still be part of my family, but I felt like I was letting them down by leaving. I was the daughter who lived the closest to my parents. I was the daughter who still went to Gridley for family occasions. I liked having a dual Gridley-Sacramento life. How did you have a trio Minneapolis-Gridley-Sacramento life?

As I drove, the Buttes popped up out of nowhere. They always seemed to do that to me on the drive from Sacramento to Gridley. They just appeared as if to say, "Hello, Margaret, welcome home." I burst into tears. Until I realized why I was crying.

I had lived my entire life in fear of sudden death. And that is not living at all.

In the twenty minutes it took to get from the Buttes to the Gridley cemetery, I wasn't able to come up with any life changing decisions or epiphanies. All I knew was I needed to get over my fear of sudden death.

I hadn't been to her grave since college. I'd never been a big grave visitor, always firm in my belief that graves were repositories for bodies and nothing more, like life-sized genealogical markers for the living. I brushed the leaves and debris away from the headstone with my hands. I didn't do a very good job. I wished I had come prepared like my sister, Katie, would have. She'd have been all *Martha Stewart* with special "grave brushes" and things, if those existed. I wiped my dirty hands on my thankfully dark sundress and sat back down on the blanket. Jennifer's family moved out of town in the early nineties, so her grave didn't see much action, and that made me feel worse and better at the same time for having brought flowers.

Her grave was in the best real estate of the cemetery. Who'da thunk it? A town with 5,000 people, but the cemetery was so beautiful there was good real estate and not-so-good real estate. When someone died people asked, "Are you burying him in the front or the back?" The front was where the old-timer Gridleyans were buried. If you weren't lucky enough to be up front, you were in the "new part."

I looked down and laughed, realizing that I'd taken one of my kids' car blankets handmade to perfection by my sister, Katie. This was just a fleece blanket, but the stitching was precise and if you folded it right, it turned into a pillow. Only Katie knew how to fold it right though, so the kids used the pouch to keep their feet warm.

I sat smiling at my sister's handiwork, until I saw Jennifer's name on the headstone again.

Jennifer Lynn Cone
July 23, 1964 – June 16, 1974

The granite was pink, perfect for a little girl. It was wrong that any headstone was perfect for a little girl. Jennifer never got to have kids. You couldn't have kids when you didn't make it past the fourth grade.

The laundry list of life markers that always came to mind when I thought of Jennifer appeared in my head. All the things she didn't get to do. Every passage of my life was marked with the thought that Jennifer didn't get to do that, from eighth grade graduation to having babies. I didn't mention it much. What was the point? It was just sad.

In the early days, after her death, my parents talked about milestones when they thought I wasn't listening. They'd comment on how well her parents were doing "under the circumstances." And how "that day must have been hard for them," when our whole class graduated from eighth grade and then high school. I invited them to every occasion, even though I knew it must have been awful. Wouldn't it have been worse to have been forgotten? To pretend she never existed? The markers got easier for me after high school, since everyone separated and had their own milestones at different times: college, marriage, babies.

But Mrs. Cone's words never left me. "Don't you forget her, Margaret. Don't ever forget Jennifer." They haunted me at times. Whenever one of my kids had a high fever or a bad headache, I made them sleep with me so I could awaken every hour to check and see if they were still breathing. It was as if I couldn't rest until they lived longer than Jennifer did. They had to make it to their tenth birthday, and I'd be home free.

Home free.

I burst into tears. I knew better. It didn't matter how old my kids were. I'd always worry that they'd suddenly die. That was what happened when you lost your best friend at the age of nine. It changed you forever. It changed our whole group forever. We looked at the world through different lenses than other people the same age going through similar experiences as us. At nine-years old, the only thing you were supposed to know about death was if you lost a grandparent. None of us had experienced that yet when Jennifer died. Our first experience with death was having our friend with us one minute, and gone the next. She just disappeared.

I sat on that pink blanket, with the little ladybugs on it, and had a full-on ugly cry. My shoulders shook, my nose dripped, and I gasped for air. But I didn't care. The cemetery was empty. I let it all out, and it felt so good to cry like nobody was watching.

And then I felt a hand on my shoulder. I was startled and a little scared at first, since I was sitting in a cemetery. I looked up and there was Anne, standing over me with tears in her eyes.

"What the…? What are you doing here?" I jumped up and we hugged.

"I should be asking you that. What are you doing here?" We sat down on the blanket.

"I just needed to come talk to Jennifer." I brushed some more dirt off her headstone, nervously, not making eye contact with Anne.

"Is that all? You've been acting weird lately, but I didn't ask since life is so hectic with the wedding plans." Her eyes searched mine. "Is this a good sign that you came to her grave to talk to her? Should I be worried?" She looked back and forth between the grave and me. I think she knew she wouldn't get a truthful answer. My talking to Jennifer, in front of her grave or anywhere, was my business and no one else's. I hated being grilled about it.

"It's not all that's going on, but it's not what you think."

Ooh, good one. Deflect away from talking to dead people and get to the real subject.

"Then what is it?"

"We're probably moving to Minneapolis." There. I said it out loud for the first time. Shit. I was so afraid that saying it out loud would make it real. Make it happen. Cat. Out of the bag.

Her eyes welled up again. "What? Are you serious?" I nodded my head. I had already cried enough for the moment. "When? How long have you known? Why? Omigod, tell me everything."

So we sat in front of Jennifer's grave, discussing the biggest decision of my life and how it seemed inevitable at this point. I told her everything. About the secret house hunting trips, how no one else in the Firm could know yet so we couldn't tell anyone. And most importantly, I told her how I didn't want her to know before the wedding, because I didn't want to distract her. I didn't want her to go through her wedding knowing it was the last party at my house. It was the end of an era. As I thought about all the great parties we'd had over the years, it broke my heart.

Our backyard was our oasis, our little piece of the California dream. I'd spent too much time and money transforming it so it was worthy of the panoramic golf course and lake views to even think about leaving. I'd been remodeling our home away from an eighties theme into my dream house. I'd had my new kitchen for only six months, and now I had to leave it.

"I guess if we leave," I said, "people will have more free time since they won't be going to *my* parties." We laughed, but it didn't make me feel any better. "Hey, what are *you* doing here anyway?"

"I was on my way back home from my parents, and I

saw your car. I was worried someone died so I thought I'd check on you. Wow. I got more than I thought. I just can't believe this."

The Gridley Cemetery was north of town, on Highway 99, Gridley's main artery. Whenever people heard that I was from Gridley, the first thing they would ask (if they'd heard of Gridley at all) was, "Is that the town with the gorgeous cemetery?" Our claim to fame: just a wee bit odd. Anne passed it regularly to and from her parent's house.

Anne touched the flowers in Jennifer's vase. "So, did she give you any good advice yet?"

I smiled but wasn't going to give her any more answers. "No. I haven't had the time to ask yet. I sat down, burst into tears, and then you drove up."

Anne smiled. She knew she wasn't going to get me to talk about it, but that never stopped her from trying. "Do you think you'll really go? Does Colin *actually* want to go to Minneapolis? I thought Midwesterners moved *to* California and never went back? Isn't that how it goes? You go west. You don't go east. I'm gonna need to talk some sense into him. How old was he when he moved to California?"

"Seventh grade." I shook my head but didn't have the answers, since I wasn't a Midwesterner and didn't understand the concept of any of it yet. Why would *anyone* want to leave the greatest state in the union? Didn't make sense to me.

"Seventh grade?" she asked. "Seriously? Shit, he's doomed. He has no idea what it's like to be an adult in the Midwest. The snow removal alone has to be a bitch. This is insane. Don't their lakes freeze up? I mean like *completely*? Don't they drive on 'em? That's crazy. You can't do this. You'll never survive. It's like the North Pole there. Has he seen *Fargo*? That's some crazy shit. He'll be putting people in wood chippers and talking in funny accents and what about gay people?" She gasped at this thought. A lack of gay people scared Anne more than putting people in wood chippers. "Do they even *have* gay people there? Oh, God. You can't do this."

"Calm down. Yes, he's seen *Fargo.* It's one of his favorite movies. We're not moving to Fargo, and we're not buying a wood chipper so I think I'm safe. They do really talk in those funny accents though. It's hilarious. It's like being in a different country. And they have gay people." I sat up, excited to tell her this news.

"Shut up. I don't believe it." Anne said, revealing her suspicion. "Are they just telling you this because you're gay friendly and you asked? Or did you meet any? I want proof."

"That's where it gets kind of weird. I met a real estate agent that I was convinced was gay, and he was married to a woman. Sometimes it feels like life in Minnesota is like the 1950's, only with modern technology. I haven't spent enough time there to put my finger on it yet. I'll get back to you."

"Hmmm…" she murmured, as she shook her head and looked at me like we really were discussing life on another planet.

"They told me that per capita," I said, "the Twin Cities are second only to San Francisco in the number of gay residents. So you'll have to come visit." I couldn't believe I was trying to sell Minneapolis to her.

"Sorry. I don't need to visit the arctic tundra, even if they do have lots of gay people. You'll just have to come home a lot."

"I already got Colin to promise that I could come home whenever I wanted, so I won't miss out on special occasions." I stared in the distance, feeling the weight of the decision again. "Anne, I've always wanted to ask you something but was too afraid."

"*You* were too afraid to ask me something?"

"I know it's stupid, but the thought of moving across the country is kind of cracking my head open with emotions. Did you ever forgive me? I mean really forgive me?" I looked down, afraid of her answer.

"Forgive you for what? What did you do this time?"

"No, I'm serious. For telling Jennifer that you were gay."

Anne sat back and rolled her eyes. "Are you serious? Why would you even have to ask me that? Of course I did, and I never thought about it again. Why on earth would you even wonder? And have you been wondering all these years? That's the craziest thing I've ever heard. Even crazier than talking to Jennifer in the first place."

"On an intellectual level, I would agree with you. That's why I was afraid to ask. I think because Jennifer was so real to me, I felt like I betrayed you. I felt like a horrible friend who couldn't keep the most important secret of your lifetime. I was worried you were going to go to Hell. I thought Jennifer might know more since she was you know. Not alive."

"Holy shit, I never thought of it that way. You're insane."

"Stop. I'm being serious," I whined as I leaned into her.

"So am I." She smiled. "You're a freakin' lunatic. You actually thought you could beat the system and ask a dead person about your mutual gay friend to make sure she didn't go to hell? Seriously, I'm not sure if that's insane or brilliant." She shook her head and laughed while staring at

Jennifer's grave. Then she got quiet and said, "Too bad she didn't give you the answer."

I was so relieved that she felt like she had nothing to forgive that I almost missed her point. "Oh Anne, no. We have the answer. We know. God would never create people just to abandon them. I believe that with my whole heart, and I know you do too."

"But what if we're wrong." She still stared at Jennifer's headstone.

"I'll tell you what I tell my Mormon cousins."

"Oh God, not the gated community thing." She groaned.

"It may only be my fantasy, but I like it. All the people who believe gays are going to hell will be in their own little gated community in Heaven. The rest of us will be in main Heaven, and there will be visiting hours in the daytime, but at sundown they have to go back to their gated community. And of course, because the gay community lives in our portion of Heaven it will be fabulous, but rules are rules, the others will have to go back at sundown."

"What's that line your mom used to say, 'from your mouth to God's ears'? I'm banking on you being right on this." She got up and brushed herself off. "I need to get back home. Do you want some time alone to figure this out, or do you want to walk out with me?"

"I'll stay. Thanks for understanding." We got up and hugged goodbye. "Drive carefully," I called out as she walked to her car.

"You too."

I looked at Jennifer's grave and heard Anne's words again, "time alone to figure this out." And I realized that was the problem. I was never going to figure this out. And that was okay. I was so freakin' neurotic, that I thought I had to figure every bloody thing out in my life. I needed to just go with my instincts and quit overanalyzing everything. "*Genius,*" I thought as I hit myself on the forehead a little too hard. I shook my head and suddenly felt so much better.

Except that my instincts were telling me I needed to move to Minneapolis. Damn, who knew instincts could be such a bitch? I finally knew what I needed to say to Jennifer.

With no embarrassment, I looked at her headstone and said, "I think I get it now, Jennifer. I'm not *supposed* to understand all of this. It's okay to be uncertain. Why I didn't figure this out sooner is beyond me. I hope it's great up there." I looked up, not sure what else to say—which was odd since I used to have full-on conversations with her. "Thanks for being my friend, even if it wasn't long enough. I hope to see you soon."

Oh, saying that worried me. I didn't want God to think I was asking Him to take me soon. "Okay, well not soon. I hope to see you after I've had a really, really, really long life." *Ooh, this was becoming like a prayer now. Did I have to be specific?* "And a really healthy life, with a really healthy family. Oh, and no more sudden deaths. I'll see you after my really healthy, really long life, and after I get to see lots of really healthy, happy grandchildren." *Okay, Meg, stop. It wasn't a grocery list.*

I looked away in embarrassment and saw Anne by my car, shaking her head, listening to every word I said. There I was, trying to talk to a headstone, and I bungled it and Anne spied on the whole thing. I didn't care. I was determined to get this right. As cliché as it was, I wanted closure.

"I'm trying to tell you that I loved you, and I was happy to be your friend. I'll try not to hover over my kids when they get sick, but I can't make any promises. And most importantly…" I leaned in, which I knew made no sense since she wasn't really *in* the grave, but Anne was still eavesdropping. I leaned in for privacy and whispered, "I never forgot you, Jennifer. And I never will." I kissed my finger and touched the headstone like I had done dozens of times when my kids got hurt. I don't know why I did it. It seemed right. For the first time ever, it seemed like Jennifer was still nine years old, but I was an adult. Like I needed to kiss her boo boo away.

I got up from sitting near the headstone, dusted myself off, and walked back to my car where Anne was standing, wiping tears from her cheeks with a proud smile on her face.

"Gosh Meg, I hope I die before you do. You are one devoted friend." I wiped my face and flung my arm over her shoulder as we laughed and walked to her car.

Breaking Up is Hard to Do

TWIRP Dance (The Woman is Required to Pay)
April, 1979, Farmer's Hall, Gridley, California
Meredith Carlin First

1979

The cherry blossoms were in full bloom and as fragrant as the perfume aisle at the drug store. Birds chirped, baby calves were born, and like my life, everything was coming alive and beautiful. I felt like all was well with the world. I wasn't crazy. I still had great friends. I wasn't afraid of Evil Sheila anymore. School was going well. And I still had the cutest boyfriend ever, although he did seem to be getting a bit bored with my whole, "I don't know what I want" thing. I was as ignorant as ever in the boy department.

I wished I was as strong as Anne. After she confessed to me in peer counseling, she broke up with Bobby. Like yanking a band-aid off, she gave him the classic, "It's not you, it's me," line. Only for the first time ever in the history of the world, it really was her. He just didn't know. He was devastated. I had to spend the first few weeks afterwards hanging around Dan with a lovesick Bobby. He would stare at Anne like a wounded puppy every time he saw her.

Then a perky little sophomore caught his eye and that was it. Anne was history. Bobby was back in the game with a new girlfriend. I heard a line from a Carrie Fisher movie where she referred to viral love. Carrie Fisher must have gone to Gridley High, 'cause viral love seemed to be spreading faster than a good case of mono.

Ro and I were walking out of school one day when Dan stopped us. "Hi Ro. Could I talk to Margaret for a minute?" He looked back and forth between the two of us. Ro looked at me in question. I looked back at her as if to say, "I don't know why he's here."

"Sure. But could you give her a ride home then? I have to get to work." Ro looked at me like *what's up?*

I shrugged my shoulders, but I knew. My statute of limitations on "not being ready for a boyfriend" had just run out.

"No problem, Ro. I can take her home." That was Dan, ever the gentleman, always the nice guy, soon to be the heartbreaker.

Ro went off to her car, and I looked up at Dan, so tall, so cute. I smiled up at him. "Hi."

"Hi." He smiled back and gave me half a hug. The whole time I was thinking, over and over, *Please don't break up with me. Please don't break up with me. Please don't break up with me.*

It didn't work.

The gentleman Dan took my books and we walked to his truck. The heartbreaker Dan said, "Meg, we need to talk."

Oh dang. I figured I had to say something, but all I could think of was Neil Sedaka singing, *Breaking Up is Hard to Do.* I choked out an "okay" and looked down at the ground like I needed to intensely study the path to his truck. Still, Neil Sedaka crooned in my head.

When we got to the truck, he opened the driver's side door for me. That seemed like a good sign. But the darn song wouldn't stop in my head. So I slid over to the passenger side, put my purse on the floor, and propped my left knee on the seat so I could face him. I figured if the darn song wasn't going to stop in my head, then it must be a sign that I was getting dumped. I might as well use my new found strength to face this as a woman. So I looked at him while my head kept playing like an AM radio.

"Margaret, I think we should see other people." There it was. Just like that. My big high school romance was over, all because I got scared of a little first base action. In my defense though, I had seen firsthand what first base led to. But Neil Sedaka would not shut up.

"Oh," was all I could say. I couldn't speak. It was all I could do not to sing right along with Neil and his down dooby-doo down downs.

"I know I said I thought we could work it out, but it's not working. Don't you think?"

I sat there with that infernal song in my head.

Do do do down dooby do down down.

"Margaret? Are you listening to me?" Dan was looking at me like I was insane, which by now I was pretty sure was true.

"Huh?" I shook my head trying to get rid of the song. It didn't work. "Yeah, I'm listening to you. I just don't want to hear it. It makes me sad. And I was in such a good mood until I saw you." His face fell, but I wasn't going to waste any time making him feel better. I had a song to get out of my head.

Come a come a down dooby do down down

"I'm sorry," he said. "I don't want to hurt you, but you said it yourself, that you're not ready. Maybe when you're older? Maybe when you can date?" he implored. I sat there with Neil Sedaka playing in my head, and Dan wanted me to let him off the hook?

Come a come a down dooby down down

Forget that! He was not going to down dooby-do down down his way out of this. I tried to be a grownup and it didn't work out, but he needed to own this. "So let me get this straight: you're breaking up with me because *I'm* not ready?" I sat up a little straighter and tried to find some confidence. Neil was still singing in my head so it was a little easier to concentrate.

Dan looked uncomfortable. Good. "Well, yeah. That's what you said, right? That you weren't ready for a boyfriend?" He shifted in his seat, and if I didn't know better I would have thought there was someone else. He looked downright guilty.

"Oh my gosh. You're seeing someone else aren't you? You're sitting here trying to use my own words against me to break up with me when there's someone else. Who is it? Who are you dumping me for?" I was pissed. Neil Sedaka could sing all he wanted. If I was going to get dumped for someone else, I was going to regain what I could of my dignity. Not that there was much left on the table at this point, what with the talking to dead people and Evil Sheila finding out and all. I'd been through a lot, not that *he* knew, but still, the least he could do was be honest with me.

"I'm not going out with anyone else," he said.

He seemed like he was telling the truth. I studied his eyes like I had truth-seeking powers. He looked at me like I was nuts.

Maybe I was. It was anybody's guess at that point.

"No one?" I was still staring into his eyes, moving my head to look at them from different angles. "Or does that mean you haven't asked her out yet? But you have your eye on someone?"

He looked down then. Dang it. There it was. Too smart for my own good. There was someone else. Dang it. And to top it off, he hadn't even asked her out yet. He was still a gentleman. How was I supposed to hate him now?

Come a come a down dooby-do down down

Oh hell no. I was not letting Neil Sedaka back in my head again.

Dan still looked down. I was crushed. He was a gentleman and polite and all, but I was still being dumped for someone else. I had to keep my eye on the ball and not let him off the hook. I was not going to feel sorry for *him*, because he felt bad for *me*.

"All right," I said, "clearly there is someone else, and you don't want to talk about it. It's a small town. I guess I'll just wait until I see her sitting in my place in this truck." Then I got sad again. I was pretty sure it was Amber, a perfectly nice girl from my class. I wanted to think bad things about her but couldn't. Tall, dark hair, and adorable, Amber was too nice to blame for this. My eyes filled with tears, and I did not want to cry in front of him. "You should probably take me home now. There isn't much else to talk about." I straightened my legs and looked straight ahead like I was fascinated with the road home, but all the while I was willing myself not to cry.

I'd like to say something funny happened then, like when he turned the radio on Paul Simon was singing *50 Ways to Leave Your Lover*, but that didn't happen. Or that maybe he got a speeding ticket on Hazel Street. That would have been awesome, but it also would have extended the already endless drive. But that didn't happen either. We just rode in silence for two interminable minutes.

We pulled up to my house and sat there for a minute. It felt so final. It felt like if I didn't get out of the truck, we wouldn't be broken up. I wondered how I could make that happen. *How could I just erase all of this?*

As I was thinking that, Dan came around and opened my door for me, still a gentleman. *Darn him.* I got my books and purse and tried to get out with minimal eye contact. He followed me.

"Meg, don't be this way. Please. Come here." He went to sit on the swing on my front porch.

"Oh, don't do that," I said. "That's mean." I didn't want him to sit on the romantic porch and ruin it. Then I'd only remember the porch with heartache and not the romantic moments we had there.

"Come here. Sit down." He motioned for me to sit by him, which I did, but not close. No contact.

"Meg, you're upset now and so am I, but you're going to see that this is the right thing for us. You said yourself that you weren't ready, and you were right. We can still be friends, can't we?" He was looking down at me with such sincere eyes. And that beautiful smile—it seemed mean for him to smile at me like that, what with the breaking up and all.

I couldn't look at him anymore. I held my books to my chest—the chest that caused all these problems in the first place. Darn chest. I figured I better answer the question or he'd never leave. "I guess." It was all I could say, and I sounded like a petulant child.

"All right. I guess I can't ask for more than that right now." He got up and walked toward the porch steps. I followed him. He turned around before walking down the steps and said, "This will be good, Meg. You'll see. The pressure will be off of you, and you'll feel better. After that, who knows?" He flashed me that smile again.

Aaaaaaaagh. I wanted to scream, "*THIS ISN'T FAIR.*" I didn't scream though. I tried to remember that I was a lady. Oh please. Who was I kidding? Again, though, I needed to answer. "Yeah. Okay." It was the best I could do.

I opened the door and didn't look back. When I heard, "I'll see you tomorrow," I waved behind me and went into the house. Neil Sedaka was singing about begging not to say goodbye. He was yelling it in my head.

Damn Neil Sedaka and damn viral love.

Crazy and the Spinster

The First Post-Title IX Girl's Soccer Team in Gridley
1976, Sycamore School, Gridley, California
Meredith Carlin First (in cheerleading shoes, not soccer cleats)
and RoseMarie Curcuru

After the last day of school, Anne and I sat on the grass in front waiting for a ride home from Ro and looking at our yearbooks. The air was thick with the June heat, but it wasn't miserable in the shade. It was almost cool on the grass. We sat with our arms behind us, holding ourselves up, deep in thought. The end of the school year always did this to me. I'm not good with endings. They make me sad. Even if I'm happy to move on (which I was, since no one liked to be a freshman), I'm always sad to see something end. It's probably why I can't imagine moving to Minneapolis. That would be an ending to a life I never asked to leave. Almost like a death. Freshman year was no exception to my stance on endings.

"You're getting sad now, aren't you?" Anne looked at me in a sarcastic way, if that was possible, and thumbed through my yearbook. "God, you always do this on the last day of school. Aren't you happy to be done with freshman year? We're not the babies anymore. Come on, smile." She always got frustrated with me when I got too emotional.

"I know. I know. In my head I'm happy, but I'm sad too. Ro won't be here next year. That could make it even worse. What if being a freshman with Ro here is better than being a sophomore without her?" The more I thought about that, the sadder I became. "What if all the good things that happened this year were because I was Rowan Monahan's sister? Oh man." I was in a full-on panic.

"Oh, you're killing me. The good things did NOT happen because you're Rowan Monahan's sister. Good things happened because you're *Margaret* Monahan, and you made them happen. Don't you realize that good things happen to you because of *you*? Not just because you're a Monahan? You work hard. You're nice to people. People like *you*. Not the fact that you're a Monahan. Who knows?

They might even like you more if you *weren't* a Monahan." She had a wicked smile on her face.

"Oh stop." I shifted on the grass and wondered if that was true. "Seriously, though. I have a big mouth and it gets me in trouble. I don't know how to control it. It's like it has a mind of its own. Like it's not fully attached to my brain." I kept staring across the street.

"Well, there is *that*," she said, and I pushed her for it. She wasn't supposed to agree with me. "It's true. But Meg, here's the thing, you mean well. You *like* people. You *genuinely* like people. Nobody, and I mean nobody, walks around wondering how you feel about them. We always know exactly where we stand with you at all times."

"That's the problem. My Grandma June always says, 'The road to Hell is paved with good intentions.' Took me years to figure out what that meant. I get it now and it describes me. I say too much. Why can't I shut up?" I stared across to the pool. Swim team practice started tomorrow. The summer was officially here.

"Well tell *me* then," she said, "'cause I don't know what it means."

I understood Anne's confusion, since I only figured it out recently. "It means that you can intend to do something wonderful, but if you don't actually *do* it, then it doesn't count. So like, when you go to Heaven and meet God, you can't say, 'I *intended* to be a good person and do great works, but it just didn't happen.' You have to actually *do* the great works. So, when I hurt people's feelings because my brain is not working with my mouth, I can't just say that I didn't *mean* to hurt their feelings. That's not good enough. I have to actually *not* say the things that hurt their feelings. That's the hard part." I kept staring. I didn't have the answer to this, and sadly, would spend the next thirty years still trying to figure it out.

This was when Anne was pure magic and wise beyond her years. "Meg, don't you know? Anyone who doesn't get how cool you are isn't worth your time. To hell with them. You need to forget that. Right now." Anne shook her head, and her conviction made me feel better. AnneMarie Calzaretta was a good judge of character.

"Look at your yearbook." She held my yearbook up for me to see. "Look at all these nice things people wrote. *'Margaret, You're so cute and popular. You make me ill. You have such a way with talking to people that you seem to get along with everyone. I swear you're my idol. I know you'll laugh when you read this but it's true. Stay that way always and I hope we have the greatest fun as cheerleaders next year. Love always, Sarah.'"* Anne paused after she read it, to think some more. "Okay. Maybe that wasn't a good example, since Sarah Seaver is the sweetest girl in the world." I nodded my head in agreement. Second only to Jennifer Cone, Sarah Seaver was born with the sweetest spirit God ever made.

Anne didn't give up. "Here's another one, *'Margaret, oh sweet little Margaret. How do I love thee? I guess that question is better left undone. I really have enjoyed the pleasure of being your classmate. I hope the feeling is mutual. I've probably given you one bad time too many. I'm really sorry for it. I hope it hasn't tarnished the love you obviously have for me. I wish you all the luck in the world and I'll be looking out for you. Love ya always, Marcus Williams. Your favorite.'* Wow. And that was from the star of the football team. Has Tonya seen that?"

"Come on," I said. "You're totally making me laugh now. He looks after me like a little sister, 'cause we had Spanish together and I helped him with his vocab. Plus, he was just joking like he knows Shakespeare or something." I was smiling hard now because even if Marcus was joking, it was pretty funny.

"Ooooooh, you 'helped him with his vocabulary'? I think Tonya totally needs to know this now." Marcus Williams just finished his junior year and would most likely rule the school next year. And Tonya was madly in love with him—even if he didn't know it yet.

"Seriously," I said, "he is such a nice guy. Maybe that's why I feel this way? I joke with people so much that I get to the point where I can dish it out but can't take it. Dang. I'm such a loser." I was getting depressed again.

"Oooh. Oooh. Ooooooh." She sounded like Horshack on *Welcome Back Kotter*.

"What?" I asked.

Anne went into her best Horshack imitation. She could do a mean Brooklyn accent. She channeled the Italian side of her blood. "Hellooohhhh. How aw ya? I'm Awnold Horshaaaaack." Then she abruptly stopped. "Seriously, listen to this one. It's from Evil Sheila. God, she wrote all big like she's your best friend, and oooh, it's right next to mine. Tainting my comments."

I smiled and shook my head at her.

"Okay," Anne said, "I'll read it, *'To a really super nice kid.'* Oh yeah, 'cause she's so grown up. Just because she turned into a tramp doesn't make her any more mature than us."

I shook my head and circled my index finger to get her to keep reading.

She continued, *"'I'm glad we got to be good friends over the years. If you ever need any comforting, ask me and I'll try to help.'* Is she serious? Oh sure, the Bride of Satan will be the first person you call on for help. *'Wish me luck with all my dreams, and maybe they will come true. Always stay in the house your in, there is something about it that urges people to raid it. Even if I bug you about being perfect, it's cuz I'm jealous. I've always been stupid, clumsy and an oaf and I'm always envying you. Well see ya. I love you (get it) Sheila.'* Okay. The only true things in those statements were that she's a stupid, clumsy oaf and you're perfect. Well, you're not perfect, but you are compared to her."

I laughed so hard my face hurt. "I'm sorry, but the fact that Evil Sheila envies me doesn't make me feel any better. It's kind of like being king of the dorks. Who really cares what she thinks?" I tried to convince myself that I didn't care what Sheila Scudmore thought of me, but the idea that she treated me horribly because she was jealous of me did give me a bit of comfort. Maybe she wasn't completely evil.

"Meg, knock it off. You've had a tough year." She shook her head as if even she was surprised and had lived through it with me.

"You can say that again."

"Meg, you've had a tough year." We laughed, even though we knew we were huge dorks. "Seriously, though," she continued. "Your only remaining sister is going off to college and ditching you alone with your demanding parents." Then Anne's voice sped up like she was reading a grocery list. "You became a peer counselor, and it was like the whole world fell apart around you. You had to deal with kids drinking, doing drugs, having sex, getting pregnant, and having abortions. And all that was with Evil Sheila. Just think if you had to deal with anyone else?" Anne laughed hard again, her own biggest fan.

I sat up fast. I couldn't rest on my hands for that. *What did she know?* More importantly, *how* did she know it? "What are you talking about?" I held my breath, worried that she somehow, knew about my peer counseling session with the minion on her friend's abortion.

"I was just kidding. Trying to test you. There are rumors," she said, not making eye contact with me.

She sounded so matter-of-fact, like everyone knew about this abortion. "I don't know what you're talking about, Anne." I didn't make eye contact either.

There we were, both staring out at the pool again. "Okay," she said. "You can play it that way. I understand—your peer counseling oath and all.

"I don't think you should joke about that, ever. How come you didn't tell me about these rumors before?"

Anne shook her head and looked at the pool again. I had sounded kind of harsh, like my mom or something. "Dunno. Thought you knew. Thought everyone knew. So anyway, that's a big year for a little girl like you." She laughed again. She loved to call me a little girl. "That's a whole lotta drama for a little half-Mormon, half-Presby-whatever girl to take in her young life."

I pushed her again. She loved to make fun of my "half-breed" status, especially the Presby-whatever thing. Presbyterian was a mouthful. "It's a wonder I'm still alive," I said. She made me *more* depressed.

"Speaking of that, there's your *other* best friend," she whispered. "The one who's not alive."

My face fell. I looked at her dead on as tears filled my eyes.

"Oh, I'm sorry. Really, I am." Her voice softened. "I thought it had been long enough that we could joke about it." She put her arm around me as I fought back the tears.

"You're right," I said. "We should be able to joke about it now. I still feel like such a loon. I'm not sure I will ever be able to joke about it." I wiped away more tears and looked out at the pool again. *Where was Ro?* I wanted to get out of here.

"No. It's my fault. I'm so sorry. You took it hard, and I forget that sometimes."

I put my arm around her. "See what I mean? 'The road to Hell is paved with good intentions.' Get it now?"

"God, I actually do. That sucks." We laughed.

"Tell me about it." I stared at the pool again.

"Do you still talk to Jennifer?" Anne's voice was quiet again, and she looked worried.

I wasn't sure what to say. If I told her I still talked to Jennifer she'd think I was crazy, or worse yet, maybe tell my parents. At the same time, I wasn't sure if I could lie effectively. I've never been a good liar. Then it just came to me. "I've started to so many times. I didn't realize what a habit it was. It was kind of like having my own personal shrink. The ultimate secret-keeper, you know?"

"That would be cool. But do you still?" She acted like she knew I was lying.

"You don't have to *worry*. I wish I still could. Remember when I went to see Mrs. Cone? The time I went without you?" I hadn't told anyone this before and thought it might distract her from the original question.

"Yeah?" She looked scared, afraid her best friend was crazy again and that I could never tell her the truth.

"She told me she talks to Jennifer all the time." I looked up to see what she'd think of that. But I knew what was coming.

"Does Jennifer talk back to her? Does she *see* Jennifer too?" Anne was mesmerized like she was watching a TV movie, live.

"I knew you'd ask that, and no, I'm the only crazy girl who got to see Jennifer. The shrink my parents sent me to told me she was my subconscious, or unconscious, I can never remember which, manifestation of what I wanted Jennifer to be to me at the time."

"Huh?"

"I know. I have no idea what that means. I just nodded a lot to her. I'm not worried about it. I figure I have my parents off my back, and Mrs. Cone didn't think I was crazy. So there. I'm not crazy. I mean, how many people do they have to judge me on this anyway?"

Anne shook her head.

"Seriously? How many nine-year-olds lose one of their best friends, then come up with a 'manifestation' of them and get caught and then sent to a shrink?"

She shrugged, still indicating she didn't know but laughing.

"So I figure I'll toe the line, be the good girl and not worry about it, but I *know* I'm not crazy." I got kind of loud by the time I said "crazy" and Anne jumped.

"You're *not* crazy." She smiled, unconvinced.

I calmed down and lowered my voice. "Really? Do you think I'm normal?"

Anne laughed again. "Well, *normal*? Come on, what's *normal*? You're asking *me* if you're normal? Really?"

We both laughed. Talk about crazy. This whole thing was crazy, but I felt better.

Right then, Dan's truck drove by with a girl sitting *right* next to him, in my spot.

I jumped up to look, and it was Amber. The least he could have done was pick a girl who was awful. I guess that wouldn't have been Dan though. This was just what I needed right in the middle of our crazy discussion.

"Nice," I said. "That's just great. I *knew* he liked her." I sat down and watched as the truck came to a stop right in front of us, with only a big tree and a bench hiding Anne and me from his view. "Dang it. They're parking right there, and I don't have time to escape." I immediately turned away so I wouldn't make eye contact, when they walked by, and whispered to Anne, "That's probably why he brought me that present. Just to soften the blow before I saw them together."

"What present? He brought you a present?" she whispered back.

"Yeah, a few days after he broke up with me there was a beautifully wrapped present on my doorstep. It had a card that just said, 'Have a Beary Nice Day,' and in it was the cutest stuffed bear I've ever seen. The card was in his writing, and he bought it from Ro at the drug store. She said he spent forever picking out just the right one. I thought it was so sweet at the time. But now I see it was just a guilt gift." I tried to sound like I was over him. "Okay. Whatever. I hope they'll be very happy together." I rolled my eyes and tried to look invisible and like I was so over him at the same time. "Is he looking?" My voice trailed off. I was pathetic.

Anne looked shocked but had to check it out for me. "Not yet." She kept staring in their direction. "He's getting out of his truck. Shit, so is she." Anne was talking out of the side of her mouth, almost like a ventriloquist. I had to hold back laughter. "He's holding her hand. Oh man, he's so cute."

My heart sank as I imagined them holding hands. He was supposed to be holding *my* hand.

"Oh, hi Meg. Hi Anne." I heard his surprised voice, as I whipped my head around and gave Anne a "what the hell?" look while trying to sound surprised and look gorgeous at the same time. It was a very tall order that I did not achieve.

"Hi Dan. Amber? Hey. What's up?" I sounded overly

friendly, overly enthusiastic, and very awkward. Exactly the opposite of the cool, gorgeous swan thing I had in mind. The ugly duckling reared her bony head again.

Anne tried to save me. "You guys going to graduation tonight? Big night for Ro." At least it distracted from me.

"Yeah, yeah we're going." Dan looked at Amber as he said it and they nodded their heads like a couple. Amber left after that, saying something about getting stuff from her locker. That left us alone with him.

Oh why can't we just have a giant earthquake right now so the earth can open up and swallow me and save me from myself.

Dan finally broke the awkward, endless silence. "So are you guys swimming this summer?"

We both nodded and murmured inane things about swim team and Anne's butterfly times. Blah, blah, blah. Our voices were sounding like Charlie Brown's parents, and I struggled to stick with it when Amber came back out. Who knew I'd be so happy to see Amber?

"Are you ready to go?" she asked Dan, sweetly.

Kill me now.

"Yeah, yeah. Let's go. See you guys tonight." He turned his cute head and walked back to his truck, not taking her hand.

I know. I was excited too, even though I knew it wasn't exactly a declaration of his love for me.

Anne quickly leaned in and said, "So, I saw in some movie that if a man still loves you, he'll look back at you after you leave. It's the ultimate sign of his feelings."

We watched after him like hawks. With heat-seeking missile powers, I willed him to look back at me, give me any shred of evidence that she was just a transitional thing, and he loved me and was waiting for *me* to grow up.

Anne watched us like a tennis match, checking to

make sure I wasn't falling apart while also keeping one eye on Dan to see if he was looking back. I stared. They kept walking away from us. If I stuck with the fairy tale analogy, I was turning back into the ugly duckling while my prince was walking off with another swan. What the hell?

Just as I was going to turn back around and save myself from more misery, he looked back at me. He looked back at me! He didn't wink or do any movie-like romance kind of thing. He just looked back at me and smiled his genuine smile. I tried not to read into it, but I was a goner.

As soon as he turned back around and got in his truck, Anne whisper-screamed, "Did you see that? He totally looked back at you. He still likes you."

"It's not just in my imagination?"

"No, it felt real to me, but what do I know? Here we are, crazy and the spinster. We're quite a pair."

I laughed. "It's a good thing we finally got cable TV or we wouldn't have anything to do this summer."

Ro pulled up as Dan left with Amber. As we got into her car, I heard Anne softly singing, "Reunited and it feels so goooood."

I pushed her into the back seat so I could get shotgun (which rarely happened with Anne), and as soon as I shut the door I joined her in the rest of the lyrics.

Ro looked back and forth at the two of us like we were insane. We laughed 'cause we knew we were. But it was okay. We were starting to like ourselves. Just the way we were. "Crazy and the spinster" wasn't so bad after all.

She's
Baaaaaaack

Jennifer Lynn Cone
1974, Artwork by Jeananne Richins

325

2008

The pool sparkled in the backyard against the morning sun over the golf course. White chairs lined the lawn area next to the pool and in front of the gazebo. The misters sprinkled along the back porch like fairies came to this wedding to keep us all refreshed. The caterers were busy in the kitchen, the band was set up on the basketball court, and the bar was ready in the pool house. Everything seemed to be in order, so I went upstairs to change my clothes before Anne and Kelly arrived.

I walked through my sitting room and bedroom and into the master bath and was startled to see a blonde woman sitting on the edge of my bathtub, looking out at the view of the lake and the golf course. The hair on the back of my neck stood up, and my skin tingled. I hadn't seen this woman with the catering people, not to mention why would she be sitting on the rim of my bathtub? The weird thing was, I wasn't scared.

"Hello. Can I help you?" I spoke softly so I wouldn't startle her. *Why did I care about startling this stranger in my bathroom?*

"Your view is spectacular," she said. "I should be used to it by now, but every time I'm back here I just can't get over it." She hadn't turned to show me her face yet, but her voice made me tingle more. *Who was this?*

She turned around and tears sprung to my eyes.

"Jennifer," I squealed and jumped and covered my mouth to stifle my squealing so no one would come into my bathroom. I rushed to the double doors of my master suite and bolted them shut, then locked the French doors to the bathroom so we could talk in private.

"I can't believe you didn't know it was me." She brushed a strand of silky hair off her cheek and smiled that beatific smile that made me feel like I was no longer of this world. She was stunning, even now in her forties. It was weird to watch Jennifer this way. She looked like she was our age but had no visible signs of aging like wrinkles or age spots. It was inexplicable to me.

"It doesn't matter how often I see you," I said. "It amazes me that I'm always surprised. I'm so glad you came today, of all days. AnneMarie's wedding day." I sat down on the edge of the tub, next to her, never taking my eyes off her.

"It's been a long time coming. I'm so happy for her and Kelly and I want to talk about that. But I need to talk about you first, Meg."

"Why?" That sounded ominous and scared me.

"I was there at my grave, when you visited. I know about Minneapolis."

The tears came back to my eyes. "Oh." I didn't know what to say, so I just looked down.

"You need to give up this guilt," she said. "You need to go. You'll be okay." She looked at me so softly that it hurt. "You made a promise to my mom to always remember me. Not to always live within a sixty-mile radius of my grave. My own family doesn't even live within a sixty-mile radius of my grave. Have you thought about that?" She laughed and her eyes shone.

I tried not to cry harder. "No, but it makes sense. I didn't realize I felt that way. You're right."

"You need to do this for your family, because it's the right thing to do for all of you. It's okay to be scared, but don't stay here out of fear of something new. And definitely don't stay out of any obligation to me."

"I guess I could look at it like college. I didn't have any problem going away to college. But what if we stay longer than four years?" I trailed off trying to wrap my brain around this. "I guess I could look at it like staying for medical school?" My wheels were turning. *How many years until retirement?* "If we stay until retirement, I guess I could look at it like college, medical school, residency, and an internship. I have no idea why that makes me feel better, but it does. It must be because it puts an end date on it. It gives me an out to be able to come back home. This will always be home to me. When you're in college, you get to have two homes: your college home and home, home. This could work..." I trailed off, lost in the thought of making this cross-country move work for me.

"There you go," she said. "Think of it like it's college. You can do this. But there's one more thing."

Fear crept into my heart again. *Were my children okay? Colin? Would she tell me if they weren't?* I nodded and hoped for the best.

"It's Cindy. She's struggling with her faith and beliefs on gay marriage. Has she talked to you?"

I shook my head. I didn't know what to think. What could I say to Cindy? No one knew I still talked to Jennifer. How would that go over? "Hey Cindy, Jennifer Cone, yeah from fourth grade. She visits me occasionally, and she's worried about you and wants me to talk to you."

"No. I haven't known what to say to her. Shouldn't I leave it to her and Anne?" I was so hoping I'd get to escape this one.

"Just call her. It will be easier than you think. She really needs someone to talk to but is afraid to ask. Call her. You'll all feel better and Anne and Kelly will have a wedding free of anxiety. Don't you think they deserve that?"

She was right. I knew it. I just didn't want to know it. I nodded, still a little speechless that she was here today.

"I've got to go. You can't stay locked up in your bedroom too long without your kids looking for you. Have fun today. I'll be watching." She gave me one last dazzling smile and was gone. Just like that. As easily as she'd arrived.

I would never get used to that.

Here Comes My Girl

Stacie Sormano and Michael Walker's Wedding
March, 2012, Lake Tahoe, California
Debbie Freeman, Meredith Carlin First, RoseMarie Curcuru

This was my first gay wedding, but I had to believe it was the loveliest ever, and not just because it was at my house and one of the brides was one of my best friends. And not just because I was thrilled with the union, loving each of the wives and so happy that they found each other. This was the loveliest gay wedding ever, because these two brides had everyone who was important in their lives together with them, with no dissent. There were no missing parents who couldn't accept their child's homosexuality.

Kelly had three grown children who were all there to support their mom and her new wife. With grown children it didn't always work that way. There was no bitterness. No angst. Just love.

But this was still California. The battle was heating up over Proposition 8 attempting to ban gay marriage so this was strictly a religious ceremony and not a legal one. I didn't know how the gay part of this crowd felt about it, but I thought it almost had more meaning because it wasn't legal. These two women committed themselves to each other regardless of the fact that the State of California had forbidden it. They showed strength of character that most heterosexual people couldn't imagine. Many straight couples didn't begin to put as much thought into their marriages as this couple simply because they didn't have to. Our rights have been in place since the beginning of time, so we sometimes take them for granted.

I watched as Tony walked Anne down the aisle, followed by Kelly and her dad. I got misty as I did at any other wedding ceremony. The garden was at its most beautiful. We had the ceremony at eleven so it wasn't brutally hot yet, and it smelled like freshly cut grass from the golf course with a hint of jasmine from my neighbor's vines in bloom.

We decorated our rustic gazebo with the same jasmine vines for both their beauty and fragrance. Vanilla candles were hanging from the top of the gazebo reminding me of that day, so many years back, when Anne came out of the closet. I looked at her, standing next to her bride, and thought about how far she'd come. Even since that day, thirty years ago, when she first told me that she was pretty sure she was gay. How was it possible that it'd been thirty years since then, when I still felt so young?

I looked at Kelly and thought about the fact that she never knew Jennifer. I wondered what it would be like if Jennifer were still with us. Being a good Mormon girl, how would this war on marriage in California affect Jen's relationship with all of us? Would she have voted against gay marriage? I liked to think the voting booth was like the confessional—completely confidential. So I chose to think that Jennifer would have voted for gay rights because voting was nobody else's business.

I shook my head to knock that thought right out. It didn't matter how Jennifer would have voted. She would have been here, and she would have been supportive of Anne. That's all that mattered. If her religion prohibited her from voting for gay marriage, she wouldn't have let it prohibit her friendships. Even though Jennifer was only with us for not quite ten years, I believed with all my heart that she would have remained a true blue friend. She firmly established that in her short time on earth. She may have been taken young, but she hadn't wasted the time that she had. Jennifer was a devoted, rule-following, faithful, sincere, sweet, smart, and funny girl—a nice girl to the core.

I looked over at Cindy Santini, beautiful with her platinum hair shining in the sun. I was so grateful that

Jennifer made me talk to her. She was right. Cindy was struggling and afraid. She was raised in the branch of the Lutheran Church that believes that it is a sin to be gay and she was having difficulty reconciling her faith with her friendship. I told her what my mom told me: you don't have to change your beliefs for anyone. You just need to love people the way God made them. It's not our responsibility to do anything more than that. That's what God is for.

She liked that. I'm not sure Anne would agree. I think she'd prefer that everyone in the world would not think being gay is a sin but I choose to look at things like this as an alcoholic would -- one day at a time.

As usual, my mind was wandering and philosophizing and not paying attention to the vows. Anne was to my left and Tonya was to my right, since we were the only attendants, just as it had been all our lives. Legal marriage or not, we were the luckiest girls in the world to have each other.

The officiant of the wedding was the same girl I danced with at Anne's birthday party. The one who looked like Bruce Vilanch's prettier, younger sister. A hilarious girl that made me laugh so hard my cheeks hurt. She was solemn today. I wondered how she came to officiate this ceremony since she was a photographer by trade, but I didn't ask questions. Since it wasn't legal anyway, she could have gotten her credentials online. It didn't really matter. Like voting, this ceremony was between Kelly, Anne, and God and nobody else.

They said their "I do's" with tears in their eyes. Everyone seemed pretty misty. There aren't really enough clichés to describe the ceremony and the love I felt all around. They all apply.

Kelly and Anne both wore wedding dresses. Nothing puffy, each wore sleek gowns that fit their styles. Anne to show off her bombshell of a figure, and Kelly's accented her delicate features and tiny waist. Anne was rarely without a cleavage-showing top these days ("If you've got it, flaunt it."), and she didn't disappoint today. She made sure she "brought the girls out for the wedding."

"Ladies and gentlemen, I present to you Kelly and Anne." The two brides kissed as we cheered and clapped. They walked down the aisle with everyone throwing birdseed at them. I figured we might as well add more tradition since it was an outdoor wedding. All the ducks and birds lived in the backyard anyway. Might as well feed them.

The party was revving up, and it was just the Gridley Girls at a table with Kelly. She was one of us now. I raised my glass in a quiet toast, "To Anne and Kelly."

Everyone joined in, "To Anne and Kelly," and we clinked our glasses together.

"Anne. It's time for the first dance. Come on," I said.

Anne took Kelly's hand and they walked to the center of the dance floor, which was really my kids' basketball court, but we dressed it up and the pretty jasmine vines all grew at one end. Jock had the mike now and was introducing them. "Ladies and gentlemen, it's now time for Anne and Kelly's first dance."

The song started and it was *Here Comes My Girl* by Tom Petty, and we squealed with delight. "Woo hoo."

I put my hand on Tonya's arm and whisper-screamed, "I *love* this song."

"I know. Me too. Look how sweet they are. It's the perfect song for them." Anne and Kelly were holding each other but still grooving a bit. They were a perfect couple dancing to a perfect song for them. I felt warm all over. And it wasn't just the champagne. It was love. There's nothing better than good friends who are happy.

Anne and Kelly waved to us to come dance with them. Colin appeared out of nowhere. He'd been to enough weddings to know. He took my hand and, I daresay, looked as sweet as Anne and Kelly; if it's possible to compare a big man with two lipstick lesbians.

He took me in his arms, and we danced like we'd been doing for sixteen years. His arms fit around me like a perfect glove. I put my head on his chest. "I *love* this song. Do you love this song?"

"Not as much as you do, but I really like it." He smiled and held me tighter.

"I want you to think of me when you hear this song. Do you think of me when you hear this song?" I didn't wait for his answer. "I want to be your girl. Do you think of me like Tom Petty does in this song? Am I your girl?"

He pushed me away a bit so he could look me in the eyes. "Of course I think of you when I hear this song. You're my girl. You've been my girl since the moment I met you." He pulled me closer again and got back on tempo. "You're my silly girl. What kind of question was that?" He shook his head like I was crazy. I was used to *that*.

I didn't care. I needed to hear it. *He thinks I'm his girl. He thinks of me when he hears this song.* That was all I needed to hear. I held him closer and smiled into his chest. "I'm the luckiest girl in the world. I get to live in this beautiful house in this beautiful setting. Every day I get to look out the window and stare in amazement at this wonderful view: nature, and the good grooming of a beautiful golf course, all in one pretty picture. I've got great kids and a wonderful career. All that and I have help with housework and laundry. Doesn't get any better than that." He laughed at the last comment, knowing how much we both hated to do housework. *Yes, I'm lucky indeed. I thank God every day for my good fortune and my wonderful family.*

The song ended, but Colin said, "Let's stay and dance to the next one." When Reunited came on, by Peaches & Herb, we laughed out loud but stayed on the dance floor. Anne yelled over to me, "Hey Meg, where's Dan Stone? You need to be dancing with him for this one."

Even Colin laughed with us. He'd heard all about Dan Stone and always said, "I like that silly fourteen-year-old Meggie. She's one smart girl breaking up with a guy who tried to feel her up. Those are *my* boobs."

He held me close and said, "I got a call yesterday."

I didn't like how he sounded.

"The economy is not good. California is getting hit hard. By comparison, life is still good in Minneapolis. I'm worried that if it gets worse here, we won't have a choice on where they relocate us. We'll have to move to the only open spot at the time. Do you want that?"

I held him close again, feeling like if I held him closer and didn't look at him, then this wouldn't happen. *I won't be taken away from my family and friends. Six generations. I was just counting my blessings. Counting them. Not taking them away.*

He broke my concentration. "Do you understand?"

"Of course I do. I just don't want to believe it." I pounded on his chest with my fists to the beat of my words. He didn't even feel it. The song ended and *Come on Get Higher* by Matt Nathanson came on. I didn't want to be thinking about all of this. I just wanted to hear the song, hold my husband, and embrace the beautiful day.

I knew I sounded more stern than I wanted. This wasn't his fault. I shouldn't blame him. But who else could I blame? He was going back on everything we agreed upon when we got married. Did he not realize that was part of what made him perfect for me? The fact that his family was here, and he didn't want to live anywhere other than Sacramento? That was an important thing to a family girl like me.

I laid my head back on his chest and tried to get lost in the lyrics. That song made me happy. It made me forget that we could be snatched from our homeland and our lives. It sounded crazy, I knew. We should have had free will, but we'd centered our lives around his career our entire adult lives. He'd never worked anywhere else. All he ever wanted was to make partner. If we had to move to save his career, I wouldn't really have a choice. I needed to do what was best for him, since what was best for him was best for the entire family. *Oooooh, why now?*

Then a part of the lyrics came up that I'd never noticed before. God was talking to me through songs again, telling me something about "if I could tell you what's next, if I could make you believe". I should have been used to it. Tears sprang to my eyes. I didn't want him to see me cry. It was such a great day. I didn't want to ruin it, and I didn't want to put pressure on him.

Yet.

I tried to soften my voice then and be a grownup, but I didn't look up. My face was still buried safely in his chest. "When do they want us to leave?"

"As soon as we can find a house, which I'm hoping will be in time for the kids to start school in the fall." He made me look at him. "It's real this time." He didn't say anything more. He just stared at me. We were standing on the dance floor no longer dancing, and he was pleading with his eyes for me to have a positive attitude. I didn't have to say yes. I needed to be positive for him.

I tried to give him that back. I delved deep into my soul to come up with some positive energy that I knew he needed. I tried to be the supportive corporate wife who would drop anything to further her husband's career. But where was *my* wife? Who was supporting *my* career? Nope. I couldn't do it. I was supposed to be prepared for this. Instead, I was in shock.

I could only think sarcastic thoughts. It was all I could do not to turn into a raving shrew or a bawling baby. How could we leave this wonderful life? All of our family lived within seventy miles of us. All of our best friends lived right in the neighborhood. All of our children's best friends were the children of our best friends. They'd never known any other world. How would we leave such a great life? How would I leave a life built for me by so many previous generations? Who could mess with *that* kind of tradition? Who did he think I was, a freaking pioneer? And speaking of pioneers: they went west, not east. Everybody knew that.

So I took a breath, raised my head, and with tears running down my cheeks, said the first thing that popped into my head. "I'm gonna need a fur coat."

He laughed. "You don't even wear fur."

"Well, clearly I'm going to have to start since you want to move me to Siberia."

He shook his head and held me tighter, while Matt Nathanson kept singing about drowning me in love. I was drowning all right.

What the hell was happening to me?

A Gridley Girl's Glossary to Seventies Pop Culture

After School Specials were ABC's answer to educating teens in the seventies and eighties on tough topics. In two short hours (with lots of commercials) we could learn everything about teen pregnancy, runaways, and divorce. Ask your mom if she learned more from *Schoolhouse Rock* or *After School Specials*. You and your mom will be best friends by the time you finish this book.

Andy Gibb: 1958-1988, was an English singer, teen idol, and the younger brother of the Bee Gees. Not quite Justin Bieber, but definitely up there.

Archie Comics first appeared in 1941 and revolved around the best love triangle of my generation: Archie, Betty, and Veronica. Betty, the blonde, middle class, good girl, versus Veronica, the raven haired, rich girl, vying for the attention of red-headed, freckled faced Archie, who drove a jalopy. He was an unlikely heart throb and probably why I'm so fond of redheads.

The Bionic Woman (1976-1978) starred Lindsay Wagner as a tennis pro who, after suffering a parachuting accident, was saved by special surgery giving her a bionic ear, arm, and both legs, hence making her the fastest runner ever. It was girl power all the way. By now you're jealous that *you* have lame TV shows while your parents had awesome ones, huh?

Black Hills Gold jewelry, popular in the seventies and eighties, depicted leaves, grape clusters, and vines and was made in the Black Hills of South Dakota. They used alloys of gold with yellow, green, red, or pink gold.

The Bob Newhart Show was a TV sitcom that ran from 1972-1978 starring Bob Newhart (whom you may remember as Will Ferrell's Papa *Elf* dad) as a psychologist. As a child of the seventies, it was my only exposure to psychology, and the nut jobs in Newhart's group therapy did not help me understand psychology any better.

The Boy in the Plastic Bubble was one of the greatest TV movies of all time for any seventies girl. Search for it so you can watch it with your mother and cry for John Travolta's character. At the same time you can cry for the real John Travolta, as your mother tells you his real life's love was in the movie with him and later tragically died of cancer. I know. This is a lot to handle in one footnote.

BYU (Brigham Young University) Idaho is a private, four year University in Rexburg, Idaho that used to be called Ricks College, which I used to think sounded a lot like Joe's Diner. Maybe that's why they changed the name?

Candies were a shoe trend of the late seventies. They were plastic and had spike heels with a small piece of leather for the sandal. They came in all sorts of colors, and I was never old enough to have any when they were in style.

Carrie (see John Travolta below) was a 1976 movie starring the incomparable Sissy Spacek in the title role that scared the crap out of every seventies kid. Based on the book by Stephen King, the film culminates in (possible spoiler alert) a lot of blood and blood curdling screams. It was my first, last and only Stephen King book (other than his memoir) read since I'm a hopeless scaredy cat and am guaranteed to have nightmares and walk in my sleep if I read or watch anything too scary. I'm scared now just writing this.

The **Celestial Kingdom** is what Mormons call Heaven. My Jack Mormon father's favorite joke is that a guy dies, goes to Heaven, and is greeted by St. Peter. The guy gets shown around all the sights in Heaven and sees a white wall with gilded hardware of beautiful angels with trumpets. They hear the most beautiful singing from the other side of the wall. The guy asks St. Peter, "What's in there? Can we go in?" St. Peter replies, "No. That's the Mormons. They think they're the only ones up here."

Chatty Cathy (Mattel, 1959-1965) was revolutionary for her time as the first talking doll. After 1965, when I learned to talk, Mattel stopped making the doll as I did enough talking for the whole world and you didn't have to pull a string.

Whenever you hear a Mormon say **"The Church,"** they are referring to The Church of Jesus Christ of Latter-Day Saints. No other church (note the capitalization) is "The Church" as they believe their church to be the one true religion. This is never said in a condescending nature, but just as a statement of fact in their beliefs.

There was a scene in an old Eddie Murphy movie, *Coming to America*, where the characters who owned a Jheri curl company all stood up from a couch and left their head prints on the wall behind them, because they had so much product in their hair. That was my Grandpa Clif. We had Grandpa head prints above every couch in our house.

The Curse was how they referred to your period in the real olden days of Jayne Monahan.

Dittos was a popular brand of designer denim and colored jeans in the seventies. Their signature look was the center seam that started at the bottom of one leg and ran up, across the butt and to the bottom of the other leg.

Dorothy Hamill was an Olympic gold medal winning American figure skater in 1976, and spawned a bigger hairstyle craze than the "Rachel" (Jennifer Aniston's 'do from Friends in the nineties). Ask your mother. If she didn't have a Dorothy Hamill haircut, she wishes she did.

Really? **Elvis**? You expect me to explain Elvis to you? I was just testing and you failed.

Erma Bombeck, revered in the Monahan family as the funniest humorist of her time, wrote a newspaper column from 1965-1996 and fifteen books. Think Tina Fey without any TV shows.

Family Affair was a TV series that ran from 1966-1971. Better than *Full House*. That's right. I went there. But shh, don't tell the Olson twins I said that. Ask your mom if she had a Mrs. Beasley doll. Quiz her. She'll be amazed at your new fun facts.

The Firm was a Tom Cruise movie from 1993 based on the book of the same name by John Grisham. It was about a young tax attorney who signed on with a firm that was hooked up with the mafia. Other than the mafia and murders, it felt like our life.

Gilligan's Island was another sitcom (are you noticing a pattern yet?) that ran from 1964-1967, but became very popular in syndication during the seventies because they played it after school. The show was about seven characters shipwrecked on a desert island. It was common for girls to wonder if they were more like "Ginger" the movie star or "Marianne" the down-home girl-next-door type. By now you know, Meggie wanted to be Ginger but accepted that she was born to be Marianne.

Gladys Kravitz was a fictional character from the sitcom *Bewitched* (1964-1972), about a witch named Samantha Stevens who married a mortal and tried to live a normal, suburban life without her powers. Gladys was the nosy neighbor who always seemed to catch Samantha performing witchcraft but could never get her husband, Abner, to the window in time to see it himself. Like *Pollyanna*, Gladys Kravitz entered American lexicon as a synonym for a nosy neighbor.

Growing Up Skipper, Barbie's younger sister was introduced by Mattel in 1975 to huge controversy when Mattel decided to age Skipper by allowing you to swivel the doll's arm to make her grow taller and grow small breasts on her rubber chest. Of course, my feminist mother wouldn't buy me a Growing Up Skipper. I saw it when I babysat. Thank God for mothers.

Horshack was one of the "Sweathogs" on the seventies sitcom *Welcome Back Kotter* that ran from 1975-1979. It was the show that launched John Travolta's career. Arnold Horshack was the class clown with a nasally voice who introduced himself as "Hullo. How aw ya? I'm Ah-nuld Hor-shaaaaack." He was also known for yelling, "Oooh, oooh, oooh" when he knew the answer to a question.

Jack Tripper was the fictional character and star of the seventies sitcom *Three's Company* (1977-1984) who pretended to be gay so he could share an apartment with two women so the landlord would let them be roommates.

Jackie-O sunglasses became the rage in the seventies in Jacqueline Kennedy Onassis' post white house years when her signature look was always capped off with oversized, round, black sunglasses

Jethro Bodine was the name of a dunce of a character from the popular TV series, *The Beverly Hillbillies,* that ran from 1962-1971, played by Max Baer. Jethro's most famous proclamation was, "I grad-ge-ated sixth grade, ma'am. Only took three years."

I really was *all* about **John Travolta**. *Carrie* was one of Travolta's earliest films based on Stephen King's first book. 'Nuff said, right? As always, read the book first.

Judy Blume is the author of my childhood teaching me everything I ever needed to know about menstruation, divorce, virginity and even (gasp!) teenage boys and masturbation. Yikes.

King Tut: Did you really think I was going to define King Tut for you? I *know* he came back on tour in 2010, so if you don't know who he is from history class then I shall quote everybody's mom, Jayne Monahan, when I tell you to "look it up."

Kristy McNichol was a child star in the seventies best known to our generation as the star of *Family* and the film, *Little Darlings*. In Gridley though, she was just "that actress that AnneMarie Calzaretta looks like."

Love's Baby Soft - A popular perfume in the seventies that smelled a lot like baby powder. Sure, you could have spent fifty cents on baby powder but usually, you fell for the commercials and spent your hard-earned three dollars in baby sitting money on Love's Baby Soft because it was cooler.

Lucy Ricardo and Ethel Mertz were fictional characters who were best friends in the sitcom, *I Love Lucy* (1951-1957), but the show played in syndication in the seventies. Starring Lucille Ball and Vivian Vance, Lucy and Ethel epitomized mad cap female best friends in American culture. We should all aspire to find our inner Lucy and Ethel.

Mary Tyler Moore and Rhoda Morgenstern were the seventies answer to Lucy and Ethel and were fictional characters starring in *The Mary Tyler Moore Show* (1970-1977).

Maude was a television sitcom that ran from 1972-1978 starring Beatrice Arthur in the title role as a fast-talking, outspoken feminist. Jayne Monahan was a fan of all things *Maude*—from her sharp wit to her long jackets. Ask your mom to sing the theme song for you.

Marge Simpson's smoking sisters, Jacqueline and Patty Bouvier, were known for their chain smoking and raspy voices in the long running animated series, *The Simpsons*.

Milli Vanilli was one of the most popular pop groups in the late eighties and early nineties until their fame turned to infamy when it was discovered that they were lip syncing.

A **Miracle Ear®** is a hearing aid that had goofy commercials which seventies teenagers made fun of while watching the only three channels available to them. If anyone displayed great hearing powers while eavesdropping, they were using their "Miracle Ear" just like the old people on the commercials.

Perry Mason was a legal drama on TV that ran from 1957-1966, but seventies girls like me watched them in syndication. It starred Raymond Burr as the fictional LA defense attorney based on books by Erle Stanley Gardner. Perry Mason won every case he tried on our television sets and that made him invincible in seventies life.

Pollyanna was a 1913 novel by Eleanor H. Porter and a 1960 Disney movie by everybody's favorite child star of the sixties, Haley Mills. Pollyanna was a young orphan (of course she was—it was Disney!) who went to live with her wealthy, stern Aunt Polly. Pollyanna was an optimistic girl who played the "Glad Game" where she'd find something to be glad about in every situation. The novel's success led to the name being used in every day vernacular such as "Pollyannaish" and "Pollyannaism."

Poltergeist was a 1982 horror film produced by Steven Spielberg that scared the crap out of a generation of kids with two softly uttered words, "They're here."

The official definition of **Primary** from the LDS website states, "The organization of the Church for children from ages three to twelve. Beginning at three years of age, children receive two hours of religious instruction each Sunday. One hour is spent with a teacher who provides a lesson for an age-specific group, and a second hour is spent in a combined group of children in instruction and singing." I would just add that it sounds boring when the Church describes it, where in real life, it's super fun.

By now you have already put *Saturday Night Fever* in your Netflix queue. Just think of Evil Sheila as you watch the opening scene when my bf, John Travolta, struts the streets of Brooklyn to the beat of "Stayin' Alive."

Shaun Cassidy was 1977's answer to Justin Bieber. Cindy Santini and I argued over who loved him more. She won because she had a subscription to *Tiger Beat* and I did not.

Sprouse-Reitz was a chain of five-and-dime (variety) stores in the western United States from 1901-1994. In Gridley, it was common for people (who weren't related to Jayne Monahan or who weren't paying attention to her in class) to confuse **Spruce Drug** (a superior store in every way) and Sprouse-Reitz and call them Sprouse Drug or Spruce-Reitz.

Five-and-Dime Stores were a concept originating in 1879 by Woolworth Brothers. Its retail stores originally sold everything for either five cents or ten cents, hence the name, "five and dime." Think dollar type stores in the olden days.

Sybil was a 1976 TV movie starring Sally Field as a young woman who experienced so much childhood trauma that she developed thirteen personalities. With only three TV channels, it would be difficult to find a child of the seventies who hadn't seen and been scared by *Sybil*.

Tab was a diet cola beverage introduced by Coca Cola in 1963 to compete with Diet Rite, owned by the Royal Crown Company. It was the drink of choice of fashionable seventies women like Jayne Monahan.

Title IX is a portion of the Education Amendment of 1972 that states: *No person in the United States shall, on the basis of sex, be excluded from participation in, be denied the benefits of, or be subjected to discrimination under any education program or activity receiving federal financial assistance...*It goes on and on but the bottom line to anyone under thirty is that girls didn't get to play many organized sports until Title IX was passed, and later legally enforced. All you really need to think when you hear Title IX is that it's the Girl Power amendment.

Then go give your mom a hug cuz she probably didn't get to play nearly as much soccer as you did growing up.

Vince Lombardi, 1913-1970, was an American football coach revered by Fred Monahan and legions like him. He is best known as the coach of the Green Bay Packers during the 1960's where he led them to two Super Bowls. The NFL Super Bowl trophy is named in his honor. He was enshrined in the NFL's Pro Football Hall of Fame in 1971.

Vinny Barbarino was John Travolta's breakout character in the TV series, *Welcome Back Kotter* (1975-1979), that gave him the chance to star in *Saturday Night Fever* and *Grease*. Think of a darker, sexier Ashton Kutcher and give him a blockbuster movie career, and you'll come close to the magic that was John Travolta in the seventies. As always, if you haven't seen the aforementioned movies, ask your mom. She'll know what to do.

Weebles were roly-poly, egg shaped toys popular in the seventies and known for their tagline "Weebles wobble but they don't fall down."

In Memoriam
Jennifer Lynn Cone
July 23, 1964 – June 16, 1974

*1971, Jennifer, in an outfit made by
her mother, Suzanne Cone*

Dear Readers,

While this book is a work of fiction, it is classified as a True-Life Novel; a relatively new genre of books based on true stories. I'd like to clarify a few things, especially for my readers from Gridley, as they will be most curious as to what is true and what is not.

With the exception of Jennifer Cone and her family, my grandparents, Clifford and Alice Carlin, my late cousin, David Breese, and Matt McDowell, all names have been changed to protect the privacy of everyone involved. After reading a first draft of the manuscript, David and Suzanne Cone, Jennifer's parents, gave me one of the biggest honors of my life by asking if I would please use Jennifer's real name. I was thrilled to oblige.

Jennifer's passing left an indelible mark on our group of friends—we were forever changed and are closer for it.

Maybe we cling to each other since we know a little about the fragility of life?

Matt McDowell does not now, nor has he ever had sweaty palms. I used his real name as a joke only for him, before he edited the manuscript, and I forgot. Whoops. Thanks Matt, for letting me leave you as the sweaty palmed boy, for always being a good friend, for editing *Gridley Girls*, for being the best first grade boyfriend a girl could ever have (lovely ring included), for being my actual first real kiss and someday, maybe, being my Tate Taylor.

If you see yourself in this book and you and I haven't personally discussed this, rest assured that I am not writing about your life. This is a work of fiction dramatizing events happening in my life. Nothing more. It is my hope that my life can help others, especially those who have lost loved ones much too soon and anyone who struggles with shame or regret.

You may already know that 10% of the profits from this book are being donated to children's charities that work to prevent catastrophic diseases through research and treatment. No child should ever be denied treatment when they are sick.

Shortly after writing the second draft of this book, I moved in behind some wonderful people fighting cancer with their six-year old daughter. Marit is eleven-years old now and has been cancer-free for almost five years. They get to live their happy ending because of research and treatments that now exist that weren't around in 1974. Because of donations like the one you made when buying this book, that research can continue. On behalf of every child, both healthy and not, I thank you.

There is something so unnatural about a parent outliving their child, that people like me struggle to make sense of it. Some would say these books are my therapy. I would agree. Thank you so much for coming with me on this adventure to find my sanity by sharing my *insanity* with you.

And remember: Y.A.L. (or Y.A.G.),

Meredith Carlin First

Acknowledgements

This book could not have been written without the support of my husband who was willing to jump on this bandwagon (gun to his head or not) after I left my job to follow my dreams. And speaking of jobs, thank you to Steve Jobs for creating the company that allowed me to learn to listen to my dreams and retire at forty, and to my mentors there who made my career easier: Craig Wells, Roben Talia, Julie Potter Edgett, Michele Nadeau, Kim Clark, Bob Sippel, Dan Walker, and Patty Hsiu.

Thank you to my kids, Cole and Alice, who had to eat too much takeout while I sat at my computer. Thanks to the best exchange student (and fake son) that any mother could ask for. Youri, you brightened the First Family from the moment you moved in with us. Most people think they have the best family, but I really do. Thanks to Dad (chick book? Really?), Paulette (you've taught me more than you know), Lori (the perfect one) and Randy, Melissa (Grandma Alice, Jr.), Mom and Dad First, Jo, Marci, and my new super-fan Ed (maybe you'll finally read the book now?). Thanks to all my nieces and nephews: Andrew (the best CIO ever), Nicole (the leader of the next generation of Carlin Girls), Trevor (my other son), David (my God-son), Danny (Justin Bieber, Sr.), Erika, Blair, Tay, Hayden, Tyler, and Brady.

Thanks to my friends and first readers who had to listen to me yammer incessantly as this book grew and formed in my head: Ida (I got it done in less than ten years!), Cynthia F., Suzy A., Lisa K., Vicki H., Tamara S., Brianna N., Jimmer, Michelle R.L., Pam M., Katie A., Cari A. & Kelley C., Alison B. (you're a great editor), Janelle P, Nancy B., Terry M., Berit and Michael, Amanda L., Kalley (great glossary idea!), and Olivia. Thanks to Kerianne and Adrian at The Firm (you thought I'd forget?) and Doug P. for your guidance. And because I promised, thanks to Dr. Stan Arellano for taking such good care of my teeth.

Thanks to Gridley Guys: Cousin Stewart Anstead for his brilliance on the cover art, and Matt McDowell, Ken Miller, Rick Buckner, and Mark Nakata for always being better writers than me, while sharing your talents to try and make me better too.

Thank you to Lisa Wedin Van De Hey and The Gridley Herald for a lifetime of support. Erma Bombeck only wishes she could have written free columns for The Herald.

To the original Group: Rose, Stacie, Melissa, Paula, Diane, Brenda, Valerie, Janet, and Maria. And to the original Sparkling Bluebirds and other Gridley Girls: Gail H.E., Jeanne T.H., Heidi McW., Lisa C. and Michelle R.Z., Karen N.H., Roxanne D.G., Julia H.M. and Erika W.D., thank you for your years of friendship and the best childhood any Gridley Girl could ask for. Thanks for helping me dig up old pictures and print them even if we weren't always cute. I hope someday you'll be able to pass this book to your daughters and granddaughters and say, "This is what it was like for us, growing up as Gridley Girls, in the olden days."

Thank you to Patti Frazee for the great book design and ability to handle all my revisions in top speed. Thanks to my editors, Virginia McCullough and Karen Lacey, and to Scott Edelstein for leading me to all three of these talents, and to The Loft for educating me and opening up my writing life. I would not be a writer if I had not grown up with role models like Beverly Cleary, Judy Blume, and later the late, great Erma Bombeck and Nora Ephron. Thank you for your example, entertainment, and influence on my life. And thanks to Kathryn Stockett who went out of her way to help me and for calling me "brave," and to Lorna Landvik for taking both my hands into hers and looking deep in my eyes before saying, "Believe in yourself. You're already there."

Thank you to Katie Rasinski and Sara Hall from St. Jude Children's Research Hospital for listening to a Gridley Girl with a computer and a dream to help families deal with their loss and more importantly, help families with dreams of good health for their children.

Thanks to John Shumate for technical support while I was writing in Elk Grove. Thank you to the wonderful team at Apple Ridgedale. You helped an ex-Apple girl keep her company going while living in the arctic tundra, unaccustomed to technical life away from Apple Sacramento.

Thank you to Rich Calzaretta for saying the seven most magical words to me. I hope you don't mind that I honored you by using your last name in this series of books. I did it with respect and affection.

Thanks to the Great Gridley educators who inspired me to write and helped all Gridley Girls and Guys to discover their full potential: Mr. Richard Erickson (and Lynn – my other parents), Aunt Martha Soares (and Uncle Brud), Mr. Harland Ramsey, Mizzz Joan Brock, Mrs. LaViolette (you'll always be Miss Gertz to me), Mr. Steven Jensen, Mrs. Gregg, Mrs. Messick, Mrs. Ernie Hepworth, Mrs. Anne Onyett, Mrs. Bettie Harp, the late Mr. Orville Harp, the late Mrs. Donna Graff, the late Mrs. Heffley, the late Mr. Olsen, Mr. Richard Stewart, Mrs. Jane Ostling (you'll always be Miss E. to me), Mrs. Carolyn Haft, Mr. Dan Soares, Dr. Earl Souza, Mr. Jim Underhill, Mr. Norm Dessler, Señor Herting, Mr. Chris Gulbrandsen, the late Mel Anglen, and the late Uncle Jack Faulk. Thanks to our real life Peer Counseling Advisors at Gridley High: Coach Larry Schutz, the late Ms. Jan Roberts and the late Miss Karen Watson, and my favorite Canadian teacher, Mr. Brent McGhie. If I've forgotten any of my Great Gridley teachers, please blame Joan for not being here to remind me.

To my mentors at Oregon State who made such a difference in my life: Dr. Jerry O'Connor, Dr. Strong and Professor Richard Weinman.

In 1978-79 Gridley, our vice principal was Ron Mongini, who recently passed away in a tragic accident and left behind a family and a wonderful companion, Lane Gehres, who means a lot to the Carlin family. Rest in peace, Mr. Mongini.

While I have no proof, I am convinced that the dreams that led me to writing this book came from my late mother, Joan Carnahan Carlin, a four-decade teacher in Gridley schools. Her dream for me to become the next Judy Blume was something I couldn't imagine. I am grateful for her support in this phase of the completion of my life's work.

Thank you to my cousins Beth Breese and Bob Breese for allowing me to honor Cousin David's memory.

Thanks to David and Suzanne Cone and Jennifer's siblings, Doug, Andrea, Shannon, Melissa, and Amanda for your support over the years. While I can't fathom the loss your family has experienced, I do know a little something about losing someone you love. Though it didn't need to be asked and it wasn't difficult, I hope I've honored my promise made so many years ago at Jennifer's graveside to always remember her. She is still with us all.

Thanks to Darcy for continuing to be my friend after Anne Hechegate, and for having the confidence in me to know that all I ever wanted was my best friend's happiness.

And finally, thanks to RoseMarie Curcuru, the best-darn-lesbian-in-the-whole-wide-world (BDLWWW). Yes, I said it. You are an inspiration to me. Thank you for bringing me such a great friend in Debbie. I look forward to one day presiding over your legal marriage in California. Thank you most of all for bringing me into the world of enlightenment, for I truly believe if everybody had a gay BFF there would be no marriage litigation and all that money spent on squashing civil rights could go to…say…feeding the hungry.

Love does not need to be litigated. Thank you for being a beautiful example of that every single day.

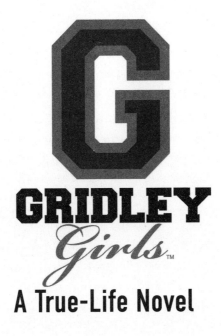

GRIDLEY Girls™
A True-Life Novel

Meredith First

A Reader's Club Guide

ABOUT THIS GUIDE

The following questions were written by fellow Gridley Girl, Chris Heinrich, of the Gaggler's Book Club in Benicia, California. She'd like you to know that she did not choose her club's name. The questions are intended to help you find positive approaches to your discussions of Gridley Girls: A True-Life Novel, by Meredith First.

1. Growing up in the late 70s and early 80s, the alcohol filled parties Meredith First writes about were familiar. There seemed to be a lack of concern about those parties from school and community (at least in Gridley, a small conservative, agricultural town). What do you think the differences are, if any, between youth experimentation and use of alcohol/drugs between now and then?

2. Ms. First writes on many teen "firsts". The onset of Meg's menses was a family affair. What memories did it bring of your first menstruation? How did family deal/discuss it? If you have young girls, how did you/ will you guide your girl through her first period?

3. Jayne Monahan, Meg's mother, was almost everyone's middle school English teacher and everyone's second mom, at least school mom. Her words still operate in adult's conscience. Who was an important non-family adult in your teenage life? What words of wisdom from that person still run through your mind?

4. How old were you when you realized a friend, family member or acquaintance was gay? What are your thoughts and feelings about gay rights and marriage? How are your views about gay rights shaped by religion and politics?

5. What were your thoughts and feelings about your religious upbringing during your early teenage years? How did your family allow you to express your ideas about religious beliefs?

6. Discuss your first kiss, first boyfriend. Meg had a series of diaries; how have you preserved those special childhood, teenage memories?

7. There is so much discussion of bullying right now. Did you have a childhood bully? Were you a bully? How is bullying different today than it was 30 years ago?

8. How old were you when you first experienced a death of an important person in your life? What were your responses? Did that first loss shape the way you have dealt with subsequent losses?

9. Meg, just recently having experienced her first kiss, is witness to Anne's much more adult-like sexual encounter with Rick. What did you think of Meg's reactions?

10. Meg sought counsel from a high school teacher who was also a local religious leader. What are your thoughts about religion, prayer and values education in schools?

11. Meg starts off the re-counting of her childhood relationships reflecting on her betrayal. Did Meg betray Anne? How hard is it to keep such important confidence?

12. Meg accepts Anne's self-revelation with calm. If you were Meg, how would you have reacted? What would you have said or done?

The One and Only FAQ

Q.

Do you think the media is trying to push a "gay agenda" on America. Is that your intention with your story in *Gridley Girls*?

A.

It's important to me to make sure that people understand that I'm never trying to push a "gay agenda" on anyone. I believe that everyone has the right to religious freedom. That's what America was founded on. It is my belief that gay marriage is a Civil Rights issue and not a religious issue. That is why I am in support of it. As an ELCA Lutheran, I do not believe that being gay is a sin. But that is my belief. As Americans, we owe every American the same governmental freedoms that we enjoy and hold so dear. I believe I was born straight, just as gay people were born gay. No gay person will ever tell you they grew up with a dream of being gay. It just doesn't happen. I dream about the day I will get go to a gay wedding and it will simply be called a wedding.

Do You Want to Help?

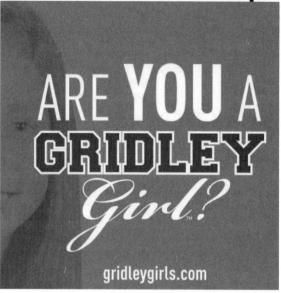

Mom always told me, "Ask and ye shall receive." So I will ask you for help. Did you like *Gridley Girls*? Would you like to help me make the world a nicer place? Or are you interested in helping me in my quest for acceptance for all? Or did you think of it as "biblio-therapy for grief counseling" as one of my readers noted? Maybe you just liked the book and want to spread the word. Either way, below are social media links and on the next page is a link to help in our campaign we cleverly call, "Get Gridley Girls on Ellen" or "G3E" if your fingers are tired. Thank you from all Gridley Girls (both in spirit and birth).

Website and Social Media:

www.GridleyGirls.com
www.MeredithFirst.com

🐦 @Meredith First

 Meredith First

ⓟ Meredith First

 Meredith First

Get *Gridley Girls* on Ellen (G3E)

Please send an email telling Ellen in 1500 characters or less, why you think *Gridley Girls* should be on her show. Share your story with her and cross your fingers.

www.ellentv.com/be-on-the-show/10/

For Snail Mail:
The Ellen DeGeneres Show
PO Box 7788
Burbank, CA 91522
Attention: Get *Gridley Girls* on Ellen!

Here's a sample letter (sic) sent to me, from Youri Maringka of Amsterdam. He made me cry and you'll see why when you read it:

Hi Ellen,

I have tried to write an email in less than 1500 characters, but I can't. I just couldn't stop talking about how great and amazing this woman is and that it would mean so much for her if she could be on your show as a guest. Her name is Meredith First. She is an author, a mother and a gay marriage supporter. And she's great in all of this. She just published her first book, called Gridley Girls. If you haven't read it yet you should! (http://gridleygirls.com/). But I'm not writing you to sell her book. I want you to know how great she is. In 2010, I came to the USA as a foreign exchange student. I lived with another host family the first semester, but the second semester Meredith took me in. And the first moment we met, I felt like home. She has always been there for me to talk to when I felt homesick and always stood by my side whenever I needed help in anything. She treated me like her own son, and I began to see her as a second mother. I still do, even though I left two years ago and we only got to talk on facebook and skype, but our contact never faded. She still sends me presents for my birthday and with christmas and even though we're thousands of miles apart, I know she'll still be there if I need her. I would love to write more, but i'm out of characters. If you want to know more about her, and I know you want to, you should invite her to your show. I know it would mean a lot to her and she deserves it! ☺

Meredith,
this last year
has been a blast I
am glad that I got to
know you a lot better this
year. Don't forget all the fun times.
Love ya,
Debbie
& I'll see you at camp.

To the Incredible Half "82"
Good luck in the
years ahead and lose
some weight.
love,
Jerd

Meredith—
You are quite the
little woman. I have
really enjoyed
your friendship and our
hair dressing sessions.
Thanks a million!
Love ya,
Carole

Meredith— I really
been great knowing you!
I hope our wonderful
friendship will last
throughout eternity.
Meredith don't forget
our love between
eachother, We have
always been pretty
close and We better
stay that way. Your
so cute and got the
best personality that
I ever known! Stay
that way please.
See ya next summer year
and have a
good summer
Love
ya,
Jimmer

Mere,
Good luck with J.P.
You guys make a great coup—
Sweet—thats you! So promise
to stay that way!
gail "80"

Meredith,
Well well well—sorry
for everything this year.
I know how you felt. Having
you in cheerleading was fun.
But—you were the one
that was out of it. Have
fun working this summer
Maybe I'll see you
when? Whee go to that
beach by Aptos when
you're with Janet.
Have fun & stay out
of trouble.
Love ya
Diane

Meredith
To a nice, sweet, pretty
maybe I should stop
I don't want to
give you a big head
I'm glad I had you
in math
Love, Kevin